The Other Fella

John Fagan

The characters in this book are fictitious and any resemblance to persons living or dead is purely coincidental.

First published 2002 by Countyvise Limited, 14 Appin Road, Birkenhead, Merseyside, CH41 9HH in conjunction with the author J. Fagan

Copyright © 2002 J. Fagan

The right of J. Fagan to be identified as the author of this work has been asserted by him in accordance with the Copyright, Design and Patents Act, 1988.

British Library Cataloguing in Publication Data.
A Catalogue record for this book is available from the British Library

ISBN 1 901231 32 1

This book is dedicated
to the memory
of our dear friend, Tony Eccles

Acknowledgements

I am grateful to the following people:

Anne Eccles and Hazel Bee for proofreading my book.

Malcolm Young, for his critical appraisal
and for pointing me in the right direction with my writing.

Daggie's Family, for lending me the photo of Billy and Jimmy.

My wife Pat, for having to suffer hours of soap dramas,
while I happily plodded on down Memory Lane.

August 1987

Tucker and Ossie stared towards the Town Hall watching the clock, which was just coming up to twelve. Then, dead on time, it chimed.
Ossie shrugged. 'Spud hasn't made it then? Maybe his flight's delayed. He'll come though, he missed the last one, so he won't miss this.'

'Five steps, that's all. It's unbelievable.' We looked on. Smithy was incredulous.

I strode across. 'Six' I said. My steps were shorter than his.
Smithy was deep in thought, and kept shaking his head. We'd seen the changes. He hadn't. It was thirty years since he'd left. Now only five of us remained, Tucker Ossie, Spud, Smithy and myself. Nacker was gone, three months after our last meeting he was swept overboard.

We spread across the street; this was it - our pitch - so narrow, eleven a side full-scale matches we'd played here and no referee, or twenty-two, whichever way you looked at it.

'How did we all cram into such a small patch?' Smithy asked, pointing to the industrial units that now cover the two Courts, Cottage Street and our block. No one answered. We were lost for words.

It was strange not hearing ships' funnels or the sirens and not seeing the armies of dockers passing the end of the street, as if going to a derby match somewhere round the corner. I came out of my reverie as we headed towards The Piggy. I could almost smell the waves of nostalgia seeping from us all and hear the echoes of our mothers' howls reverberating around darkened streets, down the back jiggers and on into shadows of dock warehouses; a beckoning call which had been passed down from great grannies to grannies, to mothers and daughters, a cry that was both primitive yet melodic and always effective.

We reached Vittoria Street junction, four middle-aged men straddling the road like we once did in our childhood days after playing out versions of High Noon.

Crossing the junction we entered the green tiled dwelling of The Piggy - the sole survivor round these parts from our formative years.

'Four pints of bitter, pal' Tucker said to the surprised barman.
We were first in and it seemed we'd caught him on the hop.

'I'll just change the barrel it looks a bit cloudy lads' he apologised.
Ossie nodded.

He still lived down town and was a recognised connoisseur of Higson's bitter.

Tucker lived in the North End; he was also an expert and Smithy, returning from Glasgow had more experience than the lot of us put together: he once had his own pub, after a career spent pursuing villains committed to breaking the law. I was out in the sticks now and lack of practice meant I just wasn't as sharp when it came to knowing what is a good pint and what isn't. Spud, well he didn't count, did he? For he'd remained an authority on the Gospels and was still engaged in spreading the good book to the Africans as far as we were aware.

'I was expectin' youse lads' the barman said, popping his head from a trap door in the floor. We looked at one another. Nothing was planned, only we knew about the reunion.

Ossie was first to speak. 'How come you knew?' He asked.

The barman climbed out of the cellar, fished in the till and passed over a note. We moved closer. Ossie slipped his half moons on. The note was from Spud.

'Sorry I can't make it boys. Dad's on his last. Dashing off to Dublin. Will be in touch.

'When did he drop this in?' Ossie asked.

'About an hour ago. A big 'eavy fella, twice the size of any of youse lads jumped out of a taxi. I thought it was the bizzies the way he came flyin' in.'

'Poor old Paddy,' I said. 'He must be gettin' on a bit though.'

'Aye turned seventy at least' Tucker replied.

'Worra bout your old fella Billy?'

Smithy thought for a moment. 'Been gone over twenty years now. His ticker packed in after Celtic hammered the Gers. We scattered his ashes at Ibrox in the goalmouth, it was his last request.'

'And yours Jim?'

'He did quite well,' I told them. 'Seven heart attacks altogether. The last one was too much.'

'It's a wonder he didn't 'ave another seven bringin' you up,' said Ossie, grinning like a Cheshire cat.

I had to laugh. Ossie was Ossie. He'd never change. We kept in touch; he was best man at my wedding. I've often reminded him he was the worst best man you could possibly have. He takes no notice.

I'll never forget his speech at my reception when he was half-shot. I cringed as he reminisced about our upbringing in town and joked about the way I'd been disciplined by dad.

Dad found it amusing however. 'The proof's in the puddin' ' he said, putting his arm round me. Later Ossie and dad got bevvied together, the first time I'd seen dad legless. He lost his false teeth and afterwards mam had a field day.

'Put two more pints on the counter, mate,' Tucker said to the barman and they were pulled.

'To absent friends.' We touched glasses. 'To absent friends ' we repeated.

Chapter 1

Recollections

My parents were local people born and brought up in Birkenhead. They were educated in the adjoining parish of St Laurence and Our Lady's, both predominantly Catholic areas of the town. I was their second child and first son, born fourteen months after our Bridie, who unlike me had fair skin and blonde hair. She was the apple of dad's eye. Her likeness to his mother, my Grandmother, was more than likely the reason for his fondness for her, but whatever the purpose he had a strong fatherly bond with Bridie.

Mam and dad were opposites in character, in temperament and in attitude, a combination often proclaimed to be a blueprint for a successful marriage. However, a child's earlier opinions may be slightly impaired, a conviction I could readily vouch for.

Dad was small, stocky, impetuous, sharp eyed and a firm believer that a man's house was his castle. Like many of his generation he ruled the roost and his final word was law.

Apart from being a proud and independent person he strangely held a deep respect for people in authority. Also, as a means of keeping fit, dad regularly exercised in the backyard using chest expanders and other contraptions for strengthening muscles. This to him was as important as 'keeping the brain alive' he often reminded us.

Mam, on the other hand, didn't resemble dad in any way whatsoever. She had olive skin, wore glasses, was hard of hearing and unfortunately possessed a very poor sense of smell. She was also mild mannered, compassionate, religious and her nature would never allow prejudices to distract from her judgement that all human beings were equal, regardless of colour or creed.

Our house was situated in a picturesque district of Birkenhead between the Vittoria and Morpeth Docks where dad worked as a docker, or 'dock labourer,' to give him his proper title. This was the moniker he used whenever he had to fill forms for electoral paraphernalia or when obtaining furniture on the 'knocker'.

A few hundred yards from our street, across the Corporation Road, Alfred Holt's famous Blue Funnel Line ships berthed and together with the docks these provided panoramic views from where we lived. Unlike many of our neighbours, whose houses were overlooked front and back, we were fortunate to have such views.

'We've got a lot to be thankful for, son,' said dad, gazing out from our front bedroom window watching pigeons and seagulls fighting over scraps of bread that old Mrs Barton placed on the pavement for them each morning. We didn't brag about our seascape view, we could have done but we didn't. Timmy Murphy did. He was always showing off about having a garden in their backyard.

'Garden' we'd say. 'Where's the grass Spud?' It was his mam's old washing tub in which his dad grew rhubarb and then the cats peed on it because it was the only vegetation in the street.

Birkenhead, for those who don't live round here, is situated on the banks of the royal blue Mersey less than two miles across the water from Liverpool and is often referred to as 'The one eyed city.' Before I go any further, I've got to hold my hands up and admit that the river isn't really blue at all, but a muddy brown colour. Still, a little exaggeration never hurt anyone, well not in my book it doesn't.

Of course the river isn't recommended to bathe in, not with all the pollution present these days, but it was different when we were kids. You see, we were street and water-wise. From an early age we knew all about the perils of meeting a Mersey 'gold fish,' though none of my mates, as far as I can remember, ever had a collision with any, or swallowed one …well not on purpose.

'Remember when we were kids an' used to mess about down at the 'oller in Brookie an' you nearly killed yourself when you fell to the bottom?' Ossie Feeley casually remarked when we were having a pint in the Queens Hotel one winter afternoon.

'Fall down … I didn't fall, you pushed me, remember? And I ended up in the Borough Hospital getting stitches in me 'ead,' I replied.

'Did I? I can't remember that,' he said. But I knew he was lying because of the way that he wiped the froth from around his mouth with his sleeve, instead of using his long horrible tongue, which he normally did. I don't miss a trick. That's why I'm known as Dead Eye Reilly. No, not One Eyed Reilly, that's our Tommy's nickname.

When I arrived home that night I began recalling and noting down my earliest memories.

1941 - 42

'Mam, Jimmy's pinched the pennies off the baby's eyes,' our Bridie
yelled.

She didn't say it was her idea for me to nick them or that she helped
me to spend the money on sweets at Robbs corner shop. She was
always a snitch; she was probably born one, well that's what I thought
anyway.

Mam didn't reply, she just lifted me under her arm, closed the door to
where our Tony lay and took both of us into the back kitchen.

'Your little brother's gone to heaven,' she told us gently, though I was
sure that he was only asleep in the front room. It was only when the
bombing started and we were carried across the street to the air raid
shelters that I missed our Tony. He wasn't in my mother's arms, I knew
then that he really had gone to heaven. I was only three and a half and
our Bridie was nearly five.

Across the next twelve months I was forcibly introduced into the
subtle art of 'nose pinching - cod liver oil swallowing,' a medieval form
of torture, guaranteed to make sure that a full teaspoon of the foul liquid
slid down your throat without touching the sides and was always
administered just before bedtime.

Food rationing became a main topic, the blackout an accepted part of
life and mam had another baby, a girl - our Bernadette.

On my fourth birthday I was taken to Cathcart Street Nursery School
and when mam left I yelled and screamed like a big cry-baby. However,
a gingersnap soon halted my floods, I was always susceptible to bribery,
even at a very early age.

Whistling bombs, followed by deafening explosions shook houses and
streets sending out underground tremors to terrify us as we huddled in
the communal air raid shelter in Queensbury Street. Shaking with fear
we clung to mam, crying incessantly and grasping for warmth and
comfort.

Tommy Duffy's mam, a larger than average lady, tried calming
everyone down, saying the raid was over and we'd soon be hearing the
'All Clear.' Suddenly a flash of lightning was followed by an enormous
bang overhead. Mrs Duffy screamed.

'Jesus, Mary and Joseph please help us' and collapsed on the bunk
almost flattening Tommy and his brother Billy. The youngest brother,
Frankie, came off worst though; his mother ended up on top of his head

almost smothering him. A short time later the sirens wailed and the air raid wardens brought us outside. We crossed the street and when mam opened the front door a cloud of dust and plaster swept past us into the fresh air. The front room ceiling now had a huge hole in it and this ran up through the bedroom into the roof so we could see the sky without even going outside. It was great. White powder covered all the furniture and mam screeched at the top of her voice. 'Holy mother of God, we've been bombed.' She threw her arms round us and we were afraid to move in case an enemy pilot lurked in the front bedroom. Then, as if by magic, dad appeared. He was on duty that night with the Home Guard but he didn't guard our house very well at all. Nevertheless we felt safer with him around.

'Where's the bomb dad?' I asked.

'There's no bomb son, just shrapnel, that's all,' he replied.

'Shrapnel, what's that Charlie?' Mam gasped, thinking it was a new type of incendiary device the enemy had invented.

He picked up a couple of pieces of jagged metal lying on the floor besides the dresser and held them in his hands. 'This is the little buggers that have done all the damage' he proclaimed and I remember at the time being quite disappointed. I wanted a bomb to show to my mates. Without proof they wouldn't believe that the Germans had nearly flattened our house.

We moved around the corner to a house in Brook Street, next door but one to Aunt Fan's. Mam was pleased to be staying in the same locality and parish.

'We're still with friends and neighbours, thank God.' She always thanked God for everything, but dad didn't. He'd fallen out with God since our Tony died and wouldn't go to church either. With mam being partially deaf, dad always raised his voice and so it was difficult not to hear them arguing in the back kitchen when they thought we were asleep.

Dad hired a handcart from Dows and moved all our belongings and furniture on his own. I went with him on the final trip to collect the last of the coal and despite the fact I was wearing a clean pair of pants he plonked me right on top. However, when the metal rims round the wheels rattled on the cobbles by the Arab Arms Hotel some of the coal bounced off the back of the barrow and it was then that I noticed Tommy Molloy's little brother Danny walking behind with a cardboard box picking pieces up, but I didn't snitch on him. They were really poor and his dad was in jail as well. Mam told us he was a constipated objector, which we thought must have been worse than robbing a bank or even murder, because nobody else in our street ever spoke about it.

Our terrace house, number two three nine Brook Street was situated between what we called the courts, but which in fact were Arrowe and Caldy Place. We had a front room, back kitchen and two bedrooms, plus a lavvie at the bottom of the yard. A green painted mangle, a dolly tub and a large tin bath hanging on a hook outside the back kitchen door completed the backyard furniture. We also had our own air-raid shelter, so compared with a number of our neighbours we were more than lucky.

A few large hairy spiders and daddy longlegs hid in the corners of the roof of the shelter, but they didn't bother me. They scared mam and Bridie though and in temper, I chased them with a candle, driving them away with the heat. When no-one was looking they crawled down the wall again, but this time I was waiting and captured them dead easy. I had a matchbox stashed away and so they became my first prisoners of war.

Next day in school I let them escape on the bench I shared with 'droopy drawers,' Maggie O'Loughlin. That would fix her for not lending me her tennis ball and clat tailing to Miss Curtis after I nicked one of her sherbet dips.

I had beeen in St Laurences mixed infant school since I was five and Ossie was in our class. He was easy to spot. You could see him a mile away. His inside leg was always redder than anyone else's was. This was caused by him peeing down his left trouser leg - though we didn't think much of it at the time because ours were always chafed as well, yet nowhere near as bad as his. Eventually we became best friends, but only because mam gave him a dripping butty every day after school.

From then on he looked on me as his brother, even though we weren't alike in any way. Besides being a lot taller than me he had loads of freckles and a mop of ginger hair, while I was smaller than average and dark skinned.

Peace time

Nineteen forty-five was a memorable year. With the ending of the war an electric atmosphere engulfed the town. Streets were gaily decorated and Union Jacks painted on gable ends and entry walls. A sort of euphoria raged throughout the population and V.E. day was vociferously celebrated in Hamilton Square. Welcome home banners were strewn from house to house as local hero's returned from battle, while sadness and not a few tears were shared for those who hadn't survived. The end of the war was hailed as the start of a new era, with everyone looking forward to a future of full employment, the end of food rationing and finally, prosperity for all those who'd suffered during the previous six years.

For us kids however, nothing appeared to change. We were still dosed with cod liver oil to keep out the cold, syrup of figs was sparingly poured down our throats at the slightest complaint of belly ache, and worst of all, we were forced to swallow thick lumpy porridge for breakfast before going to school. 'Hand-me-down' clothes continued to be handed down, we all slept in the same bed, top and bottom, with Dad's working overcoats, purchased from the Army and Navy store still used to supplement thin blankets and the oven plate remained an able substitute for a hot water bottle.

That year I was seven and with the rest of my school friends we transferred to the boys' school, passing through a wooden gate on the other side of the lavvies. This small door separated us from the girls. Unlike us they were taught by nuns as well as teachers and their head mistress, Mother Browser, paraded the playground like a hawk, with the objective of making sure the connecting gate remained closed at all times. She looked extremely strict and I for one was glad we weren't taught by nuns. It was common knowledge that whenever our ball was booted over the wall and Mother Browser was around, even the hard cases wouldn't venture through the gate to retrieve it.

There were fifty of us crammed into our class, but no one moaned, even when the heating was off. This happened frequently during harsh winter days and as soon as the pipes froze we were sent home. After our kid-glove treatment in the infants we were expected to behave ourselves properly now that we were in the boy's school.

Our class teacher, Mrs Carty, made it clear from the first day that she wouldn't tolerate any nonsense whatsoever from any of us and she was as good as her word.

As a means of punishment, the first step was a slap with a ruler and if this failed we were made to sit with our hands on our heads for ages. Should bad behaviour persist we were forced to kneel on the floor for a lesson and this, apart from hurting your knees, was truly boring. To relieve the tedium we pulled tongues behind Mrs Carty's back but were always caught. The laughter from one or two creeps always gave us away and a short stubby cane would then be brought out from the cupboard. It was Mrs Carty's ultimate weapon and she certainly knew how to use it, as first Ossie sampled it and soon afterwards I followed in his footsteps.

Our headmaster, Pop Lally, was a thin lanky man who rarely smiled. He had a terrible reputation for caning pupils who stepped out of line. From day one I decided to make it my business to stay out of trouble and not join a queue of trembling delinquents, who waited outside his office every morning.

'Who made you?'

'God made me.'

'Why did God make you?'

'God made me to know him, love him and serve him in this world and forever in the next' we droned, in singsong fashion. Father O'Hare, a dark haired Irish priest grinned. Mrs Carty sighed with relief

'Well done boys, I can see Miss Carty's doing a great job on you bunch of scallywags,' he said, winking at our young attractive teacher. We gawped in amazement. We all knew that priests weren't supposed to look at women or get married. That's what we were always told anyway. Charlie Cleary didn't like the priest's familiarity one bit. He was teacher's pet and a sniveller as well, but no one dared tell him, for apart from being bigger than any of us he had a wicked temper. Now he boldly interrupted events.

'Hey Father, it's not Miss Carty it's Mrs and she's married as well, aren't you Miss?' Father O'Hare smiled. 'Please forgive me Mrs Carty. You're a very lucky teacher indeed to have such a fine fella of a lad to protect you,' he said, glancing at Charlie.

'What's your name boy? Speak up don't be afraid.'

Charlie went crimson before glancing down at the floor, no doubt hoping to seek refuge under the desk. We'd all have done the same thing in his position, so you really couldn't blame him. It was obvious to us that he could have bitten his tongue off as we watched him nervously rubbing his nose with his finger and at the colour slowly draining from his face. He was scared stiff all right. He realised he'd slipped up when he glanced across at Mrs Carty and noticed the choked tears of laughter running down her face beneath a fluttering white handkerchief, but by then he knew it was too late.

'Cleary, Father, Charlie Cleary... an, am ...am ..sorry... father. I wasn't being cheeky an' all that, 'onest, father, I wasn't, 'onest,' he cried. His eyes were bulging as he tried to squeeze out a few drops of tears, which is difficult to do without practice.

We nudged one another and Ossie had a big soft grin on his face but I wouldn't take the chance myself just in case Cleary saw me, despite the fact he was under scrutiny himself.

'It's all right Charlie Cleary, no waterfalls please' said the priest. 'In fact, I'd say it's very gallant of you to defend your teacher, which is more than I can say for this bunch of hyenas,' he added, grinning broadly as he spoke.

Charlie glared and I know for fact he'd have half killed any of us if he thought we were skitting at him, so we all looked down at the floor.

'The meek shall inherit the world, said the Lord,' the priest continued 'and you, my little man, appear to be the apostle destined to defend all of these poor souls. Although it's a tall order for one so young, I'm sure you have the right attitude to succeed,' Father O'Hare declared. He left the classroom with Mrs Carty and we heard them giggling. We couldn't help it; they were only standing just outside the door.

Mrs Carty did her level best that first year with us thick 'uns but as long as we managed to recite the catechism and retain a basic interest in sums, composition, writing, spelling and drawing, it seemed that this was sufficient to allow us to progress to the next standard.

Attending mass remained a different matter altogether. One of the main reasons we fell by the wayside was the distraction of Sunday morning football matches played in Cathcart Street school playground.

The priests, who lived in the Presbytery around the corner from the Lauries school, paid regular visits to our class, checking progress in catechism studies. They also tried tripping us up on Monday morning to see if we'd been to mass, which I thought was a lousy trick myself seeing that we hadn't yet made our Confession and taken our first Holy Communion.

Besides, we didn't know any better and mam told us that we'd get away with all those sins Scott- free, and she never told lies. Ossie and Spud Murphy were in the same boat as I was, but snivelling Anthony Duffy never missed mass at all. The priest had promised him an altar boy's job, just like their Billy ... the creep.

After I made my first Confession and Holy Communion, it was murder, honest to God. For that's when we found out about purgatory and the devil and mortal sins and venial sins and burning forever in hell. We thought twice then before climbing over the railings to play the Proddys at footy on Sunday mornings.

It wasn't fair. They didn't have to worry about going to mass, or missing it for that matter and then getting lambasted by their fathers. Nor did they have the problem of being told off by the priests for sagging school or for pinching and telling lies.

Brookie... Our gang... Neighbours.

Our gang consisted of Ossie Feeley, Tucker Griffiths, Spud Murphy, Nacker Ryan, Billy Smith, who was the tallest and broadest and finally, me. As a last resort, we occasionally and reluctantly allowed Tich Feeley to come with us when Ossie had to look after him. Most of the time though we sneaked off, sending his mam into convulsions.

'Take Tommy with you and don't forget to look after him, do you hear our Austin?' she screeched in a high-pitched posh voice, which sounded slightly out of place in Brookie.

She had a good heart, so mam said, which was the main thing, but I know she got under ma's skin when she bragged about her upbringing in the country.

When the Feeley's first moved into the street the majority of the neighbours considered them to be 'snooty.' As far as I was concerned Ossie was a good lad, for he was the first to give me a Hotspur and a Dandy without swaps. Most of our neighbours were suspicious, however, because Mr Feeley held a permanent job on the Railways. 'He's been transferred in from Helsby for promotion purposes,' Mrs Feeley told mam and Mrs Murphy when they were getting to know each other.

'Promotion me arse,' said dad. 'Frank Feeley's only a porter at Woodside, so what was he before he came here, a bloody carriage cleaner?'

Dad could be sarcastic when he wanted and though he was honest with his opinions, at times he tended to go overboard, but that was dad. He always called a spade a spade, whether it offended or not and this, of course, didn't enhance his popularity - though if it bothered him he never showed it. Dad didn't swear much in the house, except on those occasions when he got carried away and slipped up. Then mam was into him like a viper.

'Don't be using your dockers' language in here, Charlie Reilly. This is a respectable house and don't you ever forget it. And remember, walls have ears.'

'It's not just walls have ears,' he sulkily replied, you can bloodywell hear when you want to.' But when Ma gave him one of her funny looks that was more than enough.

Of course though, it was acceptable for him to use the most common expletives, such as bloody, buggar and arse but mam rarely used bad language even when she lost her rag. However, she was prone to hurling the occasional plate or saucer at me when I aggravated her. On the other hand we weren't allowed to say anything slightly offensive. Even the odd bloody, sod or swine would guarantee a swipe across your face and as an added deterrent, the threat of having our mouths washed out with Lifebuoy soap.

Another thing, with having a mole in our house that thrived on snitching, I always had to be on my guard. It didn't matter whether at the time I happened to be an outlaw or even a pirate, it was imperative that our Bridie wasn't in our vicinity when the action began.

It was the end of 1945 when Nacker formed Brookies fifth commando unit.

He'd seen commando's fighting in North Africa on the Pathe News at the Rio picture house and from that moment we got rid of our bows and arrows, swapping them for rifles and bayonets made from pieces of wood we'd nicked from Marchbanks timber yard in Price Street during the dinner hour when all was quiet.

On our first mission we scaled backyard walls and ducked below window sills until we reached the end of Vine Street, which was in Our Lady's parish. From there we crept to our secret destination near Pats Field, while Ossie, our chief scout, trailed behind in case we were being followed by the Japs or the Germans.

Nacker showed us how to crawl on our knees and elbows, despite the pathway being full of gravel, which really hurt - though none of us dared cry.

'The first one who cries stinks,' we yelled and even if our elbows and knees were scraped raw we stuck it out, because we were real commandos, not cry babies.

On our next mission we wore balaclavas and rattled door knockers, then hid in the shadows watching angry householders look in vain up and down the street, but we were never seen. That's when Nacker declared we were the best commando unit in town.

Spud Murphy was in the same class as Ossie and me. Nacker also went to the Lauries, but was a year older than us and automatically became our leader. Meanwhile, Tucker Griffiths attended Cathcart Street School with him being a Proddy, well he was half-and-half really. His mam was a Welsh Baptist, or something like that and his old fella was a lapsed Catholic, whatever that meant. We weren't bothered anyway - he couldn't half fight and knew some cracking dens where the enemy would never find us.

Smithy also went to the Proddy school, which was known as Cathie. His dad, big Jock, worked as a boilermaker down the yard for Lairds and often had us in stitches when telling jokes, some of which were dead funny and others quite rude. Big Jock also swore a lot in the house, even in front of Mrs Smith, who he called hen and that was funny too; she had a bright red double chin and a hooked nose and looked to us more like a cockerel than a hen. At times we were dying to laugh, but not in front of Smithy, he would have murdered us. Apart from telling jokes Jock showed us some brilliant card tricks, though on occasions it was difficult understanding a word he said, especially at the weekends when he was full of whiskey.

Jock held a prominent position in the Orange Lodge and once a year joined the annual marches, which began in Liverpool and finished in Southport. On his way out he looked a real toff - dead smart in his black overcoat, bowler hat and leather gloves. For some reason, however, he always returned the worse for wear and without fail, and for what was considered devilment, he always sang ' The sash my Father wore' across the neighbourhood and then called everyone 'Fenian Bastards.'

Only Spud's dad, Mr Murphy, seemed bothered at Jock's utterances, but my dad had an altogether different viewpoint.

'There's three hundred and sixty five days in the year and if a man can't enjoy 'imself an' express his beliefs on just one of them, then there's something wrong with society,' he always said.

Mrs Smith had a different personality to Jock. She was a quietly spoken lady who hardly drank, but nevertheless seemed content with life. Usually she could be found parked on an easy chair by the window, with balls of wool on her lap, contentedly knitting all kinds of jumpers and scarves while Jock rambled on with a stream of jokes, many of which were directed at her. She'd learnt over the years not to retaliate or to criticise him too much in case 'he turned,' which usually happened when he'd sunk one over the eight and then all hell could break loose. Although he could be a demon in drink, it wasn't all one way traffic;

Mrs Smith held a crafty trump card up her sleeve. She had a few bob put aside from her needlework so that when Monday arrived and after Jock had blown his tank, she was always in a position to ration him with 'a last hour session' until pay day. Of course there was a price to pay for this and before he was allowed to leave the house for his 'last hour session' he had to perform certain domestic tasks, which under normal circumstances he would have refused point-blank to undertake.

Brook Street, like Cleveland Street and Price Street, ran north to south from the town hall, covering the parishes of St Werburghs (the Wergies), St Laurences, Our Lady's and further north, Holy Cross. Each parish had its Church of England counterpart, St Marys, St Anne's, and St James and in addition there was Holy Trinity, known to us as the Devils Church, disrespectfully named because of the fearsome gargoyles glaring down from the square-shaped belfry.

A number of dock areas had many descendants of Irish immigrants among the population and these were Catholic strongholds. In our street, however, there were more Protestants than Catholics, but most of the time there was little animosity among religious factions, with the exception of July the twelfth. That's when the Orange Order held their annual colourful processions, with disturbances seemingly confined to the other side of the water in Liverpool, around the highly populated Scottie Road area.

In our parish churchgoers went either to St Peters or to the Lauries, although quite a percentage of both denominations didn't go to church at all. Those who did drink, all drank together in the same alehouses for such was the community spirit. Dad was the odd man out; he didn't frequent either church or pub.

'It's a free world,' he said. 'As long as their families aren't starvin' or going without, a man's entitled to a bit of pleasure.'

'Why don't you go to The Piggy or the other ale 'ouses, like Mr Smith or Ossie's dad?' I asked.

'Don't ask daft questions an' you won't be told any lies,' he replied, before burying his head in the Echo.

'Stop pesterin' your father,' mam interrupted. 'You don't realise what kind of an upbringin' he's had to suffer.' She was always defensive about dad's younger days, knowing from hearsay about the harsh childhood he'd endured and the fact that he had no memory of his father who died 'of the drink'. To add to his misfortunes his mother had passed away when he was a teenager and as a result his step-sister had brought him up.

We had little doubt that his upbringing affected his blunt approach to life and was more than an influence on his stubborn attitude to many matters concerning our daily routine.

On the corner of Duke Street a scrapyard was stacked right to the hilt with used cars. It was dead easy to gain entry because there were only thin corrugated sheets around the site to keep us out. We'd only been there a short time when Tucker discovered a battered Bentley beneath a pile of other old wrecks and this immediately became our headquarters. Naturally we were all sworn to secrecy.

'Cross your hearts and swear to die,' Nacker ordered.

We wet our fingers, crossed our throats and vowed on our mothers' lives that we wouldn't tell anyone where our hideout was and that's why, whenever we were lumbered with Tich or any other nuisance, our other den at the back of the Corpy yard in Clevie was used.

We spent hours throwing 'jockers' at tin cans and empty bottles just to practice our aim and then, huddled together, we'd plan raids on other gangs' bonfire storage places. During the course of the day we made traps and collected all kinds of spare car parts to torture our enemies with after we'd captured them. It's strange but I couldn't remember us ever catching anyone, even though they were out there.

I knew they were. Spud said they were all around us, so they must have been. I believed him myself, because he didn't tell lies now, not after I dropped him in the lurch with Father Doyle. This was the first time I went to confession and told the truth about us bunking in through the fire door in the Super Picture house and then getting thrown out. Spud who was next in line after I came out of the confessional box, denied being at the Super, but later cracked under interrogation from Father Doyle.

As a penance he was given ten extra hail-Mary's for telling lies and promised Father Doyle he'd never tell lies again and that was the reason why I believed him when he told me we were surrounded by the enemy.

One time a couple of tinkers came rooting through the scrapyard and spotted us. Within seconds we had clambered into our den and as quiet as mice, listened to them talking above our trap door. 'Be jaysus they were off like rabbits, where did they bloody well vanish to?'

We smiled at each other placing one finger over our lips.

Before darkness crept in we'd set off for home, our hands and faces black with grime and oil, singing our troop song like the yanks always did in the films at the Gaumont on Saturday mornings. Even when we were Indians or outlaws, it was always our song that we sang. We were never cowies mind you, they were always the goodies, and as Ossie said, no-one would respect us if we played Gene Autry or Hopalong Cassidy all the time.

'We are the members of the Brook Street gang,
Everybody knows
We know our manners, how to spend our tanners,
We are respected wherever we may go.
And when we travel on the railway lines,
We open the windows wide.
We know how to use our feet,
playin' football in the street
We are the Brook Street gang.'

Returning from battle we were usually starving and thirsty. Nevertheless, we carried our trophies with valour and pride. These were nothing more exotic than rusty axles, pieces of tin, inner tubes or old used car tyres. If thin enough these tyres were thrown over the gaslight besides Caldy Place, while thicker ones were stacked down the jigger. Next day we'd climb into them and more often than not we fell out dizzy after having been rolled down the street.

This was a game that we eventually grew out of, the lumps on our heads and our scarred elbows and knees lessened the attraction of trying to outdo bikes and trolleys as a means of transport.

After tea we would gather round the lamp-post and throw ropes over the top crossbar and swing like Tarzan. The jungle king was everyone's idol - well he was ours anyway. The girls were welcome to Jane.

'Whoop... whoop... whoop,' Ossie yelled. 'Me Cheetah,' he screamed, pounding his chest, hopping around like Tarzan's best friend and scattering the girls who were playing hopscotch and skipping. He didn't look a bit like Cheetah, in fact to us he resembled a Yeti, or abominable snowman, but he sounded like Cheetah and that was good enough for us.

This gas lamp was the sole source of light between Cathcart and Vittoria Street. However, the dark held no fear for us and we thought nothing of wandering down to the docks or the long entries or into the shadowy trees of the park. Even more daring, we ventured down to the bottom of Payson Street where, according to legend, the area was supposed to be ridden with hundreds of banshees. Banshees failed to frighten us though, they knew where we came from and we were scared of no one whenever we were altogether in a gang.

We didn't bother with girls; they were a nuisance, unless of course a goalie was needed. Only then, if we were desperate, we'd recruit Betty Davies, a tomboy and good netball player. She lived in the Court and always wanted to play with us. There was little doubt that she was better in goal than Tucker, but couldn't dive as good as him in case she showed her black drawers. It was easier to play fullback and goalie with ten men and stop our team from gawping when low shots were fired in the bottom of the goal than to play her.

The rest of the girls kept well away from us when we were playing footy, they knew that we didn't like anyone messing about during our every-day matches. When we were bored, however, or for devilment, we often tried spoiling their games, just to get our own back because we all suffered in some way or other with having sisters.

'Don't you dare hit your sister back,' ma screamed if I retaliated after getting pushed over. It wasn't fair, they could get away with scratching your eyes out, pinching your arm, pulling your hair and worse of all, for clat tailing. I was forever getting a fourpenny one from ma whenever our Bridie snitched on me for climbing on roofs or swearing in the street.

Ossie was luckier than me. He only had one sister, Teresa, but two brothers Johnny and Tich. I was stuck with two. Spud was worse off than both of us, he was outnumbered four to one. There was Pat, Mary, Molly and Kate. Mrs Ryan had all lads, from Stephen the eldest, down to Liam the baby and going in for a football team, according to a certain nosy parker who lived nearby. In Tucker's family there was just himself and his little brother Eddie, so their house was quieter than the majority of the others.

Smithy was an only child. Whenever it was freezing or raining we went into their parlour to play with our lead soldiers. This was the only place we could escape to have some peace.

Air raid

'Keep still and stop whingin', dad growled. It was the Saturday morning after he purchased a second-hand pair of rusted hair clippers from Marriots scrapyard in Exmouth Street and was about to demonstrate his skills on my head.

For some unknown reason I was always a guinea pig when he signed the book. Mam said that if he didn't sign he wouldn't get any money at all, but he preferred working, instead of what he called 'receiving a pittance.'

It was during these periods that his ambition to escape those draconian conditions motivated in him a desire to try his hand at other occupations, such as being a barber. His frustration was understandable, for few workers would be as content as the dockers had to be, to stand in pens and be treated like cattle, then be chosen for a day, or even half a days shift. The selection procedure also left a lot to be desired, for being chosen often depended on your religious belief, popularity with the bosses, or in frequenting the right pubs. It was a totally unfair situation to say the least, but why did I have to suffer, what had I done?

'Yah! Yah! Yah!' I yelled, as chunks of hair including fragments of scalp, dandruff and other unseen aliens who occasionally lodged there, were forcibly removed.

'Shurrup or I'll give you something to cry about,' dad replied, before taking down an oil can he used to lubricate his bike with from a shelf above the mangle. He then dosed the shears with the lubricant, flicked them a few times, seemed quite happy with the result and resumed the onslaught.

'Dad there's something runnin' down me neck,' I yelled, thinking he'd severed a main blood vessel to my brain and in a blind panic attempted to escape from the clutches of the electric chair.

'A drop of oil 'asn't killed anyone yet lad. Not to my knowledge anyway, so bloody well keep still or I'll cut the bloody lot off,' he threatened, gripping me firmly with one hand and cropping my head, like he was in charge of a lawn mower, with the other.

I did as I was told. I had no choice. Dad thought nothing of scalping me. It didn't matter to him if my mates took the mickey. In fact he expected them to and for me to retaliate.

'You're no lad of mine if you can't stand up and fight for yourself,' he'd preach. However, I was a simple soul who didn't like much conflict, well not at that early age anyway.

After checking his enterprising operation, he seemed quite satisfied with the massacre, so he spat on his hand and belted me across my head.

I yelped again and screwed up my face to stop myself from crying out loud.

'First wet lad. Not a bad attempt seein' it's me first time, is it?' He concluded, shaking lumps of hair from an old ripped shirt which he'd professionally draped around my frail shoulders.

'What's that on your head son?' mam asked when I stumbled into the kitchen, searching for a mirror to inspect the injury inflicted by this latest of dad's 'Get Rich' schemes and which, I prayed, would be a one day wonder like the rest of his brainwaves.

'OIL! It's not fair, why does he always 'ave to pick on me?' I sobbed, trying to remove the slick with the rough flannel that mam used every morning to push tidemarks further down my back. As usual, however, she remained loyal and could detect no harm in dad's barbaric pursuit of personal gratification completed at my expense.

'You know what he's like son, he's only doin' it for your own good and he can't very well try them out on anyone else, can he? After all, you are the eldest you know,' she added, placing a spoonful of best butter on my baldy scalp, which I ought to have been grateful for but I wasn't. Usually a much cheaper commodity such as lard was applied, so no doubt she was trying her best to be kind to me in her own way. Unfortunately, at that particular time, I didn't know what was good for me or not.

'This'll shift it,' she confidently predicted, massaging my layer of stubble with powerful stubby fingers. However, she had no success and the oil drifted over my ears and forehead and it stank so much that I yelled even louder.

'I'm not going out like this,' I cried. Dad then intervened and solved the problem by rubbing a rag dosed with turps across my head which removed most of the oil-based concoction, though it smelt worse than before.

'Now don't be sittin' by the fire until your hair's dry son,' he wisely advised me, but I had no intention and galloped out through the back door before he had any more bright ideas.

'Hey crust'ead, whose had a basin on yer 'ead?' Franky Bailey yelled as I ventured into the street. He was off like a flash before I could get hold of him, so I looked round, picked up a brick from out of a stockpile we had ready for a raid on the Cathcart Street gang and threw it after him. Fortunately for him I missed, but with the stone being a 'ducky' it bounced about ten times before clattering into Mrs Dillon's front door. Before she had time to see who had thrown it I flew down the jigger in case I was spotted and reported on to dad. Throwing stones at one another, or 'raids' as we called them, was a pastime that most of us lads resorted to and the consequences were often severe, especially for those caught by the bobbies.

Micky Dobson was really unlucky and suffered for it. He threw a ducky which severed a spoke on Constable Jones' boneshaker bike. Unfortunately for Micky, he'd been seen by Maggie Thompson who snitched on him to his mam. The shiny stone went right through the back wheel and sent the constable headfirst over the handlebars. Dobbo cried for days after his dad tanned his behind with a horse rein. He didn't even have time to stick a Dandy or Beano down his trousers like the older lads often managed to do when faced with similar circumstances.

To rub salt in the wounds, Mrs Dobson made him go to school, even though he could hardly sit down properly. It must have been murder for him sitting on those bone hard benches, yet he never complained to us about it.

We had sympathy for his Dad though, for it was hardly his fault if he couldn't afford a ten bob fine and buy a new wheel for Constable Jones' bike. Consequently, when faced with Hobson's choice he'd executed the punishment himself and even though poor Dobbo accepted his fate, he found it difficult to grin and bear it.

It's funny, but none of us could recall Mickey Dobson ever throwing stones after that episode. Of course we all felt sorry for him. It was just pure bad luck, that apart from the fact that his dad worked for the Co-op as a coalman and used a horse and cart for delivery, he also happened to have a rein handy. In comparison, my dad only possessed a leather belt which he often threatened to use, though at that particular time his fearful voice was sufficient to act as a suitable deterrent.

The Ryans and the Murphys

It was all right for Nacker, he had it made. He didn't bother going to church, there was no need for him to go, not with Spud, Ossie and me in his gang. We supplied all the necessary information; such as the name of the Priest who said mass and the colour of his vestments so the only time he entered church was on Holy days of obligation. On such occasions we were marched like soldiers around the corner from school to church and no one escaped.

Nacker's dad, Eugene, came from Kerry and was also nicknamed Nacker. Some of his mates called him Nudger, considered much easier to pronounce than Eugene. The boss in the alehouse said he was lucky to have two manly names, but his comments didn't make sense to us. Mr Ryan joined the Merchant Navy when he was a lad and like many seafarers before him found it difficult to settle down with a shore job. He didn't seem bothered by the fact that most of his trips were 'long hauls' and often meant being away for twelve months or more, but it was the only way of life he knew. After every voyage there seemed to be an extra mouth to feed and for all that, this didn't appear to worry him, although remembering the younger boys' names appeared to cause him most problems.

Poor Mrs Ryan, with eight kids snapping round her ankles, had more than enough on her plate when he was away and always appeared at the door carrying a baby in her arms. We didn't think anything of it; babies were babies to us. We probably would have taken more notice if there weren't a new baby after Mr Ryan had gone back to sea.

Although christened a Catholic, Nacker's mother didn't worry about mass or church events and with a single-minded approach to life she did her best to instil discipline and good manners into her family. No-one could deny that her whole life revolved around her kids. She was also fanatical about calling her boys by their Christian names. Sometimes we forgot and yelled down the lobby, 'Nacker are you comin' out' and without fail, she always answered. 'You mean Stephen don't yer. One Nacker's more than enough in this 'ouse.' We always said we were sorry. I don't know why but we did.

Mam always reminded us about how tough a life Mrs Ryan had to put up with and how well she coped under extremely trying circumstances. Most of our neighbours agreed with mam's assessment.

Spud's old man, Paddy, was also Irish and came from Dublin. He worked on the buildings, drank like a fish and his face was always bright red, caused by supping too much ale, so it was said. Occasionally, Jock made us laugh when teasing Spud.

'Yer old man's got' a face like a farmer's arse, so yer don't have tae worry about a shillin' fae the meter in your house when the lights go out.'

Spud took it in good heart, but when he was alone with Smithy he tried getting his own back by skitting at Jock's blue nose. Smithy was too smart though.

'At least it's the colour of the team he supports an' not a green one,' he replied.

Spud never told his Dad what Jock said. He knew very well that his dad didn't like Jock singing on the twelfth of July and for that reason Paddy retaliated by whistling 'Kevin Barry' whenever passing Smithy's house on the way to the Lauries Y.M.C.S. in Price Street.

Mind you Spud was a bit of a nark himself you know.

'My da's stronger than yours,' he said to me one day.

'He's not yer know. My dad's got loads of 'airs on 'is chest,' I replied. I'd seen Mr Murphy watering his rhubarb without his shirt on and he only had a few little clumps and they were a horrible ginger colour.

'My da's bigger than yours.'

'Mine's broader.'

'My Da's gorra tattoo an' yours 'ain't.'

'He has and only me an' me mam 'ave ever seen it.'

I was only kidding, but that got him thinking. I knew I had him foxed. He was scratching his head and Nitty Norah had already been round our school.

That was it as far as I was concerned, he couldn't brag anymore, but he always had to have the last word.

'My da's cleverer than yours.'

'He's not ... he's thick.'

That got Spud's temper up, so he grabbed me in a headlock and swung me off my feet, catching me by surprise. I didn't even have time to wipe my nose on my sleeve, so I wiped it on his jersey instead. I know it was a lousy thing to do, but what else could I do? I was suffering with a real heavy cold at the time and my nose was running.

'Hey stoppit, what d'yer think doin' Timothy? Mates don't fight,' Mr Murphy bawled when he spotted the unusual position my head was in. Spud released me at once.

'Now shake 'ands the pair of yeh.' We did.

'No 'ard feelin's.'

'No 'ard feelin's,' I answered.

'That's much better. Here's a tanner between yeh. Now away yeh go an' buy a bottle of cream soda an' share it out,' he said.

I liked Mr Murphy, he wasn't thick. I only said he was just to get my own back on Spud. Mr Murphy was always laughing and acting the goat. He drank in The Piggy, or The Shamrock and occasionally The Atlantic with Mr Ryan when he was home on leave. One day Spud, out of curiosity, asked his dad a question, a really daft question, but only because he had nothing else on his mind.

'Hey dad how come they call Mr Ryan, Nacker?'

'He's a Kerry man son.'

'Er ... er .. wotcha mean like?'

'All Kerry men 'ave two between their ears son, ha, ha, ha d'yer gerrit?'

Spud looked blank.

'Wotcha mean da, I don't get yer?'

'Be jaysus son don't they teach yer anything in that school except bloody religion,' he muttered. It was definitely the ale talking. He'd have been battered from pillar to post if he had said such a thing in front of Mrs Murphy. She ruled the roost in their house, everyone knew, still Paddy seemed more than happy with the situation. After all he wasn't soft, there was a huge weight difference between him and Mrs Murphy, for he was like a featherweight in comparison to his wife.

'Balls...now yeah know what balls are, don't yeah? An' I'm not talkin' about football or tennis balls, either,' he continued.

Spud couldn't believe his ears. His dad never ever spoke dirty. It was more than he dared. Not in their house anyway.

Mrs Murphy prided herself on being religious. She wasn't a religious maniac, but not far off it according to my dad; but then again, his views were often biased.

Very few doubted for a minute that her house was the holiest in the street and the general view by a number of neighbours was that it resembled a shrine inside. Apart from cleaning the church on a regular basis, she was a respected member of the Mothers Guild and in her search for saintliness was hardly away from the Lauries Church.

Spud didn't know what to do. His mam was due in shortly and she'd have a fit altogether if she heard his da talking like that. He'd been told often enough that anyone who swore in their house would be struck down by a bolt of lightning; that's what his mam always said and his dad knew it. For this reason, he usually bit his tongue. However, Spud's uncertainty didn't last long, his da solved it for him.

'Now don't be repeatin' what I told yeah to yer Mammy or I'll give yeah a thick 'ear meself,' he threatened. To get it off his chest Spud told Ossie and me instead. We didn't mention it to Nacker though, just in case his old fella murdered Spud's dad when he was full of ale, so we kept it to ourselves. We believed the story about Kerry men, until years later when we found that Spud's dad was only pulling his son's leg.

After Mr Ryan docked, it was a usual routine for him to visit all of the drinking haunts in the vicinity of the docks before making the final journey home. As he staggered the last hundred yards towards his house he would normally break into song. The song or the words rarely varied; it was always the same verses of Paddy M'Ginty's goat and more often than not he'd throw all his loose coins to groups of ragged trousered kids who congregated around the lamplight. However, before they had chance to pocket their good fortune, the money was swiftly retrieved by anxious neighbours and given to Mrs Ryan next day. She always appreciated her neighbours' actions.

A few weeks later when Mr Ryan was skint or felt the call of the sea beckoning, he'd lift anchor and prepare himself for another voyage. Within minutes of leaving his house a curtain flickered in Mrs Turner's window. She was an old lady who lived in Cottage Street and probably, because she had nothing better to keep her mind occupied, spent most of her time watching the comings and goings of every visitor to the neighbourhood, whether they were friend, foe, debt collector or rent men. Whenever the coast was clear she'd emerge from behind her front door to begin her weekly gossip report with Mrs Green, her next door neighbour and another who suffered the same complaint of nosiness.

'There he goes, sneakin' back ter sea again, leavin' poor Lucy in the puddin' club,' she croaked, rather loudly, not caring a hoot if anybody heard her or not. Her lack of discretion didn't go down too well with a majority of the neighbours. After all there were kids playing outside in the street.

'Why don't yer mind yer own friggin' business you nosy old cow,' Frank Bailey's mam yelled, but her words were lost on deaf ears, Mrs Turner had a reputation of being thick skinned.

Mrs Bailey, who lived opposite in Caldy Place, often bore the brunt of Mrs Turner's vicious tongue yet she was more than capable of holding her own and retaliated at every opportunity; and she didn't mince her choice of obscenities either. Jock Smith called Mrs Turner 'Ould red lead nose', a nickname popular in the shipyard, and within a short time, those neighbours who found her activities irritating also began using this appropriate moniker.

'What's the puddin' club, ma?' I asked, thinking it was a sort of Christmas club, which at the time was quite popular, and afraid we were missing out on something.

'Worrave I told yer about listenin' to grown up conversations,' she said, before releasing a right hander that sent a cloud of dust from the seat of my trousers, gathered when crawling through a bombed house opposite the Co-op bakery in Price Street.

It didn't half hurt. She caught the chafed side of my leg but there was no way that I would cry in front of Ossie, not when his mam agreed with my punishment.

'Serve 'im right Maggie. I'd have tanned our Austin's arse me'self if he'd have used that sort of language in front of me,' she declared. I was puzzled.

'Grown-ups,' I mumbled under my breath. I don't want to ever grow up. If you don't ask, you'll never learn, so I'd been told time and time again. You ask and get belted for asking simple questions.

'What's wrong with askin' about puddin' clubs, Ossie?' I moaned when we were on our own in Arrowe Place.

'I dunno but I'm not goin' ter risk askin' me mam or me dad for that matter,' he replied

'Yeller belly,' I mutttered.

He had no bottle even then but he was cleverer than I was and besides we always stuck together, only because we were best of mates.

Jock Smith

If there was one house we loved going when we were bored, or the weather was lousy, it was Billy Smith's. His dad Jock originated from Glasgow and was good at telling stories.

'Were a' Jock Tamson's bairns,' he'd continually repeat whenever he smelt as if he'd been on the ale and had a faraway look in his eyes. He was ever so wise though, and nothing was too much trouble as he patiently answered those queries which we found difficult to understand. It was different to our house, there were no babies or girls to get in the way and we were as proud as Punch to be treated as if we were real soldiers.

'Here's the rest of yer troops Billy. Come away in laddies, yer know the way tae the parlour,' he'd say when he opened the front door to us. The parlour was always nice and warm and unlike our house didn't have oilcloth on the floor, but instead had the luxury of carpets. We were in our element, lying full stretched on the carpet listening to tales about Glasgow and the Rangers and poverty he'd experienced before the war.

'Aye boys ye widnae credit how poor we were when we were your age. We were lucky tae find a loaf in the hoose at the weekend. Mae mither was an expert at makin' porridge an' bread puddin an' we lived on that all week. Ten of us bairns, thae were, ye see. Most o' mae family were all wee 'uns. Ah dinnae know how I ended up bein' sae tall. Mind ye, I suppose a wiz always an early riser.'

We were fascinated and counted our lucky stars that we weren't as poor as Mr Smith had been when he was our age.

'Didn't yer 'ave any 'aggis when you were a lad, Mister Smith?' Spud asked. 'Me mam sez all Scotch people eat it an' it doesn't grow in England either,' he went on.

We all looked amazed. ' 'Aggis! What's that?' Tucker asked. None of us had ever heard of it. Jock smiled.

'Ach laddies, a'm goin' tae educate ye sassenachs fae a change.'

'Sassennachs... us?' we said, wondering if Jock was swearin' in Scotch.

'Now troops, a haggis is a wee animal that stays up in the Highland o' Scotland and has two lang legs an' two wee'uns.'

' 'Ow come they don't fall over then?' Ossie enquired. He was a deep thinker just like his mam. She had a high forehead and ginger hair and we all knew that's what clever people had. Cathy Murphy, Spud's sister had told us often enough and she should know, for she'd passed a scholarship to Holt Hill Convent. Besides, she had red hair herself, though you couldn't tell if she had a high forehead or not because she always wore one of those pudding hats.

'Och a'm glad ye asked that question Ossie, it shows ye've mair up top than sawdust.'

Ossie beamed.

'The reason they dinna fall over, laddies, is because they never venture on flat ground but stay on the side of the braes, an' it's far easier tae run on a slope with two long legs an' two wee 'un's than four the same size, d'ye see?'

We were mesmerised. Not only were we learning about Jock's childhood but also about wild animals and that was great. Most of us had only seen horses, dogs and cats and they weren't that wild, not round here in Brookie anyway.

Mrs Smith carried on with her darning and smiled. Jock was back in his childhood days, which was much better than leaning over the bar in The Anchor getting himself half-cut. She was happy to see 'her fella' keeping his mind occupied and amusing the boys at the same time.

'Mister Smith.'

'Yes Tucker.'

'Why did yer leave Scotland to work in Lairds an' leave yer mates an' Rangers, an ' all that, just to come 'ere to live?'

'Well son it's a long, long story which I'll tell ye all agin, but what a will tell ye, it's all tae do wi' that fine woman sittin' over there.'

Mrs Smith beamed, then reached for her handbag and we knew it would soon be time for us to leave.

'Jock yer tell a fine tale. For a moment you had me kidded there lad. I thought for a minute you were in for the night,' she said.

'Well hen, ye should know me by now, an' ye know I canna kip properly without a wee swally. A drop of the hard stuff and a wee half never killed any-one laddies, remember that. Or maybe a couple o' wee halves,' he declared, glancing gleefully at the ten bob note slipped into his palm.

The Tutor

'Manners, like water cost nothing,' dad declared one miserable day, after returning from the library, which he frequented when things got on top of him. He was an avid reader and prided himself with being 'self-taught' as he put it. Being an orphan at thirteen years of age made him a tougher character, and this handicap inserted a strong determination within him to learn the rudiments of life and pass it on to us. We were fortunate to have parents who cared, he often reminded us.

The knowledge he attained was attributed to being out of work for seven years after the general strike of nineteen twenty-six. Like many of the working class he was an ardent Labour supporter and principles were high on his priority list. He was often on strike and we as a family were familiar with his utterings, such as scab, black leg, scumbag and a few other unrepeatable descriptions of those who didn't fight for their rights.

I don't know who Socrates was, or whether he was a strict disciplinarian or not, but dad often quoted him when embarking on many of his numerous brain testing exercises. These exercises were designed to disturb dormant intelligent cells, which he assumed needed a little prompting, especially mine.

'Education, kids, is the best thing in life. It's the only opportunity you'll get to allow you to escape from the doldrums of this sort of existence, which, whether we like it or not, we've all got to live with,' he said, glancing around our tiny, sparsely furnished front room. The houses, which were Victorian built and at least seventy years old, were similar to all properties in an area where women scrubbed their front door spaces as if a competition existed for the cleanest step, and fervently polished window cills with Cardinal red polish until they sparkled. It was an environment where washing was boiled with pride, dolly pegged, then flattened through a mangle and hung outside for all to see across clothes lines which bridged backyard walls.

Apart from accommodating large families, most dwellings contained unwelcome visitors. They came in three species, bugs, mice and cockroaches. These despicable lodgers were eradicated with various types of poisonous powders and traps, but at times proved most resilient as they reluctantly travelled to adjoining houses, more often than not arriving unscathed. After receiving similar treatment they were once again evicted and mosied on. Such was life in the terraces.

I was always being told that I was thick, so I must have been. It was better than being a clever dick though, because then you'd be expected to know everything and that must have been lousy when you couldn't answer even simple questions.

Dad's questions were always directed at our Bridie who was older and obviously more intelligent than I was.

I wasn't really interested in learning. I'd had enough at school and my brain couldn't take any more, it was full up already after listening to Mrs Carty rabbiting on for nine months, but dad didn't appear to see it my way. He had no time for excuses as he relentlessly pushed forward with his quest to educate us whether we liked it or not.

On those occasions I really tried my best to look interested, even though the lads were outside our front door playing 'shots in' against Jenkins' factory wall and I loved being in goal.

'Which city is the capital of America?'

'Washington,' our Bridie answered before the question had sunk in.

'Whereabouts is Paris?'

'France.'

'Where's Berlin?'

'Germany, dad,' she smirked and by that time I had a face on me.

'Who's the Prime Minister then?'

'Atlee.'

'Okedoky Bridie, give 'im a chance an' see if he knows this one,' said dad.

I pulled tongues at her so she pinched my arm and I yelled.

'Cut it out the pair of yer, otherwise I won't ask yer anymore questions.'

I hoped he wouldn't, so I pulled tongues again, but she knew what I was up to and didn't retaliate.

'Let's think of a nice easy one for you son,' he went on, and our Bridie had a face on her tripping to the ground. I was happy then.

'What country is Tipperary in?' After some deliberation, I answered 'America, dad.'

She laughed, she would, but dad stroked his chin, looking perturbed.

'What makes you think it's in America son?' He quietly asked, which was encouraging, as he normally growled, so my confidence soared again.

'You know that song yer always singin' dad?'

'Which one?'

'It's a long long way to Tipperary.'

'Yeh worra bout it?'

'Well America's the furthest place that I know of, so it must be there,' I confidently replied and our Bridie burst out laughing again. I kicked her one, under the table, so she smacked me across my face and I screamed like a pig and woke the baby up.

'That's it, that's all I need,' dad bawled.

'When are you two goin' ter behave yourselves like other kids?' he demanded as mam appeared carrying our Tommy, the latest arrival in our family.

As everyday events took their course, life meandered on at the same pace. There didn't appear to be a consistency or a sequence, as activities, large or small passed by. Petty crime regularly took place and murders, whenever they happened, were always headline news. With most people in town leaving their front doors open, thieves were low priority, probably because there wasn't much to pinch in any case, except money in the lecky or gas meters, but if anyone attempted to knock those off they'd have been better off committing suicide before they were caught and strung up.

We were no different than anyone else, but for convenience sake, dad tied a piece of string to open our front door. However, the majority of our neighbours just left the latch off. Strangely enough the back door had a huge flat iron bar used as a locking device, so perhaps there were thieves after all...back entry ones.

'Go out an' play while me an' your mother 'ave a quiet talk,' dad yelled when sometimes I arrived home to find the string missing and the back door locked.

'What are yer talkin' about dad?'

'Mind yer own business and go an' play.'

'I wanna butty.'

'Go an' bloody play.' Nine months later we'd be lumbered with a screaming baby and stinking nappies and all because mam and dad wanted a quiet talk.

It was like a festival when the Lecky or gasman was due to empty meters. News travelled even faster than when the cops were about to raid Billy Thomson, the bookies' runner's house. We couldn't believe our eyes as the metal boxes were removed from the bottom of the meters and loads of shillings emptied onto the kitchen table. All the dodgy or foreign coins were put to one side and as soon as the coast was clear, mam dropped them back into the meter box. The collectors were always welcomed with open arms and tea was offered and supped in every household. If it happened to be Monday a slice of apple pie or a buttered scone followed, such was their popularity. Rebates were like winning the treble chance or getting paid twice in the same week.

'Now don't be goin' an' tellin yer father that the Lecky man's been,' we were often warned, but dad wasn't soft. As soon as a shilling dropped into the box though, the echo gave the game away.

'Aye Aye, when did that get emptied?'

There was deathly silence. Mam went deaf.

Shanks's pony

After twelve months in the boys' school and that first summer holiday of our young lives, we all moved into standard two. Our new teacher, Miss Brindle, a small, stocky, middle aged lady with short dark hair, believed passionately in using the cane to control unruly pupils. What we found refreshing, however, was that she had no time for snivellers and so we weren't burdened with any self-acclaimed teacher's pets. Cleary wasn't too bothered, for his earlier crush on Mrs Carty evaporated dramatically after Father Doyle suggested that 'perhaps young Cleary might be a possible candidate to champion the meek and mild' - a suggestion totally alien to Cleary's nature: he preferred belting them instead.

Before leaving standard one, Cleary had endured the final indignity when he'd received a hefty whack across his backside with a long ruler for talking in class. This ultimate punishment by Mrs Carty finally dented his faith in the concept of loyalty to any teacher.

Although the summer holidays were now long gone, the freedom of running wild for six whole weeks stayed with us, even though we were quickly brought to earth with a bump when we resumed school.

Miss Brindle made it clear that she was the kind of person who was determined to knock us into shape at all costs. Mind you, if we were well behaved she would reward the class by reading to us from a book called Gullivers Travels; and when this happened, well, you could've heard a pin drop. For Gulliver's adventures were our adventures, and as soon as we were free and out of school we let our imaginations run riot, because we too wanted to be travellers and visit wild and undiscovered foreign lands.

But then again we were already well-seasoned travellers ourselves, for hadn't we just spent the summer exploring distant lands?

Right across those six long weeks we would either catch a bus or trudge on Shank's pony to places well beyond the confines of the lanes of Birkenhead. We sought out and conquered Bidston Hill, the Nanny Goat Mountains and the Bluebell Woods, Moreton Shore - and even made it to that distant favourite New Brighton. Once we even enjoyed the added excitement of a charabanc trip to Raby Mere, which was organised by our mothers.

Early on in the holidays someone suggested we give 'the Arno' the 'once over.' The day we chose happened to coincide with a planned trek to the paradise of Arrowe Park; a location which to my eight-year-old eyes was miles out in the deepest countryside. According to some of the older lads the Arno was only a short detour from our proposed route and so it was decided we'd traipse there first, just to see what it was like for ourselves, before journeying on to Arrowe Park.

As on all our travels and adventures, mam always fussed about beforehand, making sure that I was clean and tidy.

'Tap water costs nothing,' she'd say, scrubbing my face and pushing the flannel down as far as my shoulders. 'And neither does Corporation oil,' she'd add, running the comb under the tap and parting my hair like a sissy. I hated that bit.

Then there was the question of the butties. For whatever reason, mam just couldn't cut the slices straight. They started wafer thin on one side and ended up as thick as doorsteps at the other. Mind you she more than made up for her bread slicing inadequacies by spreading loads of jam on the butties, so it would ooze out through the newspaper wrapping, sometimes making it possible to read the football results transfer - printed onto the slices of bread. Despite mam's shortfalls, I always had plenty to eat on my travels.

'Tucker, don't forget to bring yer 'aversack,' Nacker bawled, as we waited in the Court for Smithy and Tucker to appear.

Sometimes Tucker left his dad's spare haversack at home on purpose and who could blame him? It wasn't because it was bulky, or that it was awkward to carry or even that we piled our grub into it, he only objected when other bits and pieces, such as catapults, empty jam jars, string and footballs were slipped in as well. He said he felt like a Co-op cart horse, which was fair enough and so on this occasion, for once, we all agreed to carry our own butties and bottles of water.

Before we set off and to be on the safe side, Nacker advised us to nip home and cadge a few pennies from our mams just in case we happened to become stranded somewhere out in the wilds. This we reckoned was good advice coming from our leader.

For a change, the gang were free from everyday chores to make the journey and everything seemed to be plain sailing, but then Frankie Bailey tagged on behind, pestering to take him with us, though he was only seven and a bit and at least nine months younger than me. None of us really wanted him to come along until he produced a half crown given to him by his Uncle Joe as a reward for running messages. Nacker immediately displayed leader wisdom, suggesting that it was time we showed young Frankie the ropes and demonstrate to him just how smoothly our gang operated. Of course we had no objections, if Nacker said it was a good idea, then it was a good idea as far as we were concerned.

The Arno proved a washout. There was just nothing for us to do there…no swings nor tall trees to test our climbing ability, no ponds to mess about in or nowhere to catch fish. And there wasn't even a decent patch of grass to volley the football at one another. As far as we could see, the only thing at the Arno was flower gardens surrounded by sandstone rocks and a whole lot old people sitting on benches reading papers.

'This place is no good to us,' Smithy moaned. So after swigging a mouthful of water, we set off towards the Flat Lanes. We'd hardly reached the top of the first hill, however, when a thunderstorm appeared from nowhere and spots of rain as large as two bob bits splattered down on us. To escape the shower we sheltered beneath large branches of the many chestnut trees that most of the posh mansions situated along the Old Bidston Road had in their front gardens. As we stood there huddled from the pouring rain Nacker reminded us to take careful note of our whereabouts so that we would remember the location for the start of the conker season. What a leader I thought, for as well as Frankie Bailey we were all being shown the ropes.

It was Smithy and Tucker who first spotted the big church opposite the Flat Lanes and before anyone else had a chance, they'd 'bagged' it. You bagged anything you could in our gang, not that bagging anything meant much, just that you were alert, and perhaps had seen or spotted something a good second or two before the others, but when Nacker said that it looked like a Proddy church to him we told Tucker and Smithy they could have it.

As the rain eased off and the dark clouds which seemed to have followed us from the Arno were replaced by blue skies, we ambled on, wandering a few hundred yards to where a sign-post caught our attention. One of the finger posts pointed in the direction of Arrowe Park but there was no mention of the big white house, which according to Nacker was our landmark and could now be plainly seen on the other side of a valley surrounded by fields of green and yellow. 'Three miles from Arrowe, that's all,' yelled Tucker. The big white house, which was supposed to be situated before Arrowe Park looked to me as if it was three miles away, but then again I couldn't really imagine just how far three miles was.

At that moment a huge rainbow appeared in the sky, running from behind a hill on the left side and disappearing into a cornfield directly to our right. We gawped at the spectacle - we'd only seen a full rainbow with as many colours in picture books at school.

'You'd never see that down town,' Spud said in a determined way, as if to give further help to Frankie Bailey in learning the ropes.

'There's supposed to be gold buried at the foot of a rainbow,' Smithy yelled.

'Gold? Who told yer that?' Nacker asked quite sharpish.

'Me dad told me,' Smithy retorted.

This silenced Nacker; though he was our leader he couldn't argue with that. We all knew that if Mr Smith said there was gold at the bottom of a rainbow then there was bound to be.

'Okay lads, let's get goin', Nacker ordered and without a further thought we galloped like mad down the Flat Lanes, splashing through the puddles, our pumps squelching and clothes wringing wet.

We raced onwards now, not stopping for a breather or to wait for poor little Frankie Bailey who lagged behind in last place. We sped alongside some tennis courts on our right hand side, following the lane as it meandered, narrowed, then dipped rapidly near a sharp bend.

As we turned the corner Nacker, who raced in front, held his hand up and yelled for us to stop. 'This 'ill do us for now, lads,' he bawled.

Just yards away lay a large pond, shaded by a massive willow tree twisted with age. We plonked ourselves down in this haven, lying on the dry side of the bank and attacked our butties like ravenous seagulls. During the feast we followed the time-honoured practice of swapping butties, for some of us had different flavoured jams and one or two even had cheese. Smithy as usual had the best butties. It seemed that Mrs Smith always managed to have a bit of something salted away in one of her cupboards and so Smithy often had meat butties, even though the meat might only be Spam or cornbeef.

As young Frankie had only tagged on to us at the last moment he hadn't brought any butties at all. We agreed, however, to adapt the gang's 'share and share alike' arrangement and offered him some of our grub; we couldn't let him starve, could we? Of course, we were well aware that he'd broken into his half a dollar and bought a large bottle of Tizer from Maines paper shop in Vittoria Street.

Nacker, as we'd kind of expected, removed the bottle from Frankie's possession and rationed the swigs of pop - which was only fair seeing that Frankie was still learning the ropes.

After scoffing half of our butties we carefully wrapped the remainder for later when we'd be starving again, and began splashing about in the pond, pushing aside the bulrushes and reeds as we searched for frogs or newts or anything like that. However, the commotion we created no doubt scared them off and in the end our hunting skills were never really tested. In addition, the murky green water prevented us seeing much below the surface and with having no idea if there were any dangers facing us we waded further from the edge. Not that the gang were afraid of anything much anyway.

Soon our feet began sinking into the slippery mud and when the bottoms of our short trousers became wet we panicked and immediately grabbed hold of each other's hands, dragging us out of the muddy bottom and onto the bank. Frankie, we realised, had learned another lesson here, about how we all acted as one in the face of adversity.

With legs caked with damp and sticky mud we set off on what was the last stage of this adventure to Arrowe Park. We tramped alongside the fields of corn and wheat now, plucking seeded arrows and sticky buds on the way, which we hurled at each other as we tumbled along. The sky was blue, the rain was more or less forgotten and the mud was drying tight on our legs. We were now in the deepest of deep countryside where proper birds - not your 'townie' pigeons or sparrows - flew overhead.

'We are the members of the Brook Street gang,' we sang out in an unmelodious chorus and at that particular moment in time there was no one in the world as happy as we were.

Arriving at the iron gates of Arrowe Park, we stopped for a moment to gaze at their enormity, then sprinted like mad into the park towards the statue of Baden Powell which stood a few hundred yards or so away, half way along the path from the gate. The tiredness in our legs from the tremendous number of miles we must have covered to reach the end of our journey was forgotten now and the aches and pains in our young muscles seemed miraculously to have disappeared. High in the trees huge black crows screamed and fought as they protected the biggest nests we'd ever seen in our lives and we yelled even louder in our excitement.

Suddenly, as if by magic, bright yellow beams of sunlight burst through the clouds onto the darkened paths, revealing the swings and the children's playground and the open fields beyond. We shrieked louder than anyone as we raced each other to be first to reach the hanging bars, where we threw our clobber down in an untidy heap before leaping up onto the bars, swinging from one arm to the other and much better than any of those chattering monkeys we'd seen in the Tarzan picture last week.

After draining our excess energy, we finished our butties, drank noisily and thirstily from the drinking fountain, played football for a while and then re-tracing our steps we began our long journey home. Leg-weary, we reached the pond by the willow tree, slipped off our pumps and socks, dipped our hot feet into the mossy water and later began fishing for sticklebacks (or Jack Sharps, as we called them). This time, using our mams' old stockings - which were much more effective than any proper fishing nets, we caught half a dozen Jack Sharps, without too much effort or skill. Along with these, a load of tadpoles and a couple of croaking frogs were triumphantly carried off in jam jars, which were supported with the string we'd bought at Johnny Brown's chandlers shop.

Near the Seven Stiles, sharp-eyed Tucker Griffiths spotted an overgrown orchard lying well off the beaten track that had no surrounding fence or any signs of life. We all 'bagged it' immediately and christened it 'No Man's land,' a name that seemed to go well with the long adventurous journey into the wilds that we'd made. After stripping a few of the trees, we took off again heading for home with loads of apples hidden under our jerseys, which in turn were tucked into our trousers. It felt like hours since we'd finished our butties in Arrowe Park and by this time, as we were starving, we began eating the apples, even the sour ones and not long afterwards Frankie Bailey started crying because of a belly ache. Smithie bent over to put his arm around him just as Frankie let rip and almost filled his trousers. Fortunately, he managed to reach the lavvies in the top park, but stunk to high heaven. Following Nacker's example we went on ahead, just in case Frankie's mam blamed us for taking him with us in the first place - or worse still, accused us of making him eat the apples as well.

Eventually we arrived home in Brookie, tired, hungry, covered in mud and all of us looking as if nobody owned us. As soon as I entered the house mam went off like a bottle of pop; she didn't believe in a softly softly approach when the matter of dirt was concerned.

'Will you look at the colour of this fella,' she gasped to dad who having been grafting down the docks since half seven was relaxing on the settee reading the Echo. Dad too had also arrived home as black as the ace of spades and he wasn't in the mood for talking. As usual he'd bagged all the hot water for his wash before dinner and trust my luck, mam didn't have a shilling in change for the gas meter, so I had to put up with a bowl of cold water.

It didn't take mam long to remove the top layer of grime, nor was she bothered in the least about using more than an abundance of elbow grease. The whole process didn't half hurt but she was in no mood to be gentle.

'Stop screwin' your face up an' yellin'. Do yer hear me? You'll wake the baby up in a minute an' woe betide you if he starts screamin' 'she threatened.

A few tears trickled down my face. They always did when I got soap in my eyes, but ma hadn't finished yet, she had a cob on... worst luck. 'Have yer seen the dirt in 'is ears Charlie' she asked dad? You could grow a pound of spuds in there.'

'Don't tell me about it woman, he's like a bloody dog,' he replied. 'He'll roll about in bloody shite all day, just like the rest of them out there. No pride in 'imself, or us for that matter. That's the bloody trouble with 'im,' he concluded, without even looking up from the paper. Mam continued removing debris from my ears before wetting my head and grooming my matted hair with a comb that had half the teeth missing. Dad called it the cowboy comb because of its wide open spaces, but to me it was ten times more welcome than the fine tooth comb; everyone of us kids in the family hated that comb; for apart from pulling chunks out of your head, it trawled at your scalp like a mechanical scraper.

Usually this instrument of torture was kept on the top shelf, 'out of harms way,' as mam said; and was only brought down when she'd heard on the grapevine that 'Nitty Nora the biddy explorer' was entering our territory. Family pride would then dictate we should all have a good combing to try to stave off the disgrace of having Nitty Norah discover wild-life in our heads; and so we had to kneel on the floor, one at a time and place our heads across her lap. An old copy of the Echo would replace mam's inevitable pinny and our scalps would then be subjected to an intense fine-tooth grilling which would leave every would-be intruder trembling in mam's wake. There was no reprieve for any captured biddy, the death penalty was always imposed and carried out at once.

After these scalpings mam would give us the third degree to see who we had been knocking around with.

'Who'ave you been playin' with, James?' she'd demand.

'Thingy, you know thingymejig from Backo.'

'Mrs Lawton's lad?'

'No, next door Mrs Whatsername. He's in Tucker's class. You know.'

'Ah! Thingys lad ... McNamara's?'

'Yeah, 'im an me other mates.'

'Were any of them scratchin'?' the steward's enquiry continued.

After deep thought and a scratch of my head, which earned another clout, I replied.

'I dunno.'

But then I thought to myself, 'all me mates scratch their heads, pick their nose and throw stones, don't they? Isn't that what your fingers are for?'

Later, when the holidays were long past and Miss Brindle was holding us quiet and captivated with the exploits of Jonathon Swift's hero, I stopped to wonder if Gulliver had ever to face the joys of 'Nitty Nora' when he was a boy, or indeed, whether he had to suffer the indignities of the 'fine tooth comb' after he'd returned from one of his adventures.

Jess

Saturday night was always bath night in our house. The first job of the evening was to carry the long tin bath from the backyard, where it hung from a large nail and place it in front of the fire on top of a rug mam had patiently made from strips of cloth. In order to fill the bath with hot water, kettles, pots, pans and buckets were used from the four rings on the gas stove, the main source of heat in the house.

As soon as the water in the bath reached an acceptable temperature for our bodies we took it in turns to soak in the suds, knowing that we had to be quick otherwise the last one in would be bathing in cold water and inevitably start whinging.

'Hurry up an' get dried otherwise you'll catch yer death of cold,' ma ordered.

'An' don't forget your dad wants to see the fire as well,' she added. Mind you, it didn't take long to dry; the fire was always stoked right up the chimney on bath nights.

Dad loved the coal fire, but didn't like setting it. His rocking chair was almost on top of the hearth with his feet resting comfortably on the black oven range containing the fire grate. It was debatable who could get nearest the fire, our Jess or dad, although he vigorously disputed the dog's claim to pride of place.

'The bloody dog's on fire,' he would cry as steam rose from Jess's coat after she'd drifted in from the rain.

She was a funny old dog, but crafty. She didn't like the rain or snow but loved the fire, though dad wasn't having a dog dictate to him who got the best speck by the fire.

'Bloody move, will yer,' he'd growl, prodding the dog with his stocking feet. These were steaming as well, but we daren't tell him because he'd only accuse of us of siding with the dog. Jess would then move, rather reluctantly and sulkily towards the sanctuary of the back door.

Having exercised his authority, dad would now relax and rock away merrily in his chair until he succumbed to the heat and dozed off.

I was the only one who noticed Jess move. As soon as she heard the strains of dad's rhythmic snore, she stood up, stretched, then lay down again a yard away from the door. She glanced slyly at dad to make sure that he wasn't cat napping, then up she popped, stretched once more, then down again, edging nearer each time and before the fire needed another shovel of coal she was back against the grate. It was noticeable that her hearing and awareness seemed to dramatically improve during these encounters. I watched, as she kept one of her eyes open in case dad felt the heat shielded from his legs and woke up with a start. Then, without fail, she'd rapidly move. She had dad weighed up to a fine tune.

Jess was a decent house dog and good company, particularly during dark nights.

I only had to mutter 'cats ... cats,' and she was out in the yard before I could say 'Jack Robinson.'

When nature called, she was my best friend. That's if no one volunteered to stand by the back door and whistle when I went to the lavvie. Nothing seemed to bother her at all, even the sight of me sitting with the door open or the pong. To be honest she lay by my feet, keeping an eye on any movement from stray rodents or cats lurking in the entry. I didn't know whether it was because she wasn't fond of the dark, like me or just nesh.

Her loyalty, however, couldn't be faulted.

Dad got her from the dog's home in Livingstone Street, where she'd been abandoned. Someone had told him fox terriers were excellent ratters and fighters and it was this type of reputation that appealed to him. He also shared a belief that a dog had to earn its keep the same as everyone else, so she was under scrutiny to perform her house-guarding duties from day one.

Jess had also been doctored and this too, was an added bonus. Dad wasn't the type to encourage an increase in the canine population. I don't think he felt sorry for her because she was about to be put down. Dad wasn't like that. He wasn't sentimental at all. 'A dog's a dog,' he often said, but he was real proud of her after she fought Billy Marsdon's Alsation and half-killed him. I know he was. He had a big grin on his face.

Dad didn't like Billy Marsdon one bit. He was an odd-ball who chased the kids from playing outside his front door and was forever moaning and threatening to set his dog on them.

'Good girl,' dad said patting Jess's head despite blood pouring from what remained of part of her ear. She was as surprised as we were at his affectionate overtures and responded by licking his hand, which took some doing considering she'd been in a battle for her life. He returned the compliment by vigorously slapping her back. However, she didn't appear to enjoy his heavy handed reply and dropped on all fours, gently washing her wounds.

Dad had an unshakeable opinion that it was a harsh world outside and you either defended yourself or suffered the consequences and that included the dog, who, after her victory, was very much part of the family.

Following our weekly bath, after we were dried and dressed ready for bed, mam often made each of us a mug of cocoa with sugar, a commodity still rationed at the time. We lapped it up, cocoa tasted much better with sugar than saccharine tablets, a type of sweetener everyone seemed to use.

Mam always baked on Saturday night and there was nothing finer than sampling her hot scones or apple pie. It was the best night of the week as far as we were concerned. Dad would be propped in his easy chair listening to the latest news from the BBC, with the crackling wireless updating him on world events and the sports news.

'Shush kids, be quiet a minute...what's that? Ghandi's dead?' he uttered.

We immediately stopped talking. We knew if we didn't it would be straight to bed for us.

The coal fire, with an occasional log burning away, sent the heat to every corner of our front room and sometimes it was so warm that Jess retreated to the back kitchen to enjoy the coldness from the red quarry tiles that covered the floor. For us, however, we were in a world of our own, reading comics or drawing on scrap paper, while mam relaxed, passing the time away darning socks. We felt so secure in our own little heaven. Sometimes mam bought sarsaparilla, a popular drink which we all enjoyed and on extremely cold nights she would have a pan of spare ribs on the boil.

Occasionally she bought tripe from the butchers as a treat for dad. Tripe dosed with vinegar, was one of his favourite meals.

'Fancy eating a cow's belly,' I often wondered, glancing down at our Jess and shuddering at the thought of someone tucking into her fat stomach with all the nipples hanging down.

Dad had no such inhibitions as he swallowed the lumpy porridge-like concoction.

I don't know how he ate it but he did. Not even Jess was interested and she'd eat anything.

Perched at the top of our street and overlooking Hamilton Square the town hall clock smiled down at us, chiming its consistent message every quarter of an hour, day and night. At ten o'clock on Saturday night its unmistakable gong confirmed it was 'towels up' in the adjoining pubs. The streets, which were always quiet beforehand, then sprang to life.

Dad would turn down the wireless to listen to the Saturday night revellers singing the golden oldies at the top of their voices as they displayed talents which during the week had been hidden within mundane everyday existence.

'I'll take you 'ome again Kathleen,' Paddy Murphy sang and dad would draw the curtain slightly ajar to see what kind of state he was in. We'd sneak a look too and I laughed as Mrs Murphy dragged her husband by his tie as he wobbled like a jellyfish. I couldn't wait to tell Spud next morning. Following 'Good nights and God blesses,' tranquillity returned. Shortly after Mr Murphy was safely home and his front door closed, dad realised we were still up.

'It's high time these kids were in bed, Maggie. Right kids, let's have you up the dancers

An' don't forget ter give yer mam a kiss,' he ordered. This was a hint for the girls to give him a peck as well. Lads didn't kiss their dad, only sissies did. I wasn't a sissy.

'Good night dad.'

'Good night son,' he replied, ruffling my hair and giving me a playful crack on the bum.

'Goodnight an' God Bless' an' don't forget to say your prayers,' mam insisted, closing the back bedroom door while we fought with our feet to get a speck on the oven plate.

I always slept at the bottom of the bed by the window, ready to escape in case the gang wanted me. You could never tell. War may break out again and then all our gang would be needed; there was little doubt that we'd be expected to defend the docks with our commando unit. That was one of the reasons we practised our aim whenever we met at our hideout and another thing, we knew all the best specs in town to hide from the enemy.

For personal comfort I wrapped dad's army coat around me leaving the blankets for the others. Lying there feeling the brass buttons and regimental inscriptions, I often wondered if the soldier who'd worn the coat was dead or alive.

'Was he a paratrooper or a commando?' I asked myself before concluding that he must have been both.

I could even smell the battles he'd been involved in and would fall asleep fighting my way out of enemy controlled villages, shooting Germans left, right and centre and throwing hand grenades. And after we'd won the war, returning home and getting a medal from the King in Buckingham Palace.

'I'M A HERO,' I screamed out in my sleep.

'Shurrup you, before me dad hears yer and then you'll be in for it,' our Bridie yelled and so I turned over and dreamt of playing for Tranmere Rovers, then Everton and finally being picked for England.

Self defence

After a weekend of fun, the start of a new week rarely generated a great deal of enthusiasm. Like every day our routine rarely altered. We left home at twenty to nine, gave Spud a knock, called for Ossie, met Nacker at the corner of Cathcart Street and then made a beeline to Blackburn's bakery. We would each buy a couple of hot barm cakes, stick our fingers in the middle and bite round the edges, before entering the small gate situated in Pleasant Street. Sometimes a few of the older boys stood by the gate demanding our barm cakes and this confrontation inevitably resulted in fights developing.

On such occasions Nacker became our hero, as neither Ossie, Spud nor I were any good at fighting. All we could offer was vocal support. One particular Monday three of these older lads attacked us and Nacker screamed at me, pointing to a small dark lad. 'Smack 'im one Jimmy, I'll take his mates on.' I dived in head down, trying to grab his waist, hoping to wrestle him to the ground. He stood back - it seemed he had been trained to fight you see. Bang...a straight left ... right on my chin. The ground came flying towards me and stars appeared before my eyes. Groggily, I looked across and staring me in the face were a pair of grubby shoes, a black lace in one, a brown in the other with grey socks rolled down and a big dirty bleeding scab on his right knee. My nose was numb and the side of my face was numb as well.

'I'm bleedin' ter death,' I yelled feeling warm blood dripping onto my lips. Nacker immediately came across and punched the lad on his chin before taking me into the lavvies to inspect the damage. Although my shirt was ruined I was able to hide this by turning my pullover round the other way, but my nose was a different proposition altogether. I couldn't turn that round, I only wished I could.

I was taken into the rest room and Mr Robinson from standard four bathed my wounds with cotton wool before dabbing a drop of iodine on the open cut and I cried out in pain. He smiled on the sly, I saw him. Afterwards one of the older lads took me to my own class where I was made to sit at the back of the room as punishment for misbehaving and I didn't get an ounce of sympathy even though my nose was half hanging off.

'Dad will murder you when he sees what you've done to your best shirt,' our Bridie gloated when she caught me 'dossing' it under the bed. There was little or no chance of hiding the bruising under my eye or swollen nose though. I hadn't mentioned it to mam when I got home as she was busy with the dinner and I didn't want her to worry herself sick before I got myself murdered, that wouldn't have been fair.

Dad didn't notice anything different at first, my face was always grubby, but I knew he'd soon find out because our Bridie was dying to tell him.

'Have you seen our Jimmy's face dad, and his nose?' she eventually blurted out. I recoiled ready for the expected onslaught, but dad surprised us all.

'Don't be tellin' bloody tales, you,' he said, rising from his chair and lifting my chin, before announcing that it was about time he taught me the rudiments of self defence.

The following weekend he purchased an old pair of boxing gloves from a second-hand shop in Exmouth Street and my lessons began. First of all he set out to develop my stance. I found this extremely difficult as my feet seemed rooted to the ground and every time I tried punching with my left hand I fell over.

'Guard yer chin, guard yer chin, like I've just showed yer ... Come on straight left ... straight left ... uppercut ... bloody uppercut,' he yelled, dancing round the yard shadow boxing. Eventually I cornered him against the mangle but the gloves were like huge pillows and flew off my little hands. Dad wasn't put off by this small problem and decided it was time to teach me to fight bare fist.

'Punch me as 'ard as you can,' he challenged. And so I did.

'Christ that's below the belt yer little bugger,' he gasped. I felt quite pleased with myself. It was the first time I'd seen him wince, I was proud of that punch. After another half-hour of coaching, dad began complaining that his feet were getting cold with dancing in his socks and called it a day. It was a pity he was ending my first lesson just as I was getting the hang of it; nevertheless he seemed quite pleased with the result.

Just another weekend

We all looked forward to Friday. A whole weekend without school. We didn't have homework; well we did in a way, though it had nothing to do with school. The girls were trained in domestic chores while we ran messages, not only for our mothers but also for elderly people who were ill or housebound. Friday for most workers was pay day and the majority of wages were paid in little brown envelopes. Sometimes pay dockets had a habit of disappearing before reaching households, a feature considered normal to many wage earners who didn't consider it prudent to disclose take-home pay, particularly when overtime hours boosted their wages.

Friday was collectors' night too, with the breadman, coalman, milkman and cheque man eager to balance their books before the weekend. For us Catholics, we had additional visitors, the Parish Priests. At least one would call every six weeks for family visits and to see the sick or dying more frequently.

For some reason, however, the cheque man remained bottom of the league in order of priorities and mam, like many others, often stalled him for a week when funds were low.

'Mr Cline from Sturla's is on his way mam,' I dutifully reported, when spotting him pedalling in the direction of our block.

'Tell 'im I'm not in Bridie.'

'I'm not tellin' lies,' she yelled.

'They're only white ones. Will you go to the door James?' she asked.

'Course I will mam.' Lies didn't bother me, whether white or any other colour.

'Me mam said she's not in Mr Cline.'

'Tell 'er I want double next week and also to be careful she doesn't damage her knees on the cold floor.' I looked round; mam had done it again. She'd only left her feet sticking out from under the table.

'Dad, here's the priest,' I yelled as the dark figure of Father Doyle emerged from Aunt Fan's front door.

'Christ Almighty,' he bawled, pushing his dinner to one side and scarpering into the backyard to the lavvie.

Mam swiftly lifted his dinner plate and popped it into the oven just as the knocker rattled. Our Jess, who normally brought the house down whenever anyone else other than the family knocked at the door, barely moved. She appeared to have a sixth sense that Father Doyle's presence had a devastating effect on dad and more importantly on his dinner, so nothing could be done but to wait a short while before scrounging scraps.

'Good evening Maggie and how are you?'

'Very well, thank you Father.'

'And Charlie and the kids?'

'Couldn't be better thanks.'

'Any sign of Charles going to mass yet?' He whispered nodding in the direction of the backyard. Mam shook her head before giving her usual reply.

'I still believe in miracles you know Father, but when they will happen God only knows.'

'I won't stay long then,' he said. 'It's been a right cold old day on the docks and I wouldn't be too popular if Charlie's meal isn't on the table when he comes in, will I?' He added, glancing down at the shrivelled ring on the plastic tablecloth where the hot dinner plate had left its indelible evidence.

Mam retrieved a two bob bit from behind a statue of Our Lady on the dresser, placed it into his outstretched hand and he thanked her.

'Good night and God bless and say a little prayer for me, won't you Maggie?'

'I will that Father, I will indeed and I'll say a little prayer for me'self that Charlie's dinner hasn't burned,' she muttered under her breath as the priest departed up the street to the McCarthy's.

'Has he gone yet, Jimmy?' dad whispered, sticking his head round the lavvie door. I know it was lousy of me, but depending on whether he'd been in a good mood all week or not, I'd keep him sweating for an answer. This was the first time I realised I had a mean streak in me.

'Hey Jimmy look what I've got,' Tucker shouted the following morning when I was on my way to the Co-op for mam's groceries.

'Worr is it?' I asked, as he slipped the mysterious object into his trouser pocket like a pistol. 'It's a real banana,' he declared. I was flabbergasted. I couldn't help it. I was so surprised that I dropped ma's shopping bag onto the pavement, with all the empty pop bottles in. You see I'd never seen a real live banana before.

'Gis a bite,' I asked, but he declined, saying he wanted to show it to the rest of the gang first, which was fair enough. We called for Ossie, then Spud, who was busy cleaning the family's shoes in the backyard. It didn't take him long to abandon the task when he spied Tucker's prize. Billy was counting his best ollies and sorting out the ball bearings when we arrived. They were soon put away. Nacker had gone to Wallasey gas works, taking the baby's pram with him to fetch a couple of bags of coke for his mam and unfortunately for him missed out on the sighting of the first banana.

After a short discussion as to whether we should wait until he returned, we decided it would be better if we tasted the yellow bender first and let him know what it was like afterwards. Our share and share alike declaration wasn't even mentioned.

Seeing it was Tucker's banana he had first bite. Sinking his teeth half way down he bit through the thick yellow skin and grimaced.

'Ooh... Ooh,' he baulked, spitting out strands of skin which we thought was quite wasteful, seeing it was the very first banana any of us had ever set eyes on.

Johnny's grandmother, old Mrs Collins, who didn't have a tooth in her mouth and was generally assumed to be 'doo lally,' happened to be passing at the time and observed the spectacle with interest.

'What's that you'se lot 'ave pinched now,' she cackled and began laughing as she spotted the banana.

'You don't eat the skin you soft buggers. Come 'ere an' I'll show yer what to do with it.'

Taking the banana from Tucker she peeled the skin away and swallowed the lot.

'Christ' yelled Tucker 'she's ate all me friggin' banana.'

We stood there mesmerised. In one foul swoop we'd witnessed what could well have been the beginning of a real disaster.

All we recovered was the skin which we hungrily scraped with our teeth and as Ossie said, it was better than nothing seeing it was our first taste of a banana.

Nacker eventually arrived home and learnt of the calamity.

'Serve yer right,' he said, 'it wouldn't have happened if you'd have waited for me.'

We agreed ... Wholeheartedly.

Bad habits

It was just before Christmas after the decorations had been strung across the classroom ceiling and we were counting days to our winter break, that Spud was thrown out of class for breaking wind and Pop Lally caned me for laughing. The trouble with me was that I was easily amused. Spud was renowned for farting in class, but would escape detection most of the time because they were silent raspers. His family were well known for their participation in this particular function, thinking nothing of it: 'Church or chapel, let 'em rattle,' his old man, Paddy would proclaim and they all followed suit with great gusto.

You wouldn't do it in our house though, not in front of dad. He'd throw you out in the yard without a second thought. It was okay to let one go in front of mam; she never heard and had no sense of smell. With dad, however, it was a different ball game altogether. 'There's a time an' place for everything,' he'd bawl.

As a result I always took care to remember where I happened to be and not to let off when dad was around, for if he heard me there was little doubt he'd have clipped me across my ear.

Spud, however, slipped up this time when he dropped one in the classroom. It was during a period when the class was dead quiet so that even Miss Brindle would have been hard-put not to have heard it. I started tittering, which was probably caused by my nerves as much as anything else and in consequence, earned myself a rap across the knuckles with a ruler as Miss Brindle made her way to the back of the room. Everyone in class knew Spud was the culprit, that's why they all looked in his direction.

'Who's the disgusting wretch responsible for this outburst?' she demanded.

I don't know how he did it, but Spud kept a straight face, glancing over his shoulder as if the 'rasper' had somehow drifted in from further back, even though we all knew that there was only the wall behind him. 'Was it you Byrne?' she yelled, glaring at Timmy Byrne who happened to be sitting beside Spud. He immediately started crying. Timmy hated sitting next to Spud, particularly at times such as this when it seemed he was about to be blamed for something he didn't do. He was so upset that he split on Spud.

'No Miss it wasn't me, 'onest ter God, it was 'im, it was Murphy,' he wailed.

Miss Brindle grabbed Spud by the scruff of his neck, dragged him to the door and flung him out into the corridor, just as Pop Lally happened to be walking past.

I couldn't stop laughing at the look on Spud's face and as a result, I was thrown out too.

We both received four of the best and instructed to apologise to Miss Brindle for our disgusting behaviour. I was just eight and a bit and it's probably fair to assume that my decline from grace had already begun.

'Lets see yer 'ands,' Ossie and Nacker asked as we walked across the dump into Watson Street. We revealed two red stripes across each palm. Nacker had been caned on numerous occasions so the novelty had worn off. His hands had toughened up, but ours were still soft. To take the sting out of the weal's we kept blowing warm breath through our clenched fists.

At the end of St Anne Street we bumped into the rest of our gang and it was there that Nacker met up with some of the lads from his class. They began singing a common song popular with the older boys, so we joined in as we made our way home to Brookie.

'We've got chickens in our back yard, we feed them on Indian corn,
One's a bugger for screwin' the other, an' that's against the law.
Oh, Auntie Mary's got a canary up the leg of her drawers,
when she farted, down it darted, down the leg of her drawers.'

We laughed, it was dead funny, well we thought it was anyway, but how was I supposed to know our Bridie was walking behind me with her mate Frances Cartland.

'Just you wait till I tell me dad about you our Jimmy,' she yelled. Her threat, however, fell on deaf ears. I didn't care a wink when I was with my mates and I knew that dad wouldn't be in 'til half seven. If I was smart enough I'd be up the stairs before he'd eaten his dinner and besides, the baby would be asleep by that time and no way would he risk wakening him up.

The first thing I noticed as I sneaked through the kitchen for my tea was dad's hook hanging behind the back door. My heart missed a beat when I heard his gruff voice demanding to know 'what's the other fella's been up to now?' I then panicked, I must admit, for there was only one 'other fella' in our house ... me.

'Dad, he used the 'F' word, in Cathcart Street' I heard Bridie say.

'Yer what, the 'F' word... are you sure it was our Jimmy?' dad quizzed and I shook from head to toe in the back kitchen.

'Ask Frances Cartland if you don't believe me,' she replied.

I didn't know if mam was in or not. As she was the only one I could rely on to save me from getting battered, I stood without making a sound until I heard the baby chuckling.

'I hadn't used the 'F' word, had I? Of course I hadn't. I'd have remembered it. I kept count of every time I swore, so that my conscience was cleared properly before going to confession. She was at it again, telling lies,' I muttered to myself.

Without a second thought I walked into the front room and I could tell by the look on dad's face that this wasn't a smart move. He stood with his back against the fire, glaring at me. Mam was breastfeeding Tommy, our Bernadette was reading a comic and the other one, our Bridie, had a look on her face as if she just read Charles Dickens', Great Expectations.

'What's all this I've been 'earin' about?' Dad snarled. It was comforting to see his belt was still buckled up and it seemed that even Jess hadn't sensed impending danger as she lay peacefully by the front door...though events could change rapidly in our house.

'What! worr'ava supposed to 'ave done now?' I whinged.

'Swearin' in the street.'

'I didn't dad, she's tellin' lies again, she's a liar.'

'There's no bloody liars in this 'ouse, now what did you say?' he bawled.

Out of the corner of my eye I spotted that Jess was on the move and mentally began planning my own escape route ... through the back yard door, or failing that, straight up the stairs and out of the window onto the air raid shelter roof.

'Nowt dad, nowt, 'onest. Ask Ossie Feeley if yer don't believe me,' I pleaded.

'Liar' our Bridie butted in.' 'He said the 'F' word an' sang dirty songs with his mates.'

'He what... he sang dirty songs as well. What did he sing?'

'I'm not sayin'' she said ... 'I've been to confession once this week an' I'm not goin' again.'

Dad seemed more than exasperated by her reply and this suited me at the time. She hasn't done it to save my skin, I thought. She must have had something else on her conscience. Dad turned to me and glared. 'Listen to me m'lad an' listen properly. If I hear one more complaint about you from anyone, an' I mean anyone, I'll tan your bloody arse till its red raw, do yer 'ear me?'

'Yis dad.' I wasn't deaf' I heard all right. He was only two feet away, so I moved rapidly out of reach, all the while imagining the pain I would suffer if he were to carry out his threat.

I pulled tongues at our Bridie on the sly and mam smiled. She hated any upset in the house. I was like her in a way. I just wanted a simple life, to come in from school, have my tea and then go out and play with my mates. There was nothing wrong in that was there?

Given the circumstance of this interrogation and how close I'd come to a thrashing I didn't mention about getting caned at school to dad. He'd have probably exploded and given me a right roasting.

'It's a good job we were well separated from the girls' school, otherwise life wouldn't be worth living,' I muttered to myself.

Chapter 2

Action Stations

The winter of 1947 is one that is clearly remembered by anyone who lived through it. With the war only eighteen months behind us, rationing still biting hard and little for the grown ups to cheer about, it was left to us kids to celebrate and enjoy the truly tremendous downfalls of snow which covered the town like a huge white blanket for weeks on end. We kids, it seemed, were immune to the freezing smog which swirled through the streets, blocking out the dim gas lights and making any easy identification of approaching pedestrians almost impossible from only a short distance. It was almost like being back in the black-out, though this was more of a white-out, with fog to make it all the more bizarre. The depth of the snow and the fact that it lay for weeks, meant we spent days on end with wet legs, which became red and sore from the tops of our socks to the bottom of our short trousers. Mind you, this didn't deter us from rolling down snow covered hills in the park during the weekend, or skating on the frozen lake whenever we felt it was safe to do so - which was just about every time we went there.

One Monday morning shortly after the snow started blanketing the town, Mister Christie, the school caretaker failed to re-fire the boilers so that eventually the school's heating system packed in altogether. As cold draughts seeped in through the classroom we sat with our coats and scarves on, ignoring lessons and silently prayed that the large snowflakes blotting out the glass on the windows would continue falling until break time. We'd no sooner finished drinking our milk, however, than Mister Lally, the headmaster popped his head into the classroom and told our teacher to send us home because the heating system was still causing problems.

What a wonderful thing this snow was then. Within no time we were dashing through the school gates into Park Street, yelling and screaming like tribes of Indians on the warpath and pelting everyone in sight with handfuls of this fresh and fabulous stuff.

The next day, Tuesday, the heating was still off, so once again we were allowed to go home. As there was no let-up in the freezing and icy conditions this pattern continued over the coming weeks and the resulting 'holidays', well, they were magic, particularly with the snow falling like it had never fallen before.

No sooner had dad left for work on the docks each morning than I was there, right behind him, inspecting the fresh snow that had fallen during the night on the doorstep. I just couldn't contain my excitement when finding the milk bottles, delivered earlier by our milkman, buried under the new fall. It was great digging them out.

Before long all kinds of makeshift sledges began appearing with no one able to contest the fact that Tucker had the best one of the bunch in our street. His sledge could quite easily carry three of us and sometimes we'd hurtle down the hills in the park at speeds much faster than any of the trolleys (made with a plank of wood and pram wheels) used as our street transport during the summer months.

By the end of January, with no sign of the cold weather giving up its grip on the town, the road surfaces became treacherous; 'like death traps' our mother's said and slides, as slippery as glass, stretched from one end of the street to the other. Although we felt privileged to have our own ice rink outside the front doors, the whole thing, we were told, was devastating for the elderly and sick for they were confined to their homes for weeks on end by this enormous white-out.

As a result of the heavy snowfalls, access to our dens became impossible, and Nacker, true to form, came up with a suggestion to the effect that an attic in a bombed house opposite the Chinese cafe in Price Street could be our temporary haunt until the big freeze subsided. Gaining entry to this alternative gang headquarters, however, meant climbing along a thick drainpipe at the back of the house, a hazardous task even under normal conditions. For apart from the pipe being corroded, dangerous icicles shaped like huge pointed glass daggers hung above our heads from cracks in the wall where water had leaked down from a broken gutter. After slipping and sliding down the icy wall, we eventually managed to clamber in through a window, though a rope was needed to support Ossie, who, with having legs like knitting needles, always struggled to climb as easily and as well as the rest of us. Creeping up what was left of the stairs we entered the front bedroom and were delighted to find it contained an old fashioned cast-iron grate, which at sometime or other had been packed with old newspapers and now was covered with soot. This became our immediate point of interest, as first Tucker unsuccessfully tried lighting a fire, followed by Nacker, but when the room filled with choking smoke they called it a day.

Looking round to see what else could be of benefit to the gang, Nacker began a further investigation of our new surrounds and before long had discovered a hole in the loft which led into the bombed house next door. The loft spaces in both these houses, we soon learnt, had been taken over by flocks of local scraggy pigeons but they soon scattered as our mucky faces appeared on their patch.

With loads of slates missing from the roofs of both houses our natural curiosity soon got the better of us and within minutes we'd struggled through from the ceiling trusses and clambered outside. To our delight we found the roofs covered with dry snow, much whiter than the frozen slush that lay on the streets below.

From our vantage point we could easily see the prominent red brick Bridewell and morgue, located alongside the Livvie Baths and only a matter of yards from where we were perched. As everyone knew, the Bridewell was the home base for the bobbies who patrolled the district and there weren't many that'd argue that they often made our young lives a misery. Now from where we sat we enjoyed a birds eye view of the 'scuffers' as they made their way back in ones and twos to the police station after a shift spent tramping the beat. Without as much as a second thought we grabbed handfuls of snow, rolled them into balls and took aim.

'Lerr 'em 'ave it,' Nacker ordered as the cops drew level with us on the opposite side of the street. Watching the flying snowballs splatter around them, we quickly ducked and crawled for cover behind the huge chimney stack that had served each of the houses before the German bombs had done their damage during the war. It seemed obvious to us that the cops would look up towards the roof, but we felt from our position we would be almost impossible to see.

This was the first time we'd been in what we thought was 'proper action' since our raid on the Morpeth buildings and we were delighted with the way events were panning out.

The 'scuffers' shone torches and even approached our new den by the same back way that we had; but we knew there was little chance of them shinning along the drainpipe, or scaling the icy wall and climbing to the lofty position in the roof.

We celebrated the success of our raid with a swig of Tizer that Tucker had nicked from Goranges and a bite from a baking apple, which came the same way from Gladys Lewis's. Ossie as usual bagged the core.

'You can't fight on an empty stomach,' Nacker wisely declared, once again proving to us that we had indeed chosen the right leader for the gang.

On our last visit to this temporary den we removed the remaining dry floorboards to make a small fire. Within minutes, with the fire burning slowly, we crouched cross-legged in front of the glowing embers to discuss our next plan of attack. We'd already bombed the chinks laundry with a load of snowballs and targeted Johnny Brown's chandlers shop, easily escaping detection on both occasions. Ossie had also thrown a couple of large lumps of ice at Eric Elias's barbers shop, splattering the doorway and only missing the red and white pole by inches. This was his way of seeking revenge for receiving a jailbird crop instead of the short back and sides he'd anticipated. After his retaliation he felt better - or so he said.

It was the eagle-eyed Mister Chung, from the laundry who observed the curl of smoke drifting through the slates in the roof that eventually gave us away. The next thing we heard was the 'scuffers' shouting. 'Come on lads, get yerselves down 'ere. We know where you are.'

Nacker immediately ordered us to stay still and keep quiet. We all obeyed except Ossie, who in sheer panic almost fell through the ceiling at the spot where we'd removed most of the floorboards for the fire.

The injury, a scrape to the top of Ossie's leg (which had Oz crying like a big soft baby) was inspected by Spud, who declared that it wouldn't need stitching or amputating. Having completing his diagnosis, Spud farted - something he was prone to do on such solemn occasions.

Ossie didn't find this funny and called him 'a dirty stinkin' bastard.'

We all agreed that it wasn't at all funny, not when we were surrounded by the enemy and were supposed to be keeping dead quiet. Showing concern for another important matter, I reminded Ossie to put his outburst down on his swearing list for confession, but he didn't seem to appreciate my good intentions and in his temper turned on me and told me 'to shut it and mind your own business.' And there was me only trying to help him.

We stayed up in the roof space until well after six o'clock, but before abandoning our secret hide out Nacker decided to gain some slight revenge on the one he considered was responsible for snitching on us. Removing a few pigeons' eggs from the scattered nests, he climbed back onto the roof and hurled them down at the windows of the Chinese Café. Mr Chung, who was looking up to the roof where we were hiding, stepped back as the eggs showered down. We cheered as he covered his head and ducked down quickly to avoid Nacker's missiles, some of which almost landed on their target in the doorway. Gloating over the skills of our leader and bubbling with our success, we left as quickly as we could.

There was no improvement in the weather for several weeks, with the whole country experiencing the most prolonged and extreme conditions for many years. These affected everyone and everything, including the horses, which skidded on the icy roads as they battled against the elements to pull carts loaded with freight for the Railways and coal for the public. Meanwhile we small boys rejoiced, for the coal shortage had now added to the school's heating problems and to our jubilation this meant no lessons and no learning, except for ways of the street.

It was Nacker who decided that the scarcity of coal could perhaps be turned to our advantage and it didn't take him long to conjure up an idea for us to make a few bob from the fuel situation. He came up with the suggestion of going to the local gasworks and collecting coke for those unable to make the trip. Although most of the locals relied on coal and scrapwood to warm their houses, another alternative was coke. Nacker's idea was particularly enterprising and not surprisingly, when we began touting in the neighbourhood, we found many eager customers willing to pay a couple of bob for a bag of coke delivered to their house.

Pooling our meagre resources, we just scraped together the necessary shilling for the hire of a fairly decent barrow from Dow's yard in Cottage Street and so in good spirits we set off for the gasworks in Hind Street. Passing Cathcart Street corner we thought it most unusual not to see Scouse Reynolds, an old fella who would stop and generally talk to us and make up rhymes as we walked to school. We reckoned the cold weather was probably responsible for his strange absence from his usual post and trundled our hired cart along Price Street stopping only briefly by Effinghams Bakery.

'D'yer fancy a penneth of bits?' Nacker asked, but for once I wasn't hungry, I'd eaten a full plate of thick porridge before I left home and to my surprise I found my belly couldn't take anymore - or so I thought. That is until I spotted Ossie coming round the corner from Watson Street polishing a rosy apple on his coat. We stopped and called him over. He looked pig sick; he knew what was coming.

'First bite,' said Nacker.

'Second,' I yelled.

'You can 'ave a bite Nacker, but not you Jimmy,' Ossie retorted. 'You nearly bit me 'and off last week, remember?'

Ossie then cupped both of his hands tightly round the apple leaving only the tiniest of holes, so Nacker, trying to push Ossie's thumbs out of the way with his face almost flattened his nose to even get to the apple skin. Despite Ossie gripping the apple with all his might, Nacker had plenty of practice at the art of getting 'first bite,' and managed it easily.

'Go on gis a bite Oz,' I pleaded.

'No, you're gettin' none,' he replied.

'Stick it then,' I grumbled.

'I will.'

'Stick it as far as you can gerrit.'

'I will.'

'An' further.'

'I will, watch me' he replied, sinking his teeth into the apple, biting deep into the pods and then spitting out the pips with a burp.

'I hope it chokes yer,' I said.

'It hasn't,' he jeered back. 'Look,' he added sticking out his horrible tongue.

'Come on Jim, let's get goin' 'said Nacker.

We carried on to the Devils church and turned into Eldon Street with Ellis's wood yard on one side and the pre-fabs on the other. The wind hit us full blast, forcing us to stop for a second to pull down the sleeves of our jerseys over our freezing fingers. Most of the main roads were slushy but passable, allowing the cart to glide along, although we found it difficult to control when it skidded. Turning alongside Hemmingford Street School we fell in behind other would-be coke seekers. Some were pushing large prams, others had home-made barrows and so we felt quite the part with our posh handcart, despite our ragged appearance.

As we pushed on, a lad ran out of the St. Andrew's Square flats, shouted 'scruffs' at us, and immediately took off. Without warning Nacker let go of the cart and immediately gave chase. The cart tilted forward and the shaft shot upwards leaving me dangling in mid-air. The lad was probably right. I wore a scruffy corduroy jerkin over my jersey, black pants with a crudely sewn patch across the middle and grey socks with spuds in the heels. Nacker fared no better. He wore his dad's seaman's jersey tucked into grey longies and these in turn vanished down a pair of wellies at least two sizes too big for him.

Situated alongside the Central Railway Station, Hind Street sloped downhill to the gasworks, so that even before we turned the corner into the street, the stench of the coke had penetrated our running nostrils.

The end of a large queue was the sight waiting to greet us as we reached the top of the hill, but this came as no surprise, for everyone knew that Saturday was always the busiest morning of the week at the gasworks. Nacker and I ducked down out of the wind at the end of the line, huddling together to wait our turn as the queue shuffled slowly forward. It was absolutely freezing. We were only half way down the queue when someone yelled just yards behind us. Turning quickly we observed a number of men kneeling over a prostrate figure. They began covering him with sacks and within minutes an ambulance from the vicinity of Chester Street arrived, sliding to a halt besides the group who flagged it down. It was a sorry sight watching grown men holding their caps with heads bowed as the person was placed gently on a stretcher and driven away. From where we were positioned in the queue we couldn't see exactly who it was or what had happened, but when eventually reaching the coke chutes we learnt that it had been a young lad, and he'd dropped dead with the cold.

Two men lifted our sacks of coke onto the barrow for us because we were too small and weak to manage and then a couple of older lads left the queue to help push the whole thing back up hill. From there we struggled home with our overweight load, having firmly decided by this time that this specific money-making exercise was just a bit out of our league and should come to a quick conclusion.

Confession

As March approached, the importance of making our Easter duties was stressed in no uncertain terms by teachers and priests alike, causing minor panic for those of us who hadn't been to confession for months. Spud wasn't too concerned. His mam had hauled him along to benediction one freezing night after she suffered a bout of 'the jitters,' when she almost slipped on the ice outside her house. As a result, he was commandeered to support her on the short trip to the Lauries. With it being such a miserable sort of evening only the die-hards of the parish attended the service, so as a means of an incentive the priest slipped in an extra confessional session and of course, Spud was made up.

It was different for Ossie and me; we had accumulated two months of sins and dreaded the thought of going on Saturday morning. However, we were left with little choice for both of us were living in mortal sin and had we died we'd have gone straight to hell.

We weren't on our own though, for only the goodies in class, consisting of no more than a couple of dozen, hardly missed mass at all, so in a way most of us were in the same boat.

'We aren't heathens are we?' Ossie asked.

'Dunno,' I replied. 'Dunno worrit means.'

Father Doyle always said that those who missed mass were heathens. He couldn't mean us could he? We'd only missed mass on one occasion when Spud's old lady caught the flu and we played footy instead, but that was the first time in three months that we'd dodged on purpose.

All week during catechism lessons, confession remained foremost on our minds, but as soon as the bell sounded and we were set free the sacrament was quickly forgotten. However, by the time Saturday approached we were as nervous as the rest of the heathens. The church that day was crowded and to our dismay we could see there were as many girls as lads...including our Bridie.

'Trust her to be in Father Morrisey's queue,' I muttered. ' She's done that on purpose.'

Father Morrisey was a popular young priest who always joked, never lectured or gave long penances. Consequently, it was only natural for everyone to make a beeline to his cubicle to disclose their confessions. Father Doyle, who was always going on about heathens to us, had moved on to another parish in the diocese leaving Father Nugent to take his place. With being old and deaf it was deadly going to him, for he tended to shout so that everyone could hear your sins being broadcasted around the church.

Mind you, Canon Smythe, who had a reputation for being extremely strict was reckoned to be the worst of all. When we first made our confession we'd heard rumours from some of the big lads that if you went to him with your sins you'd get shot. That was the reason he was called the Canon and why we made sure to avoid him at all costs.

Before going into the church we'd always toss a penny to determine which of us would go into the confessional box first. On this Saturday I won the toss, but only because I fiddled the whole thing with a two headed penny which Billy Smith had loaned me. It was a lousy trick seeing Ossie was my best mate, though I knew for a fact that he'd have done the same thing if he'd had the chance.

After weighing up the length of queues for the various priests it became obvious we had little choice but to join those who were waiting to enter Father Nugent's booth, and confess our sins to him.

I was half hoping that he'd lose his voice or doze off and with Ossie going before me I knew I wouldn't be long in finding out. Another problem I could foresee, lay with our Bridie, and I immediately started praying that she'd be well away before I entered the confessional box. Knowing her, though, she was certain to hang around on purpose just to see how long I was in the box.

'Bless me Father for I have sinned,' I heard Ossie say. I couldn't help it. I didn't want to, but he'd left the door slightly open and I didn't have the nerve to close it properly in case it put him off his stride.

'I missed me night and morning prayers about six times Father, an' told lies a couple of times, an ... er ... an ... er.' he faltered trying not to break details of his mortal sin too early.

'SPEAK UP BOY,' Father Nugent roared. I nearly jumped out my skin.

My worse fears, I knew, had been realised, he hadn't lost his voice nor fallen asleep. Ossie hadn't started on the worse of his sins as yet and I was shaking like a leaf.

'I've stole twice and swore twenty seven times,' Ossie blurted out.

'YOU STOLE ... WHAT DID YOU STEAL ... WHO FROM ?'

'Erm ... erm a loaf ... from the Co.ee, fa-fa-father an' two bottles of milk from the dairy.'

I knew Ossie well enough to realise that he'd soon be whinging and he hadn't even got as far as his mortal sins yet.

Father Nugent was just warming up.

'HAVE YOU HEARD OF RETRIBUTION? COME ON, ANSWER ME BOY,' he bellowed.

'No... no...no I haven't Father,' Ossie cried. All eyes in the church were now fixed on our section, as we knelt with our heads bowed.

'YOU SHALL PAY FOR THE GOODS STOLEN AND NEVER EVER STEAL AGAIN ... DO YOU UNDERSTAND?'

'Yeah... Yes... Father,' Ossie squeaked, but without conviction.

'NOW THIS HABIT OF SWEARING, WERE THEY BLASPHEMOUS WORDS YOU USED?'

There was a silence inside the confessional box and I had visions of diving in through the door and dragging Ossie out'; I was certain he must have fainted. Finally there was a crackle, thank God, and Ossie replied.

'Er...I don't know what you mean Father.'

'IN YOUR CATECHISM LESSONS DIDN'T YOU LEARN ABOUT

TAKING THE LORD'S NAME IN VAIN...SPEAK UP BOY...I CAN'T HEAR YOU. HAVE YOU HEARD OF BLASPHEMY?' he bawled irritably.

'Yis Father but I forgot about that', Ossie replied and I knew then, that his confidence was returning.

'But I didn't take the Lord's name in vain, Father. I just said ordinary swear words, like all me mates,' he said, as if waiting for a plaudit from the priest. Of course we couldn't help but hear Father Nugent huffing and puffing quite loudly and I began thinking he must be really fed up, so this wasn't looking too good for me.

'ANYTHING ELSE ON YOUR CONSCIENCE, WHILE YOU'RE STILL IN HERE,' Father Nugent yelled and I waited anxiously for Ossie to finally confess to his mortal sin.

'I missed mass once Father, through me own fault,' he added hastily, as if that might soften the blow.

'YOU'RE MIXING WITH THE WRONG TYPE, YOUNG MAN. I SHALL HAVE TO SPEAK WITH YOUR TEACHER ON MONDAY MORNING,' Father Nugent declared.

I wondered then if the priest could see through the little black curtain and I began fidgeting with my fingers, as my heart sank.

'FOR YOUR PENANCE,' Father Nugent instructed,'SAY TEN OUR FATHERS, TEN HAIL MARY'S AND TEN GLORY BE'S AND SAY A PRAYER FOR ME WHILE YOU'RE AT IT, AND FOR NOW, MAKE A GOOD ACT OF CONTRITION.'

'Oh my God, because thou art so good,' Ossie began to mutter. Then he lowered his voice and started whispering so that I couldn't hear him, even though I tried my best. Everyone was now looking over, waiting for him to emerge from the box and when he did appear his face was white as chalk and to me looked as if he was about to faint. Because I was his best mate I decided to give my speck up in the queue and help him to the back of the church. For some reason the huge doors had been left wide open and without thinking we staggered through, not even blessing ourselves, so that was yet another sin to go down in the book of retribution.

That evening I attended St Werburghs church for benediction and later went to confession. Ossie came along with me for company. He didn't mind now that his ordeal was past and his conscience clear. He'd also had his tea so he was in a better frame of mind than he had been earlier in the day.

'You're a good mate Ossie,' I said. I was being as genuine as possible, although I still had a slight touch of conscience over the two headed penny. He could have it next time I decided, but only if we went to Father Morrisey for our confession.

Ambitions

'What do you wanna be when you grow up?' Tucker asked Nacker as we crossed the Penny Bridge into Wallasey during the Easter holidays.

'I wanna go away ter sea like me ol' fella,' he replied, as we threw pebbles at a green bottle floating in the dock.

'Me dad was fifteen when he went away an' he's bin to every country in the world bar none,' he continued, and we were all dead jealous because his dad had been to more places than any of ours.

'Gorrit,' Smithy yelled as the bottle disappeared into the murky water of the dock.

'I'm goin' on the railways as a train driver,' Ossie said.

'Worrabout all that steam getting' in yer eyes... I wouldn't fancy that,' Tucker declared.

'It's nowt that... It's only when you're going into stations when you stick your 'ead out you get loads of steam and besides you've gorra wear a cap.'

Tucker, who had a slight turn in his eye and was always conscious of it, seemed satisfied with Ossie's explanation, even though we couldn't really fathom out how a cap could prevent steam going into your eyes.

Still, it made no difference to us as long as Tucker was happy.

He then turned his attention to Spud. 'Worrabout you Spud?'

Spud was the heaviest in our gang and the tidiest. His hair was always properly parted and his socks were permanently pulled up. Mrs Murphy, we knew, had high hopes for her Timmy and would always ignore criticism of concern at his weight problem. 'It's only puppy fat and it'll soon drop off when he gets older' she'd reply if neighbours mentioned that he was a bonny lad, but heavy with it.

Spud didn't reply for a couple of minutes and appeared to us to be up in the clouds. None of us, however, were prepared for the shock we received when he finally answered Tucker's query.

'I'm goin' to be a priest,' he declared.

We all stopped dead and even Tucker and Billy who were Proddies, were as stunned as we were.

'A priest!' Nacker gasped. 'Since when?'

'Since Easter when I found out,' Spud replied.

'You've known since Easter an' you haven't told us, yer mates. An' what about all the knockin' off we've done an' the swearing and you've done it as well. An' what about me missing mass.' Nacker, we could see was furious, I'd never seen him so mad. Then Spud started crying. We all felt lousy, so to cheer him up Ossie said. 'Hey Spud, worr happens if you're takin' someone's confession an' you fart?'

'Or worrabout if you let rip in the pulpit?' I asked.

'Or you drop one on the altar,' said Ossie and we all laughed.

For the rest of that day we all called Spud, Father Murphy and wondered if he would indeed grow up to be a priest despite all the sins we'd committed together.

I had a secret, a secret I'd sworn never to reveal on my mother's life and now Smithy glared at me, giving me the nod as a reminder that he'd kill me if I said anything to Nacker and the rest of the lads about it, so I didn't. He'd told me sometime beforehand that he wanted to be a policeman in Glasgow when he grew up and then later a 'Tec'. This had been decided after he'd seen Humphrey Bogarte in Casablanca at the Gaumont Picture house one Saturday night.

Just imagine, I thought, Spud becoming a priest, Billy a detective in Glasgow, Nacker going away to sea and Ossie driving a train. That left Tucker and me. I suppose we'll end up on the docks like our old fella's, I thought, unless Nacker lets me go away to sea with him.

'Mam guess what?' I gasped, arriving home breathless after being chased over the four bridges by the Seacombe gang who outnumbered us three to one. Mam was changing the baby's nappy in the back kitchen. I always kept well away in case she thrust it towards me, which she often did, depending on her mood.

'You've discovered America,' she replied sarcastically, trying to aggravate me, but I was too excited to bite the bait.

'No, don't be daft mam. Y'see I know something that you don't know.'

It was my turn to tease her now, but she didn't seem that interested in my news, so I said it again.

'Guess what mam, d'yer want me to tell you something?' I was almost pleading with her now in case our Bridie got in first and told her the news about Spud.

'Wait till I've powdered the baby's bum,' she replied, dosing Tommy's crevices with a good sprinkle of Johnson's talc.

'Right, James,' she said. 'What's this priceless piece of information that can't even wait 'til you've had a jam butty.'

'Spud's going to be a priest mam,' I gasped. She smiled and I knew then that somebody had beaten me to it and told her first and I hadn't even had my jam butty yet.

Training

'I'll take that fella into town this year, Maggie,' I heard dad say one day in May when the weather changed for the better. Mam pretended not to hear. She either didn't agree with what he was his proposing, or she was having a bad day.

Whichever angle I looked at, I began imagining the various kinds of mental and physical forms of torture that he might have in store for me, but as it turned out my fears were unfounded. Dad, in his wisdom was only thinking of my welfare.

'It's for your own good,' mam said, when he proposed to teach me how to swim properly and learn to ride a bike.

As if that wasn't enough, he also suggested taking Bridie and me about the town for an education lesson in history and geography.

In theory this was all well and good, but in practice it was an entirely different matter altogether. First of all I didn't have a cossie or a bike and as for walking with dad, now that could be murder. 'Throw your shoulders back, pick your bloody feet up and stop draggin' them,' he'd bawl and if I happened to forget who I was with and kicked a tin can or a brick, he'd almost have a fit. He would then lecture me on the price of shoes and how lucky I should be for having a father who worked for his family, while I wasted his hard-earned cash kicking the toes out of my best shoes.

Regarding his walks around Birkenhead, I wasn't bothered who built the town, or who flattened it for that matter, but he knew best, for after all I was 'the other fella' and in no position to contradict him. Our Bridie, who could already swim and ride a bike, told dad that she was interested walking around the town with him; trust her, she'd do anything to get out of helping mam with the housework, but dad couldn't see through her like me, that was the problem.

After four fine days on the trot dad announced his intention of teaching me to swim. With his usual kamikazi enthusiasm he decided I was to be taught, Dockers style.

'Right son, it's down to Livingstone baths for you,' he declared.

To be honest it felt kind of strange. You see, I'd never been to the baths with him before. He, or I should say mam, had bought me a little jersey-type cossie which gave an added impetus because until then we'd always hired the corporation's own design, locally known as 'slips.' These consisted of a mini cotton cover with two straps onto the side: that's if you were lucky. The well-named 'slips' were costumes that were off more than they were on, although this made little difference. With an all-male baths on one side and the separated female on the other, nobody was bothered about seeing a few bare bums or mickeys floating around.

Dad appeared from the cubicle wearing a pre-war style black leotard costume, a sort of Tarzan type vest with one arm. Everyone was staring, but if it bothered him he didn't show it and as far as I could make out seemed oblivious to the comments about his unusual swimwear as he strolled to where I stood at the shallow end of the pool.

'Right lad, this way' he ordered, grabbing hold of my hand. I wouldn't be as bold to say that he dragged me, it was more a case of over-enthusiasm on his part as he pulled me past diving fanatics, who not only performed from the edge of the pool, but also plummeted from the balconies above. As we reached the deep end he let go of my hand and plunged into the water, splashing the dithering bystanders who were themselves contemplating going in.

At first he swam round demonstrating his own specific version of the crawl before turning over and floating on his back. When he was about six-foot from the side he beckoned to me.

I was on my own, standing on the edge and I couldn't ignore him even if I'd wanted to.

'Okay son... let's 'ave yer in now,' he shouted. 'You seen the way I dived in didn't yer?' I was confused and frozen to the spot, so I nodded.

'Hands out straight in front of yer, 'ead down, keep yer feet together, mouth shut an' drop in the water gently,' he commanded.

'Don't worry son, I'm here. I'll catch yer,' he assured me.

With one eye on dad and the other on the bottom of the pool I let myself go, just like a plank dropping over a cliff.

SPLASH! I belly flopped and sank like a stone. To my eternal relief I didn't touch the bottom and shot up to the surface, where I immediately looked around for dad. Panic overtook my disorientated senses when I spotted his bald head swimming down towards the shallow end of the pool. A feeling of self-preservation immediately took over as I flayed both arms like a windmill on full swing and kicked out my feet as if they were on fire. It seemed to me nothing short of a miracle that I moved at all and was propelled towards the direction of the edge of the pool. Someone, it seemed, was looking after me up there - but definitely not down here.

I frantically grabbed hold of the handrail as if my life depended on it, which, on reflection, I'm sure it did and then as if by magic, dad leaned over the edge and hauled me out.

'There yer are, there's nowt to it, is there lad?' he beamed. I couldn't reply for a minute, it seemed as if I'd swallowed half the water in the deep end and my eyes felt bloodshot from the powerful chlorine they used to keep the water clean.

As I hung there gasping, dad lifted me up in his strong muscular arms and for a minute I even thought that he was going to toss me back in again, so I clung to his neck like grim death until he put me down. Holding his hand I walked down to the three-foot end which was crowded with lads of my age, all learning to swim in what I'd call the proper way, with their fathers holding them under the chin to build their confidence.

I didn't half envy them.

'See that lot son' said dad glancing contemptuously in the direction of the novices. 'You'll be swimmin' miles while they'll still be learnin' the doggy paddle and why? Because of me, your father, who had the nouse to teach yer ter dive before you can swim.'

'But I thought yer had ter learn to swim first dad.'

He looked at me, shaking his head.

'You know what thought did, don't yer lad?'

'What?'

'Bloody well peed himself an' thought he was sweatin',' he retorted, before taking me back to the deep end for what he termed 'confidence boosters.'

Stage two of my trial consisted of dad swimming vigorously across the breadth of the pool with me lying across his back desperately clinging to his neck. It was great being towed along. For the first time in my life I began enjoying dad's company and my previous experiences were soon forgotten. Complacency, however, can sometimes be a strange companion and needless to say this was such an occasion. I was lulled into a false sense of security and without warning dad suddenly turned turtle, leaving me once again floundering in the water. This time he only swam a few yards away and miraculously I somehow scrambled to the side.

Dad had a big grin on his face.

'There you go lad, you can swim as good as anyone in here, now, can't yer? It's easy isn't it?'

I shook my head up and down, my ears were blocked and I couldn't speak for a minute. However, dad construed my answer to be 'yes' and that seemed to please him. He never praised me; he wasn't one for praises. His view was that it was a parental duty to teach and he took that responsibility seriously. His method in this particular exercise seemed to belong to him and him alone, but may have been a custom passed down through the Reilly family. Maybe, I reckoned, he'd read some book in the library called 'Sink or Swim'; whatever it was it worked. That was the main thing.

'God help our Tommy when he gets older,' I muttered under my breath.

'It's all in the mind son, conquer the fear of water an' you've cracked it. Whether it's six-foot or twenty foot deep it doesn't matter. The top twelve inches are the most important. Sink below that an' you've 'ad your bacon. Have yer got that lad?'

'Yis dad.'

Having delivered this sound judgement, it seemed dad's tutoring and philosophy lessons were over for the day. Changed and dressed we left the baths, walked home and turned the corner into our street, to be confronted by the unusual sight of an election car crawling along the street. From a large microphone precariously placed on the roof, a metallic voice blurted out: ' Vote ... vote ... vote ... for Percy Collick.

This was our Labour candidate.

'Let's hope he gets in,' dad muttered.

'Yeah, I hope so,' I replied.

I caught dad glancing down at me with a twinkle in his eye.

Pilgrimage

At the beginning of the summer holiday dad decided that my legs needed building up and embarked on a programme to teach me how to ride a bike properly. Without his knowledge I'd already attempted to ride his bone-shaker, with my leg through the side bars, only because I couldn't reach the pedals properly even when sitting on the cross bar.

For my abortive effort, I received a 'fourpenny one' from mam for getting oil all over my socks, but this time, however, I was about to be coached by a professional. Using our Bridie's bike I stood on the pedals while dad held onto the back of the saddle and ran up and down the street a number of times, encouraging me with words of wisdom, trying to instil a little of the confidence, which in his opinion he deemed I was lacking.

'Brake. brake ... keep yer eyes on the road,' he yelled. I responded by falling off several times, adding even more scabs to my well-scarred knees.

'Okeydokey, that'll do Jim', dad announced after an hour of ups and downs and all the while aggravating the big lads who were playing a game of shots in against Jenkins' wall.

'You've got the hang of it for now son,' he said, 'so next Sunday I'll take you for a little spin out in the countryside.'

After returning from eight o'clock mass with mam, we arrived home to find dad cooking the breakfast. Mam got the shock of her life; he'd never ventured near the stove since we'd moved into the house and as far as mam was aware, he didn't know the difference between a gas ring and a bell ring.

'What's 'appened Charlie,' mam demanded, thinking something had happened to one of the kids and he was cooking to steady his nerves.

'Bear with me Maggie, bear with me while I turn the sausages over,' he said, flipping them in the air like pancakes.

'I'm only savin' a bit of time before me an' our Jimmy set off on our journey, that's all, so I thought it would be an idea to get the breakfast ready and give you a little spell,' he added, just as the bacon caught fire and the toast burned blacker than the grate.

'Bloody 'ell look what you've made me do now woman,' he yelled, as the kitchen filled with smoke. Our Bridie, aware of the danger, dashed into the back yard and I was two steps behind her. Then Ma took over; she couldn't half move when she wanted to and within seconds had the crisis immediately under control. Dad, however, was acting peculiar and this bothered me. Whatever was on his mind, I just couldn't fathom out.

My fears and reservations were confirmed when he produced an old army haversack from somewhere upstairs and packed it with loads of butties and a couple of bottles of water. Even someone of such low mentality that I possessed had no problem concluding that these rations were well over the top for a little spin into the countryside. I couldn't contain my curiosity any longer and asked him what he had in mind.

'Whereabouts are we goin' dad?'

'Only as far as Wales son.'

'Wales! But that's miles away ' I gasped. He ignored me though and carried on pumping up the bike tyres.

We set off at ten o'clock and to my amazement, three hours later we crossed the border into Wales, just before Queensferry. Stopping by the side of the road we found a decent speck and sat on a grass verge, sampling the first of the butties. By this time my legs felt as if they were hanging off, so dad massaged them in his usual vigorous manner until they felt even worse. I was assured, however and yes - by dad - that the further we travelled the easier they would get and in my childish innocence I believed him.

'Okay son, time to make tracks,' he suddenly announced. I immediately turned my bike around towards the English border.

'Woa, where d'yer think yer goin',' he shouted. I was stunned.

'This way ... this way lad, we're nowhere near Holywell yet,' he declared, pointing in the opposite direction. Reluctantly I stood up on the bike praying there'd be sufficient downward sloping hills to enable me to rest my legs and sit on the saddle as I free wheeled down.

'There she is our Jim, St Winifred's Well...what do yer think of it?'

I glanced up the steep hill not knowing whether to laugh or cry, but kept a still tongue and pretended to look impressed instead of depressed.

'That's why pilgrims come here from all over the world to bathe an' to get cured,' he exclaimed, with what sounded like a sincerely felt conviction.

'How did he know that when he never went near a church,' I thought, but I kept my thoughts to myself. At the well there were crutches, walking sticks, wooden legs and various other aids for the handicapped, stacked neatly in a corner by those pilgrims who'd apparently been miraculously cured. This spectacle seemed to arouse dad's curiosity to the limit. Meanwhile I staggered over to the shrine wondering if St Winifred would answer a little prayer from a small boy who only wanted a cure for my aching legs and for her guidance in seeing me safely home. I knew that's what mam would do if she was in my predicament and so I removed my shoes and socks, placed my feet in the clear water and lowered my legs in, where they froze solid.

'Oh my God, they've dropped off,' I yelled at the top of my voice. Dad, who was busy reading through a list of every pilgrim from our neck of the woods who'd been cured, galloped over.

'What's up with you now?' he bawled, without even swearing - which was most unusual and even noble of him. Besides, he didn't sound as aggressive and that wasn't like him at all.

'It's me feet dad ... it's me feet ... an' me legs ... I can't feel them ... they've gone dead,' I cried in despair.

'Bloody 'ell ... I don't know ... I can't take you anywhere without somethin' happenin', can I?' he replied, pulling me out of the water in one sweep.

My feet were blue, truly blue and this was dead scary, frightening the life out of me. Honest to God, I couldn't even stand properly for a minute and to give dad his due he didn't let go of me straight away, as I sort of expected. Mind you, this was probably because the other pilgrims were gawping and it wouldn't of looked good, or cast him in a good light if I'd collapsed in a heap and died right in front of them, especially after they'd travelled all this way to seek a cure for their own ailments.

'It's a miracle dad,' I gasped feeling the warmth returning to my feet and my legs. They were now glowing as if on fire, while all the recent aches and pains had mysteriously disappeared. He responded by taking his cap off, crashing it in the direction of a blue bottle which had the bare cheek to try to enter his haversack, no doubt expecting to feast on our cheese butties. I must say, I admired the fly in a way. It had a lot more nerve than I did.

'Bugger off yer little swine,' he growled, flattening it with a second swipe. Dad's pilgrimage was over. Whether he'd requested divine intervention at the shrine or had received it anyway was debatable; however, he seemed in a much better mood as he cocked a leg over his old Marriot boneshaker in preparation for the return journey.

'Thanks St Winifred,' I said, as we left the shrine, blessing myself three times, one for mam, one for dad and one for all reluctant travellers who were forced to ride fifty miles or more, standing up. I then enjoyed the additional pleasure of sitting on a saddle with my feet on the front bar, speeding down the hill to the coast road.

We arrived back in Brookie at nine o'clock that night and although I was starving and dead tired I couldn't wait to tell mam about my miracle. It was just my bad luck that she was lying down with the baby and so I told our Bridie instead. She just shrugged and carried on with her homework, as if it was every day that a miracle happened.

Excursions

For the second consecutive year our mothers organised a charabanc to take us out for the day away from the smoke and grime of the town. Hardings, the only proper coach company in the town were unable to supply a charabanc on that particular day and so the 'Corpy' were contacted and a double decker bus was hired from them. As soon as it turned into our street we roared and danced up and down with excitement: this was the first time any of us had seen a bus in Brookie.

Although it was a Saturday we were all dressed in our best clothes ready for the trip to the seaside resort of West Kirby, a destination with greater appeal to us than the previous one to Raby Mere. On that outing Spud fell into the lake and nearly drowned even though we all knew it was his own fault.

He'd been messing about in a rowing boat when it capsized, but fortunately for him the owner was in a nearby boat and by using the 'pulling in' pole managed to hook Spud by the pants. There was little doubt his quick thinking saved Spud's life.

However, by the time Spud surfaced he'd swallowed loads of water and slimy green moss and we thought it possible that it could also contain frogspawn and tadpoles. This dilemma immediately aroused our curiosity and so on our return from Raby Mere we went round to Mr Smith to see if he could put our minds at rest. Mr Smith was having a shave when Ossie, Billy and me confronted him in the back kitchen.

'Erm...Mr Smith, can yer tell us something?' Ossie asked.

'Aye what is it lads?'

'Spud fell into the lake at Raby Mere today.'

'Aye.'

'Worr if ... say he swallered loads of water?'

'He'd be as sick as a dog.'

'An' ... worr...if ... erm ... he swallered green moss?'

'Hmm ... that could block his lungs.'

'An' say he swallered frogspawn and tadpoles dad,' Billy hurriedly got in before his dad lost his patience. Mr Smith nearly nicked himself with his cut-throat.

'Ach let me see. That's a wee difficult question ye've given me there son, just give me a minute or two,' he said, swilling his face under the cold water tap.

'Ma' honest opinion laddies is that in a few days time or maybe a wee bit longer, the frogspawn will hatch and Spud will have wee tadpoles swimming round his belly and then have wee froggies coming out of his bum.'

'Told yer, didn't I,' said Ossie.

Me and Billy were flabbergasted.

'Wouldn't it be funny if they came out when he's in bed or in class,' Billy joked, and I thought to myself 'what a great idea' as other weird conjectures fired my imagination.

We were disappointed though, for nothing out of the ordinary happened throughout the following days, despite our constant concern. Ossie suggested that Spud's Sunday roast dinner had probably seen them off. We were inclined to agree.

Not all of our mams came on the outing to West Kirby, just half a dozen and for their sins they became foster mothers for the day. Obviously they were given permission to chastise us in any way necessary and it came as no surprise when Mrs Feeley took it upon herself to keep her beady eye on us, seeing we were Austin's friends.

With the bus being a double decker, our team took over the top half and no girls were allowed upstairs, although one or two tried sneaking up to see what we were up to.

We knew they were spies and under orders to report on us to the old ladies who occupied the 'mind your own business seats' besides the conductor, so we chased them downstairs.

We passed St James church in the north end of the town and caught sight of the windmill on Bidston Hill, which brought back memories of one of our previous expeditions.

'There's Biddy 'ill...an' 'the Rhods.'

'We've bin there 'aven't we lads?' Tucker yelled excitedly.

'Yeah and to Tam O' Shanter's cottage. That's when the sheep dog jumped over the wall an' we legged it, remember?' An worrabout the cave an' the Devil's chair?'

'An' remember when I bagged that orchard near the Flat Lanes,' Smithy reminisced.

'Yeah an' Frankie Bailey filled 'is kecks.'

'No I didn't. I nearly did, but I didn't, ask me mam,' Frank cried, but

Now we could dig up all the treasure that the monks had buried on Little Eye. There were gold ingots, trunks filled with diamonds, emeralds and stacks of golden coins, plundered from Spanish galleons that had floundered in the sinking sands. It would now be our treasure. Tucker was the first on the island. Standing on top of a sandstone rock he waved his green shirt, because of course, we didn't have a flag.

We all cheered, wakening a few sunbathers up who moaned about the noise, but there are always casualties in war and so we took no notice.

As the sun beat down on our heads and shoulders we lay in shallow pools surrounded by rocks to cool off, even though we still had our trousers on. 'They'll soon dry off before we get back' Spud said. Although we felt like stripping off, we couldn't go bare skinned out here, not like we would back down at the docks when it was quiet and there were no ships in.

'Yah!! ... yah!' Mickey screeched shooting out of the pool, a crab hanging onto his braces.

'Let's see it,' said Nacker who knew all about crabs. He wasn't half cruel though and thought nothing about snapping off their legs and using them for bait whenever we fished under the floating bridge, but as no-one in the gang knew how to hold crabs other than Nacker, we had to accept his skills and knowledge.

'It's only a baby crab, an' look it can't hurt yer even if yer put your little finger in his pincers,' he boasted.

'Ouch yer bastard,' he yelled, tossing it high in the air and towards the tide, which looked as if it was on its way in.

'Frankie-ee, Frankie-ee,' a faint voice echoed across the sands.

We looked towards the shore but couldn't make out anyone in detail, all we could see was a mass of people and they were over a mile away on the edge of the high tide-mark.

'That wasn't yer old lady was it Frank?' Tucker asked.

'Yeah I think so.'

'Frankie-ee-ee.'

'ALRIGHT I'M COMIN' ,' he bawled. We decided to leave at once. You didn't argue with Mrs Bailey. We all knew that she wouldn't think twice about belting any of us if she thought fit and that was a chance none of us were prepared to take. She was such a hard case that even Mr Bailey, who was over six foot tall, wouldn't say boo to her unless he'd first swallowed a good drop of Dutch courage and then he'd deeply regret it the next morning.

It was swiftly decided that the other two islands would have to wait to be discovered and explored until we came out this way again.

'Frankie-ee-ee.'

'I'M COMIN'.'

'Frankie-ee.'

'BLOODY 'ELL...she'll murder me when I get back.'

We could hear the girls screaming even before we'd reached the edge of the tide's littered trail and no one shouted louder than Maggie Dobson who was yelling

'Here they are...here they are.'

From out of the crowd, Mrs Bailey, distinctive in her bright yellow frock, burst through, broke into a run and headed straight towards us. Frankie tried hiding, first behind Nacker and then Spud but was pushed aside like a hot potato. In desperation and fear for his life he fled in the direction of the boating lake. Meanwhile we trooped towards the grown-ups, not knowing what to expect.

'Look at the state of you our Austin, you're a disgrace and you lot too,' Mrs Feeley hissed before walloping Ossie a good fourpenny one across his backside. The girls were all laughing, which in our eyes wasn't on, so Nacker in defence of Ossie boldly interrupted. 'It's only sand Mrs Feeley an' it'll fall off as soon as we're dry.' Mrs Feeley didn't appear to appreciate our leader's intervention and gave him a real filthy look before grabbing hold of Ossie once more. 'Get those trousers off at once,' she demanded.

'But there's girls 'ere mam, I can't take me pants off in front of them,' he cried.

'Put this round you,' she said passing Ossie a thin white towel no bigger than a tea towel. Ossie stood with his back to the sea wall and dropped his pants. Our attention, however, was diverted by the sound of Mrs Bailey's loud voice echoing right across the beach as she pulled Frankie through the sand by his ear, which from our position looked as if it had stretched to twice its normal size; needless to say floods of tears were running down his face. As a good-will gesture and to get back in the grown-ups good books, we made our way across to the paddling pool, washed the black mud and sand from our feet and legs and swilled our faces in the salty water.

Then Nacker deliberately upset Ossie by snatching away his towel and throwing it onto the embankment wall. In a fit of rage Ossie threw a tantrum because everyone in the paddling pool had a good view of his white bum and pink mickey.

At six o'clock we began gathering together all our bits and pieces and shoved them into a kitbag belonging to Mister Bailey. He'd been in the Pioneer Corp during the war, although he didn't see much enemy action with having to dig lavvie trenches, so Jock Smith told us one night.

Before leaving our paradise we were herded together by the adults and counted, just like our teachers did at school. Satisfied that we were all accounted for we made our way down the promenade, but before turning the corner alongside the chip and putt green we sneaked a final look at the three islands that were now surrounded by the incoming tide. Stopping briefly as the rest of our party carried on walking, we once again marvelled at the height of the Welsh Mountains in the background. 'We'll be back 'ere, don't worry,' said Nacker.

As soon as we arrived at the car park we were surprised to find it crowded with all kinds of charabancs, but our bus was parked on the far side which was just as well because as soon as the driver's attention was diverted with the convergence of bodies clambering for seats, we smuggled a huge lump of sandstone onto the bus. Sandstone, always in demand back home, was used to scrub pavement flags outside the front doors. When the bus came to a halt near the lamplight by Caldy Place, we took our treasure and broke it into pieces to share between us.

'Here's a present for you mam,' I said, handing her a nice square corner piece.

'Thanks son that's very thoughtful of you.' She hugged me tightly and planted a wet sloppy kiss on my forehead. I was happy that she was pleased with the present, then using my sleeve I wiped away the dribble. 'It's the thought that counts,' mam always said. That's why I always brought her something back from my travels that cost me nothing or next to nothing.

Johnny Feeley

Mr Feeley was a smart man, in fact he was probably the smartest fella' in our street. It wasn't because he wore a Railway uniform and never looked dirty like those who worked on the docks or shipyards did. Rather, it was simply a case of him being fanatical about appearance. Ossie's eldest brother Johnny shared his father's passion for clothes, even though he had a slightly different taste. He favoured bright coloured suits with open neck shirts, a stark contrast to his father's sober looking clothes. Ossie, on the other hand couldn't care less what he wore and wasn't in the least fussy about whether he looked smart or not. He was too small anyway for Johnny's cast offs, so all his clobber came brand new.

Johnny was our hero and Ossie shared him with me, but only because I didn't have an older brother and it was obvious that everyone needed one of them. I was even allowed to call him 'our Johnny,' which he didn't seem to mind. He was dead old though; nearly eighteen and he teased us every time we were in Ossie's. However, he still treated us as if we were older than we were and we loved that.

'Run and get me a Seven O'clock blade young Jimmy,' he'd ask and I'd be there and back from Kelly's corner shop before he'd had time for a swill. We would then watch him shave and he always stuck his soap filled brush across our faces, but that didn't stop us waiting for him to slice the pimples off his chin. As soon as the blade touched his face the blood seeped through his skin and poured down his neck and he never flinched a bit. We were amazed at his bravery. At moments such as those we were dead proud of 'our Johnny.'

Johnny worked for Bentleys pawn shop in Conway Street and was very popular with the manager who clearly appreciated the way that his young charge would use his discretion, which was something that went down well in the 'pop shop' business. Johnny had been at Bentley's since leaving school and was on first name terms with most of the regular customers, which was another pointer in his favour. As a result of his skills in this area he was occasionally left in charge of the shop, an arrangement that suited him fine, for unknown to us he'd begun taking an interest in the opposite sex. To make himself look older and more distinguished he grew a moustache in the hope of attracting the attentions of a couple of young girls who worked in the cake shop on the opposite side of the road.

One day when we were at a loose end and fed up, Ossie suddenly said 'Let's go an' see our kid an' see if we can scrounge a tanner off him.' We stopped by the lights outside the Meadows pub, directly opposite to Bentley's pawn shop and piped Johnny in the shop window. He was wearing a striped shirt, velvet waistcoat and gleaming shoes, but we couldn't fathom out why he kept moving things round as if he owned the shop. Another thing we noticed was his 'tash' which was much darker than normal, when it more closely resembled a small dollop of dried horse manure.

Ossie rattled on the window, Johnny ignored him and so Oz hammered again, this time on the glass door. Johnny quickly turned round and gave us a wide grin exposing his snow-white buck-teeth, which according to Mrs Feeley were his main assets in the good looks department. Suddenly he did a very strange thing and began acting oddly, which baffled us completely. One minute he was speaking to us and the next thing he was waving across the road, blowing kisses with his hand. We swung round, but couldn't see anyone or anything for that matter.

'He's not goin' doo lally is he, like old Mrs Collins?' Ossie asked, before we went inside.

'Dunno...let's ask 'im.'

'You ask 'im.'

'No, you said it first.'

'No you did.'

'Okay boys what's troublin' yer,' said Johnny, real grown up like, so we both spilled the beans and told him we were worried by his crazy actions. He laughed, then admitted that he fancied the girl in the cake shop opposite and she fancied him too. So the mystery was solved, he wasn't a loony after all, waving to no-one and we were delighted. We didn't want him carted off to the lunatic asylum at Chester in a loony bin, did we?

After crossing the road we called in at the cake shop with the thripenny joey that he'd given us. We knew he was watching us because the window trap in Bentleys was still open.

'Worr'ave yer got for thripence?' Ossie asked a dark girl. She kept looking out of the window across the road and we reckoned she was the one that Johnny had his eye on.

'There 'e is again,' her mate shouted before the dark girl had a chance to serve us.

We turned around as Johnny appeared in the window once more, this time holding a small brush to sweep the shelves.

An older lady emerged from the back of the shop remonstrating with the girls and totally ignoring us. We weren't too bothered, we only had threepence to spend anyway.

'That young man's goin' ter fall through that winder the way he's goin' on, an' then what will 'is poor muther do?' the other lady said.

'He shouldn't be showin' off then, should he?'

'Yer wanna stop eggin' 'im on then.'

'He thinks he's it ... 'cos he works in the pop shop,' said the dark one.

We glared at her and nearly got our tempers up and said something then.

'Tater gob,' they bawled together, laughing and skitting. That was it as far as we were concerned.

'Right boys what was it yer wanted?'

'Nowt. We wouldn't buy nowt from 'ere now even if it was on fire. That's our kid yer talking about,' we both repeated, walking out of the shop and slamming the door with spite. We then set off down Watson Street to Crinnions greengrocers for threepence worth of apple fades.

Footy

It was a derby game, Everton versus Liverpool and organised by the older lads. The match, held on our other pitch which was further up the street by the carpet cleaners, was played with a tennis ball because the Casey happened to be punctured. As for the pig's bladder, well that had been pinched from Frankie Bailey's backyard. The bin men, it seemed, always got the blame when anything of value vanished and were prime suspects for the disappearance of one of our prized possessions. Mr Feeley got the bladder from a mate who worked in the Lairage and had proudly presented it to us before our last big game, which was between Tranmere and New Brighton. The pig's bladder proved a lucky omen for us as we had won four-two, with no windows smashed. The result, attributed to the unfortunate pig's sac, had come in a game which for a change lasted a full ninety minutes.

The Casey was an entirely different matter to the pig's bladder though. Made up of thick patches of leather it became as heavy as lead when it was wet, so that heading the ball was kept to a minimum in case your head came into contact with the lace, then it would knock your brains out, or in, whichever way you looked at it.

'Keep it down, keep it down,' the older lads screamed when the ball ventured over the kerb and rattled someone's front door. If it happened to hit and break a window the street would be deserted within seconds, with the unfortunate householder left to rely on the honesty of the team to have a whip-round to pay for the repairs.

Before the start of a game we all stood in a line while the captains picked the teams, a nerve-racking experience and slightly different from our usual puddin' and yock selections which was straightforward for us ... for if you were a pudding, then next to you would be a yock, then a pudding and so on. No one was left out, even if there were thirty of us in a line. I suppose in a way I felt just like dad waiting for selection in the pens outside the dock gate.

'I'll 'ave 'im ... no we don't want 'im in our side ... he can't kick a ball straight.

No not you ... next ter you. Come on Tich you're with us.' This process continued until the squads were selected, with those unfortunate enough not to be chosen left to stand behind the goals and retrieve the ball when someone volleyed it down the street.

I was in goal for Everton and Spud was full-back. The rest of our gang, with the exception of Nacker, were playing for the reds. 'My ball, my ball,' Ossie screamed as he hurtled down the left wing like Billy Liddell. Unfortunately he then hit Spud side-on and disappeared down Mrs Cotton's lobby. The ref didn't see the collision and we didn't think too much of it either. After all it had been a fair challenge and we simply presumed Ossie would come flying out of the lobby just as quickly as he'd gone in, if not faster.

It was a well known fact that the Cotton's had the reputation of being a strange pair who didn't like intruders of any kind. That, it was argued, was why they didn't socialise with any of the neighbours and, rightly or wrongly, it was assumed that they thought themselves a cut above everyone else. Worst of all, they failed to draw their curtains when old Mr Jones was buried and this was an unforgivable act in the eyes of a majority of the older neighbours.

With ten minutes to full time Ossie was finally missed, not that his contribution or skills didn't amount to much, but the loss of a winger clearly meant the reds were down to ten men. However, the game continued and finished three goals each at the final whistle. With Ossie's coat still remaining where it served as a goalpost a search party was launched to see if he'd fallen through the floor in the Cotton's lobby. Spud ambled across and tentatively rattled the door, which had been closed since the tackle, while the rest of us remained under starters' orders to leg it to the Feeley's for reinforcements.

When Ossie opened the door with a big beam on his face and eating a buttered scone we almost fell over with shock.

'Worrav you bin up to?' Tommy Collins asked. His family lived next door but one to the Cotton's and had never spoken to them in the four years since the Cotton's moved in. What's more, it was common knowledge that the Cotton's had two grown up children, but never spoke about them. Putting two and two together it was assumed that the two sides failed to keep in touch because of personality clashes, while Mrs. Turner, another neighbour, stuck the boot in good style by claiming that the kids had been abandoned.

Ossie, however, put the record straight by informing us that 'Tommy and Amy Cotton lived in New Zealand and were coming over next year to see their parents and Mr and Mrs Cotton had asked him to go with them to meet them off the train.

It seemed that Ossie had landed in the hall with such ferocity that Mr Cotton, who was down the backyard in the lavvie, thought a bomb had dropped. Oz banged his head so hard on the bottom of the stairs when he landed that it knocked him clean out. Mrs Cotton, a former nurse, brought him round with a cup of sweet tea and as he supped it she then produced photos of her son, who, similar to Ossie, had freckles and ginger hair. As a result the Cottons had treated Ossie like the prodigal son returning home.

'The jammy bugger's landed on his feet again,' Tucker sulkily declared.

We agreed. Ossie was always jammy. Hadn't he been the first in our gang to break his arm and get plaster of paris! We were dead jealous because everyone wanted to sign their name on the cast, and wasn't he as sick as a parrot when we had a battle with the mob from Bentick Street and Billy Thomson, who was cock of their gang, grabbed Ossie in a headlock and then poured red ink over his plaster, ruining every one of his autographs.

There's nowt as strange as folk,' Mrs Murphy said, when she heard about Ossie's experience at the Cotton's.

The Walks

Neither the weather nor anything else for that matter would deter dad from continuing his walks around the town. He always insisted that physical and mental exercises were the best thing in the world for us and, most important, cost nothing. According to his way of thinking, if your brain and body were active you were obviously progressing.

Naturally, on those occasions I didn't break my neck with enthusiasm and volunteer to join him on the treks, but on the other hand I couldn't defy him otherwise he'd have assumed I wasn't interested in learning. Of course it would have proved disastrous if I had been foolish to admit my innermost feelings to him, so I kept quiet.

Treks always began on Sunday mornings and for once I was determined to outshine our Bridie who seemed to know something about most subjects on dad's agenda. I was crafty though, well I thought I was, for I had the answers to some of the questions he was likely to ask up my sleeve ... some things she'd never know about, I gloated to myself.

Recently, on a day I'd sagged school, I sat besides the locks and successfully identified and then memorised the type of flag on every cargo ship entering the port on that particular day. 'Let's see her beat that one,' I thought before we set out.

'Right kids, we'll go as far as Hamilton Square and walk along to Lairds,' dad announced. My face immediately fell. He glanced down at me.

'What's up with you m'lad?' What's your long face for?'

'Nowt ... I just wanted ter go down an' see the ships in the docks that's all dad.'

'There'll be plenty of time to see those before the year's out,' he replied.

'All those ships I'd taken the trouble to learn about will be gone by then,' I cursed under my breath.

'That's John Laird's statue over there,' dad said, pointing to the statue on the far side of the square.

'Yeah I know,' I sulked.

'Whereabouts did he com....'

'Scotland,' our Bridie butted in even before he had time to finish the question.

In temper I booted a tin can lying on the pavement.

'Hey, watch those bloody new shoes m'lad,' dad scowled, but I think he understood my frustration because he told Bridie to let me answer the next question.

'Who designed the park?'

'I know ... I know ... er ... erm.'

'Joseph Paxton,' she yelled and silently I cursed, I knew that one myself.

'Let 'im answer this one m'lady,' said dad trying to be fair to me.

'What else did he design? I'll give yer a clue ... It was in London, an' a football team.

You should know that one Jim.'

'It's easy...it's CRYSTAL PALACE,' I bawled.

'Well done son.' I was made up. I could tell by her face that she didn't know it.

We walked down the floating bridge and gazed across the water at the Liver Buildings. Almost immediately dad gave us a running commentary about the India buildings, the Cunard and overhead railway that ran from Bootle in the north to Dingle in the south end. He often travelled on this unique transport system, known locally as The Dockers umbrella, when working at the many docks that stretched along the other side of the river, so he knew it like the back of his hand.

The Mersey was alive with ships of different flags, while ferry boats brimming with day-trippers ferried them in the hundreds across the river to where we were standing at Woodside. With Woodside being the main terminal on our side of the water, during the summertime it was always congested with buses ready to transport throngs of excited tourists to destinations such as Chester, Arrowe Park, New Brighton or Moreton shore.

We glanced over the river at the Irish boats, moored to the left of the Pier Head and from our position could clearly see the large funnels above the adjacent buildings. To me they looked enormous. The fresh salt air blowing from Liverpool Bay stung our faces and before long my eyes began watering and then my nose started running, so I began doodling.

'What are yer doin' messin' around with yer tongue for?' dad growled.

'Dunno.'

'Put it away then.'

'Ossie can touch his chin with his.'

'That's bloody useful.'

'An' he can lick 'is nose as well.'

'So can a bloody dog.'

Dad was getting agitated with me I could tell, so conveniently I changed the subject.

'Ossie's goin' to Ireland for his holidays dad.'

'Is he now. We'll go ourselves next year, if God spares us,' he replied and both Bridie and I smiled together for the first time that day. He wouldn't expand on his statement despite our continued pestering, but we were thrilled at the prospect of our first holiday, even though it was a year off. During our walk we'd learnt about the benefactors of the town and the streets named after them. Dad also listed the many

Scottish architects who were responsible for the design and layout of buildings and streets.

We arrived home just before tea time. I couldn't wait to tell the lads about our forthcoming holiday and also Mr Smith about the Scottish pioneers who had designed the town.

Mam wasn't too pleased about the proposed holiday and dampened our spirits straight away telling dad to grow up and be realistic.

'It's stupid you promisin' the kids a holiday when you don't know whether you'll be workin' or not yerself Charlie,' she moaned.

'Well then, we'll just 'ave to wait an' see, won't we,' he replied.

It was obvious to us that he was now having second thoughts.

'Ar ... eh dad, that's mingy. Spud's been to Blackpool an' Tucker's been to Llandudno, an' we've been nowhere,' I whinged, but I knew that whinging wouldn't alter anything.

All we could do was hope that he'd be fully employed over the next twelve months, but judging by previous years the proposed holiday didn't look very promising at all.

'I'll tell yer what then, as soon as the weather picks up I'll take you kids as far as Southport, how about that?' dad suggested seeing the disappointment in our faces.

'Not on the bikes Dad?' I gasped in horror, immediately remembering the painful experience of my bike ride to Holywell

'Don't be so bloody daft. We've only got two bikes, soft lad. I wish you'd use your bloody 'ead an' brains that God gave yer,' he added.

'There you go,' mam interrupted. 'You don't know how lucky you are to have a father who takes you everywhere, now do you? Some poor kids don't even have that, an' besides, nobody round here goes on holidays anyroad - unless their goin' to their auntie's or uncles,' she added. 'Holidays are reserved for people with money an' you wouldn't like to be show-offs, now would you?'

We didn't reply to mam's lengthy speech and show of loyalty to dad who beamed and patted the dog's head with satisfaction. This was his way of showing that he fully approved of mam's display of solidarity for him.

Pongo

Dad was as regular as clockwork with his bowel movements. At eight o'clock every night he headed down the yard to make his will. Mam often said you could set the time against the town hall clock when he was making his institutionals.

'Institutionals? what's that dad?'

'Constitutionals, thick-head,' he replied. I nodded, still no wiser. Why grown-ups used such long words instead of simple ones just didn't make sense to me.

Late one night I was in the back kitchen playing with Jess when dad ventured out to the lavvie. He wasn't afraid of the dark, like me or our Bridie or mam, and he didn't whistle either.

'JESUS CHRIST. WHAT THE BLOODY 'ELLS THAT,' he yelled, flying back in through the kitchen door like a whirlwind, pulling his pants up over his John 'L's.

'WHERE'S ME FLASHLIGHT?' he bawled, snatching the lamp from his bike and galloping back out in the yard again ... which I felt took some doing.

Whatever it was out there didn't bother dad, he was brave and I was dead proud of him, even though he called our Jess outside to back him up.

I crept out and stood on the backyard step, watching him flash the beam around the lavvie and by the bin, but our Jess just wagged her tail and her attitude didn't appear to impress dad.

'GERRIT GIRL ... GERRIT.'

But Jess didn't know what she was supposed to get, so she sniffed behind the mangle, ran round in circles a couple of times, barked, and then in desperation to please, jumped up and down on the entry door.

'Bastards gorr away,' dad muttered and I heard him, but I wasn't bothered.

We all swore ourselves when we were on our own, which was okay as long as it wasn't in front of women or girls. It was then that I noticed Tucker's cardboard box lying on its side with the net gone and my heart missed a beat. 'Pongo ... Pongo, he's escaped,' I cried and dad gave me one of his looks, the kind he gave when he was about to get his Irish paddy up.

'WHO THE BLOODY 'ELL'S PONGO, WHEN HE'S OUT ?'

I was so upset I didn't answer him straight away.

'AM I TALKIN' TO MYSELF OR WHAT!!' he roared.

I spluttered 'Tucker 'ill kill me. His pet toad's escaped, an' I'm supposed to look after it while he's away at his nan's.'

'TOAD, WHAT BLOODY TOAD ... WORR 'AVE I TOLD YOU

ABOUT BRINGING OTHER PEOPLE'S TROUBLES INTO THIS HOUSE ?'

Whaa!! whaa!! I yelled as dad grabbed me by my ear and crashed his hand across my rear end.

'I'll give you bloody whaa,' he bawled.

'I'll give you somethin' to whaa about,' he repeated, as I sampled another dust raiser.

Mam appeared on the scene after our Bridie told her dad was half killing me in the yard and my skin was saved. To be honest, it was the first time in my life I was glad I had a sister. 'That'll do Charlie, that'll do for now,' mam bawled.

I rushed over, flinging my arms around her waist and felt the flour from her pinny stick to my face.

'Mam, mam, dad's flushed Pongo down the lavvie,' I cried. 'Tucker will murder me when he finds out.'

'It's okay James, it's okay. Just say a little prayer to St Anthony when you're safe in bed an' who knows, perhaps Pongo may turn up on the doorstep tomorrow mornin.'

She was great was our mam; truly religious, I know. Dad called her holy Maggie because she had so much faith and really did believe in miracles.

Next morning as I was getting a shovel of coal from the air raid shelter, something moved. 'JESS, JESS,' I bawled at the top of my voice.

'RATS, RATS. GERRIT JESS.' Then the miracle happened, right before my very eyes, as Pongo jumped out from amongst the coal and leapt nearly three foot further than he ever jumped before and Jess shot back in fright. I grabbed Pongo, but he kicked out at first and soon gave up. I'm sure he knew it was me because he croaked loudly. He seemed as relieved as I was; even though, with black coal-dusted skin he was now unrecognisable. I carried him inside and swilled him under the tap. He didn't flinch one bit as the cold water tap blasted the coal dust from him; the cold water didn't seem to bother him, like it would have bothered me.

Mam smiled when I told her about my miracle, but dad grunted. He had no belief or sense of humour when anything interfered with his daily routine or constitutionals.

Aunties

'Hey mam, how come we don't have any grannies or ninnies like everyone else?' I asked after Spud had spent the weekend at his grandma Murphy's in Lower Tranmere and she had taken him all the way to Blackpool for a day out, just before the end of the school holidays.

'They're all dead son, worse luck, but none of us can live forever, thank God.'

'That's lousy isn't it mam,' I replied; only because all my mates had grandparents and I felt left out.

'You'll 'ave ter put with all your auntie's instead, James and count your lucky stars you 'ave them, because there's many a poor child doesn't 'ave any,' she replied wistfully.

In addition to Aunt Fan who had one son, our Frank, I had aunties spread all over town who were mostly mam's sisters. I was therefore, never short of refuge should anyone chase me, which I suppose was better than nothing seeing that I had no gran's or grandad's to visit. I would often call on one of my aunts just for the sake of calling and was welcomed more or less with open arms, but for some reason my aunties always seemed to pose the same kind of questions.

'How's your mam son?'

'Is your dad alright?'

'My word you're the picture of yer mother James. You've even got her colour 'asn't he Fred?' Aunty Molly always seemed to remark on the occasions that I popped in to see her.

Uncle Freddie, a man of few words, very rarely acknowledged my presence when I called to his house and as far as I could remember never answered her questions, which I suppose he classed as being mere trivialities.

'What's your dad doin' these days, is he workin' ?' he always asked in his usual dull monotone voice.

'No, he's on strike Uncle Fred,' I replied truthfully. Nine times out of ten he would mutter, for me to hear. 'Half that crowd down there don't bloody want work, they're just lazy buggers. Greed, that's all I put it down to, pure bloody greed.'

I didn't reply, I just looked ahead. Dad wasn't fussy on him anyway.

'Your Uncle Freddie's gorra big chip on his shoulder,' my dad would often say. Aunt Molly on the other hand wouldn't have a word said against any of her immediate family; regardless as to whether the criticism was right or wrong.

'Hey that'll do from you,' she would leap to the defence of the Reilly's. 'You're talkin' about my sister's 'usband an' James's father you are, now cut it out. An' while you're at it, why not take a decko at your own crowd,' she went on.

Uncle Fred never rose to the challenge or retaliated. He was under the thumb and had no bottle' so my dad said.

Uncle Fred's way of dealing with his wife's onslaught was to leap from his armchair, grab a newspaper, head for the lavvie and slam the kitchen door on his way out.

Frustration, Aunt Molly put it down to, ever since he'd lost his job with the Corpy after he refused to go on the bins. This to his way of thinking was a step down the promotion ladder, especially after he'd conscientiously driven the binny ellie for three years.

My cousins, our Billy, who was two years older than me and Chris and Maureen immediately dived into his chair to enjoy the heat of the fire while I finished eating a dripping buttie Aunt Molly always made for me.

Another of mam's sisters, Aunt Julia, lived in a terraced house in Wallasey off Wheatland Lane. At the rear of her house, on the far side of the entry, someone back in time, with innovation, had built a wash house. After school on Mondays, it was to this working class luxury that I would trek with mam across the four bridges pushing a pram full of washing.

I loved that walk through the dock estate; it bubbled with activity and I was instantly transported into a different world. There were ships of all flags berthed on either side of the docks and tugs scurrying backwards and forwards through the locks, with dockers laughing and joking alongside make-shift canteens. Steam engines shunting L.M.S carriages puffed and clattered on railway lines that ran parallel with the pavements. Coolies ambled along in single file, chattering away in their native tongue, carrying large bundles of second-hand clothing on their heads. Meanwhile lorries laden with huge carts and wooden boxes of every imaginable kind of freight stretched up in lines leading to the docks. It was magic.

I hardly spoke a word to mam on these trips; I was mesmerised, day-dreaming most of the time of far away places and determined to sail there one day, maybe with Nacker, who could say! No wonder Mr Ryan had gone to sea. 'I only wish my dad did,' I thought to myself. Then I'd know all about ships when I left school.

Aunt Julia was a widow and older than mam. She had four girls and wasn't used to a scruffy urchin like me parading around her house as if I owned it. Her home was dead posh compared with ours and a hundred times more tidy. I thought I was the big shot, showing off in front of the girls until Aunt Julia collared me.

'Sit down James,' she hollered and I did as I was told. I had no choice, but when she wasn't looking I pulled funny faces behind her back making my cousins giggle. Aunt Julia knew what I was up to. It seemed to me as if she had eyes in the back of her head.

'Stoppit! You'll end up sticking like that you naughty boy,' she scolded. I felt my face flushing up and the girls began laughing again.

'When are you goin' to train this fella of yours our Maggie? He's out of control already and not even nine years old yet. If I had him I'd train him with a poker,' she added.

I shuddered. 'As long as it's not a hot one,' I thought. Mam, true to form, played on her deafness. I was made up.

'You want to seriously think about gettin' those ears of yours seen to, our Maggie.'

Ma smiled. 'I'll give it a bit of thought, our Julia, when I find time,' she said,

As we walked home mam remonstrated with me. 'You'll 'ave to behave yourself in future when you go to Aunt Julia's, d'yer 'ear me James? She's not used to lads an' she's had a hard life bringin' those girls up on her own, an' thank God she's done a good job.'

'Okay Mam...I'll remember that next time. By the way Ma, how's your ears?'

She tutted, her eyes were smiling, she heard me all right.

'I don't know who you take after,' she replied, but I knew she was joking. Mam could see right through me and I felt, at times, that I could see right through her.

My favourite aunt lived in the North end of the town and had six lads and two girls. There was our Tommy, Mickey, Robbie, Bernie, Tony, John, Mary and our Sheila. Aunt Florrie Murphy, no relation to Spud's clan, waddled like mam and was slightly stouter. I used to meet her outside Pegrams grocers in Watson Street to help her with the shopping. We'd wait to catch the ninety-four bus up to her house in Tees Street and despite the large number of dockers waiting at the bus stop they made sure that we boarded first and Aunt Florrie had a seat.

Uncle Peter originated from Gerrard Gardens, off Scottie Road in

Liverpool and was crippled with arthritis. He rarely moved from the easy chair without the aid of a walking stick, but in spite of his handicap he still managed to keep an orderly house. Dad thought a lot of him and often walked to Aunt Florrie's to enjoy interesting conversations with Uncle Peter on Sunday mornings for an hour or two. Uncle Peter, an ex-merchant navy seaman, had amassed a great deal of knowledge on his travels and he willingly shared all of this with anyone who was prepared to listen.

He was as wise as an owl, however, and knew all the strokes, even when our John sent me on a spying mission to see if he was asleep. He would then pretend to snore.

'Is he asleep,' John would whisper to me.

'Yeah.'

'Are yer sure?'

'Yeah, definitely.' Our John always took my word. After all, I'd taken my first Holy Communion, so why should I tell lies? He sneaked through the front door and just as he was about to help himself to a ciggie his dad's walking stick would crash down, almost taking his fingers off. I'd slipped up again. I was hopeless playing out a spy and Uncle Peter knew it.

Aunt Florrie always treated me as her youngest son and although her lads were in their early twenties and late teens - with the exception of John who was fourteen - they always 'mugged' me when it was time for me to leave. Uncle Peter as observant as ever, rattled his walking stick on the floor, interrupting the concentration of my gambling cousins who would be engrossed in a game of poker and announced. 'Young Jimmy's goin' now.' The card school was halted for a few seconds while I collected half pennies and pennies from those who weren't playing so well and usually a sixpence from whoever was on a winning streak.

Of course to my way of thinking I'd earned every penny of their generosity, for it was me that accompanied Aunt Florrie on pious excursions to Holy Cross Church, crushed between her and Mrs Daley who was equally as stout, and then escorted for a dose of benediction and hymns while they enjoyed the peace and quiet of the house.

Aunt Florrie, like my mam, had a loud and tinny voice, which in her favour made up for its lack of quality. Like many of the mothers who found the sanctuary of the church a pleasant outlet from the running of large families, Aunt Florrie used the visits as a pleasant break from bickering arguments which sometimes disrupted the harmony of the card school.

'Hail queen of heaven, the ocean star, guide of the wanderers here below,' the congregation wailed and this set me off wondering what I was doing there and what the lads would be up to down town.

Aunt Mary wasn't our real aunty, but had been mam's best friend since they were in service together in the early 1930's. Living close by she always assumed the role of surrogate mother when ma was heavily pregnant or in labour, taking it upon herself to run the show and sort things out. She was never one to tolerate nonsense from any of us, including dad, who called her deadpan Mary, the Greek wrestler, but behind her back of course. Now and again she'd wind mam up, telling her 'You're far too soft with them Maggie, you've got to put them in their place properly an' that includes Charlie.' This advice was never given in front of dad; he'd fall out with her at the drop of a hat - but only when mam wasn't pregnant. For once we sympathised with his point of view, because apart from Aunt Mary being twice the size of mam she had none of her patience either.

'Come on shift yer feet,' she'd moan at us, quietly, but aggressively, so that if by chance we were absorbed reading comics we could easily find our feet swept along with the rest of the debris on the floor, or be belted with her mop.

Aunt Mary was so strict that even our Jess would stay out late until she'd gone and occasionally missed out on her dinner. This for a dog, according to dad, showed a lot of intuition. 'She knows which side her bread's buttered best,' he often observed.

'I think that'll do us for now Maggie, we'll make 'im the last,' our Bridie overheard dad say to mam after the arrival of our Tommy. Bridie tried explaining this important conversation to me and indeed I rubbed my hands with glee, even though I wasn't too sure where Tommy had come from in the first place. All I knew was that he screamed all the time and I couldn't wait for him to grow up and act normal like us. Then hopefully we wouldn't have to put up with Aunt Mary's ' ruling our roost' ever again.

Sagging school

Nobody in our house ever volunteered to light the fire except me. I'd been dying to have a go for ages, but no one would listen and despite my cheerful enthusiasm my services were forever getting rejected. I always ended up with the simple task of emptying the cinders in the bin, not a very inspiring job considering the talent that I knew I possessed. However, once I reached my ninth birthday and had been expertly coached by mam in the fundamental art of setting the fire out, I was deemed responsible enough and given the task as a Saturday duty; this show of faith pleased me immensely.

I'd always had a fascination for fires for as long as I could remember and was blissfully aware of dad's strict instructions to 'keep the matches out of the reach of the other fella.' This, I suppose, to my infantile way of thinking always made the need to succeed even more of a challenge, and in consequence I went to great lengths to find the hide outs so that I could empty half the box into my trouser pocket.

I delighted in dropping flaming matches like dive-bombers onto pieces of wood floating in the Park Lake or the docks and then watching the white smoke fizzle out as they plunged into the water. The lads would also drop bombs down the metal grids which lay under the windows of most of the corner shops and were elated if they set fire to the scrap paper or empty cigarette packets lying a foot or so beneath the surface. Naturally, our cries of delight incensed the angry shopkeepers who chased and cursed us for placing them in the position of having to throw buckets of water down to prevent the fire from spreading.

All eyes were on me that first Saturday when I set and lit the fire. I was real proud of myself, even though mam was the only one who had faith in my ability.

After applying the match to the sticks I held the Empire News across the shovel just as mam had instructed me to. Amazingly the paper failed to catch fire until the draught sucked it in against the shovel and then, without warning, it burst into flames sending burned and blackened pieces of paper floating up around the hearth. Immediately I shoved the rest of the burning paper up the chimney with my bare hands and surprisingly it didn't even hurt or singe them.

Within a short period of time the sticks caught fire and yellow flames with blazing sprays of sparks set the coal alight. Then particles of soot, lodged half way up the chimney, glowing red from the heat of the flames, dropped down like bombs splattering the grate. I was made up - these were real bombs, much better than those that the gang dropped down the grids.

My fire even excelled any that mam or dad had lit, for theirs tended to smoke and smoulder for ages before the coal started hissing.

'Well done James, you've done a good job there son,' mam said.

Although at first she had serious reservations with dad about him delegating another of his jobs to me, mam now appeared happy with the outcome.

I revelled in mam's praise and felt like a dog with two tails, even though I'd dabbled with fires before, you know, but of course not in our house.

The summer holidays were over in no time and upon our return to the Lauries we were given a cautious welcome by our new teacher, Mrs Burgess. I was now in standard three and academically hadn't progressed since standard one. One of my first priorities was to try and worm my way in by sitting next to Ossie as I'd done the previous term. Life was easy sitting next to Oz, for if I struggled with any difficult questions he'd always find a means to help me and show me the answers, usually on the sly. This arrangement suited me admirably until it was time for exams and then I fell to pieces, as Miss Brindle confirmed when emphasising an apparent lack of interest on my Standard Two school report. Dad almost hit the roof when reading my sub-standard effort and threatened all kinds of annihilation if I didn't buck my ideas up during the coming term. After spending a few nights in solitary confinement, I promised on my mother's life to pull my socks up and improve my dismal record in future.

However, my memory seemed to slip my mind upon returning to school and even dad's punishment was forgotten as I scurried to the back of the room trying to grab a speck next to Ossie, but Mrs Burgess was far too experienced a teacher not to notice the scramble for the back seats. Even though I managed to sit next to Ossie, one of her first tasks was to move me away and place me next to Cleary.

Our mutual dislike was obvious, for when in bed with the devil you have little choice but to act like the devil. One of Cleary's tricks was to throw paper aeroplanes behind teacher's back when she was writing on the blackboard and foolishly I began tittering, placing me under suspicion straight away. It was probably bravado or maybe because I enjoyed showing off that I accepted the blame, or it could have been just plain cowardice, but for whatever reason I was no match for Cleary. Despite the fact that I'd been trained how to fight by dad, my record wasn't worthy of note, two fights two defeats, both emphatic.

Bare-fist fighting after school was quite common among the older lads but our attempts were just skirmishes. We were inclined to push, shove and try to wrestle our opponents to the ground, an action guaranteed not to cause serious injury.

Poor Spud, who was the quietest of our gang, stayed behind one night to have an extra half-hour lesson. He was confused with spelling and his reading wasn't up to scratch either, so Mrs Burgess, a dedicated teacher, offered to give up her own time to teach him in the quietness of the classroom without the usual distractions.

We were playing in the Court when he came along Brookie with his head bowed low and tears running down his rosy cheeks.

'What's the matter Spud?' Ossie asked. Spud hardly ever cried, well not in front of us he didn't if he could help it. Ossie did, he was different from Spud, he'd whinge if you pinched his bum, even when we were messing around.

'Cleary belted me an' called me a sissy,' Spud sobbed.

Nacker arrived with Smithy and Tucker and when they saw the state Spud was in suggested going round to Cleary's end to sort him out once and for all. We agreed to make the numbers up and immediately headed for the Morpeth buildings, an ancient block of Victorian flats and certainly no place for the faint-hearted. Nacker led the way, closely followed by Tucker, Smithy was next, then me and finally Ossie; he trailed behind in case we were ambushed. He wasn't soft, there were some hard cases in the 'Morpho's' and although he hadn't been trained to fight yet, he certainly could run. Fortunately for us, Cleary wasn't to be seen anywhere so we retreated, screaming obscenities and throwing bricks down the narrow street, scattering a number of mongrels and hoping that one of them would strike Cleary's dog who was amongst the pack.

On the Saturday morning Spud knocked on our door just before nine, something I found rather strange; he didn't normally get up until ten unless we were going to the matinée in the Gaumont. However, at that particular time we'd been barred for three weeks for holding two fingers up in front of the projector, a gesture, that didn't go down too well with the management.

'Me da said could I borrow yer boxin' gloves?' he asked. Dad was busy messing about with a cobbler's last in the yard and I was happy myself. There was no way he could involve me with that experiment I thought, although I fully expected my shoes would be the first pair he'd mess round with.

'Dad, Spud wants ter know if his dad can borrow the boxin' gloves?' I asked. Dad put his hammer down and shoved the last out of the way; an obvious sign he'd had enough of it for the day.

'D'yer want me to teach yer son?' he said to Spud, flexing his muscles and loosening up.

'No thanks Mr Reilly. Me da wants ter teach me 'imself, so can I borrow the gloves please?'

'Of course yer can, of course yer can Spud. If your old fella's strugglin' come back an' see me, won't yer?' He insisted. But I knew dad was disappointed, I could tell by his face and as soon as Spud had gone he sarcastically remarked. 'Paddy teachin' that lad of 'is ter box, worra a joke, he couldn't box kippers himself.'

'His dad used to be a boxer,' I indignantly leapt to the defence of Mr Murphy who I happened to like and, what's more, just to be argumentative.

'What! Yer mean the horizontal champ. Listen son, an' listen carefully. Spud's ould fella, who I've known since he came across from Dublin, only had four amateur fights an' never lasted a round. What does that tell yer?'

I didn't answer, there was no point in pursuing the conversation, dad was in one of his funny moods, which was confirmed when he picked up the last and hid it in the shelter when mam was looking the other way.

By mid October I was sagging school on a regular basis, having first developed the habit in Standard Two. Nacker, who was in his final year and studying for the scholarship, suggested we have a long weekend by taking Friday off. Without as much as a second thought I agreed. I was easily led and didn't need my arm twisting up my back to refuse. Ossie and Spud declined the offer, as they had more sense. Tucker, who was off school with what was diagnosed as growing pains, said he would join us. As I hadn't experienced any of these growing pains at that particular time I was unsure of the symptoms or whether they hurt or not.

'To the swings,' we yelled as soon as we were safely through the park gates and out of view of anyone who could snitch on us for sagging school.

'Last one there stinks,' Nacker bawled, so racing like mad over the hills and across the cinder pitch we reached the deserted play area within minutes. This was the life; while our classmates were being taught lessons in musty surrounds, we lapped up the freedom of playing in fresh air on the May-pole and monkey bars, before heading towards the top park to see if there were any sign of conkers, even though the leaves hadn't turned orange yet. Despite the fact that Tucker was suffering with growing pains it didn't prevent him from climbing the trees and shaking the branches with all his might. I wasn't as skilled as Tucker so I copied Nacker and hurled lumps of wood, severing large sections of the tree, which couldn't have done the tree much good.

Tucker spotted the uniform first and yelled as loud as he could. 'PARKIE ... PARKIE!' Catching sight of the park bobby peddling furiously towards us we scattered towards the lower park. Luckily for us we managed to disappear into familiar territory by the rocks. There was nothing down for us if the Parkie caught us. He was ruthless. His preference for punishment rarely changed, a crack across your chops was his speciality and you couldn't complain. It seemed that anyone wearing a police-type uniform had a good enough reason for cracking you one. Nobody ever interfered, it was just one of those things as far as everyone else was concerned

After leaving the park we made our way to another of our favourite destinations, the docks. Although we knew that the school boards who patrolled this area on bikes could be lying in wait for us, it didn't deter us one bit. Glancing to the top of Park Road East, lorries loaded to the hilt queued right down to the Vittoria dock, carrying cargo with exotic destinations written on huge wooden crates, names we found fascinating.

We entered dock estate and I was dead nervous, for apart from avoiding the school board I always feared that life wouldn't be worth living if I happened to walk into dad. As a precaution I kept a low profile, hiding wherever I could until safely across the four bridges on the Seacombe side of the docks. My nervousness, however, rapidly disappeared as soon as we caught sight of the lock. The lock, a massive barrier spanning the whole of the dock, held calm water on one side and the Mersey's turbulent tide lower down on the other. With our pockets weighed down with stones we crawled along on our hands and knees, as you'd expect commandos to, and began bombing the crabs or anything else that clung to the edge of the lock. As soon as we were fed up we threw stones into the dock and tried guessing the depth of the water by noting the number of bubbles floating up. This was the place to learn; we didn't need to go to school, we learnt better our own way, so Nacker told us.

After messing about on the locks for a while and discharging our stones, we decided to explore the dock that surrounded the flour mills. Tucker had heard on the grapevine from his mates in Cathie that peanuts had been taken there on barges and anything to do with food, as far as we were concerned, was always worth looking into. Racing each other down the side of the quay we jumped over rope as thick as our legs and darted in and out of large bollards scattered alongside the half-busy dock. Nacker, blazing the trail with Tucker just behind him, leap frogged over the larger bollards, but I had no chance; there was no way my short legs could straddle them, so I settled instead for the simpler side-saddle alternative.

The barges were berthed alongside a huge shed and to our surprise nobody seemed to be working in the vicinity. Unable to believe our eyes, or luck for that matter, we crawled across the tarpaulin and attempted to lift the hatches, but they proved far too heavy for us. After a while we gave up the chase. Before leaving though, Nacker vowed to bring his mam's carving knife with him the next time we came down this way and as he said, 'slit open the tarpaulin to see for himself what was inside.'

With it being a warm and clammy day we removed our shirts, moseyed across to the Alfred Dock, found a quiet section where we stripped off to our bare skin and dived into the green oily water, coming up by the steps without swimming. Feeling as clean as if we'd just come out of Livvie Baths, we used our clothes to dry ourselves and then played a game of pirates inside an old wreck that was lying at the far end of the quay. At half four we set off for home.

Everything seemed normal in our house. Mam was cooking the dinner, Bernadette was reading comics, Tommy crawled round the floor and our Bridie whinged about the noise, which I kind of expected. She was studying for the scholarship and it came to a point where I couldn't even open my mouth without getting told to shut up. I was fed up with the whole palaver. And all this fuss, for what? Dad was paranoid over her passing and backed her up on every occasion. At the time I wished I were deaf like mam. Then I could talk to my heart's content without having to look up and pull a face when I was getting bawled at. Mam didn't know how lucky she was.

Ossie was in the same boat as me, but their Teresa wasn't quite as bossy as our Bridie and besides, his brothers' took his side, which made a big difference. We now appreciated what Spud had gone through when their Cathy was sitting the scholarship. It must have been murder for him with having four sisters and his mam to contend with. 'No wonder he eats all the time an' wants ter be a priest with 'aving to put up with that lot,' Ossie said and I tended to agree with him.

'I wouldn't go to those extremes me'self though,' I answered.

'You a priest Jimmy, no way on this earth,' Ossie replied.

'You'll end up a heathen the way you're heading.'

Downfall

After morning prayers Mrs Burgess began her daily routine by removing from her desk the school register. As usual she diligently ticked in blue ink those present and red ink those absent. Allen ... in miss ... Atherton ... in miss ... Byrne A ... yis miss ... Byrne B ... BYRNE B, she repeated, glaring at the back of Bernie's head ... 'ere miss ... 'Pay attention, do you hear? ...Yis miss'. Byrne P ... in miss. Cannon ... miss. Cleary ... here miss. Connolly .. .CONNOLLY. 'He's got the measles miss,' a chorus responded from the section where he normally sat during his rare appearances.

'Who was it that brought his note in last time?' Mrs Burgess irritably demanded scanning through her list of excuses which appeared to be increasing daily, before resuming. Curtis ... miss. Doughty ... 'ere miss. Duffy ... am 'ere miss ... Feeley ... 'here miss' he yelled raising his hand up as high as he could, showing off as normal. Then Spud farted and Ossie flushed crimson. We all laughed ... Mrs Burgess removed her glasses and glared at everyone in class.

'The culprit responsible for such disgusting behaviour should be ashamed of himself,' she bawled and Ossie gave Spud one of his dirtiest looks, hoping it would enable the teacher to detect Murphy straight away; Mrs Burgess, however, had other means of detection.

Half an hour later she belted Spud with a ruler for nothing. Ossie smiled and put his thumb up.

By November time I was well down the slippery road to self-destruction, my truancy becoming such a habit that I was now sagging school at least three days a week. Only for the fact that Tucker was a good writer and an expert on excuses I'd have been rumbled long before. He was a much better writer than mam, but he had to be careful not to make the notes too perfect and threw in a few spelling mistakes, which he thought older people would be more likely to make. Ossie, or Spud for that matter, didn't mind leaving the notes on Miss Burgess's desk, but both had misgivings about my own lack of interest in the whole procedure.

Apart from 'sagging' school I began pilfering, a more serious habit that would have definitely earned me the biggest hiding of my life. There was no way I could ever forget the number of times that dad drummed into me not to take anything that belonged to someone else. However, like an ostrich with its head in the sand, the last thing I thought about was the consequences of my foolishness.

Peter Donnelly, a hard knock from Payson Street who was in the same class as Nacker suggested that we raid the Co-op bakery in Price Street. 'It's as easy as wink to knock off,' he told us, so without a further thought we set off on the short journey to the bakery.

In single file we crept along the cinder path that separated the bakery from a building in St Anne Street which housed the bread vans and headed towards two double doors facing each other. It was common knowledge among the lads at school that across this passageway the bakers transferred hot bread on trolleys to the vans.

At weekends the drivers escorted the trolleys from one building to the next. This was to limit the threat of being ambushed by unscrupulous school kids, but during weekdays, when everything was quiet, the trolleys lay invitingly across the space between the two buildings.

No-one seemed to be near as we reached the trolleys and within seconds we were away with a hot loaf tucked under each of our jerseys. As we legged it along Vittoria Street towards the park entrance the heat from the bread seeped through our shirts, mingling with the sweet smell of the crust and although we were tempted to stop and bite the corners off, like we normally would when going for our mothers' bread, we didn't chance it.

Once through the park gates, however, we systematically devoured our loaves, starting at the four corners and working our way round. The dough in the middle we fed to the ducks and pigeons which had now surrounded us like swarms of bees.

Nacker anticipated that the loaf would probably last us for the day, but to be on the safe side he suggested that it might be a good idea to help ourselves to a variety of fruit, placed in boxes outside the greengrocer shop in Conway Street.

After leaving the park we fell into line with another of our favourite yet dangerous pastimes, namely, cadging lifts by hanging onto the back of lorries. We'd wait for a lorry to pull up at a halt sign, then creep behind, grab hold of anything that would support us and hang on like grim death until it stopped at the next set of traffic lights. Sometimes we fell off before the lorry reached a junction and quite often scraped our arms and knees, yet it didn't deter us. As far as we were concerned there was no greater feeling than speeding along busy roads, grimly hanging with one hand, swapping across to the other and feeling the wind bite into your cheeks with the draught sweeping from under the lorries swinging your feet. This was another obsession I found difficult to discard.

Finnigan ... 'ere miss. Gardener ... miss. Hanlon ... HANLON ... 'ere ... 'ere miss. 'Murphy Thomas ... here miss. Murphy Timothy ... everyone hissed ... 'ere miss, Spud growled. Nolan ... in miss. O'Grady ... O'GRADY ... norrin miss. O' Loughlin ... 'ere miss. Quinlan ... 'ere miss. Rafferty ... here miss. Rainer ... 'norrin miss' Reilly ... REILLY ... 'he's absent again miss.' Ossie dolefully replied. 'I want you to take another letter to his parents, Feeley. Please collect it before you leave class this afternoon.'

'Yes miss.' Ossie was petrified. The last letter he'd brought, Nacker grabbed it from him and threw it in the dock. I remembered it well, it was the time we were chased and almost caught by the school board who had been on our trail all day.

In addition to 'sagging' school I had also stopped going to mass and to anyone with a scrap of foresight it must have been apparent that I was treading on thin ice. I didn't dwell on the consequences for one moment and the latest letter went down the lavvie, again unopened.

'REILLY... come out at once' Miss Burgess yelled. I was accused of disrupting the class, but this time I was innocent. Of course I couldn't bubble Tony Connolly the real culprit, he'd have only called me a snitch and that's one thing that I wasn't, so taking the only way out I accepted the blame.

'I've had enough of your nonsense Reilly,' the teacher screamed, taking a short cane from her desk and rattling my palm with a succession of blows.

'OUCH ... OUCH ... OUCH ... OUCH ... OUCH,' I bawled, even though it didn't hurt. Everyone started laughing and this infuriated her even further.

Having now reached the end of her tether, Mrs Burgess dragged me out of the class and hauled me before Pop Lally, the headmaster. As he began reading my attendance record I quaked in my shoes. I then watched him scan through the lists of excuses supposedly written by mam. He was a clever man - far cleverer than any of us, including dad - and it didn't take him long to recognise that these masterpieces were simply fakes.

'Who wrote these letters?' he demanded his eyes almost popping from his head.

Although I was shaking like a leaf I couldn't snitch on Tucker even though he was a Proddy and had nothing to do with the Lauries or Pop for that matter. As usual, whenever I couldn't see a way out of a problem I took the easy way out, looking down at the floor and not answering.

I was given four of the best, with two of them on the tips, for refusing to answer his question, and I don't mind admitting that the punishment brought tears to my eyes. Worse news was to follow, however, for he then announced he'd send for my parents, and that's when I really panicked.

Mam always said that I was born under a lucky star and in this instance I suppose she was right in a way. That week dad was working over the water at the Gladstone dock, our Bridie had gone to her friends for tea and so only mam, Bernadette and baby Tom were in the house when the call came that Pop Lally wanted to see her at once. Despite numerous death threats from mam, I stubbornly refused to disclose the reason for the summons, desperately hoping she'd calm down on the short journey to the Lauries.

Leaving the kids in Aunt Fan's capable hands she then marched me round to the school holding the top of my jacket just in case I wriggled free and escaped, which strangely enough was something I'd seriously contemplated attempting as soon as we left home. On our arrival I received a further roasting from both Pop Lally and Miss Burgess in front of mam and was threatened with expulsion. The headmaster also intimated that he would be having a quiet word with the priest, a disastrous threat considering I'd missed mass on so many recent occasions. I was scared stiff now and after profusely apologising and swearing on my mother's death that I would never sag again, we set out on the journey home.

Mam was embarrassed; her face flushed red with anger, she resumed her grip on my jacket collar, cracking me across the back of my legs every yard of the way home. I wailed as if I was being murdered and I could have been for all the notice people took.

'How did they know I was guilty? Just because a grown-up was battering me didn't necessary give them the right to judge me,' I cried to myself.

'Just you wait till your father gets in, just you wait m'lad,' mam bawled. I don't know why she always said 'just wait' because no one in their right mind would sit and calmly wait to be murdered, now would they? And I had no intention of waiting myself, I was too busy working out all possibilities of whereabouts I could hide until dad cooled down and let his dinner digest. Of course living in a two up and two down terrace house limited my scope considerably.

Dad turned into our street and with him being bandy like me, I could recognise his familiar walk a mile away, but although under severe pressure I didn't let my duty to mam get in the way of my immediate demise. Taking off like a rocket I dashed home, yelling that dad was on the way, giving her time to have his dinner on the table when he arrived. Without a moment to lose I darted down the jigger and within seconds scrambled into the dark shadows of our air raid shelter, confident no one would ever find me until I was dead. Then they'd all be sorry they'd battered me or listened to our Bridie clat tailing or done nothing when Pop Lally scared the life out of me and all because I'd sagged school twenty two times.

Then there'd be my funeral, with me lying pale and cold in my coffin in our front room and all my mates coming round to see me and I could hear them talking.

'Poor Jimmy,' Ossie would say. 'He was me best mate. I didn't mean ter snitch on 'im to Mrs Burgess,' and he started crying which I expected him to.

Spud stood there staring down at me and I knew what he was thinking. He was sorry he hadn't learnt the last rites before becoming a priest. He was also dying to fart, but given the circumstances he knew that he daren't, not in front of me lying in my coffin and knowing that I always laughed when he dropped one. He just couldn't take that chance now.

Nacker came in with Tucker and Smithy and quickly announced that this was the end of the Brook Street gang. I felt like shouting 'No ... no ... not our gang,' although of course my lips wouldn't move.

Our Bridie peeped through the door from the kitchen, yet wouldn't come in and I could swear she had a tear in her eye, though I wasn't certain so I wouldn't bet on it. Then at last, when my mates had gone mam and dad came and stood by my coffin. Dad hadn't had a shave yet or a wash, but I noticed he still had his belt on.

'Just nine an' a bit ... that's all he was,' mam wailed. The tears swelled in my eyes when I thought about Christmas coming up and then my birthday with all the presents that I'd miss out on.

'Aye' dad said. 'He looks peaceful lyin' there, doesn't he?'

'Who's goin' to light the fire now our James is gone?' mam cried, and Jess looked at her with those soft doleful eyes and licked her hand before trotting into the back kitchen to park right in front of the gas oven which was full on.

'He'll miss out on Ireland too,' dad muttered.

I began sobbing uncontrollably. 'I always wanted to go to Dublin an' to Kerry an' to kiss the Blarney stone an' to see the Mountains of Mourne where me dad's family came from,' I yelled and my shirt was soaked with tears now. I'd been in the shelter for hours, it was getting dark and it seemed like ages since dad had been to the lavvie.

'FRANKIE,' Mrs Bailey screamed. I knew the street would be soon deserted.

I was freezing now.

'I wonder when they'll find me body,' I cried as the back door opened and I heard our Bridie's voice.

'Our Jimmy's in the air raid shelter again mam.'

Mam came scurrying out.

'Nip upstairs an' see if your dad's asleep,' she ordered.

'Why, what's he been up to now?'

'Get goin' an' mind yer own business an' do as you're told,' mam replied angrily.

Bridie scattered and within seconds reported back.

'Yeah ... he's snorin'.'

'Go an' put the kettle on an' close the door after you.'

'James are you alright?' mam whispered.

'No ... I'm dyin' mam,' I cried.

'Come on out son. You don't want to be dyin' all on your own in the dark now, do you?'

'No mam,' I sobbed, appearing through the shelter doorway, my eyes all red and puffed up and my nose running like two candles, covered in coal dust.

'Eee ... I don't know what I'm goin' ter do with you,' mam declared, wiping my nose with her pinny and hugging me despite the state I was in.

'Now listen to me James. If you promise never, ever to sag school again I wont tell your father on you this time, do you hear?'

'Yis mam ... I promise ... I promise 'onest ter God,' I whimpered.

Mam stripped me to my bare skin and scrubbed me down in the back kitchen with hot water from the kettle so that even my little mickey didn't escape the rough flannel.

Next she put a clean shirt on me and announced I'd have to wear my best trousers for school the following morning because of the state that my other pair was in. I couldn't really argue, even though I hated wearing my best clothes during the week. I didn't notice the chill of the cold red floor tiles as I stood forlornly by the kitchen door feeling extremely sorry for myself. Mam lifted the tail of my shirt and tapped me on my bare bum and I didn't object as I normally would when she lifted it in front of our Bridie. I was too upset.

'Come on in from the wars my little soldier,' mam said 'and I'll make you a nice cup of cocoa and a piece of toast done on the fire.'

Our Bridie craftily sneaked a glance at my swollen eyes, wondering what mischief I'd been up to this time, but of course I wouldn't tell her.

'Mam ... mam ... quick,'our Bridie yelled, shaking her awake.

'What is it?' mam whispered, trying not to disturb dad who had to be up at six o'clock because he was travelling across the Mersey to work in Liverpool.

'It's our Jimmy, he thinks he's dead an' I can't get to sleep with him shouting.'

'He'll be well and truly dead if I've got to bloody well gerr up,' dad roared.

'It's okay Charlie I'll see to him,' mam muttered, coming through to the back bedroom where she felt my forehead.

'Go asleep son, you'll be all right now,' she whispered gently.

'What's the matter with the other fella now?' Dad asked when mam climbed back into bed.

'It's all right Charlie, he was just haloosikatin that's all,'mam replied.

Dad tutted a few times. 'Halucinatin' my arse,' he muttered before turning over.

Not only did Miss Burgess notice a distinct change in my behaviour;

I could even see it myself. The lads, however, didn't realise the near death experience I'd encountered and were totally oblivious to my change in ways, no doubt putting it down to a phase I'd been going through at the time.

I was still well behind in my studies but decided that from now on I'd ask questions about anything which I couldn't fathom out on my own. Ossie took some beating though; whenever Miss Burgess or the priests asked questions he'd raise his hand higher than anyone in the class would, eventually standing up just to get noticed.

'Here miss … here miss ... here Father ... over here Father,' he would snivel, though half the time he didn't know the answer anyway.

The whole exercise was just snivelling for attention, there again it didn't bother me; I struggled to keep up with easy questions never mind the hard ones and don't forget, it was all my own fault and I had no excuse whatsoever.

The catechism books in our third year got thicker and the questions became harder and the more I tried the worse it seemed I became.

'What's adultery Father?' I asked when we were being questioned on religious studies.

'Well Reilly, adultery occurs when, say a man or a woman who are not married commit a sin by going with each other. Do you understand?'

'Yis father,' I replied, though it was all double Dutch to me - but not to Ossie.

'Father … please ... Father,' Ossie yelled for the umpteenth time.

'Yes, what is it now Feeley?' Father Nugent replied irritably.

'Is that the same sin as thou shall not covet thy neighbour's wife?' he asked, showing off as usual.

'More or less Feeley, more or less, but I really think you're too young in this class to completely understand the proper meaning. What I suggest is that you worry more about venial sins for the time being.'

When dad was having his dinner nobody spoke. He needed time to eat his meal in peace and depending on his mood we all waited until he'd read his paper, been to the lavvie and lit his pipe before we spoke. When he was comfortably settled in front of the fire, he would then patiently listen to any upsets or problems that required his judgement. With our Bridie sitting the eleven plus in the near future she more or less absorbed his full attention and that was all right by me, for I was in a comfortable position of not needing any advice or guidance whatsoever, or so I believed.

'Hey mam have you ever committed adultery?' I enquired innocently, just to show dad I wasn't thick and had been learning as well as our Bridie had.

Mam simply smiled, she knew I was seeking attention. Dad, however, exploded.

'WHAT WAS THAT YOU JUST SAID, M'LAD ?'

'Nowt. It was nothin' important dad. I was only asking the priest in school today about adultery an' what it meant an' all that and Ossie wanted ter know about coverin' your neighbour's wife ... that's all.'

'I don't bloody believe what I'm 'earing 'ere' he growled. Suddenly I had a sinking feeling that maybe I shouldn't have tried showing off in the first place about my new found knowledge.

'Did you 'ear that Maggie ... a bloody priest talkin' like that to nine year olds. The bloody world's gone soft if you ask me.'

'Take no notice of him, he doesn't understand what he's talkin' about Charlie.'

'I know that Maggie, but it's not very nice hearing your own son asking his mother if she's committed adultery ... now is it? And in front of me ... 'is bloody father as well.'

I didn't know what all the fuss was about so I went into the back kitchen out of the way, muttering to myself. 'That's what you get for trying to impress dad. In future I'll not bother asking anything important. He'll be sorry when I grow up an' know loads of things and I won't bother telling him nothin'.]

Bonnie night

Across the weeks before bonfire night there was always one or two unscrupulous shopkeepers who would illegally but willingly sell fireworks to us under-aged lads. The gang would scrape together what few pennies we could muster and naturally select those fireworks that made the loudest bang, or caused the most mayhem. At the same time of the year 'winter warmers' became a fashionable accessory and a popular item for small boys, especially in the dark nights. These simple devices consisted of a tin can with holes punched in. This was then filled with old rags soaked in paraffin, with a longish wire attached as a handle to the top at each side. Once lit the can was then swung in a circle and of course, the faster they were swirled the more they'd burn. Eventually when the fuel ran out, or when the makeshift wire handle snapped - as occasionally happened - the can was then simply hurled down the street to be brushed up on the following morning by the Corpy cleaner, for 'easy come easy go' was our motto.

One Saturday afternoon, we trooped along to our den in Duke Street to discuss tactics and at the same time practice blowing things up with our explosives. On this occasion, however, we were expecting trouble from the North End gang so rather than suffer the humiliation of another defeat as we did on our last visit to Dukie, we came armed with sticks and stones. There was no way we were going to be caught out again, Nacker said, after their mob chased us down Clevie showering us with a barrage of stones.

They must have caught wind of our gang or heard us chanting as we headed up the Corporation Road, for when we turned into Dukie the scrapyard looked as it always did, quiet and empty.

After dropping into our secret hide-out and emptying our pockets, we counted the stock of fireworks that we'd collected between us. To our surprise the arsenal consisted of a dozen cannons, eight torpedoes, six rip raps, four rockets and ten ordinary bangers.

'We've enough explosives to blow half the town up,' Smithy gasped, shaking the fireworks next to his ear as if they were sticks of dynamite before climbing back into the fresh air. Nacker, who led the way, wedged two large cannons into a small tin can, set light to the blue fuse, and we didn't need telling twice as we scattered behind an old battered meat van without doors. An almighty explosion shattered the silence and the can shot higher than the telegraph pole on the corner of the yard. We waited for a moment to make sure our bomb hadn't alerted any snoopers, but all was quiet, so we emerged, delighted that such a small device could create so much noise.

Out of curiosity Ossie split open a number of fireworks and began pouring the precious gun powder into the army barracks that we planned to blow up, which in our imagination was the enemy headquarters. After attaching a small piece of tatty string dipped in oil like they did on the pictures we lit it. Once again we darted behind the old van to watch the explosion devastate the small wooden fruit boxes into a thousand pieces. We celebrated our victory by jumping up and down and screaming like banshees.

Next morning Nacker smuggled a 'cannon' into school, waited for Spud to go into the bogs, lit the fuse paper and slipped it under the door for a laugh. The door burst open and poor Spud came hurtling out with his trousers round his ankles. Everyone in the playground cheered at the sight of his pink mickey, except for Pop Lally who as usual could be seen wandering around the playground looking for trouble. Of course he was livid and tried his utmost to find out who the culprits were. For a change no one snitched, and being close by I quickly moved out of the way to avoid his angry looks. I wasn't sure if he'd suspected me or not, but there was no way I was going to chance it.

As bonfire night approached we met in the back jigger by the side of Jenkins workshop. Most of our planks were by now stacked safely on the roof out of sight of the enemy gangs. It was decided that everyone would go hunting for 'bonnie' material except the unlucky minder who was detailed to 'keep nix' in case we were attacked by rival mobs. The one unlucky enough to be chosen had a responsibility requiring nerves of steel, and a task which wasn't for those who were scared of the dark, nor was it a job for the likes of me who couldn't fight. I'd have been labelled a sissy if they'd known I was scared stiff at night time, or that whenever given this job I always brought our Jess, taking her away from the comforts of the fire and telling dad that she needed a walk to relieve herself. Jess didn't mind in the least providing no-one let a banger off near her.

Days before November the fifth the tempo increased and to help our scavenging operation, younger lads from the neighbourhood were allowed to join our gang. Apart from scouring the docks for wooden crates, we stripped floor joists in bombed houses, collected rubbish from backyards that needed shifting and brought anything back with us that was flammable.

During the war bonfires weren't allowed for security reasons, but as soon as peace was declared they were lit throughout the land, emphasising peace as opposed to evil flames of hatred experienced during the blitz. Surprisingly, effigies of Hitler or Mussolini were never burnt, just poor old Guy Fawkes.

On the big night Guy looked a pathetic figure, having been constructed from sacks filled with straw and wearing Dobbo's old man's ripped donkey jacket with Mr Griffiths' worn out trilby stuck on his head. He was then plonked in an old wooden table chair, tied with thick rope and placed in a prime position near the top of the pile, ready to be cremated, just for committing a crime against the state. Upon hearing his sad story we felt a great deal of sympathy for Guy Fawkes. He was a rebel and rebels were high on our list of heroes at that period of time.

Our bonfire, set in the middle of the street, was promptly lit at half six and even before the town hall clock chimed seven huge flames shot up engulfing the 'Guy' within minutes. Brimming with excitement we yelled as sparks from burning timbers leapt higher than the carpet cleaner's factory roof while all around us thunderous explosions disrupted the heavens across every area of town.

Meanwhile, against his better judgement, dad purchased five bobs worth of fireworks from Connolly's paper shop. He'd speculated his cash, buying two rockets, five cannons; two rip raps, a Catherine wheel and Roman candle, with a few sparklers for our Bernadette. When he arrived home he scrutinised each firework as if it was something special and afterwards compared their performances with those of our neighbours. He was just as bad as we were for excitement on bonfire night.

Placing a rocket in a milk bottle he ordered us to stand well back out of the way, but I could have told him before he lit the blue tip that he'd be disappointed. We'd fired two similar ones and they hardly cleared the roof of the black fella's pub in Clevie.

'Bloody 'ell another damp fizzler,' he moaned, watching the rocket barely lift above thirty feet into the air before crashing down onto Jenkin's roof.

'What are you laughin' at?' he angrily muttered, but I couldn't help it. I was just one of those kids who laughed at other people's misfortunes, but never my own, I must add.

Before lighting the Roman Candle he placed an old leather working glove on his hand for protection and as soon as the firework was lit he began swinging his arm in a circular fashion, a method proving an instant success, so we cheered as showers of colourful sparks illuminated the pavement outside our house. At least one of his purchases wasn't a waste of money. After enjoying his thirty seconds of fame he generously passed it across to me to hold for the last ten seconds.

Meanwhile as the bonfire raged and flames shot above roof tops, the intense heat began causing concern to a number of the older people who worried about their windows cracking, but with the fire at its peak nothing could be done, so it burnt on.

During the course of the evening gangs from other parts of Brookie arrived, joining the revelry and atmosphere we ourselves were enjoying. Bangers exploded and ships' rockets furrowed across the sky, dropping distinctive showers of red stars, while smoke from the many neighbouring bonfires drifted down Brookie like a mist of heated smog.

Dad, as usual, wanted to see how the rest of the town folk were celebrating, so it came as no surprise when he asked if we fancied traipsing as far as Woodside, some ten minutes walk away. As soon as we turned the corner by Hamilton Square Station, Bridie challenged me to race her to the floating bridge, so we both sprinted downhill while dad trotted behind. Within a matter of minutes we were standing on the edge of the river leaning against the barriers. From our vantage point we witnessed the ferryboats leaving the landing stage and ploughing through the Mersey's crimson water, while the sky over Liverpool displayed a mass of colourful stars with exploding rockets of every variety.

We stood for ages gawping, without getting bored, our patience even surprising dad, until eventually the cold wind seemed to penetrate the thin clothes that we were wearing, and then it was decided that we make tracks for home.

Back in Brookie the bonnie still burnt, but not very high or as fierce. We noted that some of the older neighbours had brought chairs out onto the pavement to enjoy the last of the November heat, while others stood round poking away at the fire trying to liven smouldering rubbish that wasn't as flammable as the bone dry timbers that had blazed earlier on.

After ten o'clock when the pubs emptied the fire had almost diminished, but it didn't deter celebrations continuing, with those of musical ambitions performing their talents for all to hear. Dad finally set off the Catherine wheel on the back entry door, a pretty impressive spectacle for us, although he got no pleasure or plaudits from anyone else, which disappointed him in a way, but there was little he could do about it. We knew that there was nowhere else to set this particular firework off because it burnt the paint in a huge circle and the rent man wouldn't have been too pleased if he'd have used the front door.

As usual dad ended the evening with his annual sermon, a speech we'd come to expect. 'What a bloody waste of money. Five bob gone up in smoke, just like that. That 'ill be the last time I buy any more of that rubbish.'

We smiled. 'Til next year,' I muttered under my breath.

The following morning a large black smouldering ring covered the spot where our massive bonfire had been and, simultaneously, from households up and down the street, Brookie's dogs, all of the Heinz variety, gingerly emerged after their night of terror.

A couple of hours later a Corpy man arrived with a small wheel bin and began the task of clearing up the mess. There was little chance he'd be interrupted. Private cars rarely came down our street. The only transport likely to enter was bin lorries, funeral cars or occasionally, a Black Maria.

Christmas

December was great for us, but a worrying time for parents. With money scarce many families struggled to make ends meet. Some folk joined Christmas clubs by saving a couple of bob a week in local corner shops to add a little extra cash for the festive season, and for others celebrations were kept to a minimum because of the poverty. Naturally any additional source of income was welcomed with open arms.

From a very early age the most important number entrenched in kid's minds was their mother's Co-op divi number. From as long as I could remember I could rattle off 80252 easily. Before making my Saturday trip to the Co-op, mam always issued the same instructions. 'Don't lose the list an' don't stop an' talk to anyone. And keep your eye on that ten bob note an' don't screw it up either, do you hear?'

'Yis mam.'

'What's me divi number again?'

'80252 mam.'

'Now don't forget to collect the little blue slip an' watch me change.' The divi always came in handy and was a blessing in disguise, especially at Christmas time, so it was vital that receipts were kept to avoid any disputes. For the cheque man, the festive season was not only the season of goodwill, but also the time of the year when caution was thrown to the wind, a period when families relied on a little credit to celebrate the occasion. Dad wouldn't hear of mam going into debt, he'd rather have done without, but although he had an inkling of the goings on behind his back, he was inclined to turn a blind eye, and so mam, rather than cause friction, tried keeping her dealings with the cheque man 'on the quiet' from him. Like many families she tended to deal with Sturla's, one of the more popular local stores and this was a shop I loved going to whenever mam purchased clothes. I was fascinated by a pulley system carrying customer's cheques. The cheques were placed in little containers and shot along wires, at amazing speed to the cashier.

'Here's ours mam,' I yelled, following our canister as it dived up and down, taking various routes from one counter to the cashier and back again. It was a fascination I never tired of.

As Christmas approached dad relied on the market for bargains. He was particularly impressed by the antics of a dark skinned, charismatic character named Eli. Apart from his showman routine, he was famous for his bargains and held the distinction of being the most popular trader, with a store on the outside of the main market.

The market remained the main hub of the town and every Saturday morning vans and lorries emerged carrying pots, pans and crockery from the Potteries; fresh vegetables and flowers from Shropshire; meat, poultry and eggs from Wales; and from different areas of Cheshire and Lancashire, shoes, clothes, carpets, lino and every commodity imaginable.

Eli was in a class of his own, for not only did he sell all types of unusual toys and even dolls that could talk, he also stocked a variety of games, household goods, exotic gadgets from overseas, all bargains in their own right. As a result, you had to be up bright and early to get anywhere near his stall. Quite a number of folk watched his performance out of curiosity, others because they were skint, but dad had other reasons, he was shrewd and weighed up every transaction. No-one gave anything away for nothing, not in his book anyway, so within a short time he had all the stooges decked and those who accepted free gifts to get the crowd interested. Despite all the shenanigans he still ended up buying bargains himself, but only when the time was right to make an offer.

The school holidays, whether Easter, Summer or Christmas, were always exciting periods and of course the last day was celebrated with howls of delight as we galloped out of the school gates, smacking the sides of our pants just as we did after watching a cowie picture at the matinee on Saturday morning.

We weren't the only ones delighted to be free; the teachers seemed as relieved as we were to be given a welcome opportunity to recharge their batteries in readiness for the next slog at the beginning of the coming term.

Our Bridie couldn't wait to tell me that Father Christmas didn't exist, but I didn't say I already knew and that Tucker had already told me when he called round on Christmas morning. He'd only found out himself that day, after his dad fell over the cat and dropped the presents he was carrying, sending them clattering down the stairs. The noise not only disturbed the rest of the family but incensed his mother who began screaming at the top of her voice accusing Mr Griffiths of taking his spite out on the cat. And all because his dad had been on the ale since lunchtime. The moggy, a Persian type with a big head and the only feline pedigree in the street disappeared from sight, her departure spoiling the Christmas festivities for the whole family. Poor Mrs Griffiths was so upset about Pixie going missing that she couldn't concentrate to cook the Christmas dinner, so it turned out a miserable day all round for the family.

Just after mid-day Tucker brought his jigsaw puzzle round to our house to play with and as soon as mam found out he was starving she squeezed an extra dinner and he gobbled it like he'd never seen food before. After eating our Christmas dinner we spent a few hours searching for the cat. I even took our Jess to track her down and Jess hated the sight of That Pixie Griffiths. She'd never forgiven Pixie for scratching a cob out of her nose when the moggy happened to wander into our yard by mistake, so Jess was as keen as we were to locate the missing cat. She had a score to settle.

'PIXIE e.e.e ... PIXIE.e.e.e,' Mrs Bailey yelled, after kindly offering her services to a distraught Mrs Griffiths, which on reflection may have been a bad move.

If Frankie, her own son, never immediately responded to her war cry, it was doubtful if a cat and a genuine pedigree would be enthusiastic and come strolling home. Unfortunately there was no happy ending for the Griffiths family, Pixie had vanished into thin air.

Later in the evening, when I happened to mention to dad that I didn't believe in Father Christmas, he hit the roof and blamed our Bridie for telling me.

'You've ruined all the excitement for him now,' he bawled, but our presents were usually predictable and I wasn't too bothered myself. I didn't mention about Tucker telling me first, because he'd never shouted at Bridie before and I wanted her to experience what it felt like to be bawled at for a change.

Before mam turned off the bedroom lights on Christmas Eve we'd hung one of her stockings at each of the corners of the bed. Next morning, within minutes of wakening, the room was in a state of chaos as we grabbed our own individual stocking and emptied the contents onto the bed. Predictably, these consisted of tangerines, apples, sweets (that's if there were enough ration coupons), a couple of small toys, thin story books and a variety of nuts requiring a hammer or flat iron to break the shells (Dad didn't believe in making life too easy for us.). If dad had enough money we received a boxed present wrapped in brown paper placed on the floor at the bottom end of the bed. This could be a jigsaw puzzle or a football album for me and a sewing set for Bridie, but the excitement of getting something different seemed to thrill us most. Our Bernadette, who was easily pleased, usually ended up with a cloth doll and a few packets of Dolly Mixtures, whereas baby Tom, well he didn't understand what all the fuss was about and so mam bought him new clothes.

Apart from the annual feast of turkey and Christmas pudding (with a couple of sixpences thrown in by dad), mam bought more food than she would normally purchase during any other period of the year. This once a year extravagance could also have its pitfalls. Sometimes if I left food on my plate this really infuriated dad. Leaving food was something that got right under his skin and I always seemed to be on the receiving end of his reactions.

'Eat it all up m'lad. Your eyes are bigger than your belly,' he moaned, even though I could hardly move.

'But dad, I'm full up already an' can't eat anymore,' I pleaded.

'Eat it ... come on gerr on with it. You were bloody starvin' a minute ago, so gerrit down yer,' he commanded. Reluctantly, in an attempt to avoid a crisis, I'd try and find more space to accommodate the remaining food, or if he wasn't looking drop it slyly onto the lino for Jess. She was always a loyal friend and good minesweeper and as far as I could remember never once let me down.

'There's people starvin' in the world an' the other fella's wastin' food,' dad continued, but as mam wasn't into politics, a few 'tuts' usually assured him she agreed with his point of view.

'But it's only Christmas pudding' dad,' I whinged.

I couldn't have said a worse thing; my reply gave him the cue he was looking for and a chance to practice a series of proverbs he'd memorised to a fine art.

'Only' he said. 'Now ONLY is a very important word in the English language, are you listening our Bridie?'

'Yes dad,' she muttered, glaring at me and for once I couldn't blame her.

'If only I'd ate me pudding I'd be now outside playing with me mates,' I thought.

Dad began. 'Only a fool an' his money are easily parted.' We both looked blank, for a change.

'Proverbs, kids, proverbs,' he went on and it became obvious we were cornered until nature called, or perhaps a miracle might occur and a priest payed a surprise visit, though at Christmas time that would be unlikely to happen.

'A bird in hand?'

'Is worth two in a bush,' we drawled, showing very little enthusiasm.

'There you are see how easy it is when your father teaches yer?'

'Never put off until tomorrow what you can do today. That's one for you Jimmy.'

'ME, dad .. .why me? ... it's not fair ... you're always pickin' on me,' I moaned.

'Shurrup an' listen an' learn,' he growled.

'Empty barrels ... make the most noise,' he almost sang, again looking in my direction and I thought to myself 'if I'm supposed to be thick how can I make that much noise.'

Mam, who appeared not to be listening, fidgeted uncomfortably in her chair. Then it dawned on me. That's how he knew when the Lecky man had been to empty the meter. He was crafty; this was his way of getting his little dig in and at the same time letting us know that you couldn't kid him.

As New Year approached dad promised we could stay up late to enjoy the atmosphere of the celebrations taking place in our street. However, on previous years, unknown to him we'd sneaked into the front bedroom as the bells tolled midnight, pulled the curtains across and watched most of our neighbours singing and dancing in the street. This time there was no need for us to sneak across the lino to the front bedroom window. With having dad's permission we both looked forward to the novelty of seeing how the grown ups celebrated the begining of a brand new year. 'Let's hope next year's a better one than this one's been, eh Maggie,' dad lamented as he sat by the fire after reading the last edition of the Echo.

'Who was it that let last New Year in?' He continued.

'You did Charlie?' mam said. 'If my memory serves me right, you went out the back door, picked up a piece of coal from the air raid shelter and came round to the front.'

'I didn't you know. That was the year before last,' dad replied, as if pondering to himself.

'I know, who it was' he finally answered. 'It was Pete Connolly, remember? He knocked on the door right on the stroke of midnight and invited me to their house for a drink.'

'You're right Charlie,' mam agreed. 'No wonder we've had no luck this year.

Fancy us allowin' someone with a mop of blonde hair to let the New Year in,' she tutted.

During the course of the evening, just after listening to Dick Barton on the wireless, dad taught us how to play chess, a game he frequently played during dark winter months. Mam brought out the best tablecloth and began setting the table. Besides making a variety of butties she had also baked a large bun loaf and to our surprise dad produced two bottles of booze, one of sherry and the other port, 'just in case visitors called to the house,'he said.

Before slipping outside at five minutes to twelve dad placed a couple of logs on the fire, gave mam instructions not to open the front door until Big Ben tolled the New Year in, closed the door behind him and vanished into the darkness of the street.

At the stroke of midnight, as Big Ben chimed simultaneously with the town hall clock, sirens and hooters erupted from every ship berthed in the docks and even those anchored on the Mersey, could be heard in the distance keeping up the momentum.

The knocker suddenly thudded three times, dad's familiar signal, but mam wasn't prepared for the shock she received when opening the front door, for standing next to dad was a coolie wallah. Judging by the expression on his face it was little wonder that he found the whole situation strange and amusing.

'It's okay Johnny, in you go first,' said dad, easing him through the front door.

Mam shook hands and wished the seaman a happy New Year and we did the same.

Dad poured a glass of sherry and mam offered the stranger a piece of bun loaf. After finishing the family offering the seaman bowed and said something in his native tongue.

'Salaam a lago, salaam al ickam,' I confidently muttered. Mam and our Bridie looked at me in horror, but dad smiled.

'Salaam al ickam,'the seaman replied, bowing once more. Dad shook hands wih the stranger and then he was gone. 'Well done Jim,' said dad. He was pleased as Punch that I remembered his lessons about Lascar seamen who toiled on the Blue Funnel line.

Dad held a high degree of respect for 'coolie wallahs,' as they were called, often describing them as being extremely poor hard working individuals who were occasionally exploited by large unscrupulous shipowners. He also threatened to cut my hands off if he ever caught me begging.

This was something a number of kids were inclined to do when coolies were seen walking towards the docks with bundles of clothes on their heads. 'One pen John,' we'd chant, trotting alongside with our hands held out, but as soon as dockers intervened we scattered.

'Well Maggie you can't complain next year about not 'aving a dark stranger bringin' yer good luck, can yer?' said dad smiling at his ingenuity.

Mam grinned and chuckled. 'It's a good job our Fanny didn't come through the back kitchen door ... she'd have had a duck egg.'

'By the way Charlie have you made your New Year's revolution yet?' she continued.

Dad smiled and shook his head.

Although the pubs were no longer open, the atmosphere remained electric as groups of people danced and crooned outside open doors, but no one could argue that there wasn't a more livelier house in the neighbourhood at Hogmanay than Jock Smith's. He yelled to everyone in sight to pop in for a wee dram and although worse for wear, he nevertheless was in a buoyant mood. Tucker and Billy beckoned me so I joined them and stood beneath the lamplight watching dad greet our neighbours with a handshake. Almost everyone was drunk including Paddy Murphy and Mr Feeley, who appeared to be holding each other up and were singing 'It's a long way to Tipperary.' Dad, who didn't require ale to sing, moved between them, making it a trio.

Dad always fancied himself as a singer, informing us on numerous occasions how good he'd been when he was a member of Our Lady's choir. His self-praise fell on deaf ears though; we were tone deaf and didn't appreciate his enthusiasm for music. On the other hand Tucker's mam, Mrs Griffiths, who hailed from South Wales, had a great singing voice and played the piano equally as well. Opening wide her front door she serenaded the neighbours with her touching version of 'Land of Our Fathers,' but not many joined in for at the same time Jock began singing 'I belong tae Glasgie,' in his deep gravel tone. As everyone appeared to favour the Glasgow national anthem, Mrs Griffiths' settled for second best. She wasn't bothered though, Pixie had returned home unscathed. After spending four days on holiday in the dock area chasing rats she opted for the comparative comforts of Mrs Griffiths front room and of course, the easier and more docile opposition of Brookie's canine assortment. Pixie had also arrived during the middle of the night, thus avoiding Mrs Bailey's ear-shattering shrieks; her shrewdness emphasising the difference between a mongrel and a pedigree.

Amidst the revelry, rockets lit the sky and the odd firework spluttered and exploded as celebrations continued. A lone voice sang in the distance 'Land of Hope and Glory,' but faded after just a couple of lines. Dad had a wee 'un' with Mr Smith, for Auld Lang Syne, while we sat on the step stroking our Jess, who, for the sake of a little fuss, braved the flashes and bangs.

It was a wonderful experience for us, watching our neighbours enjoy themselves for one night of the year and putting aside hardships, past and present.

Chapter 3

1948

After Christmas was finally over and we were fed up with the festivities, Tucker and Smithy joined the Boys Brigade. The B.B. held their meetings and practice sessions in St Peters Hall just around the corner in Cathcart Street, and although we tended to poke fun whenever they marched as far as the church on Sunday mornings, I suppose we were envious in a way because they always looked smart in their uniforms.

We were pleased, however, when Tucker declared he was learning to play a bugle and Smithy the drums, news that considerably fuelled our curiosity. It seemed strange to us the way our gang began to develop a cultural aspect of activities, a total contrast to natural instincts that favoured mischievous pastimes.

Spud owned a very small mouth organ which at one time or other had belonged to his Uncle Muffer. Spud inherited the harmonica after his uncle unfortunately lost his teeth while attempting a solo display when departing from the Queens Hotel, apparently, as rumour would have it, worse for drink. Tripping over the pavement near the park entrance he almost swallowed the mouth organ and was extremely fortunate that Johnny Feeley happened to be passing at the time, otherwise it would have lodged across his throat and could seriously have affected his drinking hobby. With the Borough Hospital being close by he was admitted to Casualty and after a small operation came round minus his teeth.

Uncle Muffer, a strong-willed type of person, resumed playing the mouth organ as if nothing had changed, but became increasingly disheartened after his drinking pals complained about getting splashed by sprays of Guinness. Reluctantly, and in order to retain his popularity with his friends, he passed the harmonica on to his nephew Spud who treasured it as if it were a crown jewel.

We all had took turns at playing the mouth organ, but with the exception of Nacker (who had a natural gift for anything musical), we couldn't raise a note. Of course it was an accepted fact that he was the only one in our gang who could play the clappers (thin pieces of slate), a poor man's version of 'the bones,' with both hands and that took some doing.

Apart from Sunday morning's top wireless show 'Family Favourites,' music - or musical instruments for that matter - didn't play a great part in our development at home.

The nearest we came to melodic aspirations was wrapping a piece of tracing paper around a comb and blowing it with our lips, but when it tickled our enthusiasm soon waned. Obviously, as a family we weren't musically orientated, but this didn't stop dad seizing the opportunity of slipping across one of the quips he'd heard at work.

'They're all musicians in our family,' he'd say, waiting for a response and when no reply was forthcoming, he'd carry on and answer 'except the sewin' machine an' that's a singer.'

Dad always laughed at his own jokes; we didn't, they weren't funny in any way, unless of course I was after a threepenny Joey for sweets or something like that and then I'd pretend he was indeed funny.

Sometimes he spoke of the nicknames given to certain dockers and many made us laugh. Being a cowie at the time I was fascinated when he casually mentioned working with the Gun Slinger who'd shoot off at eleven, but other names such as The Lazy Solicitor who was always asleep on the case and the Broken Boomerang who never came back, amused our Bridie who had a different sense of humour than me.

Very little seemed to change upon our return to school. Those who sat with their mouths open continued catching bubbles, day-dreamers remained in the clouds, the head scratches scratched on hoping answers to difficult questions would surface through their fingers, the head workers sat at the back, with the clever ones in the front, and the remaining thumb suckers, thick-heads and mischief-makers made up the numbers.

As usual at this time of the year the classrooms were freezing and apart from pupils suffering with the usual complaints of head colds and runny noses, there were some really poor lads who didn't possess shoes. Naturally Pop Lally was informed and although we saw the headmaster as a strict type of person, he also had a soft spot. On occasions such as these he used his influence by contacting the Saint Vincent de Paul Society, a charity offering assistance to poor families, requesting their help. Due to his intervention the lads were given a pair of black heavy boots; but boots, or even shoes for that matter, didn't suit these particular lads, we were used to seeing them in their bare feet and to us they didn't look comfortable with their feet covered up.

Miss Burgess appeared to have forgotten my previous indiscretions, an oversight coming as a surprise to everyone including me, but when she called me out to clean the blackboard I got some filthy looks from those pupils who believed that behaving badly was something that didn't pay. Ossie was made up though. He seemed pleased that I'd changed my ways, although he knew that I was still influenced by Nacker, who continued sagging school despite Mr Robinson caning him persistently for under-performing and constant absenteeism. Mrs Ryan didn't bother too much about her son's record, for as far as she was concerned there were far more critical things in life than school.

During the cold spell Nacker kept the fuel bill down by helping himself to a few buckets of coal from the dock sidings long before the workers arrived and afterwards lit the fire before the rest of his brothers came down from the cold bedrooms.

He'd also think nothing of nicking a loaf or two from the bakery, but like everything else, that could be attributed to circumstances at the time.

Meanwhile, Mrs Murphy, by using her religious influence, convinced the priest that she had a prospective disciple in her family and her perseverance finally paid off when Spud was invited to join the Duffy brothers, serving as an altar boy. He looked angelic enough on the altar, but the vestment was far too tight on him. With having a fat stomach it lifted up in the front, but we were used to seeing his pot-belly, having seen him in the raw many times when we swam in the docks or at Livvie baths. He didn't seem to mind us skitting at him and surprisingly took no notice even when Ossie said he liked his frock.

Nacker was wary of Spud though, but he had nothing to worry about; Spud still swore and never refused any apples that we knocked off, so he was still one of us.

The only difference as far as we were concerned was the fact that he'd had 'the call', whatever that meant, but we didn't want it anyway. Someone had to have it otherwise there'd be no priests and that could cause all kinds of problems for us. For a start there'd be no St. Laurence's and we'd all have to go to either Cathie or Trinity Street School and then what would we do? None of us would have a clue to where we were, or what we'd do next, because we'd be mixed up with the Proddies. So in a way we were glad he'd had the call and not us.

'Boys, be quiet and have your dinner money ready,' Miss Burgess ordered before opening the dinner register. Those who could afford to pay queued up and received blue coloured tickets and the rest, whose fathers were dead, in prison, on strike or out of work were given a free red ticket. At twelve o'clock, dead on time, we were escorted to the canteen, an asbestos type pre-fabricated building in Price Street, just a five-minute walk away from school. Some of the food was quite palatable, but others, such as sago pudding (frogspawn), lumpy custard, or semolina we found hard to swallow and left it for the pig swill bin; and the pigs were welcome to it. With free milk and school dinners most of us had something substantial in our stomachs, yet as soon as half four came around we would all be ready for a jam or dripping butty.

The docks were busy during January so the New Year started promising for dad. For a change he managed to work four nights overtime a week, so being an opportunist I took advantage of the situation and decided to strike while the iron was hot.

'Can I 'ave a pair of football boots for me birthday, please dad?' I asked, giving him sufficient notice in order that he bought me something I needed and not what he supposed was good for me, but typical of dad when caught without his guard, he swiftly replied. 'You'll get what you're given an' be thankful for small mercies m'lad.'

I sincerely hoped and prayed that size four would qualify for dad's small mercies.

Until my birthday I continued wearing an old pair of Ossie's boots handed down from Johnny, which had leather bars instead of studs and were two sizes too big for me. There was no point complaining, they were better than nothing anyway. One thing about dad though, he'd never forget a birthday card. If nothing else there'd always be one from him and mam on the table whenever any of our birthdays occurred, a custom we reciprocated on his. For some reason the verse always seemed important to him; he'd never consider buying a card unless the message meant something.

Luckily for me he succumbed to my request and for my birthday I received a pair of size six football boots, predictably two sizes too big. I was expected to grow into them and grow into them I did.

'Take care of those boots an' make sure they last yer,' dad instructed.

I dubboned them as if they belonged to Tommy Lawton.

Although the year started brightly enough for dad, dark clouds began forming and before the beginning of March he was again out on strike.

Time to batten down the hatches,' he philosophically announced, comments we expected with no money coming into the house. During the week he'd be away on picket duty, often arriving home in a bad temper and cursing someone or other who'd scabbed the dispute. At weekends he was a different person altogether, resuming his mania for walking and aggravating the life out of my feet and then telling me off for not taking care of my shoes. I tried many ruses to avoid capture, including playing football after mass and arriving home late, but he was always waiting. I couldn't win. Once on the road there was no turning back or surrender, I had to like it and lump it.

It was amazing what local knowledge he'd absorbed on both sides of the river, even as far as Chester, a city he knew like the back of his hand. I relished the day he'd lose his desire to visit new districts, but deep down in my heart I knew I was clutching at straws.

Dad's first dabble

'If a job's worth doin' it's worth doin' properly,' dad announced, having successfully repaired a pair of soles on his best shoes. He'd somehow mastered the intricacies of using the last, after purchasing a pair of self-adhesive soles from Higgins' cobbler shop.

'Worra bout that?' he proudly declared, holding them up for all to see, and apart from protruding slightly over the original soles they did indeed looked passable ... in the short term.

Dad was pleased as Punch with his effort, but my heart missed a beat when he demanded to see what could be done about my black pair. The heels were well down, but this I could credibly explain with all the walking I'd done recently. However, there was no way I could account for the fronts, which resembled a book of pages and caused by toe-ending a football. I tried disguising the damage by plastering shoe polish across the fronts, but at close range this wouldn't fool anyone, let alone dad.

'What the bloody' 'ell 'ave yer been doin' with them m'lad?' he growled, his mood changing unbelievably within seconds, and that's when I put on my 'scared stiff' look. This occasionally had a favourable effect on dad; he had a soft spot though he didn't like showing it too often in case it was seen as a sign of weakness.

'They'll 'ave ter do yer 'til Easter, that's all,' he sighed, picking up his pair of best shoes and giving them the once over again.

With Easter only weeks away and dad still pottering around, mam used a little psychology to convince him the front room and stairwell could do with freshening up with a coat of paint and wallpaper. The house hadn't been decorated since we'd moved in and a spring clean was well overdue. Now seemed an ideal time with him being out of work and riding the crest of a wave following his cobbling success, so mam craftily grasped the opportunity with both hands.

Dad chose the pattern wallpaper, a colourful, distinct floral type from a stall on the inside of the market. Arriving home with eight rolls and a bucket for emulsion he rattled furiously on the front door knocker. We knew why he'd come the front way. It wasn't a case of showing off, well not in his eyes anyway.

It was all to do with pride and letting people know that although he was on strike he had enough money to decorate the house. That's why he didn't use the back door as he normally would.

We waited till he'd eaten his dinner and out of curiosity listened as he discussed with mam plans for attacking the decorating assignment. He sounded even more convincing when declaring his intention of causing minimum disturbance and mess and it was difficult not to be impressed. It was still hard to imagine dad having the patience to tackle wallpapering though, and besides, most decorators we'd seen wore white 'ovies' while his were always black and greasy.

Stripping the walls became his first priority, a simple task according to dad. We were allowed to help tackle it, but were totally unaware that the wall had been continually papered over. This novel idea of the previous occupants to insulate the walls in this manner resulted in the diameter of the room being reduced by a good half inch less than when it was first built. It was now like cardboard and far too tough for our small hands to have much affect, so dad intervened, attacking it as if tearing the hide off an elephant.

'Bloody laziness, that's all this is. Why people can't do a job properly in the first place beats me,' he muttered. 'Patience, that's all it takes, just bloody patience. If a job's worth doin' it's worth doin' properly,' he reiterated. I glanced at mam, who like me had permanent twinkles in her eyes and she smiled, as if knowing what was going through my mind.

After devastating the walls, pulling half the plaster off and sweating like a pig, he clutched mounds of the now decimated pre-war wallpaper and dumped it in the backyard. Mam, the kids and our Jess, breathed a sigh of relief.

Unfortunately with it being such a small house there was nowhere for them or the dog to seek refuge while dad was on the rampage. It was okay for me though, I shot round to Ossie's out of the way, although I heard dad remark 'where's that bloody fella goin' now,' as I opened the door ready to move off.

Dad was stripped to his vest when I came back. He didn't say much, he didn't have to. I had a good idea he was sorry he'd started the job in the first place, for not a lick of paint or strip of wallpaper had been applied yet. I'd have liked to have helped him, but he'd already spurned an offer to burn the old wallpaper in the backyard so there wasn't much I could do except keep out of his way. His next plan of action was to work through the night and paint the ceiling. I felt really sorry for our Jess; she'd be the only one to witness his performance which had all the ingredients of being a turbulent night. I didn't envy her prospects. It's a good job that dogs can't talk, I distinctly remember thinking as I climbed up the stairs to bed.

It wasn't dad's fault. He'd never decorated before this and wasn't properly organised. He had only a small emulsion brush, not designed for pasting wallpaper and was also without a stepladder. This meant improvising using a chair or table to stand on.

All was quiet during the first half-hour, except for clattering noises as chair legs came into contact with the dresser. Classical music drifting from the wireless could be heard in the background so everything appeared to be going to plan. The full moon was shining through our bedroom window and for amusement I made silhouettes with my hand and fingers on the dividing wall, just as we did in the flicks until we were caught and thrown out. Suddenly the silence was shattered by an almighty crash, followed by an even louder yelp with dad bawling.

'GERR' OUT OF ME BLOODY WAY.' It didn't take a great deal of imagination to realise that Jess had foolishly parked herself behind dad's makeshift step-ladder and the inevitable happened. She wouldn't do it on purpose, I knew that. She wasn't that kind of dog. More than likely it was her way of showing affection seeing that dad was all on his own down there while we were tucked up nice and warm in bed, though unfortunately not really appreciated when he was in that kind of mood.

'LOOK AT THE BLOODY MESS YOU'VE CAUSED ... YOU BLOODY SWINE,' he yelled and although Jess wouldn't be aware of the actual words, I think she got the gist of the message. In blind panic she ran upstairs, knowing full well it was definitely out of bounds to her.

I clambered out of bed and sneaked down the top three stairs. Over the top of the back kitchen door I watched dad wiping up the emulsion with his brush and I even managed to give Jess a quick stroke before being spotted. Within seconds I was back into bed, snuggled into dad's R.A.F overcoat, the latest fashion in eiderdowns on the docks.

I may have heard dad going to bed, I wasn't sure. I was dreaming about our Jess who was talking and answering dad back. It was dead funny honest to God. Dad was arguing with the dog and mam was saying 'I told yer Charlie she'd turn on you one of these days.'

I really enjoyed it. Jess getting the last word in, which infuriated dad. Then I woke up.

'Good God,' mam exclaimed, when she went downstairs next morning, but dad was still snoring after his arduous night, which was just as well. Mam was in a fearful mood. Now curiosity is a terrible thing when you're dead tired, but I allowed it to get the better of me so I followed her down to witness the results of dad's labour of love and to make sure Jess hadn't suffered a nervous breakdown. I needn't have worried about the dog; she was an expert in self-survival and somehow had managed to whimper her way out of the house, probably before dad had completed a second coat on the ceiling.

In the front room spots of white paint transformed most of the furniture and even the black grate hadn't escaped the spray. Apart from smudges of emulsion on a cushion where he'd relaxed, his easy chair seemed to have evaded the main shower. Mam picked the cushion up and threw it down in disgust. I thought her action a little unkind; after all he'd been on his own all night so he was entitled to a rest at some period. She also seemed to have forgotten he was accustomed to working the welt on the docks and being a man of principle he'd never forfeit a hard-won concession, no matter what the occasion.

Dad appeared at half eight full of the joys of spring until he noticed mam's long face. He abruptly stopped singing as her tempestuous attitude knocked him right out of his usual routine, dampening his spirits dramatically. He loved singing on a Saturday morning. It was a habit he'd developed over the years and although his voice left a lot to be desired he was happy as Larry, with mam often proclaiming 'he's better in a good mood than a bad,' but now she'd put him in a rare old bad one.

'Now what's the matter with yer?' He muttered, glancing at the ceiling that had dried streaky white, but was nevertheless a huge improvement on its previous yellow colour. She'd wiped most of the mess off the furniture, so in fairness to him he was more than satisfied that he'd done a good job and as far as he was concerned she was moaning for the sake of moaning. To add fuel to an already raging fire he was now in the process of psyching himself up for the second phase of his decorating programme, so mam's intervention couldn't have happened at a more critical time. There was no doubt that she'd dampened his enthusiasm of implementing his next task after a weekly visit to Livvie public baths; it looked ominous that we were in for another dose of silent nights.

In the frosty atmosphere we ate in silence, enduring cold lumpy porridge for breakfast followed by aptly burnt toast with tiny speckles of white emulsion, just about visible to the naked eye.

I began my Saturday chores by lighting the fire followed by a journey to the Co-op. Dad walked alongside me on his way to the baths, moaning about ma's attitude. I just listened and kept my mouth shut. It didn't do to take sides.

When I returned with the groceries, the rolls of wallpaper were laid out on the table, with a bucket full of paste, made up from cold water and flour on the floor near by. Mam, who was getting ready to take our Bernadette and Tommy out shopping, placed the kettle and teapot ready to brew on the stove, this was her way of implementing a peace offering to dad, who hadn't at that time returned from his weekly soak. She knew this was a fifty-fifty chance really, for a lot depended on whether he'd managed to avoid the huge queues that gathered for the small number of slipper baths available. Dad was always short of patience and didn't like queuing at all.

After 'munging' into a jam buttie I left the battle scene and made my way to Spud's house. Our Bridie, also anticipating the atmosphere was likely to become volatile gathered up her homework and headed for Aunt Fan's.

Mr Murphy, who was doing some press ups in the backyard with Spud when I called, welcomed me in his usual jovial way.

'Come on in young Jimmy. You're just in time to do a few exercises with me an' our Timmy here, an' we'll see if I can make a foine pair of men outa the two of yeh, at all.'

He always said 'at all ... at all' after every sentence, but then so did loads of fella's including my dad. Mr Murphy, on the instructions of his wife, was trying to get the puppy fat off Spud, but you could tell from the way he kept glancing at his watch that he was doing it under sufferance until the pubs opened. Anyway Spud was quite happy the way he was and I couldn't imagine him giving up six barmcakes a day to lose weight just to please his mam.

After twelve o'clock we called for Tucker and Smithy. Ossie had already gone to the Balaclava pitch in the park with Tich to try and teach him to play football properly. Nacker was out with his classmates so we moseyed up to the park for a laugh. Tucker had been given a smashing present by his auntie for Christmas. It was a tin peashooter capable of firing up to thirty feet, and as to be expected, we'd come prepared with loads of 'ammo' in our pockets. Our first victim was an ould fella with a baldy head, parked on a bench opposite the lake reading a daily paper. We crawled up the hill behind Tucker, who was more experienced than any of us and watched as he caught the victim a beauty right on the 'napper' first time. He rubbed his head and looked up at an over-hanging tree with bare branches sprawled above the park bench.

Tucker fired again, this time pinging the newspaper. The ould fella immediately jumped up turned around, dashed towards us and we scattered. He had a boxer's wide nose and real mean features, one of those fella's you wouldn't say boo to even if he stamped on your toes on purpose.

Ossie was easy to locate, he was playing with Tich so we popped him a few times before he realised we'd arrived. We left after a short game of 'shots in' and headed for the swings. It was Tucker who spotted a few older girls messing around on the seesaw and couldn't resist peppering them, but once again fortune remained with us. They happened to be three hard cases from the North end of the town and we were more than lucky to escape with our lives. They couldn't half run and chased us out of the park by the Borough hospital. It's a good job they didn't catch us or we could've ended up in casualty department, a ward familiar to each of us at one time or another.

It was about five o'clock when I arrived home, the morning drama completely forgotten. The string was missing so I thoughtlessly hammered on the front door.

My memory was rapidly restored when dad's booming voice yelled for me to go round the back. Entering the yard Jess welcomed me like a long-lost friend and I knew at once that she wouldn't be out in the cold if all were well inside the house. We had a close affinity our Jess and me. I always took her sixth sense into account and this had saved my skin on numerous occasions in the past. I therefore decided to tread carefully before dashing into the house, instead of by my usual method of entry.

The table, together with the dresser, had been relegated to the back kitchen, drastically restricting the walking area, an essential detail when plotting imminent escape routes. My critical eye observed the half-full paste bucket, so I knew dad was still working. Mam, Bridie, Bernadette and Tom were huddled round the fire and dad was enjoying himself eradicating masses of bubbles with the help of a tea towel and looking every bit a professional. I thought he'd done extremely well myself. One wall almost complete, another papered half way across, quite an achievement since eleven o'clock. Not unexpectedly the pattern match was low priority. A few flowers had lost their stems and one or two were growing out of the heads of others, but there weren't any known horticulturists in Brookie so he'd get away with that slight error of judgement. Mam beckoned me into the kitchen for dinner and warned me in no uncertain terms not to aggravate dad while he was concecratin'.

'I'm goin' out to play with the lads after me tea mam,' I mentioned matter of factly.

'Whereabout are you goin' on such a cold night as this?' she asked.

'It's a secret I can't tell yer. I promised Ossie on me own life that I wouldn't tell anyone an' you woudn't want me to die yet, would yer mam?'

'No son I don't expect I would, but the way things are goin' on someone round here is likely to.'

I devoured my dinner like I'd never seen food in my life, taking advantage of the fact I was in the kitchen and out of sight. There was no way I could enjoy my meal eating like a steam train in front of dad; he'd go bananas.

'Hey slow down lad an' take your bloody time. You haven't got a train to catch,' he often chastised and rather than cause friction I always did as I was told.

Mam looked exasperated. 'I don't suppose you'd like to stay in and give your dad a hand?' she asked.

I couldn't say no even if I wanted to, she looked fed up so I offered my services to paste the wallpaper and to my amazement dad accepted.

'Don't forget to put plenty on around the edges,' he instructed and so brimming with enthusiasm and a fair amount of confidence I began a pasting exercise, allowing dad to complete the easier task of depositing the paper on the wall. He was managing quite well, three pieces positioned without any of them sliding to the floor. This surprised mam because prior to my assistance he'd cursed everybody from the manufacturer to the retailer, then the landlord and of course the walls themselves.

'There's nowt to this wallpaperin' lark is there son?' he called out to me.

'My God,' I thought to myself 'he's not contemplating taking this up for a living.' I conjured up a vision of us as 'C. Reilly and Sons, decorators and demolition experts' and tried imagining dad walking in front of a barrow wearing bib and brace white ovies and me behind, carrying the step-ladder.

'Stop your bloody day dreamin' an' pass us another one Jimmy,' he yelled, startling me for a second. I duly obliged, making sure there was an abundance of paste on the full-length piece and handed it to him as he was admiring the last piece he'd put up. I knew he was doing two jobs at once, something he'd always preached to me that I shouldn't do, still, who was I to interfere? And of course, he wasn't looking what he was supposed to be doing either, but how could I stop the paste from dripping onto the chair he was about to stand on.

'JESUS CHRIST,' he yelled. This was followed by a loud thud. Peeping surreptitiously around the kitchen door, I saw the length of wallpaper, like a crumbled rug, covering dad as he lay prostrate on the lino. Incredibly he then scrambled to his feet covered in paste from head to toe, even before we could count him out at ten. I looked across at mam and knew by her eyes that she was dying to titter. Unfortunately I hadn't learnt the art of self-restraint and burst out laughing; I couldn't contain myself. Dad, however, could never see the funny side of things; he just hadn't the sense of humour me and mam had.

He glared in my direction, screwed the paper into a huge ball, moved like lightning towards me and then slipped on the paste! Those vital seconds allowed me to escape through the back door and with our Jess by my side I galloped down the street, reaching Kelly's corner shop within seconds. Mam was right, I was born lucky. I looked up at the stars and tried counting them.

It was our Bridie who found us. We were sitting by the bus stop outside the Falcon Laundry. I was clocking the cars going towards the town hall with Jess guarding my feet in case a rat ran up my leg and attacked my goolies. Nacker had told us that a mate of his dad's was bitten in just that manner when sailing from Africa: He'd apparently had his balls removed so when we were down the docks or by our den we always kept tight hold of the bottoms of our trousers. That's why our Jess and me respected each other. I made sure she was always fed properly and she guarded me when I was on the lavvie, or anywhere else for that matter.

'Dad's gone to bed so it's alright to come home now,' Bridie told me. I was quite happy where I was, but decided to go home because I knew mam would be worrying herself sick. Beside, I was cold and hungry. Mam was pleased to see me. I had a huge smirk on my face. She laughed, but not too loudly in case dad wasn't properly asleep. Mind you he'd worked hard, the room was almost finished apart from a few patches and this would be hidden behind the dresser, which didn't matter if it was done properly or not.

Next morning when we returned from 8 o'clock mass dad had finished the papering in the front room. He was now in the process of introducing a coat of red gloss paint to the kitchen door. This, judging from its condition, had never experienced or benefited from any kind of paint from the day it had first been hung. We were all impressed by dad's apparent skill, for it had only taken two days. Not bad considering his temperament.

'When are you goin' ter do the kitchen dad?' I asked enthusiastically.

'When Paddy gets his eye back.'

'Worrabout the landin' Charlie?' said mam, taking a chance that he seemed in a good mood and hadn't snapped my head off.

'You kidded me last time Maggie. Once bitten twice shy,' he answered coolly.

'Right kids we'll go for a walk when yer ready,'dad said, ending the conversation. After visiting great Aunt Polly, Aunt Sarah, and dad's stepsister Aunt Nelly, we traipsed along familiar routes up Holt Hill and into Donkey Town. From this high position we enjoyed panoramic views of Lairds shipyard where the 'Rio Belon' and 'Rio Belgrano' were being built for Ellerman Shipping Lines.

'The finest shipbuilders in the world,' dad enthused, proudly narrating a running commentary on almost everything built in Lairds, from the 'Alabama' confederate naval ship to famous vessels such as 'The Prince of Wales' and 'The Mauritania.'

been run over by a train and was lying in the mortuary in Price Street. I was rooted to the spot, not daring to move in case Mrs Feeley collapsed and mam needed me to run for an ambulance. I coughed and they both turned round.

'Ah, there you are James, have you seen our Austin?' Mrs Feeley asked. I sensed the urgency in her voice. I knew then that Ossie's dad had popped off.

'I'll go an' get 'im straight away Mrs Feeley,' I replied, dashing off through the kitchen without even stopping to put my coat on.
Their house was only two minutes up the street ... it took me literally seconds to reach.

I went round the back way and found Ossie messing about with a bladder from Billy Smith's casey. 'Quick your mam wants yer straight away,' I yelled. I couldn't break the bad news to him then, even though I was dying to tell him. It wouldn't be fair would it? He recognised the sense of urgency in my voice, dropped the bladder, which had too many patches on it anyway and galloped like mad to our house. Breathlessly Ossie dashed into our front room with me trailing behind. 'Sit down Austin, I've something to tell you,' said Mrs Feeley. Diplomatically mam took the cups out to the kitchen and so I followed out of respect.

'WHEN!' I heard Ossie shout. I stopped immediately. I didn't half feel sorry for him. Fancy being told your old man was dead and in your mate's house as well.

'Come away from that door James an' stop listenin' to other people's business,' said mam. She was sort of buttering a piece of bread for me, which I thought was kind of tactless seeing that Ossie was hearing bad news in the front room.

'Mam, when's the funeral?' I gasped. I couldn't hold onto my emotions any longer.

'What are yer talkin' about James and who 'ave you got dead and buried this time?'

'Er ... I thought erm ... er ... I thought it was Mr Feeley,' I stammered.

'Don't talk so dammed stupid. Johnny's been called up for the R.A.F, that's all and poor Mrs Feeley is beside herself with worry. So keep your thoughts to yourself, do you 'ear?'

'Yis mam.'
I was dead chuffed that there'd be no funeral. It was always a miserable time when anyone died in our street. You weren't allowed to play out and all football matches were abandoned until after the hearse had gone.

Easter duties an' all that

Easter was late that year so mam said; though it didn't make the slightest difference to us. We still had our Easter duties to do and Lent was forty days whether it was early or late. Mam had given up taking sugar in her tea which was easy because it was still rationed and we were also encouraged to give something up, although it was difficult decision to make. Sacrificing sweets was an option, but sometimes forty days passed without getting any and what about refusing an uncle Joe's mint ball from Tucker's dad when he managed to buy them on Friday nights. Smithy would be made up eating our share. We decided to ignore that idea straight away. Giving up breakfast in the morning was a thought, the porridge wouldn't be missed, yet how could any of us manage without our toast? I clearly remembered sleeping in one morning and missing my breakfast and barmcakes from Blackburns. By the time ten o'clock arrived my belly thought my throat was cut. I couldn't go through that trauma again.

Nothing was ever simple for us. Why couldn't we give up throwing stones or playing kick-the-can, or even footy? On second thoughts we couldn't give footy up, the derby games hadn't been played yet. It was Spud who solved the problem. We'd give up going to the pictures on Saturday mornings he suggested. That way there'd be no detrimental risk to our health. Little wonder he was going into being a priest, neither Ossie nor I would have thought of that one. Tucker and Smithy said we were mad though. They couldn't understand all the rigmarole that we had to go through every year, but it was no use us trying to explain it to them. We didn't know ourselves and we were Catholics.

With mam being religious she loved holy picture cards and without fail I always bought her one from McGuiness's corner shop for Easter. She had loads in her prayer book, almost fifty-two the last time I counted. Sometimes when I was bored, or whenever temptation got the better of me, I'd remove them from her prayer book to see if I could make a deck of cards, with the intention of playing snap. Unfortunately for me there wasn't anyone in our house to play with and no way would I trust our Bridie, so as an alternative game I shuffled them up and tried getting three Saint Anthony's in one hand. He was mam's favourite saint. She had more pictures of him than anyone else and it was always Saint Anthony she prayed to when losing something or other, after developing a habit of placing certain items out of harms way then forgetting whereabouts she'd put them. That's when St Anthony came to her rescue. He hadn't let her down yet, so she said, but I lost my conkers once and he never answered my prayers, which made me think that he only helped his favourites.

I hated going to confession at Easter time. It was all very well if you were a regular customer like Spud, who now went every week since becoming an altar boy. For me it was different however. Through my own fault, I'd slipped down the road considerably and as a consequence had accumulated three months of sins, but worst of all, I'd lost my little notepad which I kept all my records in.

I knew near enough how many times I'd missed mass and how many loaves I'd pinched, but swearing, telling lies and not saying my prayers could have been hundreds.

Seeing as I was in a bit of a quandary I decided to seek Spud's advice, knowing he was the nearest I'd get to discussing absolution of my sins with apart from a priest. Ossie was mooching around so I told him to push off out of the way for a minute, because he was listening and skitting, which was lousy considering he was supposed to be my best mate. I expected more from him. He knew my position but appeared to be enjoying the predicament I'd got myself into.

'Worr if I can't remember how many times I've swore?' I asked Spud.

'Don't worry … it's not important.'

'Worr about lies an' missin' me prayers Spud?' Ossie tittered so I tried booting him, but missed. 'That's nowt Jim, they're only venial sins and the priest's not bothered too much about those.' I didn't mention how many times I'd missed mass. I didn't have to; they knew themselves about my absenteeism. I was grateful however, to Spud for his advice and immediately halved the number of venial sins I thought I'd committed. This eased my conscience considerably.

Funnily enough the church always seemed packed before Easter. Well it wasn't really funny when you weighed it up. It depended how long it had been since your last confession and the length of time that the priest kept you in the dark. This could be a daunting experience causing no end of embarrassment when you re-appeared. All eyes would be staring, and everyone nudging one another wondering what misdemeanours you'd committed and yet you could have been talking about football or the weather or anything for that matter for all they knew. Still it made no difference, you were condemned and all because you were in the sin bin for ages.

Easter was supposed to be the time of year for fellowship and friendship, a time for good friends to show their true colours, such as entering confession first and easing the pressure from those following. That's if you had good friends. I found it lonely myself, I was friendless.

Despite many crafty manoeuvres, including arriving early at church, I still couldn't kid Ossie like I'd done in the past. Unfortunately for me he still remembered the double-headed penny and refused point blank to go into confession first. I even promised to give him my tin whirly bird that flew higher than anyone else's did and still he wouldn't budge. Spud also declined. Consequently I was left with little choice but to be first to face Father Morrisey in the dreaded confessional box.

My mind was in turmoil as I knelt, waiting for the red light to flash over the centre door leading into the little room where Father Morrisey made himself comfortable while preparing for a bombardment of sins. I often wondered if he was allowed a drink or a jam butty or something else to eat when he was in there on his own. If it had been me listening to confessions I'd have been starving by the time they'd all finished.

I again went over the sins that I'd committed and gradually reduced them each time. Then I thought of the bread I'd pinched and also Ossie's experience when he had to make retribution for stealing a loaf. I remembered going with him to the Co-op bakery and sneaking along the passageway where the trolleys came through. He legged it to the doorway, threw a tanner towards the drivers and was back into Cathcart Street within seconds. I hid behind a pillar and watched the astonishment on their faces.

'What was all that about Teddy?' I heard one of them distinctly ask.

'Dunno,' said his mate.

'P'raps he's simple,' he added, rubbing the tanner on his lapel.

'Heads or tails?'

'Heads.'

'Tails, hard lines Tom,' and then they were gone.

I counted under my breath how many loaves I'd knocked off. Five times six, that's three bob I gasped. Then I began working out in detail how much I'd eaten, which surprisingly reduced the amount dramatically. Eight corners times five equals forty, then there were the crusts and the sides, which left the majority of the dough in the middle. This I'd compassionately fed to the ducks and the pigeons in the park.

They would definitely have starved without my intervention I reasoned with myself. I was quite pleased now that I was examining my conscience properly before entering the box.

The light eventually flashed and I stood up. For some reason my legs felt like jelly. As expected Ossie had a huge smirk on his face, so before closing the door I turned round put my thumb on my nose, waggled my fingers and pulled tongues. I felt much better then. Maybe it was with going into the dark from the light, I couldn't tell, but suddenly I tripped over my laces and hurtled head first towards the corner where a window shutter separated the priest from me.

'OUCH ... OUGH ... OUCH ... ME 'EAD,' I cried and the shutter swiftly opened. I looked up and stared into the ashen face of Father Morrisey.

He didn't recognise me for a moment, without his specs on. It didn't take him long to recover though and even when I held my hand across my face he must have guessed my name.

'James Reilly, what on earth do you think you're playing at?'
I didn't like saying that I wasn't playing at anything father. After all he was a priest and it could have been a sin frightening the life out of him like that. I wasn't sure what to do for the best, so I kept my mouth shut and whimpered for sympathy.

Pulling myself together I knelt down then grabbed hold of the shelf and peered into the mesh curtain, but the knock on my head must have shaken me, because I felt real dizzy.

'Bless me ... bless me ... bless me father,' I stuttered.

'It's okay James. Take your time, take your time.'

'For I 'ave ... I 'ave sinned. It is .. .it ... is ... it's ... three ... three ... three.

'Weeks?'

'Yis father,' I gratefully replied.

'Since me last confession.'

'I 'ave told a few lies father ... I've swore a number of times ... I ..   I .. I've stolen father.'

'What did you steal my son?'

'Bre ... bread father.'

'It's okay... All young boys are greedy and take more than they should do, so take one slice at a time in future.'

'Yis father.'

'I've missed ma ... ma ... mass as w ... well father. Oh me 'ead, oh me 'ead.'

'Take it easy child. How many times have you missed?'

'Oh ... oh ... er ... erm ... er.'

'Once or more?'

'Yis ... yis ... father.'

'St Patricks day?'

'Yis father. Oh me 'ead ... me 'ead.' I cried.

'Make a good act of contrition and for your penance say five Our Fathers and five Hail Mary's.'

'Oh my God, I am very sorry that I 'ave sinned against thee and I will not sin again.'

'Go in peace and tell your mother to check that forehead of yours James.'

'Yis father.'

I stumbled out with a wide smirk on my face. Those waiting to make their confession stood up to let me pass and Ossie tried to dead leg me on the sly, but I was ready for him.

'Missed' I whispered. He opened his mouth to curse and then realised he was in the House of God and we all knew that swearing in church was one of the worse sins you could ever commit.

I grinned, then knelt down between the benches just across the aisle and as quick as I could rattled through my penance and almost skipped out of the church. I was dead chuffed; Ossie hadn't been into confession yet.

Spud was laughing when he came out, but Ossie had a face on him. I was playing 'heads in' with a couple of lads who were waiting for their dad.

'You fell over on purpose,' Ossie growled, refusing to kick the ball back when I passed it to him.

'I didn't yer know, I tripped over on me laces.'

'Yer did ... I know you.'

'I didn't, an' look at the lump on me 'ead.'

'Swear on your mother's life then.'

'I swear on me mothers life.'

'God forgive yer Reilly if your mam drops dead. You'll go straight to 'ell, wont he Spud?'

'Yeah, but he could be tellin' the truth Ossie. Just because you were in there for ages doesn't mean he's lying.' Ossie didn't reply but I knew he had a cob on, he never called me by my surname.

I had a shilling on me so I offered to buy the chips from Fletchers chippy at the corner of St Anne Street. I didn't want to fall out with Ossie. Johnny was going away soon and Mr Feeley promised both of us we could go to Woodside to see him off.

Johnny swaggered up our street carrying a posh brown leather case with Ossie and me strutting either side of him, showing off in a way. He'd also shaved his tash off in an effort to make himself look years younger. We were made up because Johnny would soon be flying aeroplanes and no one else that we knew had flown them before.

Out of curiosity a few neighbours watched our little procession, with Mr Feeley walking behind us dressed in his uniform looking as solemn as a funeral director. Mrs Feeley stood on her step waving with one hand and drying her eyes with the other; mam and Mrs Murphy stood either side of her giving moral support.

Dad couldn't be bothered.

'The war's over ...What's all the bloody fuss about' he said. 'And I don't know what you're standin' there for when there's plenty of jobs to do in 'ere woman.'

For a Sunday, mam was kind of sharp.

'Mind your own business Reilly. Just because you have no friends it doesn't mean that I haven't.'

'There's no show without Punch,' he bawled. The front door slammed loudly, again bearing the brunt of his temper.

'Will you be flyin' bombers Johnny?' we asked. His face lit up exposing an array of ivory type gnashers spanning from ear to ear. We thought at first it was for our benefit, but were mistaken. To our surprise a dark haired girl appeared from behind the number ten bus, all dolled up wearing a bright red coat and 'lippy' to match.

'Hiya,' she said, walking over and linking Johnny right in front of us ... and even in front of his dad.

Mr Feeley didn't turn a hair. He must have known. We were shocked, so we trailed them real close to see if he kissed her, but from our position he didn't. Johnny boarded the train and leaned out of the window. It was then that we noticed he had a red smudge on his cheek, we nudged each other. He gave us the thumbs up and waved like mad as the train pulled out. Within seconds, Johnny's fluttering hand disappeared in a cloud of steam.

'Remember me?'

'Er ... erm ... no,' we said.

'I'm Marlene from the cake shop, remember me now?'

We both looked stunned then nodded.

'Call in on Monday after school an' I'll keep a bag of bits for youse.'

'We will, thanks.' We never refused a gift horse in the mouth.

Mr Feeley took us into his shack at the end of the ticket office and gave us a bob between us. 'Now Austin I want you to promise me that you'll not mention a word about Johnny's girlfriend to your mother.'

'Course I won't dad.'

'And you as well Jimmy.'

'On me mother's life I won't Mr Feeley.'

'Never say that Jimmy. You'll not forgive yourself if anything happened to your mother.'

'It won't Mr Feeley, it won't, because I'll never tell anyone about Johnny's girlfriend, that's why,' I replied.

Jess's demise

Dad's work situation hadn't improved. He was either on strike or signing the book so any suggestion or ideas about holidays weren't even on his agenda. He constantly worried about Bridie passing the scholarship and if she did how and where the money would come from to buy her uniform and books, although in a way, he always seemed confident that ultimately he would meet the expense. I wanted for nothing myself - I had my footie boots and a new pair of galoshers that mam had purchased on the cheque - they were all I needed. Our Bernadette and Tommy had new clobber, bought before Christmas, so dad, as far as I could make out, was worrying unduly.

Mam didn't worry at all, she wasn't the type.

'God's good we'll not starve,' she'd say, but dad, of little or no faith, didn't share her opinion and would respond in his down to earth way:

'The church won't feed us when we've no bread in the house.'

With both mam and dad having conflicting points of view, we kids had a choice of who to side with. This wasn't a problem for me; I tended to go along with who was likely to be of most use to me in the next minute or so.

Although the light nights were always welcome after a miserable winter, the dark evenings had some compensations and advantages for small boys like me. To dad's annoyance I continued hanging onto the back of lorries and with him having so much time on his hands he eventually became paranoid over my habit. I just couldn't understand why he took the trouble to bother. The library was still open and the number of times that he'd preached about it being a scholar's free paradise would fill a book. And what about the Grange Road shops? They didn't close until half five and he loved mooching around there for bargains even though he was skint. So why the sudden interest in my bit of fun?

Ossie's dad didn't seem to bother, nor did Spud's. Then again, Spud only jogged on the binny ellies going to the Corpy yard, which unlike other wagons had a rear platform to support him and went dead slow. Sometimes when he felt more adventurous he'd hang onto the back of the L.M.S horse and carts going to the Morpeth dock. Depending on their moods, the driver's wouldn't bother too much about carrying an extra passenger. Occasionally, however, they would crack the whip against the back of the cart and that's when Spud would drop off and scarper.

The distance from Conway Street to the docks was too short to gather any sort of speed, but jogging a lorry down Clevie or Pricie was a different proposition altogether, for there was a good half mile to cling before the first traffic lights. This was a task I could manage quite easily, though it's fair to say that Ossie often struggled. With his left hand much weaker than his right we sometimes lost him. This usually happened if one of the wagons hit a bump in the road and on those occasions he arrived home with his knees bleeding and elbows scraped. Then Mrs Feeley would give him a fourpenny one. I'd experienced a number of similar clouts myself and at times had even tasted the belt. The belt was still better than a clip over the ear though, for that stung for ages. Like everything else however, by the time next day arrived the pain would be forgotten and new pursuits underway.

Determined to put an end to my dangerous occupation, dad instigated a plan that called for placing look-outs on different street corners. Aunt Fan, together with his chief informant, our Bridie, was recruited, though mam wouldn't be cajoled into his scheme at any price. She had better things to do with her time than watching lorries pass along the main roads, so she said, and besides her eyesight wasn't too clever. She could only see a short distance and it was her opinion that I'd soon grow out of the habit anyway. After deliberating for a while she announced that it wouldn't be right for me to get a hiding if she couldn't be sure if it was me or not hanging on the back of lorries. I could see the sense in this logic myself, even though I shouldn't have been listening in the back kitchen when dad was discussing his battle tactics.

I think Jess's addiction first developed after we'd rescued her from the dogs' home, for within days of arriving in Brookie she began chasing the coalman's horses. From this she progressed to running alongside the bin lorries, barking like mad whenever they moved along the street and although I tried curbing her habit she wouldn't take a blind bit of notice of me. Of course she'd never do it in front of dad, for like me she was aware of his temper and valued her life too much. In her defence though, every other dog in the street had similar faults and it wasn't unusual to find lumps of coal or tin cans strewn across the pavement that had been thrown by angry drivers delivering or collecting essential commodities.

Another thing in Jess's favour was her reluctance to mix with other dogs, a characteristic that pleased dad no end. No way did he approve of her sniffing other dogs' bums or of them sniffing hers - he had no time for that nonsense.

'GERRARAVIT.' One simple command and they all knew exactly what it meant.

One night he nearly had a fit when he found two dogs stuck together right in the middle of our front step. We thought he was about to have a heart attack the way he flew through the house and into the backyard, only to dash back with a bucket of freezing water to throw over them.

'BUGGEROFF UP YER OWN END,' he bawled.

I wasn't sure if it was the cold water or dad's voice that separated them. But it worked ... they scattered.

We always jogged lorries after school. Ossie joined Nacker and me as we walked up to Argyle Street to wait for a suitable wagon to stop at the junction of Pricie. Within minutes a lorry laden with cargo for the docks had pulled up. Soon we were hurtling towards our end of Brookie, hanging on comfortably without a care in the world and for once even Ossie hadn't lost his grip. However, disaster soon struck just as we were level with the Co-op bakery. I don't know whether she'd heard us laughing or sensed our presence, but Jess came bounding after the lorry. To make matters worse dad was standing in the doorway of Snow's chemists shop on the corner of Vittoria Street and it was a pity that Jess didn't see him, otherwise there would have been a different story altogether. Without slowing down she shot across the busy junction causing a second lorry to brake, just missing her by inches. The driver cursed Jess in front of dad, who for a change was lost for words.

He couldn't say anything of course without admitting that Jess was his dog and one thing which was very much against his natural instincts was biting his tongue.

When he arrived home mam knew by his face that he'd reached the end of his tether and her worst fears were confirmed when he refused to eat his liver and onion dinner. He just loved that meal and had never been known to leave a scrap.

'Just wait till that fella comes in,' he bawled 'and that bloody dog as well.'

Mam was so worried she instructed our Bridie to slip to Aunt Fan and ask her to pop in for a cup of tea and a chinwag, so that hopefully her presence might defuse the situation

It was unusually quiet when I wandered in at five o'clock, but I knew by mam's colour that all was not well. Our Bridie was nursing Tommy, Bernadette looked frightened and Aunt Fan stood by the table as if ready to take off. Jess wasn't in her usual spot so our mutual vibes were missing. Dad had his arms folded and a face like thunder. Fortunately for me I'd left the back door open.

He didn't speak; he didn't have to. Suddenly, he leapt towards me. Anticipating his move I was like greased lightning and out of the back door, slamming it behind me as away I galloped. One thing I could do was run, having gained plenty of practice during the occasions that I'd fled from the 'scuffers'and the schoolboard.

I called in at Tucker's house and we played Ludo and Draughts while waiting for the dark to creep in. When I thought it was safe for me I headed home. Sneaking on tiptoes the last few yards towards our house I ducked and crawled under our front window just like we did when we played commandos.

The curtains were open slightly so I peeped in and was shocked to see our Bridie and Bernadette were both crying.

I had to look twice … I couldn't believe my eyes. 'Fancy her crying over me,' I said to myself. 'And me believing she hated me,' I mumbled, feeling a lump come into my throat.

There was no sign of dad. 'Maybe he's gone to bed early,' I thought.

Mam came in from the kitchen carrying Tommy. She looked upset too so I decided to end their misery for after all, they'd suffered enough already worrying over me and besides, I was starving!

I knocked on the door, ready to face the music.

'Where've you been, m'lad?' mam muttered. I looked at our Bridie and if looks could kill I'd have dropped dead on the spot. 'She's soon got over her grieving for me,' I said to myself.

'Jess's dead and its all your fault,' she yelled.
I couldn't move for the shock. My eyes filled up. I nearly choked on my tears.

'Where? ... When?' Mam came across and put her arms round me, but I was sobbing uncontrollably.

'It's not your fault James.'

'It is,' our Bridie cried, so I sobbed even louder.

'Shut up Bridie. He's not to blame. Shush... shush.. James. Your dad'll be 'ere in a minute.' Dad came in through the front door the anger no longer in his face.

'It's her alright ... hit by a bus.'

'Are you sure Charlie?'

'Positive ... hit by one of our own.'

'Not the Wallasey bus then? Not the number ten?'

'No, the ninety four ... killed outright.'

'Oh my God.'

'WHA! WHA!' I wailed. 'Poor Jess ... Poor Jess.'

'That's what she gets for runnin' after buses,' dad said sharply.

'Don't be so hard Charlie. Can't yer see the kids are upset.'

'Worr about me,' he complained 'I've 'ad no bloody dinner yet.'

'Where is she now dad?' I cried, for I couldn't bear to think she'd be all-alone in the morgue in Price Street.

'I've put 'er in a sack outside the Corpy. They'll see to 'er in the mornin'.'

'Well at least she's not lyin' in the gutter as if nobody owns her,' said mam.

'Aye, that's worr I thought. Oh by the way, here's 'er collar. No good leavin' it there.

You never know round here, some bugger could pinch it an' it cost me three bob on the market that bloody did.'

WHA! WHA!

'Aw ... right, that'll do. Now cut it out.'
I sat snivelling on the couch. Our Bridie went upstairs and mam removed dad's dinner from the oven.

'Come an' 'ave a dip of me gravy son.'

'No ... no thanks dad I'm not 'ungry.'
Jess's collar was on the floor by the front door, where she used to lie down. I started crying again.

'Now what's up?'

'Who'll go with me to the lavvie now our Jess's gone?' I wailed.

Dad tutted loudly, then blew on his dinner which was steaming hot.

'An' worr 'appens if a rat runs up me leg an' bites me balls an' me mickey when I'm out there?'

'HEY, BLOODYWELL CUT THAT LANGUAGE OUT IN 'ERE. Who 'ave you been playin' with m'lad?'

'Mr Murphy sez it...so does Mr Smith.'

'Well you don't use that kind of language in this 'ouse. Not in front of your mother or sisters.' I carried on crying.

'It's yer privates ... 'ave yer got that me'lad?'

'Yis dad.'

'I wanna go the lavvie, now.'

'Bridie, come an' stand by the back door while Jimmy goes the lavvie,' mam shouted.

I threw my snake belt onto the kitchen floor, just in case it fell down the lavvie in the dark. As soon as I sat down I missed our Jess and all my emotions seemed to spill out. I couldn't stop crying.

'PRIVATES..PRIVATES..PRIVATES..ARSE, ARSE...ARSE..ARSE, ARSE, ARSE, ARSE.' I yelled, I didn't care.

The only response I got, however, was from old Mrs McCormack who I heard breaking wind in her lavvie, three doors away. And I didn't even laugh.

When I walked back inside Bridie looked at me strangely and whispered that she knew how I felt, but then dad bawled for us to shut the door. He'd heard Mrs McCormick as well, which wasn't surprising for she sounded just like a China boat entering the dock with its funnel releasing full steam.

'There's no bloody need for that, not when I'm 'avin' me dinner,' he complained.

'She's gettin' old Charlie, an' it's only the salts she takes, that's all,' said mam.

'Salts ... salts ... bloody somersaults yer mean,' he growled, pushing his dinner to one side before standing up and turning the wireless on full volume. He always responded in a similar way when he wanted to blank out rows or disturbances in the street.

'I'm not listenin' to anymore of that bloody crap,' he concluded, turning the radio up full blast.

It was strangely quiet in bed that night. I couldn't sleep and tossed and turned all night, and our Bridie never complained once.

News travelled fast in our street. Next morning the lads called around to our house more or less at the same time, wanting to know all the gory details of Jess's last hours, but I couldn't help them. They'd heard rumours that Berty Robinson's black mongrel had chased Jess up Charles Street and this had caused her to run in front of the bus. That was as good as murder in their eyes. Berty was taking his dog out for a walk when we confronted him, but he vehemently denied Buster's involvement and when Buster jumped up and licked us we decided he wasn't to blame, he was too friendly. So we put the blame on Cleary's dog, for just like his owner he had a nasty streak.

'I'm sorry tae hear aboot yir aunt,' Mr Smith said when I was in their house that night.

'She was a dog Mr Smith,' I replied.

'Ach a know, wee Jimmy. I had two of the auld buggars me'sel when I was your age, but ye still have ye wee feelin's all the same.'

'Dad she was a dog,' said Billy irritated by the fact that his father had once again been drinking heavily on the way home from work. Mrs Smith hardly spoke a word.

'Ah know what ye sayin' son. D'yer think ye old man's thick or something?' I had two aunts who were dogs so don't tell me anything aboot what the wee man's goin' through, because I know all aboot it.'

He staggered into the kitchen for a swill before getting ready to resume his session with his mates in the Dolphin. Mrs Smith whispered to us to go out and play. We took the hint.

Scandal in the street.

Nothing really exciting happened over the following weeks. We were back at school; Dad and Mr Griffiths managed a few days over at the water in the Alexander dock; Mr Murphy travelled down to London to work on a building site not far from Buckingham Palace; the Yard was busy, so Jock had plenty of overtime; Mr Ryan voyaged down the South American coast and Ossie's dad diligently blew his whistle as he guided trains in and out of Woodside station. Our mothers followed their normal routines. The next holiday period, Whitsuntide, would soon be on us and if we were lucky from then onwards summer days would drift pleasantly in.

The house didn't seem the same without Jess, and despite pleas for another dog from our Bernadette and Bridie, dad was adamant he'd had enough of dogs to last a lifetime and his word, as usual, was final.

'Can we have a cat instead, dad?' Bridie suggested.

'No yer can't, I don't trust them buggers. They're too bloody sly for starters.'

For once I agreed with dad. Since Jess had gone I'd caught Pixie Griffiths a couple of times in our air raid shelter using it for her droppings and stinking the place out. I shifted her with the brush thinking that she'd never have taken liberties if our Jess were here.

We were playing cricket by the court and Ossie was about to bowl to Nacker when after three short paces he stopped abruptly. We looked round to see what had distracted him, but apart from the old folk nattering as usual outside their front doors nothing peculiar seemed to be out of place. This was probably tactics or an attempt to kid us, we decided, as Ossie returned to his marker and proceeded to run the full ten paces as if intending to deliver a full toss - a speciality he'd recently developed. Nevertheless we knew something was bothering him because for some reason he kept staring towards his own house, which was no different to anyone else's, except that Mrs Feeley had placed a plant pot outside to get some fresh air. She was obviously unaware that the abattoir was about to release the rops and the stench always drifted down Brookie this time of year.

After finally bowling Nacker out, Ossie shot off saying he was as dry as a bone and was nipping home for a drink of water. While waiting for him to return we crashed down on the kerb and it was then that I spotted Marlene leaving the Feeley's house. At first I couldn't believe my eyes, for only Ossie and his dad and me knew about her - and that she was Johnny's girlfriend - and I'd told no one. It now looked as if the rabbit was out of the bag and Mrs Feeley knew the secret too.

Joey Bailey, Frankie's older brother wolf whistled as Marlene fled down the street and even the old women who had been absorbed in everybody else's business stopped gossiping, their eyes following her panic stricken flight. I noticed everything from where I lay sprawled and wondered what was happening in the Feeley's house and why Marlene looked as if she couldn't get away quick enough.

Ossie rejoined us and we resumed playing until bad light stopped play.

'Somethin's goin' on in our 'ouse,' Ossie said to me before we parted for the night.

He looked really worried and that wasn't like him at all.

'What d'yer mean like?'

'Marlene was in our 'ouse talkin' to me mam an' dad and she was cryin'. I only asked what was the matter an' me dad told me to bugger off out an' play. It's somethin" to do with our Johnny, 'cos me mam was sayin' he'll 'ave ter come 'ome now. So I don't know what's happenin'.'

'Pr'aps she's nicked some money from the cake shop an' is in trouble with the cops' I suggested.

'Yeah, 'pr'aps she gave it to Johnny to stash an' he's been caught.'

We were only a few yards from Ossie's house when we heard an almighty row that stopped us both dead in our tracks. Ossie's mam was screaming at the top of her voice. A few doors opened down the street and heads popped out. The wireless in our house suddenly came to life with loud music drowning out some of the conversation, though not all of it.

'Why didn't you tell me about her?' Mrs Feeley yelled. Her words were precise and clear.

'What will my mother say when she hears about it?' she cried. It appeared that we were hearing a one sided conversation for Ossie's dad hadn't said a word, but then he started bawling at his wife.

'I don't give a damn about your mother or anyone else for that matter. He's our son an' he won't be the first to dip his wick an' come unstuck.'

'Don't be so dammed coarse Frank,' Mrs Feeley screamed, only louder this time. After this we couldn't hear what she said because her sobbing drowned the words. We placed our arms around each others shoulders and walked down the street towards Cathie.

'I told yer they've been dippin' in the till,' I said, but Ossie was quiet and didn't answer straight away.

'What's the matter Oz?'

'Dad said he's been dippin' his wick. It's funny but I don't remember any candles goin' missin' out of our 'ouse.'

'Pr'aps Marlene's nicked them from hers,' I suggested.

'Yeah 'pr'aps yer right' he replied.

'Mam, there's a row goin' on in Ossie's,' I hollered as soon as I went into our house. Mam didn't answer though dad did. 'That's their bloody business and we don't want ter know about it,' he said, turning the wireless up so loud that even mam could hear the latest news.

'BUT JOHNNY'S BEEN DIPPIN' HIS WICK,' I yelled, keen to break the news before it was in 'The Advertiser' which was due out on Thursday and then everyone would know.

I'd seen some vicious looks on dad's face during my short time on earth but not like this one.

'WHAT WAS THAT YOU'VE JUST SAID?' he roared full voice, so that even the wireless appeared to be switched off. Mam jumped, almost dropping her darning needles. Our Bridie was upstairs doing her homework and Bernadette had gone to Aunt Fan's, which left our Tommy as the only possible witness to murder and he, being a baby, didn't understand a word that was going on.

'Dunno.' I muttered.

'WHAT WAS THAT YOU JUST BLOODYWELL SAID?'

'Dunno dad 'onest.' I was being honest. I knew what I'd said, but I didn't know what it meant, is what I would like to have said. However, I had no intention of repeating it.

'GET UPSTAIRS TO BLOODY BED BEFORE I TAKE ME BELT OFF TO YER.'

I didn't need telling twice. I was off like a flash and sat on the top of the stairs listening.

'Did yer 'ear what that bloody fella's just said Maggie?'

'No Charlie. What did he say?'

'That Johnny Feeley's been dippin' 'is wick.'

I heard mam laugh. So it was all right after all. He was just picking on me again.

'Go on,' she said. 'I wonder if he's put her in the family way?'

'I'm not interested me'self,' he replied. 'It's the other fella that bothers me. I don't know what the bloody'ell I'm goin' ter do with 'im the way he's been actin' lately.'

'He'll grow out of it,' said mam.

I didn't know what I was supposed to grow out of, no one ever told me anything.

When Spud and I called round for Ossie next day we didn't go into the house as we normally would. The house was more or less empty, except for Mrs Murphy who was with Ossie's mam. When the door opened, Mrs Murphy told us to go and play somewhere else. Seeing Tich was on his own we took him with us and wandered round to Tucker's to give Mrs Feeley some peace and quiet. Mr Feeley and Teresa were also out so Ossie's mother was able to share her troubles and woes with her neighbour and confidante, Mrs Murphy.

We arrived to find Tucker practising his bugle in the backyard and reading some sheet music. The squiggly lines didn't mean a thing to us, but the bugle sounded all right and as far as we knew no one had complained about the noise so we assumed Tucker must have been improving. Mr Griffiths was sitting nearby smoking his pipe, with Eddie perched on his mam's knee and Pixie the cat lay sprawled on the step enjoying the morning sun. Meanwhile, just around the corner, Ossie's mam was pouring her heart out to Mrs Murphy and she in turn told my mam about Marlene and Johnny. Of course we knew nothing about the going's on: we were too wrapped up in our own problems to worry about anyone else's.

There was always plenty to do on a Saturday morning and in addition to my regular jobs, dad's working hooks needed to be taken to Dows workshop in Cottage Street to be sharpened. As usual, Spud took a sack round to Gladys Lewis's for the weekly cabbages. It was a well known fact that the Murphy's ate more cabbages than any other family in our street, which was something to do with their meticolism, or so mam said. Smithy had already left with Spud to buy lettuce leaves for Bluey his pet rabbit, and Ossie and Nacker were in the park after completing their weekly tasks. As usual we arranged to follow them round later.

It wasn't to be a lucky day for us. To begin with some scally pinched Smithy's casey from the Balaclava football pitch in the park after Spud toe-ended it over the hill. We spent hours trying to find the thief, with Nacker threatening to kill him stone dead if he found him. The culprit managed to escape, however, but the biggest problem we faced was that the loss of our ball placed the end of season Cup Final in serious jeopardy.

Back home in Brookie it was obvious something was happening. We'd clocked a number of older women nudging one another whenever the Feeley's were passing by and on numerous occasions heard Johnny's name mentioned. Ossie had also picked up snippets of information from their house about their kid being in real trouble, but despite his intense interest he still couldn't find the reason for all the secrecy. Spud also heard whispers going on in his house and I listened in ours, though I had to be extra careful when dad was around. He'd hit the roof if he ever caught me ear-wigging. I knew for a fact that I would have never heard the last of it - he just hated nosy people. There was no point telling him that we only wanted to know what kind of trouble Johnny had got himself into so that we might be able to help him, because he just wouldn't be interested.

Next day Johnny Feeley arrived home after his basic training. We didn't know he was coming until he turned into our street, otherwise we'd have 'kept nix' to make sure the 'scuffers' weren't around. He looked thinner and tanned, but for some reason didn't seem to be happy to see us even after we'd lumped his suitcase from the corner of Cathie to his front door. Ossie followed him into the house, but was chased back out despite the fact he was dying for a pee. Strangely enough there wasn't a soul about on any of the neighbours doorsteps, even though it was a really fine day.

A few minutes later we were shocked to see Marlene entering the court linking a heavily built older woman. They went straight into the Feeley's house. This was too much for Ossie.

'I'm burstin' for a pee,' he said and dashed off down the back jigger.

While he was away we played 'kick the can' with the sole purpose of aggravating Pat and Mary Murphy, who were hopping around on one foot with Norma Ashton enjoying a game of hop scotch. Our favourite trick would be to time their final hop and then kick the can at them knowing it would spoil their game. We thought this was dead funny, but they didn't. It was tit for tat really - they always got their own back by throwing our football over backyard walls whenever the ball rolled near them. We didn't like that one bit, but then again girls had a different idea of fun to us, that's why we never played with them.

While we were acting the goat with the girls, a grim looking Mr Feeley came hurrying down the street and dashed into his house. Within a minute or so Mrs Murphy came rushing out of the Feeley's, to be quickly followed by Ossie who was unceremoniously ejected. 'SCRAM ... GO AND PLAY OUTSIDE,' his father yelled, slamming the door into poor Ossie's face before he landed on the pavement outside.

We looked around startled - Ossie was crying his eyes out. He lay flopped on the kerb like a red setter dog, his big ginger head buried in his arms. We legged it towards him. Spud knelt down and I followed. We both put our arms round Ossie's shoulders together, for don't forget we were the only ones who knew there was something going on in their house. Nacker stood nearby watching Ossie's tears. He never cried, he was too tough to cry and anyway leaders never cried.

Tucker and Smithy arrived passing a tennis ball to each other. They didn't know what was going on either. 'What's 'appened Ozz?' I asked, squeezing his shoulder tightly.

'It's ... it's our ... it's ... our .. J ... Johnny,'he sobbed.

'What's the matter, 'ave the cops arrested him?' I yelled. The gang moved in closer then, they knew it was important.

'No it's worse than that,' he hollered.

Nacker took over.

'Okay Oz ... it's alright ... fill us in ... let's know what's 'appened eh.'

'Our Johnny's got ter get married 'cos Marlene's 'avin' a baby,' he wailed.

'Is that all ... me mam 'as one every year,' said Nacker. It didn't seem all that bad when he put it that way, but still I was shocked. I was about to dash home and tell mam about Johnny when I realised it was Saturday and dad was in the house. I knew exactly what he'd say, or more precisely what he'd do and as it was too early to go to bed, I decided to keep my secret until mam was on her own.

Meanwhile Ossie continued whinging as he made his way down the street to Mr and Mrs Cotton's. He always called on the Cottons when he was fed up, upset or in trouble.

Over the following days Johnny and Marlene were headline news. As was to be expected, sympathy for Mr and Mrs Feeley oozed from the worried neighbours. Apart from the shame of the unexpected news and the fact that Johnny had just turned eighteen and Marlene seventeen, there was the prospect of a mixed marriage to consider. This situation appeared to bother the Catholic fraternity more than the Protestants and then dad, as usual, offered his unbiased opinion.

'He won't be the first and won't be the last. An' I don't know worr all the fuss is about over mixed marriages. It doesn't matter whether you're Catholic, Protestant, or a Welsh Baptist. You either go up there or down here, whichever way you look at it,' he said.

'God forgive you Charlie Reilly,' mam retaliated. 'Fancy speakin' like that and in front of the kids as well,' she said, blessing herself at the same time.

'They don't deserve such bad luck, a nice hard workin' family like them,' said Mrs Turner, trying to ferret a bit more information about Marlene's background from Mrs Bailey, of all people. Mrs Bailey was probably the last person in the neighbourhood to approach regarding other people's business.

'Nobody deserves a shotgun weddin' but that's what you should 'ave 'ad you nosy old cow,' Mrs Bailey replied. Smithy, who was standing on their step, heard this and told us about it. None of us had ever heard of a shotgun wedding before. I was sorry that Nacker wasn't with us at the time, otherwise I wouldn't have had to have asked mam.

'What's a shotgun weddin' Mam?'

'I'll tell yer when you're older son.'

'Does me dad know then?'

'If you know what's good for yer, you won't ask 'im.'

I didn't bother asking. I decided to use my brains and wait until the wedding.

'Then I'll see for me'self if anybody is wearing holsters on their belts or not,' I muttered under my breath.

Invaded

Dad saw it first, or thought he did. It was early morning and he wasn't quite awake at that time. He didn't mention about his sighting in case he scared mam and the girls, so he asked me on the quiet if I'd noticed anything strange, knowing quite well how sharp my eyes were.

I'd spotted a couple of cockroaches sneaking under the old cast-iron boiler in the corner of the back kitchen, but they were doing no harm to anyone and dad had seen most of them off anyway.

This was after he'd put on his cap for work one morning and he found a few of them asleep. Surely there was no need to stamp on them just because they crawled on his head, I thought. It was his own fault really; he only had himself to blame. If he'd have been working with soda ash they wouldn't have bothered kipping in his cap in the first place, but with Tate and Lyle sugar what else did he expect?

Later on I began searching for anything strange. The problem was that I didn't know what I was looking for because dad wouldn't tell me straight out, so I was forced to use my imagination. I removed the small bamboo cane I'd hidden at one time or another in my secret den at the back of the cistern in the lavvie and prodded behind the stove. All I discovered, however, was loads of grease and a few money spiders that quickly vanished through a crack in the plaster. Peering tentatively down the hole beneath the sink where our Jess used to sniff I couldn't see anything there either. Finally, I stuck my head under the cupboard where dad kept his tools and old newspapers for the fire and once again drew a blank. Frustrated I scratched my head and wondered what to do next.

Maybe dad's imagination was getting carried away, I thought. It was only a thought though. No way on this earth would I suggest it. He was never wrong and I had no intention whatsoever of contradicting him regarding his eyesight. Then I had a brainwave. Perhaps the mystery invader was lurking in the air-raid shelter amongst the coal heap. Swapping the bamboo cane for the yard brush I systematically began poking the handle into mounds of loose coal and slack, but nothing happened, so after ten minutes I decided I'd had enough. Apart from the stink, I was also covered in coal dust and as mam was due shortly I treated myself to a quick 'cats lick' in the sink before joining the lads who were playing a game of skipping with the Barker sisters.

They had a heavy rope stretched across the street with two of the Barker girls holding each side and singing:

'The man wants a bride, the man wants a bride,
ee I adio the man wants a bride.
The bride wants a baby, the bride wants a baby,
ee I adio, the bride wants a baby.
The baby wants a pram, the baby wants a pram,
ee I adio the baby wants a pram.'

Ossie came out of his house, so out of respect we stopped singing with the girls just in case he thought we were being funny. We weren't though, no way would we hurt his feelings for the world, but we stopped just in case he thought we were.

Spud then suggested going round to Smithy's to play a game of 'nearest the wall,' a game in which we threw coins on a pitch. It was a simple game, for whoever managed to get his coin nearest to the wall took the winnings. Sometimes Smithy's dad left loads of half-pennies in his overall pockets for us to play with. As usual, the gambling game didn't last because once again we fell out arguing about who'd got the winning throw and so we called it a day. Spud was happy though - he was showing three pence profit.

It was just beginning to get dark as I made tracks for home. As I trundled up the back jigger I heard dad's rising howl even before I reached the entry door.

CHRIST ALMIGHTY ... WHAT THE BLOODY 'ELLS THAT?' He bawled. I entered the yard and saw mam standing by the kitchen door. She almost jumped out of her skin as dad hurled the brush over the back jigger wall, hitting the gable end of Tucker's house. Dad's face was white with rage so I naturally thought twice about asking him what the problem was. Then I noticed his hands were black and caked with coal dust. He suddenly exploded.

'BLOODY CAT SHITE!' he snarled, pushing past mam and me in an effort to reach the sink. I don't know what possessed me to burst out laughing. I suppose it was my sense of humour, I couldn't help it. The trouble was dad heard me.

'I'll give yer a bloody laugh. I'll give yer something to laugh about,' he ranted, but he didn't understand I laughed at anything and I wasn't laughing at him, honest.

As he made a bee-line for me mam intervened. In her eyes I'd done nothing wrong and so like a good centre half she placed herself between us, held her hand up and wagged her forefinger under dad's nose. He took one look at her face and that stopped him dead in his tracks ... I knew it would.

'BLOODY CATS ... I'll swing for them,' he growled and at that moment I was half-hoping Pixie Griffiths would appear on the backyard wall and call his bluff, but she didn't.

Mam tried a little diplomacy in an attempt to take the sting out of the situation by quoting one of her many superstitions.

'You know it's supposed to be lucky if you tread in it Charlie.'

'Lucky! Lucky me bloody arse,' he growled. He couldn't take a joke and I knew for a fact that he would only have seen the funny side of the situation if it had happened to me. After tea he was still sniffing his hands.

'Cats ... bloody cats,' he muttered and I started crying. I couldn't help it, I was thinking of our Jess.

'What's up with you now?'

'Nuthin'' I said. He wouldn't understand that I was still grieving. After all it was only three months since she'd been killed and most people I knew grieved for years when one of the family died.

Mrs Feeley, Mrs Murphy and mam were sitting in our front room when I came home from school. Dad was at work, otherwise they wouldn't be supping tea and gabbing at that time of day, I thought to myself. Mam gave me a drippin' butty and told me to go out and play. I was only half way up the street when I heard her scream.

'JIMMIE ... EE.' I couldn't believe my ears. I'd only left the house a minute earlier and mam was calling me in already. As there was a distinct sense of urgency in her voice I turned and ran as fast as my legs would go.

'Perhaps Ossie's mam had fainted ... she didn't look too good,' I thought. 'As long as it wasn't Mrs Murphy, she weighed a ton. I couldn't imagine any ambulance driver picking her up on a stretcher.' The door was wide open so I dashed into the front room and got the shock of my life, Mrs Murphy and Mrs Feeley were standing on our best couch, our Bridie and Bernadette were hugging each other on dad's chair and Tommy was perched on the table with his shoes on. Mam had a brush in her hands, which she threw at me before jumping onto the couch. Amazingly it didn't snap in the middle.

'WHAT ... WHAT'S THE MATTER,' I cried looking round in fear.

'Mrs Feeley's just seen a mouse or a baby rat run under the dresser,' mam screamed.

'A RAT,' I yelled, dropping the brush and grabbing the bottom of my trousers.

'Where's yer garters mam,' I gasped, without realising they were all depending on me to chase the rat. 'It won't harm yer son, just belt it one with the brush,' mam yelled.

Immediately I swung into action, flaying the brush under and over the dresser and then under the table. In my excitement I hit the lampshade and they all screamed. Our Tommy was crying his eyes out which really got to me, so seething with temper, I knelt down and shoved the end of the brush right under the couch. The 'invader' ran out. I must be honest, I jumped with fright at first, but it was only a little mouse and I didn't have the heart to kill it on the spot, well not in front of mam and everyone else. Keeping up the pretence I crashed the brush down on the floor and the mouse flew into the kitchen where I watched it disappear down a hole under the sink.

'I've never been so scared in me life,' said Mrs Murphy stepping down and releasing the pressure from the couch. I had a feeling she'd also released a different kind of pressure myself, because there was a right pong, for which our poor Tommy got the blame.

I was hailed as a hero and soaked up the adulation. I knew it would only last until dad came home.

Dad tucked into his dinner; I didn't speak - well nobody did when he was eating. Our Bridie was upstairs out of the way, doing her homework, Bernadette experimented with a box of crayons bought for her birthday and little Tommy crawled in front of the fire, but the guard was up so it was safe for him to do so, which was the main thing

I was waiting for dad to ask mam what kind of day she'd had, a question he always asked, but trust my luck - on this occasion he didn't bother - he read the Echo instead and began dozing in front of the fire. Mind you, at the time he was working, unloading soda or bag ash, an unpopular cargo that burnt into clothing and irritated the skin. The whole operation required strenuous energy and it really took it out of him, lumping the two hundred weight bags. No wonder he was tired when he came home.

I was about to go to bed when mam finally mentioned the mouse and my heroism, but by that time the pleasure of my gallantry had evaporated. Dad, to give him his due, appeared to appreciate my courageous action and declared that together we'd sort out the rodents on the following Saturday morning.

Next day when the date and details of Johnny's impending wedding day was announced, the whole thing caused quite a stir amongst a certain section of the neighbourhood, with the twelfth of July being chosen as the date for the register office event. Marlene's dad, a leading figure in the Orange Lodge, had insisted in no uncertain terms that there'd be no wedding unless it was held on King William's Battle of the Boyne day. Mrs Feeley was upset and naturally objected but was overruled. Mr Feeley agreed with Johnny, who accepted the fact that as he was partly responsible for the situation in the first place it was his duty to appease Marlene's parents and honour their request.

Of the Catholic neighbours, only Mrs Murphy appeared to take the news personally and voiced her opinions accordingly. 'God love yer Renie. I know what you're goin' through and you above everyone else doesn't deserve it. Well nobody does. I just can't believe your Johnny would turn out like this and after all you've done for 'im.'

'Thank God that I've only got our Timmy to worry about,' she continued 'and he's had 'the call' as yer know, so I'm blessed in more ways than one. Never mind Renie, God's good; I'll offer a decade of the Rosary up for you tonight when I'm at Benediction.' This generous offer was her way of cheering Ossie's mam up, but Mr Feeley remained in the dumps and made no comment about Mrs Murphy's good intentions.

It came as something of a surprise to a number of the neighbours to hear the news that Marlene's dad was a personal friend of Jock and both were members of the same Order of the Orange Lodge. Dad said it was small world. Normally he didn't bother passing comments on other people's business, yet surprisingly on this occasion offered his opinions after hearing July the twelfth mentioned.

'That's rubbin' salt in the bloody wounds,' he said. 'I've got nothin' personal against Orangemen me'self. They've got their beliefs, we've got ours.'

Mam looked astounded at the 'we've got ours.' I knew what she was thinking. Maybe a miracle was about to happen and dad was contemplating making a religious comeback. It soon became obvious he had no such intentions.

'I can't understand it me'self,' he went on. 'Fancy forcin' a Catholic to get married on King Billy's day. That takes the bloody biscuit that does.'

'What's an Orangeman, dad?' I asked, when he'd finished speaking.

'Phew ... Christ don't you bloody start. You ask the most awkward questions at times.

I don't know who the 'ell you take after m'lad.'

I didn't think it was awkward myself. I'd seen yellow men, brown men, black men, white men, but never orange men - unless you would call Spud's dad orange, though he was more like a tomato.

Mind you, occasionally dad's face was redder than his and at times resembled a blood orange. 'I wonder if dad's an Orangeman,' I thought. It was all too complicated for me and I didn't fancy asking him anyway.

On the Saturday morning after I'd finished my messages I joined dad in the yard to see what he had in mind to get rid of the mice. Mam had taken Tommy and the girls shopping and for a change we had the house to ourselves.

'Put the kettle on son,' dad ordered. It was the first time we'd resumed our partnership since the wallpaper fiasco and I felt quite at ease. After all, I was always led to believe that there's no better bond than that between father and son.

When the water had boiled he quickly removed the kettle from the stove and poured the steaming hot water down the hole beneath the sink. I held my hands over my ears; I just couldn't bear to hear the squeals of the tiny mice as the scalding water burnt them alive in their little den. Dad was indifferent - he was hard as nails.

'That 'ill cure the buggars,' he said.

'That's a funny way of curin' anybody,' I thought to myself.' Nothing happened though; the water filled the hole yet no dead bodies floated out. Dad scratched his head - he always did when failure stared him in the face. 'What the bloody 'ells 'appened to them?' he muttered.

'When I put the kettle on they may 'ave sneaked out an' dashed into the air raid shelter,' I suggested.

'Hmn ...You maybe right there son.'

'Okaydoky Jim, give me the shovel. If they're in there, I'll bloodywell find 'em, don't you worry about that lad,' he said.

He'd only shovelled a few buckets of the coal we stored in the shelter when he jumped back startled and came out with a right mouthful.

'BLOODY CATS ... SHIT HERE ... SHIT THERE ... CAT SHIT EVERY BLOODY WHERE.' I didn't laugh, though I was dying to, as he flung the shovel down the yard.

'I'll bloody cure them if it's the last thing I do' dad roared and I thought to myself, he hasn't cured the mice yet, now he's after curing the cats. I knew of course that he tended to be over ambitious at times, but God help any moggy venturing on the wall, especially Pixie Griffiths; dad's temper was really up this time and there'd be no stopping him.

'Stay here an' keep yer eye open,' dad barked, before going off in a right mood to Johnny Brown's, hoping no doubt to purchase something to see the cats off. Fortunately Brown's didn't sell arsenic, so he ended up buying two extra large mousetraps, one for the mice and one for the cats.

That night he set them up, attaching a nice piece of Cheshire cheese to each. I watched as he craftily placed one trap just inside the shelter with the other laid invitingly under the sink.

Lying in bed I found I couldn't sleep. I was waiting for the thunderous crash of the spring as it decapitated the poor mouse. I imagined the severed head flying through the air, landing on the stairs with its eyes staring up at me when I came down in the morning and shuddered at the thought.

Then there was poor Pixie Griffiths. I knew her better than anyone, but that didn't matter to dad. He had no favourites when he was on the warpath. 'What happens if she gets half her nose caught in the trap?' I thought. Mrs Griffiths will go mad; it was common knowledge that she loved the cat more than she loved Tucker's dad.

Mr Griffiths was like dad - no feelings. I couldn't blame him though, Pixie was spoilt and scratched him every time he went near Mrs Griffiths, that's why he had no time for her. I knew for certain that dad wouldn't put up with her for one minute, she'd be cat meat by now.

I wanted to say a little prayer that neither the mice nor the cat would fall for dad's lousy scheme, but I didn't know the patron saint for cats, or for mice for that matter, and I couldn't wake mam up to ask her because dad would skin me for spoiling his vicious exterminating plan. Then there was the cost of the traps. They'd cost him six bob, so he wouldn't thank me for that either.

I woke up next morning and crept gingerly down the stairs, keeping my eyes half-closed in case I trod on a mouse head. I glanced under the sink and couldn't believe my eyes. The cheese was gone but the spring hadn't moved. I dashed outside in my bare feet and looked in the shelter. It was the same. The cheese had gone yet the spring was in place.

'Dad ... dad,' I shouted, running up the stairs and bursting into the front room.

'What ... what's the matter,' he mumbled, half asleep.

'Guess what's 'appened?'

'WHAT?'

'Guess?'

'BUGGER OFF AN' STOP ACTIN' THE GOAT.'

'The cheese 'as gone an' the traps are still set,' I cried, trying not too appear too joyful in case he thought I had something to do with it, which I did, in a way, by saying my prayers to the unknown patron saint of cats and mice.

'Just wait till Monday,' he moaned. 'They'll be going straight back to 'im. 'Sellin' me bloody dummies.' We were about to go to bed early that night ready for school next day, when suddenly dad sprung it on us.

'There was never any of this trouble with mice or cats when we had the dog,' he said to mam.

Our eyes lit up. 'Can we have another dog then dad?'

'I'll think about it. We'll see..we'll see.'

We went to bed without any fuss. All we could talk about in the dark was getting another dog. We fell asleep delighted.

Paddy's misfortune

Although I'd started my third year at school on the wrong foot, since Christmas there were signs of improvement. Nevertheless, I didn't hold much faith of finishing in the first thirty in class. I was forever day-dreaming, that was my trouble according to Miss Burgess, but then all my mates day-dreamed. How could you plan your future if you didn't? Besides it was far more interesting to day dream than to learn arithmetic or write English. Then I received my report.

```
┌─────────────────────────────────────────────────────────────────┐
│             BIRKENHEAD EDUCATION COMMITTEE                        │
│                                                                   │
│        St Laurences Primary School    Boys' Department            │
│                      SCHOLAR'S REPORT                             │
│  Name. James Reilly.              Summer     Term 1948            │
│  Class 3  Containing 50 Scholars    Position in Class 38th        │
│  Times Absent 52                    Punctuality Good              │
├──────────────────────────┬───────┬──────────────────────┬────────┤
│ SUBJECT                  │       │ SUBJECT              │        │
│ English Language         │ 12/20 │ Geography            │ 8/10   │
│ Reading                  │ 15/20 │ History              │ 6/10   │
│ Spelling or Dictation    │ 13/20 │ Nature Study         │ Good   │
│ Composition              │ 12/20 │ Art                  │ 6/20   │
│ Mental Arithmetic        │ 15/20 │ Handwork             │ 14/20  │
│ Arithmetic               │ 15/20 │ Recitation           │ 9/10   │
├──────────────────────────┴───────┴──────────────────────┴────────┤
│ Class Teachers Report                                             │
│  James has ability, but lacks concentration. His conduct in class │
│ has improved since Christmas.  However, due to extreme truancy,   │
│ his position in class reflects the seriousness of this problem.   │
│ Headmasters Remarks. James must do better.  Truancy disgraceful,  │
│ must improve.                                                     │
└─────────────────────────────────────────────────────────────────┘
```

Like a piggy in the middle, I walked home from school flanked by Spud and Ossie. Nacker joined us at the corner of St Anne Street. I knew he had no chance of passing his Eleven Plus after finishing forty fourth in class. Even I had beaten him by six places. Ossie who finished third and Spud seventh in the class held their reports with pride, showing off in a way. I didn't mind though, I only had myself to blame. Nacker screwed his report up and tossed it into the gutter. I wanted to follow suit, but I couldn't. I knew that Mrs Feeley and Mrs Murphy would be bragging about how well Ossie and Spud had done and mam just wouldn't have believed me if I said I'd lost my report on the way home from school.

Mam always said trouble came in three's and at that moment in time I realised she was probably right. First of all our Jess was killed outright. Then Johnny slipped up and had to get married. It now looked highly likely that I would be the third. I didn't dare to contemplate my fate.

Nervously I entered the kitchen and held my report out. Mam was busy with the tea, but had an inkling that I was the bearer of bad news. She knew me by now - my face gave me away.

'Before I read it James, is it good or bad?' she asked.

'Average mam.'

'Tut ... tut ... tut.'

I stood back out of range just in case a fourpenny one was on its way, but mam surprised me. She didn't lash out.

'Someone's got ter be top and someone's got ter be bottom,' she said, placing my report in her handbag.

'I'll try me best to do better next year mam.'

'Good. Do that and make me proud of you.'

It was only now that I found out that our Bridie had arrived home and already told mam she'd finished second in class in a mock exam. This news made it almost a certainty she'd pass the scholarship. Dad, as anticipated, was elated with our Bridie's results, though to give him his due, he still enquired about my performance.

'How did you go on son?'

'Okay dad.'

'Good, glad to hear it.'

While dad tucked into his dinner I ambled into the kitchen, retrieved my report from mam's handbag and shot down to the lavvie to stash it in my little hidie hole behind the cistern.

Although Mrs Murphy looked sick with worry, she wasn't the type to burden anyone else with her problems. Spud, on the other hand, couldn't keep a secret if his life depended on it.

'Guess what?' he said to Ossie and me.

'Gis a clue?' we replied, almost at the same time.

'It's me da.'

'Yeah worra bout 'im?'

'He's gone missin'. '

'Go way ... since when?'

'Me mam hasn't heard from him for over a month now. An' he's sent no money either.' We were shocked.

'Pr'aps he's lost 'is memory or maybe he's in jail in London,' I suggested, trying my best to look on the bright side for Spud's sake.

'Pr'aps he's dead,' said Ossie. I gave him a filthy look like mam often gave dad, but it didn't work, Ossie still had a big soft grin on his face. The colour suddenly drained from Spud and he looked to me as if he was about to collapse on the spot, so using my nouse, I suggested taking him home to mam. She'd talk to him. She'd know what to say.

Dad was messing about in the yard trying to mend a puncture on our Bridie's bike and as usual was covered in oil. I didn't pass any comment. I was learning to keep my mouth shut now I was getting older.

'What's up Spud? You don't look very happy,' Dad asked.

Spud began spluttering so I helped him out.

'It's 'is dad ... he's gone missin' in London and Ossie thinks he's dead.'

'Since when as Ossie worked for Scotland Yard?' dad answered sarcastically.

We went inside and mam made a pot of tea and Spud ate the last slice of apple pie. I didn't mind though, I wasn't all that hungry and besides, my dad wasn't missing; Spud's was and he could be dead for all we knew.

'Look son, take a tip from me. Don't tell anyone round 'ere about your business,' dad said. Although this advice was just how dad saw things regarding keeping your nose out of matters that don't concern you, I couldn't believe my ears, I wanted to know everything. He'd now spoilt it again.

'Tell your mother if she needs any help to come round and discuss it with Mrs Reilly, okay son?' he concluded and went back into the yard.

Mam nipped out and bumped into Mrs Feeley in the entry. Ossie had already broken the news.

Mr Feeley volunteered to escort Spud's mam to the Bridewell. He looked real smart in his tweed suit, but strangely small and thin walking alongside Mrs Murphy.

'It's a good job dad's working,' I thought. Mam might well have popped his brown suit in at Bentleys and then there'd have been a right commotion, especially if he'd offered to take Mrs Murphy to the cop shop.

The desk sergeant was sympathetic and told them that loads of fella's went missing in London for one reason or another and said not to worry. After taking details he promised to phone a colleague to check out Mr Murphy's digs and as soon as he had any news he'd relay the information to Mrs Murphy. Three days later a bobby riding a bike appeared in our street and halted outside Spud's door.

I flew inside to let mam know. Dad was out. He wouldn't have been interested anyway.

The 'scuffer' went into Spud's house. After a few minutes he came out again, cocked his leg over the crossbar of his bike and slowly peddled down the street towards the Bridewell. Even before he'd turned into

Vittoria Street Mrs Feeley was knocking on the Murphy's door. I watched from our step, wondering if Mr Murphy was dead or not.

I told mam that the policeman had left and within seconds she'd slipped her cardigan over her shoulders and nipped across to the Murphy's house. She came back saying nothing, while I hung around like a starving cat, waiting for snippets of information. Dad came in from work, ate his dinner and then mam told him that Paddy Murphy was in jail. I was listening in the kitchen and was made up. I was the only one who'd got it right out of all the lads. By sheer coincidence, Mrs Murphy received a letter next day from Paddy's mate, with a newspaper cutting inside:

'Patrick Murphy, aged 36 of no fixed abode, was sentenced to thirty days imprisonment at Clerkenwell Court today. Murphy was found guilty of being drunk and disorderly and resisting arrest.'

'Holy Mary mother of God. The shame of it. Just wait 'til he gets 'ome,' Mrs Murphy gasped when she received the news. Dad, as usual, was more philosophical.

'I take me hat off to Paddy,' he said. 'At least he managed to keep his problem to himself without broadcastin' it to everyone round here and you've got to look on the bright side 'cause he's not dead, although he'll probably wish he was when he comes home to face holy Mary.' Mam was right again. Trouble always came in three's.

Kerry

'Is the Birken'ead News here yet?' dad asked for the umpteenth time. He couldn't wait to see our Bridie's name in the paper, though I couldn't understand what all the fuss was about. After all there were hundreds who'd passed the scholarship. Granted, not many of them were from our end, but once he'd read the newspaper it usually went on the fire or was cut into squares and was stuck on a nail in the lavvie. Not this one though, as soon as the results were published he was like a dog with two tails. In addition to making sure mam and me had seen it he showed it to Ossie, Tucker, Smithy, Spud, Aunt Fan and he even read it out to our Bernadette. Mam could tell by my face that I was fed up with the whole palaver.

'He's only excited, that's all. You'll 'ave to be patient, James. After all, Bridie's the first of the Reilly's who's passed the scholarship.'

'She's not yer know,' I shot back, 'worrabout me Cousin Sheila from Beckwith Street then?'

'Oh yeah. I forget about her. Now don't you dare mention it James, you'll only spoil your dad's day.'

'Only two girls an' three lads passed from the Lauries, eh Maggie?' dad proudly announced, removing the column with a pair of scissors and placing the cutting into his leather wallet next to his union card.

'By the way where did you finish in class Jim?'

'Er ... er ... er. I forget just now dad.'

'Forget? Forgot already. That reminds me, I 'aven't seen your report this year m'lad.'

In his own way he was only trying to be fair; just showing that he had my interest at heart as well as that of our Bridie's. But I panicked and seeking an escape, blurted out. 'I gave it to mam. You've seen it haven't you mam?'

'Yes ... He's not done too bad considerin'.'

'Good. Whereabouts is it then?' dad persisted.

'I've put it up somewhere Charlie. Where it is just now I can't remember, but I'll find it. Don't worry; I'll say a little prayer to St Anthony an' it'll soon turn up.'

Dad tutted and cursed under his breath, rather than tell mam straight to her face that he didn't believe in St Anthony, or miracles or saints, or anything religious for that matter.

Grasping the opportunity, I slipped through the back door to the lavvie and made sure that my report was well out of harm's way by prodding it alongside my conkers and other 'thingys' behind the cistern. 'I hope St Anthony doesn't know this doss,' I muttered under my breath.

It was only fair that Bridie should choose our new dog. She'd passed the scholarship and although I was mad jealous when dad suggested he preferred Bridie to go with him to the dogs' home, I didn't want to make too much of an issue out of it. My school report still hadn't turned up despite mam's fervent belief that it would eventually, so naturally I didn't kick up a fuss.

I waited patiently for dad and Bridie to arrive from the dog's home and no sooner had they turned the corner into our street than I was alongside them within seconds. At first I thought they'd been unable to get a dog until I noticed Bridie was carrying a brown and white puppy beneath her coat.

'Let me carry 'er,' I moaned sulkily. Bridie was aware of my disappointment with not being allowed to choose the puppy and for once she was almost nice to me, handing over the brown and white bundle. As soon as the puppy nibbled my ear I forgot my misery and shouted: 'now we've just got to find a name for her.'

'Worrabout Cissie?' I suggested. Dad seemed unimpressed.

'Don't be daft lad.'

'Worrabout Molly then?'

'No, pick somethin' with a bit of character.'

'I know ... I know ... Lassie.'

'That's a bloody sheep dog. She's only a mongrel don't forget.'

I thought long and hard and then remembered Spud telling us about his auntie's dog in Ireland. 'I've gorrit dad ... I've gorrit... I know one. Worrabout Kerry?' I yelled before anyone else came up with a better name.

'Hmmnn ... I think yer might be right there son.' I was as proud as Punch. 'Yeah. Kerry sounds about right Jim. Mr Ryan's a Kerry man an' he's as tough as old boots.'

'Father Doyle's from Kerry as well, yer know dad,' I said.

'Exactly.'

As Johnny's wedding day loomed nearer Mrs Feeley appeared more relaxed, though Mr Feeley gave the impression that he had to support the world on his shoulders. The wedding was deemed to be a family affair so only close relatives were attending. Johnny had been given compassionate leave from the Air Force and arrived home on a forty - eight hour pass. Ossie told me his Auntie Jane and Uncle Eugene were coming over from Ireland for the wedding and this piece of news interested me. I still hadn't fathomed out what a shotgun wedding was, but then neither had Ossie and so I arranged to call at their house on Saturday morning on my way to the 'Co-ee' to see if I could make sense out of it on the actual day.

When I got there I found Ossie in the backyard brushing his uncle's black suit, which considering the amount of white hairs on it, looked as if it had travelled over on the cattle boat. His Uncle Eugene, a large red-faced man with a huge belly, came into the yard from the kitchen. He was wearing thick bright green braces, but there was no sign of a belt. There's no chance of him carrying holsters with a belly like that, I thought. A few minutes later Ossie's Aunt Jane came into the yard looking for the lavvie. Compared to her husband she was only tiny and despite the fact she had her hair tied up in a bun (like the women in all the 'cowies'), for the life of me I couldn't see any resemblance to Calamity Jane.

◆

We heard a car beep. 'The taxi's are 'ere,' Ossie yelled and I took off like a whippet, hoping to be first to see them pulling up by the lampost; taxi's were a rare sight in our street. I wasn't quick enough though, Mrs Bailey beat me to it. Doors opened, heads popped out and quite a few of the older women began congregating in groups.

Uncle Eugene came out of the house with Aunt Jane on his arm. You could tell they were Irish, they were the only ones that were smiling. Mr Feeley ambled miserably behind. He looked, as they say, as if he'd seen a ten bob note on the pavement and someone trod on his fingers when he bent down to pick it up. Mrs Feeley followed soon afterwards, quietly closing the front door. Teresa linked her arm while Ossie held up the rear.

With the front door now closed, some of us were wondering where the groom was, but Johnny, who after all was the reason for this memorable occasion, didn't bother using the front door with the rest of his family; instead he left by the backway, sneaking into the car when everyone was admiring Mrs Feeley's costume. The taxi's moved off in the direction of the Town Hall for the actual ceremony, but much as I taxed my brain I just couldn't remember there being a church in or near the town hall. There again I didn't know everything. Dad did, but I wouldn't dare ask. He'd only accuse me of being nosy when I was really being inquisitive. In the end I counted eight people in the taxi's, including Ossie and the two girls, and swiftly came to the conclusion that there wasn't half enough for a decent posse.

Ossie's house was strangely quiet that night; there wasn't a sound to be heard.I'd been to a wedding before; it was at Aunt Florrie's when our Mary married Bob. The 'do' then at night time had been great. Everyone enjoyed themselves, dancing and singing inside the house as well as outside in the street. The music had been loud and lively, with plenty of cakes and trifles for us, which, as you'd expect we scoffed as if there was no tomorrow.

But this 'do'? I just couldn't understand it myself. A wake was livelier than Ossie's brother's wedding.

'Mam ... what did you say a shotgun weddin' was like?'

'I didn't. Why?'

'Nothin's happenin' in Ossie's. It's as dead as a graveyard that's why.'

'They probably decided to have a quiet weddin' after all,' she replied.

Mr Murphy had been home three days before anyone realised. It was my eagle eye that spotted him first, though he didn't look any different to me; I couldn't tell he'd been in jail. True, his hair had been cut short, but apart from that he was full of the joys of spring and by the weekend was back to normal, drinking in the Piggy and whistling rebel songs as he passed Jock's house. There was no way that he'd had a barney with Mrs Murphy on his return otherwise the whole street would have known he was back from London.

One person who did celebrate the events at Johnny's wedding was Jock Smith, and not surprisingly he was in a right old state and could hardly walk up Cottage Street, let alone sing. Indeed, without Mr Bailey's help he wouldn't have made it home. Mrs Smith, taking advantage of the situation, dragged him through the front doorway and settled one or two old scores by clocking him a beauty that left him with a swollen black eye. Billy told us about it next day and with us being Catholics we swore on the Pope's life that we wouldn't mention it to anyone. Tucker also swore on the Pope's life, which was only fair, for after all his dad was a lapsed Catholic.

Moreton Shore

Moreton shore was perhaps one of the most popular places on the Costa del Mersey after the war period. During summertime folk with little money found it an affordable way to spend pleasant days at the seaside away from the grime of towns and cities. Trains and buses, full to capacity, arrived and within minutes the crowds would disperse carrying haversacks, tents, prams, go-chairs, footballs, cricket bats, skipping ropes and numerous other outdoor games, not forgetting food for the day. They converged in their masses towards two large fields and in no time these were transformed into a village of tents of all shapes and sizes. Clothes were swiftly discarded and replaced with bathing costumes of every variety. No one appeared bothered about fashions as they legged it over the embankment onto sands that stretched as far as the eye could see.

With dad not having regular work all year he bought a cheap tent from the Army and Navy store and we joined the exodus ourselves. After nine o'clock Mass we set off on our bikes to get a decent speck on the common. Dad rode in front with a haversack strapped to his back. The tent was in a kitbag hanging over a bracket above the back mudguard. I rode behind on our Bridie's bike with strict instructions to yell if the tent looked as if it was going to drop off. Forty minutes later we arrived. My legs didn't ache anymore - they were much stronger now after dad's unique fitness programme.

'Is it easy to put up Dad?' I asked after rolling the tent out of the kitbag.

'Course it is, any bloody fool can put a tent up. Watch me carefully - you may 'ave to do it yourself one of these days.'

'First of all we spread it on the grass an' air it out. Okay?'

'Yis dad, but worrabout the groundsheet?'

'Shush ... don't interrupt ... I'm concentratin,' he replied, trying to sort out different pieces of rope which were knotted together, some with metal pegs attached.

'Right ... whereabouts was I up to. Let's see. Yeah that's it, the guide ropes.'

'Worrabout the groundsheet dad?'

'Shurrup about the bloody groundsheet will yer.'

'Okay. Pass me those four wooden poles son an' see if there's two couplin's in the bag.'

'Couplin's! Worra they?'

'Those two metal rings ... look, there, in front of yer eyes.'

Dad joined the poles together, I was impressed. He somehow wangled them through the tent, guiding a nail on each pole through a tiny circle on the top. Standing back he seemed mighty pleased with himself. I was pleased for him too. After all he was showing me how to do the job properly. I appreciated that.

'Okeydoky... We now come to the part when I need your help Jim.' I was made up.

'I'll hold the front ... you take the back ... Okay?'

'Okay dad.' I couldn't hide my elation. Me and dad working together as a team.

Wait till I tell me mam ... she'll not believe it.

'When I say lift...lift...okay?'

'Yis.'

'LIFT.'

I lifted the pole, it wobbled a bit.

'HOLD IT ... HOLD IT.'

I held as tight as my four-foot frame would allow, but it still wobbled. Dad, without any problem at all, pushed his pole a couple of inches into the ground. Next minute he gripped mine and shoved that in as well. It stopped the wobbling and held steady.

He eased himself slowly to the front. The wind was getting up and his pole began moving. In sheer panic he almost swarmed up it, pushing it further into the ground and swiftly gripped the guide ropes at the same time.

'Where's the mallet Jim?'

'Erm ... er ... in the 'aversack dad.'

'It bloodywell would be,' he said, holding the guides tightly and slowly retreated backwards towards the haversack.

'Gorrit,' he gasped, easing himself to the front again.

'Throw me a couple of pegs, son.'

'I can't dad.'

'Wotcha mean, yer can't.'

'They're still in the kitbag.' I could tell he was getting annoyed, the way he glared at me.

He crawled back again, real commando style, the lads would have been made up if they could have seen him now. I was myself, but I didn't say anything just in case he lost his concentration and the pole fell down. I gripped my end even harder.

'Are yer ready ... now don't let go of your end ... hold it tight d'yer 'ear?'

'Yis dad, I've gorrit,' I yelled, feeling the adrenaline spreading through my body like molten lava.

He backed up ever so slowly, gripping the guides with one hand and the mallet and the peg in the other, while I held the pole tightly, stretching on my tiptoes for maximum height.

Without warning, my feet began leaving the ground. I was being lifted and suddenly I hurled forward right on top of the tent.

'CHRIST ALMIGHTY,' he yelled. I lay sprawled across the tent on my belly. I looked up. Dad's arms and legs were fluttering in the air, but I couldn't see his face or his head properly. They were hidden behind the saddle of the bike ... my bike.

I visualised the wallpaper saga in February and pictured him flinging my bike and screwing the tent up in a ball and flinging that too. Then another miracle occurred. They always seemed to happen to me when I was in peril. A young couple passing by intervened and kindly offered to help to put the tent up. Dad was grateful and humble.

'Thanks very much indeed. It's not easy when you're strugglin' with a lad this size is it?' he said. As expected I was to blame again. Ten minutes later I emptied the haversack while dad went to meet mam and the kids off the number twenty-two bus. I chuckled loudly.

'Are you alright lad?'   Startled, I looked up at a face peering through the tent flaps.

'Yis thanks.'

'Yer not goin' doo lally are yer?'

'I don't know ... I'm not sure ... I could be,' he laughed and was gone. Dad reappeared an hour later looking agitated and far from being amused.

'Have yer seen yer mam an' the kids?' he asked.

'Me..d'yer mean me?'

'Course I mean you. Who the bloody 'ell d'yer think I mean?'

'Oh ... er ... no ... I thought you were meetin' them?'

'I told your mam to catch the eleven o'clock bus, where she's gone to God only knows.'

There were literally hundreds of tents spread out across the field, many the same size and colour. A number had various flags fluttering above, providing perfect identification from the road. We were novices. Ours was just a khaki blob blending in with many more in similar positions, mam had no chance of finding us despite dad's meticulous instructions should she get lost. He suggested it might be an idea for me to go to see if there was any sign of them, but only after ensuring that I had my bearings right. Observing the number of telegraph poles from right to left and counting my steps to the roadway I was able to determine exactly were our tent was.

While I put my pumps on dad fiddled round with the primus stove, pouring methylated spirits into a small well and setting it alight with matches. It kept flaring up, going out, flaring up and going out. He added more meths, lit it again, it went out. He cursed under his breath, poured more in, it went out. Then in temper, he almost emptied the bottle, flooding the well. Some spilt setting fire to the grass. He stamped it out. I had visions of him blowing the tent and the field up. I couldn't get away quick enough and legged it as fast as I could, half expecting an explosion behind lifting me through the air towards the convalescent home opposite. Thankfully, there was no bang.

Mam was easy to spot. Even from the railway station I could tell her walk. She waddled along pushing the pram, with our Bridie, distinctive by her blonde curly hair walking one side and Bernadette the other. I ran up and joined them.

'Dads going mad ... he's waited hours for yer an' he's in a right mood,' I blurted.

'It's a pity about 'im now isn't it. All he's 'ad to do is put a daft tent up where as I've 'ad to feed the the kids and get them ready. Then the bus was full so we had to traipse to Park Station for the train. Just let him start me,' she said. 'He'll never hear the last of it.'

I never mentioned the performance regarding the tent. I could have done, but I knew it would do me no good, so I kept my mouth shut.

'There's our tent,' I said to mam whose face was red as a turkey with the sun and the weight of the clobber plonked on top of the pram. We could see dad a mile away.

He was still bent over the primus, stripped down to his vest, his bald 'half dollar' glowing in the distance. He had no success. The water was luke warm in the kettle. I knew he wouldn't succeed. He was dead unlucky with new or secondhand gadgets. Surprisingly he never cursed ... out loud.

'You've got to show people consideration when you're out 'ere,' he said, but I knew he was dying to bawl and shout and call the person he'd bought the primus from all the names under the sun. I was pleased at his consideration for others and sincerely hoped he'd bear me in mind in future when deliberating over his natural instincts. Seeing dad's change in attitude I volunteered to go for a pot of hot water from a cafe near the lighthouse, a fair distance away. My unselfish gesture allowed Bridie and Bernadette to see how far the tide had crept up the embankment, a mission I'd looked forward to carrying out myself.

After eating our butties and gulping bottles of watered-down orange juice, we enjoyed a game of rounders with a family from Walton who'd pitched their tent next to ours. Unlike us they were well organised, which impressed dad. He seemed pleased with the constructive advice given about all aspects of camping and I knew he was influenced, I could tell by his face. Our neighbour was also a docker and had positive views on life, giving them plenty to ponder over and debate during the day. Mam, on the other hand, naturally talked about kids and reminisced about days gone by. We ran around playing tick ourselves. Soon the tide ebbed and miraculously the common emptied. It was like V.E. day on the flicks as crowds shot over the embankment towards the cockle beds. We were first amongst the raiders and within a short period had as many cockles as we could carry, or possibly eat.

Dad announced at half six that it was time we made tracks. The tent came down much quicker than it went up, without any complications at all. After stowing everything in the kitbag we moved off.

'Good luck, maybe we'll see you again sometime,' said dad.
'Yeah I 'ope so. Good luck to you as well.'
'Ta ... rar!!'
'Ta ... rar ... see yeah then,' we all shouted.
'Nice fella that,' said Dad. 'You can learn somethin' everyday if you want to,' he declared when we were biking home. I was surprised at his declaration. I thought there were very few subjects he wasn't conversant with. Dad wasn't infallible after all.

Standard Four

As the summer holidays came to an end the main topic in our house seemed to be about Bridie going to Holt Hill Convent School. Apart from buying the school uniform, text books and a satchel, there were other items to consider and unfortunately dad was stony broke, a situation he'd never admit to anyone. Mam, like many other mothers, had little choice but to go into debt and on this occasion she managed to pursuade the cheque man that there were funds available to allow us to have one on the drip at five bob a week. Returning to school after the summer holidays, like Christmas, was always a peak period for issuing cheques. Regrettably, Bridie's uniform could only be purchased at Robbs, an up-market store, which, unlike Sturlas, didn't operate a cheque system. Dad, not one for admitting defeat, somehow struggled to buy the uniform and then cousin Sheila helped ease the situation a fraction when she passed on her used satchel.

As for me, I was easily kitted out. All I required was a new pair of grey pants and a shirt, but our Bernadette needed new clothes now that she was at the Lauries infants school, her enrolment adding an extra expense to mam's meagre budget. One other topic causing concern was the training of Kerry, the new pup. That was dad's department. He did all the training in our house.
Being in standard four meant this was my final year in the Lauries and those who possessed any academic aspirations, would, with a certain amount of luck, progress to grammar school or other colleges of further education. There was little doubt in my mind that I'd follow the path of the main stream and drift into the secondary modern school. Spud was different, he'd studied extremely hard and indeed turned out to be one of the cleverest in our class, inspired no doubt by his sister Mary's

success. He now used a smattering of languages such as French and Latin, subjects not taught in the Lauries, so presumably coming from Holt Hill Convent. Ossie thought that he was cleverer than Spud, but he was far from it and he didn't like it one little bit when Spud showed off by practising his limited French.

Such ability aggravated the life out of him, particularly as none of the Feeley's had ever won the scholarship, so Oz was more or less on his own with no-one in his family to turn to. Although I was blessed in having our Bridie as a role model and potential instructor, it was debatable that I would be able to learn much from her; our aspirations and objectives in life were in completely different directions.

For the first time since I'd started school we were about to be taught by a male teacher - Mr Robinson. Unfortunately for us he was still smarting from the abysmal Eleven Plus results his class had obtained in the previous year, a failure which was profoundly reflected on his personal tutoring methods. He made it quite clear and in no uncertain terms that he was determined to make up for his shortfall and there was little doubt, as far as I could see, that we were in for a rough ride during our final year.

My progress since I began school in Standard One had plummeted from a position of being tenth in my first year, to seventeenth in second and then slumped to thirty eighth place in my third. At this rate, I'd worked it out, I'd be fifty-sixth this year and there were only fifty two in class. I knew the onus would therefore be on me to pull my socks up, otherwise I could see myself ending up as dunce of the class and dad would never forgive me if that happened.

Even as the thought passed my mind I could imagine him saying 'a bloody dunce in the family ... I, Charlie Reilly, have reared a bloody dunce,' and then telling mam that I must take after her side of the family, because Bridie's obviously a Reilly through and through and there's no dunces on that side.

The thought bothered me so much that I vowed from that moment on to pay attention in class, not to day-dream and to do what dad instructed and shake my lazy bones in the mornings.

I knew there was no chance of me passing the scholarship, I just wasn't clever enough and besides I didn't want to go to St Anselms College, they played rugby there. I couldn't kick one of those funny shape balls if my life depended on it and I didn't know the rules anyway. Footy was my game and with a bit of luck I sort of hoped I'd be chosen for the Lauries school team this year.

Nacker was now at St Hugh's Secondary school, my likely destination next year. 'The Yosser's', being the only Catholic secondary school in town, always had above average football and boxing teams and it was in the latter sport that Nacker excelled; without doubt winning trophies was expected at St Hugh's.

Marlene, Ossie's new sister-in-law moved into their house after she'd had a row with her own mother. The Feeley's were fortunate inasmuch that they could manage to accommodate her, for unlike many of the 'two up and two down' houses in which the majority of their neighbours lived, they were lucky to have the luxury of a parlour and a lobby. Although slightly inconvenienced at first, after a little reshuffling Mrs Feeley eventually found room to squeeze Marlene into the downstairs room and from that moment on it was all systems go 'til the birth.

Ossie wasn't sure if he was going to be an uncle or an auntie, he said. The outcome depended on the baby, so he told us. Oz was more than welcome, for as far as I was concerned our Bernadette and Tommy were more than enough for me. I'd seen and smelt enough stinking nappies to last a lifetime. I remembered the time mam was breast feeding the babies and it definitely brought the worst out in her. She thought nothing of squirting milk over me for a laugh and seemed to find it extremely funny. I couldn't see anything to laugh about and later I'd end up swilling my face under the cold tap, that's how much I hated it. Ossie had it all to come, let's see how he liked it.

Dad on the warpath

'Don't use all those papers for the fire,' dad ordered when he began to train Kerry. The pup was only a few months old and was in the early process of learning where and where not to do her business. We knew that dad would have preferred to train an older dog to enable him to exert a little more pressure and save time teaching her right from wrong, but with a pup it was different. He only had himself to blame though. In his excitement at the prospects of Bridie passing the scholarship, he let his emotions rule his head and consequently we'd ended up with a very young bitch which hadn't even been doctored.

As usual we were expected to observe certain rules when dad resumed the role of animal trainer, and to obey his precise instructions. 'Don't feed the dog too much, especially last thing at night. Put her out in the yard before goin' to bed. Take her for a walk around the block in the mornin's. Pick your socks up off the floor an' don't leave anything around for her to chew. And leave the rest to me.' His first commandment almost spelt disaster for me and I came within a hair breadth of being skinned alive.

Dad decided to go to bed at nine o'clock because he had to be up early for work, while I was content to play with Kerry by the fire, harming no one. She was enjoying herself, licking my hands and sucking my fingers - trying to remove the last trace of the Blackpool rock, which Mr Griffith had given to me. It was obvious to me that Kerry was starving, so I said to mam. 'Look I can feel our Kerry's ribs.'

'James, you can feel everybody's ribs if you try hard enough,' she replied, not taking a blind bit of notice of me.

'Look mam she's starvin' an' she's nearly licked me fingers off,' I gasped, showing mam my spotlessly clean hands. This was a rare sight to me, let alone mam and she seemed convinced by this clinging piece of evidence.

'Give her a few spoonfuls of mince out of the pan, but don't forget to let her out before you go to bed otherwise your dad will go off his head altogether when he comes downstairs in the morning,' she replied. I poured a drop of mince on Kerry's plate and she devoured it within seconds. I was right, she was starving and so I topped her plate up a few more times and she scoffed the lot. If you've been starving yourself as I had many times it was easy to understand ravenous hunger. I still wondered where she put it though, for after all she was only a small pup and if I'd have eaten that much I wouldn't have been able to move an inch, but with Kerry there was no problem whatsoever. We went back into the front room where she curled up by the fire, resting her head against my sweaty socks. She appreciated me, you see.

I know dad always insisted that a dog has only one master, but I still couldn't see the harm in her having two. After all I had a different nature to him and I'm sure Kerry understood this in her own way.

Mam fussed around as usual before going to bed, filling the kettle and making sure the bread and marge were handy for dad's toast in the morning. Normally she was up bright and early to give him his breakfast, except when he was working over the water. On those occasions he always insisted on looking after himself.

Following the first of dad's instructions, I opened the back door to let Kerry relieve herself. She was scared of the dark and my heart went out for her because I knew how she felt and don't forget, I reasoned, she was only a pup. After squatting for no longer than a second she legged it back inside, the lure of the fire proving far too great of a temptation.

I carried out the rest of dad's orders to the tee. She'd been outside in the yard - the back door was bolted - I'd placed pages of the Echo all round the kitchen floor - I'd filled her water bowl and made sure that dad's old army great coat was down properly for her bed. What else could I do?

Mam said 'Good Night and God Bless,' before making her way upstairs leaving me with the responsibility of ensuring the fire was safe and everything was locked up. I gave Kerry a playful tickle and she responded by licking my hand. The fire was safe, yet still threw out a fair amount of heat. I don't know why, but seeing that she was enjoying the last of the fire, I thought it would be a shame to move her out into the cold and damp kitchen and away from the warmth of the front room. In a rash moment of childish affection I decided to let her to stay near the fire for the night; and to cover myself, I left the light on in the front room. At least then, I thought, she'll be able to find her way to bed, without worrying about the dark.

Feeling extremely pleased with my act of kindness I trotted up the stairs two at a time and climbed straight into bed, thankful that my feet were as warm as toast and for once I didn't need help from the oven plate. It's funny though, but later on I remembered saying my prayers that night and it was the first time in weeks. Maybe it was those that saved me. I'd like to think it was. If that was the case I might have prayed every night afterwards.

Usually I heard the stairs creak when anyone was on them, but not on this occasion. I was about to take a 'penno' for Everton when dad's voice blasted me from the land of dreams and nearly bounced me out of bed. 'MAGGIE ...WHAT'S 'APPENED TO THE LIGHTS DOWNSTAIRS?' There was no immediate response from mam, so he came bounding up the stairs like a tornado.

'MAGGIE ... MAGGIE ... have you gorr a shillin' for the meter?' he roared.

I sat up in bed, wide-awake now. By the sound of things she didn't have one and alarm bells began ringing in my head. She always put a bob in the meter last thing at night and I suddenly remembered I'd left the light switched on before going to bed. Dad bounced down the stairs cursing.

'WHAT THE BLOODY 'ELLS THAT?'

I slid my feet out of bed.

'YOU DIRTY STINKIN' LITTLE BITCH,' he yelled.

'Kerry ... it must be Kerry,' I muttered to myself. She was the only one downstairs. Then I realised she was alone with dad. I panicked and in desperation crept to the bedroom door. Everything had gone quiet. He hadn't trodden on her yet or she would have yelped.

'COME 'ERE YOU LITTLE SWINE AN' I'LL SKIN YER,' dad yelled suddenly. I heard the sound of the brush being flayed, followed by a pitiful yelp.

'GOTCHA, GOTCHA, I'LL BLOODY TEACH YER.'

I couldn't stand it any longer. I galloped downstairs just as he was about to rub her nose in it. The stink was terrible, but to have your nose rubbed into the mess must have been murder.

'Leave 'er alone she's smaller than you,' I yelled at her tormentor, before realising the enormity of what I was saying, and who I was saying it to. Dad dropped Kerry and glared at me in amazement.

'WHO D'YER THINK YOU'RE TALKIN' TO, YOU 'ARD FACE LITTLE SO AN' SO?'

I was speechless as he moved towards me, but my reaction wasn't. I shot upstairs and dashed straight into the front room. Mam was in bed. I didn't know if she was awake or not ... I prayed she would be ... where could I hide? I had only a split second to make up my mind. Behind the curtains? No, too easy to spot. In the wardrobe? No, he'd look in there first. I dived under the bed just as he burst into the room.

'WHERE IS HE ...WHERE IS HE?' he yelled.

Old Mrs Casey from next door rattled her walking stick on the wall, as she often did when things got a bit noisy in our house. Dad took no notice. Mam never moved as he looked under the bed.

'HEY YOU ... GERROUT FROM UNDER THERE,' he bawled, making a grab for my leg.

In utter desperation I kicked out, creating another disaster as my foot caught the pole, which slowly toppled over.

Just then the town hall clock chimed the half-hour.

'BLOODY 'ELL I'M LATE FOR WORK.' Dad clattered his way down the stairs again, yelling out what he had in mind for me when he came home. I crawled out from under the bed; breathing fast and sweating like a pig. Saved by the bell, or The Town Hall clock, in this instance... but only for the moment.

'Mam are you dead or what,' I cried. She moved her head to reveal the top sheet that she'd pushed into her mouth. Her eyes were wet, not with crying but with laughing.

I pulled my trousers up, slipped my braces over my shirt and went downstairs. Mam followed me down, which was just as well. She was lucky, I thought, with having no sense of smell; the stench very nearly knocked me over. It was so strong I almost vomited and to cap it all, I found that Kerry had vanished.

'James, see if anyone's light is on. '
She had to be joking, I thought. Everyone in our block would be awake after the noise this episode had created Still in my bare feet I walked round the court to see if Jock's light was on.

I was in luck. He was up and so I rattled the door.

'Hello ma wee man,' he greeted me, 'what are yerr doing up at this oor o' the mornin' and with nae shoes on yerr feet?'

'Dad's gone out in a sweat 'cos theres no lecky on,' I replied.

'Och ... ah ... see.'

'So 'ave yer got a shillin' for two tanners please, Mr Smith?'

'Aye ... course I have. Here ye are wee man, awa ye go and put yerr shoes on.'

'Thanks Mr Smith, I'll do that.'

I was back home within minutes and was pleased to discover that the house already smelt much better after mam had washed the kitchen floor using loads of Aunt Sally disinfectant. Our Tommy was crying for something to eat now and while mam made a pot of tea I slipped on my pumps and went looking for Kerry.

I found her in Cathcart Street, crawling round as four dogs tried to get at her.

'BEAT IT,' I yelled looking for a brick to throw at them. Cleary's horrible dog Dempsey was among the pack. He growled and went for me. Fortunately, from out of the blue a docker appeared and tried booting him. He just missed, it was a pity. I hated that dog.

The whole family was up when I arrived back home with Kerry. By now mam had set the fire and left it ready for me to light. She knew this was my job and I liked striking the matches and seeing that all went well.

'Can I stay off school mam?' I asked.

'Don't you think you're in enough trouble as it is, without anymore,' she replied

It was worth a try, I thought. I didn't expect her to say yes, but she knew what was on my mind.

'You'll 'ave to apologise to your dad as soon as he comes in, you know that, don't you son?'

'Yeah I know. D'yer think he'll kill me mam?'
'Well up to now he hasn't managed it, but you're runnin' out of lives and a cat only 'as nine,' she reminded me. I nodded, fearing the worst.

I had a terrible day at school. It seemed as if everything that could happen went against me. In the short time we'd been in Mr Robinson's class it became obvious to us all that he was what we called 'dead sly.' He appeared to know all our moves and there was no way we could kid him; even by pretending to write when actually we were doodling on bits of scrap or on our blotting paper.

I'd always experienced problems with smudges right from the day I'd started school and for some reason or other my handwriting was always particularly poor. Of course, being a sloucher never helped, for no matter how careful I tried to write, a blob of ink somehow replaced full stops at the end of each line whether I used a new nib or not. As a result I used more blotting paper than anyone else in class, an extravagance that appeared to infuriate Mr Robinson. Then again he just couldn't miss the footballers either. They were drawn on the blotting paper, quite creative, I thought; though Mr Robinson didn't appear to appreciate my artistic talent.

'Out in the front Reilly, OUT. Now show everyone your hands.'
I held them up. They were no different to anyone else's, four fingers and one thumb on each of them. Everyone scanned their hands to see if they'd caught whatever I'd caught, but they seemed as baffled as I was.

'Look carefully boys at Reilly's right hand, at his fingers in particular.'
Ossie stood up, leaning his big ginger head over Frankie Connolly sitting in front of him.

'I know sir ... I know worrit is,' he hollered.
'Snivellin' buggar,' I said under my breath.
'Good boy Feeley. At least we have one alert pupil in this class. Now tell the rest of us what it is you have observed.'

I was as curious as everyone else and was dying to know what mysterious infection I'd contracted. 'He's got ink stains down everyone of 'is fingers Sir. An' on 'is shirt cuff,' he added. 'That's right Feeley. Now Reilly hold up your exercise book.' I did as I was ordered. The whole class started laughing, just because I had smudges on each page. 'QUIET! Mr Robinson thundered. A full inkwell used in less than two hours Reilly. Little wonder that we are forever in need of funds from the Diocese.'

I could see that he was enjoying my predicament and even after he caned me he seemed to be still smiling with satisfaction. Ossie looked the other way as I returned to my seat, even though I glared at him.'What a mate,' I thought.

That afternoon I received another caning for dozing off. 'They'd doze off if they'd have been up as early as me and had the kind of day I've had,' I mumbled under my breath and I still had the worse to come.

Obviously I didn't dash up the street to welcome dad as I would have done in normal circumstances. Instead I skunked down the jigger in the hope of catching a glimpse of his face in order to see what kind of mood he was in before he got home, but I missed him. It seemed as if my luck had deserted me altogether and so, plucking up what little courage I could muster and taking a deep breath, I entered the house by the front way. No sooner was I through the front door than mam gave me the nod.

'You've got something to say to your father haven't you James?' Dad looked up from his paper. Instinctively, I noticed his belt was still on his waist. It was the first place I looked.

'I'm sorry for answerin' you back this mornin' dad,' I wailed, turning on the tears, a feat that by now I'd got off to a fine art after many earlier abortive attempts.

'I SHOULD BLOODYWELL THINK SO. If you ever, ever, speak to me like that again I'll tan yer arse so hard you won't be able to sit down for a week. NOW GERR UP THEM DANCERS SHARPISH! '

I did, without even pausing to say goodnight and God bless. I was happy to slip away ... happy that my luck hadn't deserted me after all.

Uncle Ossie

Mr Ryan was due home. It was more than twelve months since he set sail and in all probability this would be the first time he'd return without having the problem of remembering his newborn's name. During his absence his family hadn't increased, an almost surprising fact that didn't go un-noticed by our mother's, who were enjoying the last of the summer evenings, perched on chairs outside front doors and chattering away as usual. Nothing seemed to change much in our street except the speculation of these women and about the goings on around them.

'Perhaps he's tied a knot in it,' Mrs Bailey chuckled, nudging Spud's mam who came back with an equally sharp reply. 'There's no chance of Paddy tyin' a knot in his.'

'Nor my fella,' said Mrs Baines.

Mam joined in the laughter. 'Charlie's no chance of tyin' a knot in his either.' I was standing by the court and as the wind was blowing up the street I heard every word that was said; I was intrigued. 'Hey mam,' I shouted, 'me dad's good at knots, he can tie any knot you care to mention.' That's all I said, but my words of wisdom didn't go down too well. 'Scram big ears; quick;' mam snapped. She had that mean look on her face, so I shot off and headed for Ossie's house.

I could always tell when Ossie was pleased to see me by the way he put his arm round my shoulder when I walked up the lobby. He was moping a bit and told me he was fed up with all the palaver he'd had to put up with since Marlene had moved into their house. His mother was now talking of nothing else but the birth of their first grandchild and his dad was just as bad. Johnny didn't know how lucky he was, being far away in the Air Force, Ossie said.

What's more, he complained, there was Mrs. Smith to contend with. She'd hardly been off the doorstep since discovering that Jock was a personal friend of Marlene's dad. Day after day now she was back and forwards, bringing woolen clothes for the baby and every time she landed Ossie had to give his speck up on the couch. Having to sit on the floor all the time was getting on his nerves, he moaned.

Of course I sympathized, but told him straight that as far as I was concerned he still had the worse to come. He didn't believe me though, he never did at first and how could he know what it was really like with a baby in the house.

Dad always said there'd be no show without Punch and as usual was proved right; for the impending baby was now creating quite a show. Mrs Murphy, we learned, had joined forces with Father Morrisey in an attempt to pressurise Marlene into having the baby baptized a Catholic. Ossie's mother, however, refused to get involved; saying there was enough friction between Mr Feeley and herself over the birth of a child of a mixed marriage without complicating the problem further. Meanwhile, mam, heeding dad's advice, sat firmly on the fence, saying that the whole thing had nothing to do with anyone except the parents of the baby. Paddy Murphy wasn't as strong willed as dad and he sided with his wife. It was obvious to all those following the events with interest that Mr. Murphy had only done this to try to get back into his wife's good books and without anticipating the ultimate consequence, he'd backed her all the way. This added and unexpected support had given Mrs. Murphy the impetus she needed. What had started out as a minor difference of opinion soon developed into a full-scale screaming match, with Mrs. Murphy, Mrs. Feeley, Marlene's mother and Mrs. Smith as the protagonists, and the rest of the street unbiased observers. Craftily and in the best traditions of the church, Father Morrisey kept a low profile for the time being.

The squabble played right into dad's hand. 'Bloody religion, there's more wars through it than anything else,' he declared. 'It never bloody ceases to amaze me,' he continued. 'If there's a God up there he must be laughin' his socks off lookin' down at those daft buggers arguein' an' fightin' over where to baptize a child that's not even born yet.'

Mam didn't even condemn him for speaking about God in that way and this surprised me. I couldn't understand it, though what I really worried about was whose side I should take in the conflict between Smithy's, Ossie's and Spud's family. It could be one of the toughest decisions of my life. Of course, unlike grown-ups we kids never really fell out over stupid things like babies; there was more pressing every day problems to worry about now that the football season was well under way. A few days later Ossie came tearing round to our house screaming with excitement

'Mrs Reilly, Mrs Reilly our Johnny's 'ad a baby girl.'

'That's very rare Ossie,' mam replied with a smile. ' I'm very pleased to hear the good news. Tell your mother I'll slip across to see her later.'

Despite obvious pressures from both families, Johnny and Marlene went their own way by refusing to bow to tradition and decided to leave the decision of baptism until Sophie was at an age to make her own mind up. Their judgement remained a talking point for months to follow and for some strange reason Father Morrisey failed to appear in the street for his usual six weekly home visits. Dad rejoiced at his absence; he was able to enjoy his dinner in peace without having to make himself scarce by taking an early constitutional.

I seemed to spend less time with Ossie or Spud during certain months of that final year in the primary school. The fact remained that preparation for the Eleven Plus became a matter of the utmost importance to a minority of lads in our class; but for the likes of me, well I ran with the herd. Foolishly, I'd come to the conclusion that it would be fruitless for me to wear my brain out when I knew for certain that I had no chance of achieving a place in St Anselms. Miracles only happened if you prayed for them according to mam, and I was happy not to pray. Smithy and Tucker therefore knuckled down to their studies, with their eyes focused on the possibility of landing a place at either the Birkenhead Institute or Park High School, both prestigious colleges.

A strange kind of harmony appeared to reign in our house during the same period. Since Bridie had been going to Holt Hill we hardly had a cross word with each other and I became so intrigued by the strange sounds she made when she practised her French homework that I tried to join in. This unexpected turn of events even surprised dad, and immediately he set out to nurture my new-found enthusiasm.

'There you are son, you can learn anything if you want to,' he encouraged gently.

I didn't tell him, or mention to our Bridie that all I was after was learning just enough to show off.

'Parlez vous Francaise, Ossie?' I asked as I left his house one night.

'Worra yer talkin' about.'

'I'm not tellin' yer,' I smiled. That got him going.

'Stick it then.'

'Et maintenant, Oz, vous etes un oncle, n'est pas?' I'd spent some time practising that one.

'Are you mad or somethin'?' Ossie was clearly shaken.

'Au revoir Oz', I waved as I left

'Bugger off,' uncle Oz shouted as I ran off home.

Chapter 4

1949

'Well now Maggie, I wonder what this year holds out for us.' Dad was in a reflective mood at the beginning of January after mam had just given her verdict on events in the previous twelve months.

In mam's humble opinion, in the main 1948 hadn't really been an unlucky year, with the exception of the loss of our Jess whose demise was declared as nothing much more than a natural hazard and part and parcel of everyday life. There weren't that many dog owners in Brookie who took their dogs on leads, so the risk of an animal being knocked down by a vehicle on the main roads always remained quite high; and substantially higher if the animal habitually chased after lorries and cars like Jess.

It had also been something of a mediocre year for dad. Dock work had only been spasmodic, and so the New Year 'good luck' Coolie the year before had only been partially successful.

Unfortunately the New Year had started out with what dad considered an ill omen and was marred by the appearance of Uncle Fred. Judging by the state he was in when staggering into our house, he'd certainly been on the town and was well and truly plastered after celebrating his reinstatement to his job at the 'Corpy.' To cap it all and much to dad's annoyance, he set 'first foot' and let the New Year in. Mam wasn't too bothered about this however; he was tall, dark but not very handsome. Then again, as she said 'two out of three isn't too bad'; she'd settle for that.

Despite being cold January was a good month for us and there was no better place in the winter than the park. Days before our return to school, after the Christmas holiday, we'd trudged through the snow drifts that lay on the hills surrounding the lakes, before making our way to what we called The Rocks. This area was always a good speck for finding pieces of sandstone which we considered as good as anything to test the thickness of the ice formed across the lakes. After discharging these primitive testers which left gaping holes in the ice, we messed about until it was time to head for home and on the way, we threw snowballs at everything that moved. Before leaving the park and following our leader's instructions, we gathered a varied array of tree branches suitable for catapults. This was after Nacker had told us they were dead easy to make.

From the park entrance we made our way down Vittoria Street, heading straight to Smithy's backyard where Mr Smith's shed contained all kinds of weird and wonderful tools, mostly originating from Lairds. Without a shadow of doubt we felt this was the ideal place to make catapults. First of all we opened the jaws of the massive vice that was bolted down on Mr Smith's work-bench and by using fret saws and a jack knife we set about the task of trimming and shaping the branches. Within a short period of time we'd made more than enough frames for all the gang. From old shoes, which came from the time we were collecting rubbish for the bonfire, we removed the tongues. These would be used for the slings; however, the most essential part of the final product missing was the elastic.

As usual after the Christmas excesses we were skint, with not even a tanner to buy the elastic between the lot of us. It was Tucker who came to the rescue with a brainwave that found us slicing pieces of an inner tube from an old bicycle tyre that belonged at one time or another to Johnny Feeley. After a number of feeble attempts to stretch the tube and make it function like elastic the idea was found to be a complete waste of time and as a last resort someone suggested we should all return home to our respective houses, search in boxes and cupboards and seek out bits of elastic or even rubber bands (which were often used as garters to keep our mams' stockings up). We agreed to meet up later to report on how this part of the plan had fared.

The whole idea greatly appealed to my sense of adventure and so after eating my dinner as fast as I dared, I pretended to go out into the yard to play. I knew for a fact that mam usually kept a roll of elastic in her dressing table drawer, but this meant creeping upstairs on my tiptoes and hoping that on the way down I wouldn't bump into anyone.

Unfortunately the roll had strangely vanished, so while in the bedroom I tested a pair of mam's old garters, curious to see if they'd do the job and although I pulled them this way and that, testing their elasticity, they were too thick and tatty. Hurriedly I shoved them back in the drawer. 'There's no way I'd take those along,' I muttered to myself, 'and have the lads skitting at me mam'.

Monday had always been washing day in our house for as long as I could remember and following a weekly routine, mam I knew, always tended to dry the girls and her own knickers on the fireguard. Of course I'd never taken much notice of this before, but now that we were into catapults and the need for elastic was paramount, the whole thing became an altogether different matter. When the coast was clear I ambled over and picked a pair up, they were mam's. Using all my skills and guile and without drawing attention to myself I gently tested the strength of the elastic in the legs. 'Not bad' I thought. Surely mam wouldn't miss the elastic in one leg.

I was just about to test a pair of our Bridie's when dad walked in. Not surprisingly he almost took off on the spot. 'What the bloody 'ell d'yer think you're playin' at m'lad?' he bawled. I dropped the knickers in sheer panic.

'Nowt dad ...'onest ... I thought they were scorchin' that's all,' I gasped, but I knew he didn't believe me, I could tell by the way he was glaring. It seemed as if he always had a sort of sixth sense when I was up to something mischievious.

After tea I met up with the lads, congregated in Brookie under the lamplight, to report my failed attempt and was quietly pleased to find that no one else had been successful. During the conversation about how things had not worked out, I just happened to mention the strength of the 'lazzie' in mam's drawers, when Nacker suddenly interrupted, in a state of some excitement.

'I've gorrit lads, let's raid the clothes lines in Cottage Street,' he said. 'I'm sure we'll get some from there.'

He was a born leader, there was no doubt about it; he had a vision far greater than any of the rest of us could have ever hoped to achieve.

To accomplish our objective, it was decided that all that was needed was a pair of pliers, so after Tucker raided a pair from his dad's shed we set off on our mission. Starting at the bottom and working our way up the jigger, we crawled across the tops of backyard walls like silent assassins. Tucker and Smithy crawled on the left-hand side, with Nacker, Ossie and me on the opposite. Spud was a bit too fat to climb, so his appointed role was to 'keep nix' at the junction of the entries. We were so quiet even those using the lavvie didn't hear us. On one occasion when someone strained and broke wind, Ossie me-owed. It was hard not to laugh at the face he pulled; he was just like a big ginger tom. Not that I would have told him though - he was touchy at times about his red hair and freckles and in the past he'd been known to lash out.

We covered half of the jigger without success. There were loads of sheets and towels but no drawers. Then Tucker signalled - three low whistles - and we stopped crawling. Nacker beckoned with his finger and we both climbed across to the other side of the wall while Ossie dropped down to join Spud, that was the plan. Tucker pointed to a massive pair of knickers propped on their own, the clothes line sagging under the strain. Nacker edged slowly from the wall down into the yard, using the dustbin as a support, while I crawled on the dividing wall ready to carry the 'clouts' as soon as he passed them up to me. He'd undone the pegs but the drawers wouldn't move, they'd frozen solid to the line.

I quietly slid down the wall into the yard to join him and by each taking and dragging a leg we managed to free the drawers. Like the dried carcass of some old cow, the loot was then shoved over the wall to the waiting Smithy. Ossie and Spud set off at once carrying the spoils down the jigger together, unaware, until they reached the light at the junction, that they were holding the massive bloomers by the crotch. You'd have thought Spud had been electrocuted the way he reacted. Ooh ... FRIGGIN' 'ELL,' he yelled. 'I've 'ad me 'ands on them,' but it was only the shadow of the moon that fooled him into thinking that the crotch was a different colour to the rest of the knickers.

After Tucker had meticulously cut the lazzie from the legs and the waist, Nacker calculated that we'd got enough of the precious material for at least six good 'catties.' Having no use for what remained of the drawers, we decided to have a laugh and stood them behind Dobbo's backyard door, hoping his old man would trip over them on his way in from the Dolphin Pub.

A bobby on his bike appeared next morning in Brookie and stopped outside Mrs Turner's house. Jock Smith spotted him through the window and his first reaction was to wonder if maybe she'd popped off. Fortunately she hadn't. After a few minutes the copper came out of Mrs Turner's, walked over to where Jock had come out for a better look and asked if he'd noticed anything suspicious on the previous evening. 'If she canna tell ye, nobody else will,' he replied truthfully.

The cop approached Mrs Bailey, asking the same question. She couldn't help him, but with her usual cunning astuteness soon managed to find the nature of his enquiries. 'Someone was pinching knickers off clothes lines,' he told her. It seemed there was a pervert on the loose in the community.

When this piece of news eventually reached dad, he shook his head in disbelief.

'I don't know what the world's comin' to. It's a poor look out when decent people can't hang their underclothes on the line without perverts

pinchin' them. Personally I'd break them in two halves with me bare
'ands if I caught them,' he growled.

I remained quiet, not saying a word and just carried on eating my
meal. Suddenly he glared across at me as if he'd been stung by a bee.

'You wouldn't know anything about it would yer m'lad?'

'Me? Course I wouldn't dad.'

'Are you bloody sure?'

' 'onest dad. Course I'm sure.'

I knew he had his doubts by the way he scrutinised me.

'I'd rather 'ave a bloody thief than a liar,' he grimaced.

I didn't reply. I was a thief and a liar and knew my life wouldn't be
worth a bean if he ever found out.

Most folk showed a fair degree of sympathy for Mrs Turner and the
theft of her drawers, though not everyone shared the neighbourly
compassion for the elderly woman. Mrs Bailey for instance, jibed away.
'If she spent a little more time in the back winder, instead of huggin' the
front she might've spotted who pinched her drawers in the first place.'

Jock, however, took a much lighter view of events.

'Who ever nicked them deserves the George Cross,' he declared,
chuckling away

Dobbo's old fella, unlike Jock, didn't seem to see the funny side of the
situation. After consuming more than his usual quota of Guinness, he'd
left the Dolphin and began the short journey home along Cathcart Street
towards Brookie. Nipping down the jigger at the back of his house he'd
tripped over the propped up remains of Mrs Turner's drawers and almost
dislocated his knee. In a drunken stupor, his befuddled brain had
assumed that someone had left a sheet of cardboard against the entry
door and he staggered into his kitchen carrying it.

Unfortunately for him his wife had not gone to bed as early as she
would normally have done, otherwise he'd have got away with his
serious error of judgement. Being a woman of an envious sort of nature
she shot out of her chair and attacked him with a kitchen knife. Lady
Luck certainly shone on Mr Dobson that night, however, she missed
him by a mile and plunged the knife into his working jacket hanging
behind the door. The next day and within no time at all the whole of the
street had accused him of being the pervert. Frankie was delighted; he'd
waited years to gain retribution on Mr Dobson for the hiding he'd
received after the incident concerning Constable Jones's bike.

My eleventh birthday, the fifteenth of February, was no different to any previous one, except that I received three birthday cards which was at least one more than I had the previous year. I also received a new pair of shoes even though I'd have preferred a pair of shin-guards seeing that I was now playing for the Laurie's footy team. Down to earth as ever dad told me not to be a baby and to stick cardboard or comics down my socks like everyone else and not to be so fussy; but then he'd never played football and didn't even like it for that matter, so how would he know what it was like to get booted on the shin.

'You'll 'ave to buck your ideas up now m'lad seein' there's only a matter of months before your final exams,' dad remarked casually a few weeks later. Ever the super optimist, he still believed I had a chance of equalling our Bridie's success, but all his dreams were only pipe-dreams. I knew it, mam knew it and our Bridie knew it. Of course I had to appear enthusiastic, for he simply would not have tolerated me openly accepting defeat at this early stage, under any circumstances.

The eighteenth of March, the day after St Patrick's day, is a day still embedded in my memory. By that time of the year the worst of the winter would normally have been behind us, but a severe outbreak of frost at this late stage unfortunately inflicted extreme damage to the water main and drainage system in our section of Brookie. Consequently, the pipes supplying our lavvies were first to be affected and the water ceased abruptly.

In his haste to leave the frozen toilet, dad almost pulled the chain off the cistern as he tried to get it to flush. This caused the whole thing to crack and as a result buckets of water had to be carried to the lavvie every time nature called. It was an inconvenience he found most irritating and after weeks of moaning he finally confronted the landlord and a new cistern was eventually ordered.

On the day that the plumbers arrived I was wrapped up playing football for the Lauries and a cistern, old or new, was of no concern to me. Unfortunately Dad signed the book on that day and was off work and at home, which goes to show that fate plays lousy games at times. Curious by nature and suspicious of any strangers who came into the street, dad was just as wary of the plumbers and watched carefully as they removed the cistern in record time.

I was outside practising my right-footed goal scoring efforts when the plumbers uncovered my hidie-hole. Besides my old school report, two wizened conkers, mam's knitting needle, a rusty jack knife, a pigeon's egg (which was blown), tongues out of old shoes, a catapult and spare elastic were also revealed. The secret hoard amused the plumbers, but not dad, he was livid.

Carrying my report, the catapult and the elastic into mam, he plonked them on the table. 'Just look what that fella's hidden in the lavvie,' he bawled before reading my report for the first time.

'Christ Almighty ... 'Ave yer seen this Maggie?'

Mam, as faithful as ever, didn't crack on that she'd seen the report beforehand and acted out the innocent.

'What is it Charlie...what's up with it?'

'BLOODY THIRTY EIGHTH IN CLASS LAST YEAR!! AN' SAGGED SCHOOL WHAT DOES THAT SAY ... FIFTY TWO TIMES.? THAT FELLA WAS HARDLY AT SCHOOL MAGGIE.'

'I think he was goin' through a bad patch at the time Charlie that's all,' she replied, trying to calm the issue. 'He's been as good as gold this term, no trouble at all, accordin' to Mr Lally his headmaster.'

'It's no use you coverin' for 'im,' dad told her sternly. 'He's gone too bloody far this time. By the way, 'ave yer seen this?

Where d'yer think that's come from? I'll tell yer from where. From old Mrs Turner's knickers, that's where it's come from.'

'Don't jump to conclusions Charlie. That elastic could 'ave belonged to me.'

'Then he's a bloody thief.'

'Don't say that, he's just mischievous. It's a phase he's goin' through, he'll grow out of it.'

'Phase ... phase me arse. You're tellin' me he'll grow out of it. I'll bloody knock it out of 'im ...watch me.'

Mam sighed, giving Bridie the nod. Bridie responded by nipping outside on the pretence of going to the lavvie. Dad had the last word. 'Just wait till he gets in. He wont know 'is arse from 'is elbow when I've finished with him.'

Turning the corner from Vittoria Street, our Bridie came hurtling towards me, yelling, 'I wouldn't go in if I were you, dad's found your hidie-hole in the lavvie and he's goin' to batter you.'

I stopped in my tracks and my normal hunger pains that were driving me homewards mysteriously disappeared. My first consideration was to wonder what time would be safe for me to creep into the house without alerting dad, not a difficult task knowing how regular he was with his 'constitutionals'.

'Me dinner will have to wait,' I muttered to myself. This was something

I could afford to miss anyway and there was always Aunt Fan to rely on, if I could sneak past our house without dad spotting me through the window. I knew she'd feed me a butty and tide me over until the current crisis was past and that if by some chance I could persuade her to pay us a social visit, just a couple of minutes prior to my re-entry, it might be enough to throw dad off his stride. Having decided on this as a possible plan of action, I immediately began practising my scared stiff look, hoping that it would make Aunt Fan realise that her presence in our house could make a difference to me between life and death.

Creeping into Aunt Fan's presented no problem whatsoever, nor did scrounging a butty, but my 'frightened for my life' performance was just not going to work. She couldn't for the life of her help me out she said, because there were far more important things for her to do, especially as she had to take young Frank to the doctors.

As I anticipated, dad was in the lavvie when I made my re-appearance. It was a bit like a death-watch in the front room. Bridie had abandoned her homework and prepared to move to a safer position, while mam was hurriedly washing Tommy's face with a flannel. He, it seemed had sensed the air of anxiety hanging over the place and was screaming his head off. Our Bernadette was gazing at me with her big blue eyes. She was five now, but knew already, from past encounters, that the peace was about to be shattered.

I began edging towards the back kitchen so that I could sneak upstairs when disaster struck. In my haste to avoid capture I took my time and was undoing my laces properly instead of slipping off my shoes as I normally would. Those vital seconds proved my downfall and I walked straight into dad.

'GOTCHA YOU LITTLE SWINE, ' he roared.

I rapidly moved backward hoping the front door was still open, but my luck had finally deserted me. His belt was off quicker than Billy the Kid ever drew a pistol and before I even had time to blink he'd cornered me fast up against the front door.

'I'LL BLOODY TEACH YOU TO TELL ME LIES AND STEAL OFF POOR OLD WOMEN,' he bawled at the top of his voice.

I'd never seen him in a rage like this before and to be honest I wasn't too keen to see him like it again. Every time he crashed his belt anywhere near my vicinity I yelled, yet somehow he failed to make any direct contact with my body.

'NO DAD ... OUCH .... DAD ... DAD IT WASN'T ME 'ONEST ...

OW ... OW ... OW.' The belt buckle knocked flakes of paint from the front door. Mrs Casey from next door had turned her wireless down and I kept yelling for the entire world to hear. Our Bridie was crying (or so I was led to believe afterwards), while Bernadette went white as a sheet and little Tommy clung to mam, making it difficult for her to intervene. Kerry fled into the kitchen, perhaps wondering why she'd swapped the sanctuary of a dogs' home for a madhouse like this. Meanwhile I was screaming blue murder every time the buckle hit the door. To avoid his swings meant that I was swivelling my body back and forwards, out of the way of the large threaded bolt that held the door knob in position.

Now and again though, I felt it digging into my back and it didn't half hurt. I was terrified, even though I realised later that the belt had hardly touched me, but the noise was frightening. I'm certain dad knew all of this, yet it didn't matter to him. He was on a mission - he was in charge to control - as long as the effect served the purpose and his authority was asserted - all was well.

Mam finally grabbed the belt and I slumped to the floor clutching my back where the bolt had dug in. I was feeling for blood, but was disappointed; I couldn't find a trace to show for my injuries. All that I suffered, it seemed, was a slight scrape of broken skin. My face, however, was blotchy red with genuine tears and a few crocodile ones that had slipped in as well.

'That 'ill bloody teach yer,' said dad, satisfied that justice had been seen to be done the proper way. There were certainly no half measures in his book, for 'Spare the rod, spoil the child and suffer the consequences,' remained his philosophy.

When the dust finally settled and a semblance of normality was returned, dad scanned my report in detail. He was more rational now, changing his tactics and adopting a psychological approach in an attempt to eradicate the problems I'd encountered with my studies. I could have saved him hours of probing though, by declaring I was lazy and thick, but this would have caused more aggro. Instead I told him of my difficulties in understanding some of the lessons. This was the worse thing I could have said. I had now made a rod for my own back.

If that's the case son, we'll help yer. Won't we Bridie?' He declared in triumph.

Rebel

As soon as he'd eaten his evening meal dad had that look of determination on his face, a feature which usually spelt trouble for me. Mam removed the best table cloth, folded it and put it in the dresser drawer while dad rolled up his sleeves, placed pages of the Echo over a section of the wooden table and immediately ordered me to produce my exercise books for inspection, before assuming the role of tutor. Our Bridie, who had already taken a seat at the other end of the table, undid the straps of her satchel, removed her text books and spread all the fancy pens and pencils she'd acquired in front of her ready to begin her homework lessons. Meanwhile I fiddled around looking for the place where I'd hidden my homework, but to my dismay, mam discovered it dossed behind the bread bin.

'Right son, let's get started' said dad, removing my three thin grubby exercise books from a brown paper bag I'd found crumpled under the sink. He scanned my arithmetic book without making any sort of comment and then flicked a few pages of my composition book, tutting as he normally would when something didn't live up to his expectations. Finally he opened my history book and shook his head from side to side. 'Your bloody writing's a disgrace an' look at the stains 'ere. You've got ink an' grease over every bloody page. At times I find it hard to know who exactly you take after m'lad. You're certainly not like your father or grandfather ... the Reilly's that is,' he quickly emphasised. I looked over my shoulder at mam, but she was busy washing little Tommy's face and hadn't heard him.

'Me pen's no good dad, it's the nib, look,' I protested showing him the nib of my one and only wooden pen, with distinctive bite marks displayed on the other end. 'Rubbish, a good tradesman never blames his tools. Did you 'ear that our Bridie? Just give me one of your books over for a minute love,' he said. Glaring at me as if I was to blame for dad interrupting her concentration, she hurled her best writing book across the table. Dad opened her book, ignoring her show of temper and turned to me. 'Now that's what you should be aiming for Jim, neat and tidy and no excuses, so for a kick off I want you to buck your bloody ideas up. D'yer 'ear me?'

'Yis dad.'

The following night dad continued his torturous instructions with lessons he thought were decisive to improve my chances of enhancing my position in class. Although he excelled in subjects such as history and geography, religious and mental arithmetic issues were low on his priority list, or didn't appeal to his taste.

After a few weeks his educational regime began crumbling. Apart from stifling my natural instinct for freedom, the lessons began causing behaviour problems at school. I didn't know whether I was coming or going; Mr Robinson said one thing, dad said the opposite. I contradicted Mr Robinson, I received the cane. I disagreed with dad, I was sent to bed. I was in a no-win situation and that's when I decided to rebel, just like Nacker's hero, the outlaw Jesse James.

'Dad, what's thirty nine, minus eleven, plus eighteen, divided by two, multiplied by four?'

'How the bloody 'ell d'yer think I know!'

'Well, where did St Patrick come from then?'

'What d'yer want to know that for? What bloody good is that to yer anyway?'

Spud was right. This was the way to beat him. I'd memorised those questions all day, even though I didn't know the answers myself, nor did Spud; yet it worked.

'Sir..Sir, me dad told me to ask yer what ensign is flown on a ship of convenience?' I asked Mr Robinson next day.

'Ship of convenience?' he muttered, looking totally baffled. He didn't admit defeat straight away, but quickly changed the subject, stating that he was pleased that some fathers took an interest in their children's education. Spud beamed, winked at me and put up his thumb. His plan was working ... we were made up.

A few days later there were signs that dad's enthusiasm was beginning to diminish, as he grumbled about working all day and not having the time to read even the Echo before commenting. 'D'yer know what Maggie, I'm beginning to think I'm wastin' me bloody time an' effort with the other fella, 'cos I can't see an ounce of improvement in 'im whatsoever.' Mam didn't answer, nor did I. There was no point disagreeing or protesting. It seemed as if he finally accepted that it was far too late in the day for me to improve my bleak record; although if he'd have listened to me in the first place I could have saved hours of his time and hours of mine.

Bridie was pleased at dad's lack of interest and made it known, in her roundabout way, that she was bored stiff with the whole episode.

Bad habits continued to occupy my life over the following months, with jogging lorries one of my main weaknesses and trawling round the docks in school time, another I found hard to discard. Both were to be responsible for my ultimate downfall.

Tommy McCann, who lived in Hilton Street, asked me if I fancied taking a trip to the floating bridge after school to catch a few crabs which he said was the favourite bait used for fishing by his brother Billy. His older brother had recently taken up sea fishing and for company, as much as anything else, he'd promised to take us along with him to Egremont shore to show us how to fish for 'flatties'.

Despite crawling across the pontoons, a dangerous occupation under any circumstances (one slip and it was highly likely that we would have been swept out of sight into the Mersey), neither of us managed to catch a single crab.

By the time six o'clock chimed on the Town Hall clock, we both felt the fangs of hunger drawing us home so we called it a day and made our way in the direction of the traffic lights at the corner of Hamilton Square and Argyle Street. Although Tommy was much taller than me he knew that I was at least three months older than him, so when I suggested 'bumming' a lift down Clevie he agreed straight away.

This section of the Square with its decorative gardens and dense bushes provided a perfect cover to hide from observant drivers and was always considered, by most lads of the town, an easy spot to jog a lift. The lights were just changing to amber as a lorry approached, but without showing any intention of slowing down the driver recklessly accelerated and shot across the busy four lane junction, causing a posh sports car travelling on his inside to violently swerve and screech to a stop. We heard the driver of the sports car curse and watched him raise his fist in anger as the lorry sped away. However, we had a far more important mission on our plate as we crawled on hands and knees towards the back of the silver vision parked just yards away.

Crouching low we carefully eased ourselves onto the chrome rear bumper, feeling it slightly sag from the weight of our frames, but despite our cautious approach the driver for some reason or other glanced in his mirror, glared at our mucky faces and took off like a jet plane.

Even though the lights at Vittoria junction were changing to amber he ignored them. The next set at Duke Street were on red and instead of slowing down he drove even faster, just like a madman, flying towards the Penny Bridge at a hundred mile an hour, or so it seemed to us.

Within a matter of minutes we were speeding along the road to Wallasey village, lost in unfamiliar territory. Tommy who had been sobbing his eyes out since we'd shot through the North End was terrified and scared to death and I felt no better. Approaching the roundabout at Leasowe junction the driver momentarily changed gear and in what I thought was a moment of madness, Tommy released his hold on the spare wheel. I glanced over my shoulder and caught sight of a bundle, resembling a sack of rags, bouncing up and down the road like a jack in the box - it was Tommy.

The driver again accelerated and the car, with brakes now screaming and screeching, jetted towards Moreton while I frantically clung for dear life, gripping the spokes on the spare wheel for all they were worth. A lorry suddenly pulled out in front of us - we swerved - I lost my grip - flew through the air and landed on a gravelled footpath. I rolled like a rubber ball not feeling a thing until a poplar tree halted my momentum.

I lay for a couple of seconds wondering if I was dead or alive. A dog barked - glanced at me - cocked his leg and peed on the tree. This can't be heaven I thought. God wouldn't allow dogs to pee where they liked. Maybe it's hell.

Someone whistled and the dog waddled off. I moved my arm to examine my injuries. My head was still on that was the main thing, thank God, mam would have had a heart attack if I came home without that, I thought. Gingerly I checked my hands and was grateful to find that I had two, but my fingers were bleeding. My legs were in the right position. I lifted my left one first, it corresponded with my left foot and then I tried raising my right and thankfully that was okay. My elbows and knees were cut to ribbons and I had a lump the size of a duck egg on the back of my head, but apart from that I'd escaped relatively unscathed. There wasn't much left of my jacket, trousers and shoes, they'd taken a battering and were now in tatters; five miles from home, I was in right state.

I began the long journey hobbling like an ould fella with gout. I knew all about gout, Paddy Murphy had early stages of the disease, which he called 'a touch of the old salmon trout'.

A few passers by glancing at my sorry state wisely kept their distance. Who could blame them, very few people in their right mind would approach a scallywag in my condition.

I staggered on wondering how far Tommy was in front of me, half expecting to trip over him as I turned each corner. As darkness fell and travelling no faster than a tortoise, I realised it would be well past midnight before I reached the top of Brookie, let alone our end.

My befuddled mind started racing. I began thinking of home. First of all mam, she'd be worried sick and by now would have sensed something was wrong, dad, he'd be shouting and bawling and going even more hairless, but our Bridie and Bernadette would be rubbing their hands with the prospects of having more room in the bed. Our Tommy was too young to miss me but Kerry would, she'd miss me all right. She now realised that I was her real master.

With being so wrapped up in my own sorrows I hadn't given any of them a thought until then; I was sorry I had. I should have waited until I'd travelled a few more miles and then I wouldn't have had them on my plate as well.

Meanwhile, back home mam was in a frantic state. She knew I'd never miss my dinner, maybe a jam or dripping butty, but not my dinner. Dad came in at half seven and told her to stop panicking. 'He'll come round the corner any minute now, just wait and see.' Mam waited and by eight o'clock even dad began feeling uneasy. He nipped round to see Spud and then called at Ossie's house. They confirmed I'd attended school and gone crabbin' down at the floating bridge. The news startled dad. Ossie took him to Macker's house where they found Mrs McCann in a right state. Billy and his father were scouring the town looking for us, so dad tried reassuring her in the best way he could think of, by saying that Tommy would be alright with me because I was level headed. Ossie almost fell over and choked on the spot, he told me later; he'd never have thought dad capable of telling barefaced lies. By the time nine o'clock chimed, a number of neighbours were searching the streets around the park while dad and Mr Griffiths paid more attention to the dock areas. Nacker and Tucker tried our old dens, though the night was darker than usual and even Mrs Bailey gave her support. Standing in the middle of Brookie, she yodelled from the bottom of her lungs.

'JIMEEEE ... JIMEEEE ...' which, as usual, was a powerful enough signal. There was a good chance I might have heard, but no way on this earth could I have been able to reply.

When dad returned from the dock estate he was still reluctant to go to the Bridewell just in case I was up to mischief, so he delayed that option until all other avenues had been exhausted. This decision proved to be the right one, for unknown to him, Dobbo's old man, who had taken it upon himself to search the Corporation Road, found Tommy. As he neared Duke Street he spotted a small figure crouched against a telegraph pole and at first thought it was a tatty dog or a lost Guy Fawkes.

The tears were flooding down Tommy's face and he was so exhausted that he could hardly walk. Paddy, together with dad, carried him between them from our house to Hilton Street and on the way home he told them everything about our disastrous adventure.

At a quarter past eleven I staggered round the corner by Whartons garage, my feet as heavy as lead. I burst out crying. I couldn't help it. It was a spontaneous reaction. I was delighted to make it home and purely from a self-preservation point of view, I hoped that no one with a hint of conscience would dare batter or chastise a ragged, starving, bloodstained tearful lad.

I don't remember much about being found, my mind went blank again, it always did at critical periods in my life. I was lifted like a bag of spuds by Jock Smith, carried into our front room and plonked on the couch.

'By God wee man yerr in a tidy state,' he said, rubbing my head as if wishing me all the luck in the world, and at the time I felt as if I needed it.

Mam placed a bowl of hot water on the table and began bathing my wounds. Dad arrived home rather subdued. He was glad to see me, I knew by the look of relief on his face, although I still expected a severe reprimand. He sat down by the fire exhausted. Kerry licked the back of his hand and he didn't push her away even though she'd previously been licking her privates. He was so tired he didn't notice, otherwise he'd have whacked her one, he didn't like that sort of thing. I smiled, I'd seen her and she lifted my spirits enormously. Mam put some best butter on my lump and watered-down iodine on the cuts and scrapes. I jumped, not daring to yelp in case I disturbed dad who was now resting near the fire with his eyes closed. I devoured my dinner in record time and then dad stirred.

'I hope this 'as taught you a lesson m'lad,' he muttered.

'It 'as dad ... 'onest it 'as.'

I'd learnt my lesson all right. Never again would I be daft enough to jog a lift on the back of a sports car.

The bumps and scrapes, according to mam, were in need of medical treatment so early next morning she took me on the number six bus to the Children's Hospital. My wounds were painted with loads of iodine and I was given a few injections in my bum. Afterwards I attended the hospital twice a week as an outpatient and rejoiced, it was the first time I had a legitimate excuse for being off school.

During that period I was grounded and forbidden to play outside in the street after eight o'clock; I couldn't complain however, missing school more than compensated for my early nights.

Shrove Tuesday (duck apple night), Ash Wednesday, St Patrick's day, Lent and Easter passed by with all the usual drama associated with the Holy period. Meanwhile Mr Robinson relentlessly pushed to the limit those pupils of standard four whom he considered had serious claims for passing the scholarship and made sure that the rest of us benefited from his determined pursuit for a high success rate

Last year's abysmal record still hung over him and he, more than anyone, was aware that another bad result would see him off altogether. To satisfy dad's high set of standards, Kerry had now been thoroughly house trained in all aspects of obedience, but of course there was little he could do when she was on heat and attracting every dog in the neighbourhood. He implemented certain rules to keep her from following her natural instincts, such as locking her in the yard or back kitchen, but the door only had to be open a fraction and she was away. This lack of discipline infuriated dad, particularly when he encountered packs of stray dogs parked in front and at the back of the house as he arrived home from work. They soon scattered, however, when he bounced out of the house and charged at them swinging his belt like a demon let loose. After a while he got fed up chasing the dogs up and down the street and so did we.

He couldn't afford to have Kerry doctored and intimated having her put down. His threat, however, upset Bridie and Bernadette who complained that he was picking on her 'cos she was a girl, but I kept out of the argument myself. With being prime suspect over the disappearance of mam's shopping bag, I had enough on my plate. Shortly after my confinement period had elapsed I had been up to mischief again, but thankfully my Easter duties were behind me.

Rumours persisted that even more barges loaded with peanuts were berthed down the waterfront nearby and the temptation proved too much for a number of the local lads. As darkness fell I joined Nacker and a few of his mates from school and we headed for the docks. The barges didn't take long to find, or for the big lads to lift the hatch covers, but no one anticipated that the nuts would be half way down the hold and out of arms reach. As I was the smallest in the gang, one of the lads dared me to drop into the hold, fill the bags with one hand, cling to Nacker's legs with the other and pass up the nuts.

I was more than happy to agree to the challenge. Within seconds I'd leapt into the mound, grabbed hold of Nacker's legs and slowly began sinking into the nuts. Everything was going well; I'd easily filled half a dozen bags without too much of a problem and although up to my waist in nuts I wasn't a bit worried. Suddenly, out of the corner of my eye I noticed a movement to my left-hand side. Gripping Nacker's legs even more firmly I turned my head and caught sight of a couple of large rats scurrying in the dark. In sheer terror I dropped the bags, shoved my free hand into the nuts and grabbed hold of the bottom of my pants to protect my goolies at all costs. I had visions of the rats shooting up my trouser leg, biting my balls off, making off with them and then sinking without trace. Panic-stricken I yelled 'HELP ... HELP.'

'What's goin' on over there?' a muffled voice responded in the distance. The lads froze, unsure what to do for the best. From the shadows of an adjacent warehouse a dock policeman appeared, flashing his torch towards the barge. The sight of the bobby immediately stirred the gang into action and straight away they tried pulling me from out of the nuts. Their efforts were in vain though, for I was stuck and hardly moved. Nacker panicked, and without thinking of my plight began kicking out, whereas I clung to his legs, holding on for dear life. Meanwhile the policeman arrived at the scene and the lads scattered in all directions.

The copper grabbed hold of Nacker with one arm and yanked me out with the other. Tears swelled up in my eyes, more out of relief for being saved, rather than the shock of being caught by a copper. Woefully we stood on the quayside watching the policeman remove a notebook from his top pocket and begin wetting his pencil with his tongue.

Nacker looked across to me and nodded ... I nodded and then took off like an Olympic sprinter, dashing towards the railway lines near the beginning of the four bridges. Eventually I reached Brookie where I hid in the shadows of Jenkin's machine shop with my heart beating like a steam engine. A few minutes later Nacker joined me. He'd been chased along the Corporation Road and finally lost his pursuer after darting down the familiar jiggers between Hilbre and Lynas Street. Although we'd managed to escape from the copper, both our mam's shopping bags were lost during our getaway.

A few days later dad, somewhere along the line, heard about young villains playing on the barges and pinching nuts. Although I had a feeling in my heart that mam had her suspicions, she didn't over elaborate too much about her missing shopping bag.

'It'll turn up ... it always does. St Anthony's never let me down yet' she said to our Bridie.

'He'll need to perform a miracle to find that one,' I thought at the time.

Third time unlucky

The Whit holidays were now over and the big push for the final run up to the scholarship exam resumed. Spud and Ossie spent a number of evenings together going over different subjects, each hoping that their joint effort would help to achieve a grammar school place. Meanwhile I drifted along with the rest of the class, content with the prospect that my new secondary school would be Saint Hugh's.

Following the flack she'd received over the none-christening of baby Sophie, Marlene seemed as if she'd settled in quite comfortably with her in-laws, although a slight degree of friction could always be detected whenever Mrs Murphy happened to be in her company. Spud's mam, who wasn't the type for giving up the chase too easily, continued badgering Ossie's mother to twist Johnny's arm to have Sophie baptised in the Catholic faith, but her convictions fell on deaf ears. Mrs Feeley stubbornly refused to budge on any of the suggestions that Mrs Murphy thrust at her. Never again would she interfere in Johnny's affairs, she told mam.

The baby girl, born with the Feeley's features, red hair and freckles was, according to the family, the identical image of Ossie when he entered the world. Delighted with the compliment, he spent many hours pushing the baby round the park in a posh new pram despite having to run a gauntlet from the lads for being a sissy, but strangely enough the insults didn't seem to bother him one bit.

A week before the exams Mr Robinson dislocated his shoulder in an accident at home and although there was a certain amount of sympathy for our teacher, a minority of the class were elated at the news. The celebrations, however, were short-lived; to our dismay, Pop Lally replaced him. The headmaster, who had different methods of teaching than Mr Robinson, began by treating us as if we were all capable of passing the Eleven Plus. Then he discovered that a large number weren't as bright as he was led to believe and that's when he really turned the pressure on those of us who were inclined to loaf around.

During exam day an eerie atmosphere seemed to hang over the classroom and strangely enough not a word was spoken by any of the class. Mind you, with Pop Lally parading along the aisles between benches, glancing over huddled figures as if willing the nervous types, who constantly scratched their heads or picked their noses, to concentrate on the exam questions set before them, it was little wonder it was so quiet. I was as relieved as much as everyone else when the exam finally ended. Ossie and Spud were confident they'd done quite well and I was equally pleased that I performed better than I had in previous years.

Walking through the Lauries' school gate for the last time felt kind of strange, but the strangeness was soon forgotten as we raced one another down Park Street to begin our days of freedom. School days and exams were swiftly stacked to the back of our minds as we re-visited old haunts during the holidays. Now that our gang was back in action and the cricket season underway, the first place we headed for was a sloping pitch just beside the bandstand in the park. It was on this very pitch that our first full scale match was played and, like all games across the summer period, rarely ended until the sun went down.

Apart from improvised makeshift stumps and a pair of worn-out leather gloves, the only proper gear we possessed was a battered old faded red corky with distinctive teeth marks, souvenirs from scaly dogs that didn't know the difference between a tennis or a genuine cricket ball.

During the warm Sunday mornings of June, Tucker and Smithy, who were now accomplished players in the Boys Brigade, marched up and down Cathcart Street from St Peters hall. We hung round on the corner of Cottage Street and jeered every time Smithy belted the drum, even though his parents stood nearby watching their son's achievement with pride. This wasn't a case of jealousy on our part; we only heckled because we had nothing better to do.

As the heady days of June drifted into July, thirteen became unlucky thirteen for a couple of our closest neighbours. The day after the 'Glorious Twelfth' the melting pot finally boiled over in our street when Jock, still recovering from his previous day's celebrations, bumped into

Paddy Murphy near the Court and exchanged opinions which both found insulting.

'Who were you callin' a Fenian bastard last night?' Paddy growled.

'If the cap fits yerr ... you wear it' snarled Jock.

'Purr 'em up,' said Paddy. Within seconds coats were off, shirts removed and stripped to the waist they attacked each other with venom rarely seen on Saturday mornings.

'FIGHT ... FIGHT,' Frankie Bailey yelled. Dropping the game of marbles that we were engrossed in at the time, we dashed round to the field behind Brookie where the air- raid shelters used to be and stopped dead in our tracks; Jock was squaring up with Paddy and a circle of onlookers were baiting them on.

I was stunned - I didn't know who to shout for - I liked both of them, they were my mates' dads. I felt sorry for Spud and Smithy as they stood back with Nacker and Tucker unsure what to do for the best. Using my initiative I legged it home as fast as my legs could move; I didn't want to miss too much of the fight.

'Dad ... dad ... quick.' I yelled. 'Mr Murphy and Jock are fightin' on the dump.'

Dad was repairing his bike and didn't need much of an excuse for a break. As we trotted through the back jigger into Cottage Street front doors opened and women young and old strained their necks to see who was involved in the barney; and as expected, Mrs Turner's top window curtain was slightly ajar.

The crowd was roaring as we neared the venue, with some spectators perched on backyard walls and then dad, without slowing down, pushed his way through the circle surrounding the fighters; I was two yards behind, following in his shadow.

Jock was dancing around throwing straight lefts, ducking and diving, his footwork excellent. Paddy adopted a crab-type stance, swinging both hands expecting to catch Jock with a wild sucker punch. He appeared considerably muscular since the short break at his Majesty's expense, but Jock was equally as broad and at least five inches taller. It was a clean fight, no head- butting or kicking, which was to be expected, so dad didn't intervene. He was more interested in the styles and stances of the fighters. Like me, however, he didn't know who to support and so as a compromise resorted to shouting 'nice one Paddy' or 'well hit Jock' thus remaining neutral. Paddy hit the deck twice, dad winced.

'I told yer he's gorra glass jaw son, didn't I? He's bitten off more than he can chew this time.' Paddy glared, staggered up and struck Jock down with a mighty swing. The crowd roared. Dad was as surprised as everyone else. 'He's got lots of bottle that lad,' he muttered. I looked on, thinking to myself how opinions change in such a short time. According to dad, Paddy couldn't box kippers, was the horizontal champ, had bitten more than he could chew and now had lots of bottle. 'How did he expect me to make my mind up when he couldn't make his own up,' I thought to myself.

'COP'S ... COP'S' someone yelled. The fight stopped - spectators prepared to run. No one appeared. ' False alarm lads - its okay carry on - false alarm.' The fighters tore into one another again.

'WATCH OUT!' the bout stopped once more. Mrs Murphy and Mrs Smith appeared barging through the circle, twenty-eight stone of raw aggression between them. The supporters rapidly moved.

Paddy and Jock were both standing covered in blood and sweat, all anger seemingly dissipated.

'GET HOME MURPHY before I flatten yer,' Spud's mother yelled. Paddy shrugged, glanced at Jock, smiled, walked across and shook hands. 'No hard feelin's?'

'Nae hard feelings ... Yerr bone heided Fenian ... Ge' ye'sel cleaned up an' we'll go fae a wee swally.'

'Men,' said Mrs Smith 'they're worse than young lads.'

As inconspicuously as we could we slipped away. Before arriving at the jigger I asked dad what he thought of the fight, just to clear the confusion my mixed up mind was experiencing.

'A good draw would be a fair result,' he said.

'What d'yer think of Paddy now dad?' He knew what I was alluding to; I could tell the way he looked. 'He's still gorra glass chin an' leaves 'imself wide open, but he can certainly wallop, which is always an advantage.' I was pleased in a way with his reply. He at least acknowledged that Paddy was no easy walkover.

'The main thing son is that they shook hands. That's a good sign. Say your piece, air your differences and then forget about it. That's what life's all about, don't bear grudges.'

I was surprised at dad's philosophical points of view; distinctly contrary to those he previously possessed. In two short minutes he'd suddenly forgotten his ongoing feud with Mickey Bannister. They'd fallen out six years previously over a difference of opinion at the docks and were like two enemy warriors whenever they met; and what about falling out with the priest in the Lauries, he'd never been to church since. I didn't mention this either, he wouldn't like it one bit. Maybe he was mellowing. I kept that thought to myself too.

When tar bubbles began rising between the cobbles in the street, a few of the older residents predicted that the beginning of July was showing signs of being the hottest time for some years. For ventilation purposes most neighbours left their doors and windows fully open to allow what little fresh air blowing through the town to cool down houses.

During this hot period dad was working at the East Float, sweating it out on a vessel unloading flour and was due home at half seven. As usual, as soon as the ships' sirens heralded the end of day shift the main streets leading from the docks would be crammed tight with dockers hurrying home.

Brook Street, the third street from the dock estate, couldn't have been more conveniently situated for dad's workplace and was just a matter of a few minutes walk away from home. Most nights, if playing nearby, I made a point of meeting him as he turned into Brookie. I'd then retrieve his hook and gallop down the street swinging it above my head like a tomahawk.

Sometimes, I wandered across to the other end of town and missed him, as I did on this occasion. I'd been having a great time with Ossie, messing about near Miller's scrapyard in Adelphi Street. Later, when balancing on top of the old railway wall opposite the yard, I slipped and scraped the crust off a large blistered scab on my right knee. I'd never seen so much blood in my life. Holding my breath I watched the blood ooze down my leg and within seconds it had covered my socks and shoes. With tears dripping down my face I hobbled home as if gangrene was about to set in straight away. It was beyond me how such a small leg like mine contained so much blood.

'D'yer think me leg will fall off before I get 'ome,' I cried to Ossie as we passed alongside the Devil's Church in Price Street. He mumbled 'Our Johnny loses more blood shaving.'

'But Johnny's older an' got longer legs.' I snapped. He didn't reply ... he didn't have to ... I could tell by his attitude that he was in one of his funny moods and I was wasting my time talking to him.

Both of us heard dad's booming voice as soon as we reached Arrowe Place. 'With luck I'll see yer later Jim,' Ossie said, before walking on ahead of me.

'Yeah I hope so,' I shouted to him. I heard mam defending me as I neared our front door.

'Forget about it Charlie, just for once. He's been in enough trouble lately as it is.'

'He wants a bloody good tanned arse that's worr he wants,' dad's famous medicinal remedy rang out for all to hear. I stopped outside Aunt Fan's, wondering whether my survival instincts remained intact or if they'd drained out with all the blood I'd lost walking home.

Suddenly I lost my nerve and took the cowardly way out by asking Aunt Fan to help me walk the last few paces home. I hopped on one leg across the short distance between houses, this to my way of thinking always looked far worse than hobbling. Aunt Fan laughed just like mam would, although I couldn't see the funny side of it myself; particularly with not knowing what I was supposed to have done this time.

We opened the front door and dad glared. I just about managed to hobble inside and glanced at the scab hoping it was still pouring with blood. I was sick as a parrot though; for some reason my leg had stopped bleeding. Still, I was confident there was sufficient dried blood to convince dad that I was seriously hurt. As I entered the front room he totally ignored my wounds.

'WHAT'S THIS?' He bawled, holding a brown square shopping bag similar to mam's.

'Er ... er ... erm ... it looks like a shoppin' bag dad,' I stammered. Then it dawned on me, it was a shopping bag ... it was mam's. St Anthony had only answered her prayers, the lousy sod, and dropped me right in it.

'GET UP THOSE BLOODY STAIRS...RIGHT AWAY.'

'But worrabout me leg it's hangin' off',' I cried.

'GET GOIN' BEFORE I TAKE ME BELT OFF.'

I stumbled past mam, crying my eyes out. 'You'll all be sorry tomorrow when I've got no leg and you have to push me round in a wheelchair like old Mr Connolly up the street,' I whimpered.

By the middle of July, with the constant sunshine on our backs, we were as brown as berries, except for Ossie who was as red as a beetroot and as Spud remarked, had more freckles than the whole of the Feeley's put together. Nacker, like his dad, was tall and thin and had darker skin than any of us; he was also the fastest runner in the gang. Sometimes we ran, sometimes we walked, as he led us on outdoor activities to every swimming pool in the area. The furthest we ventured was Hoylake baths, then New Ferry, New Brighton, The Guinea Gap, Byrne Ave and of course our local Livvie baths. Needless to say we were all fairly

decent swimmers, having learnt from an early age that if the docks held
no terror you could swim anywhere.

Late July and early August always remained the months when news
of the scholarship results were announced in the local paper, the
Birkenhead News, and invariably sales increased as families eagerly
scanned the columns for names of pupils with high hopes of passing for
grammar schools. On this occasion, however, dad didn't show as much
enthusiasm as he had during previous years, although in a way he was
still interested to see how the rest of the lads went on.

There was good news for Spud and Ossie who passed with four others
from the Lauries, a figure delighting Mr Robinson; nine percent was
considered more than a reasonable success rate for his conscientious
effort. Smithy also won a scholarship to Birkenhead Institute, so out of
our gang, with the exception of Nacker, only Tucker and myself failed.
I was happy for the lads and quite pleased with my achievement. Dad
was happy for Ossie, Spud and Smithy, but unhappy with me. It would
have been a waste of time telling him I didn't want to go to St Anselms
in the first place, even if I possessed the brains, which was obvious to
everyone except dad that I didn't. I rejoiced, on the sly of course, but
my-couldn't-care-less attitude really annoyed dad.

He'd never let sleeping dogs lie and had a slightly different way of
persecuting and picking on me for my failure. The Echo printed an
article about gangs of lads breaking into lifeboats of vessels berthed in
the docks and receiving borstal sentences. He immediately brought up
the subject about stealing from barges and hinted at my particular
involvement. Finally he mentioned the mystery of how mam's shopping
bag happened to walk over the four bridges to Wallasey, all on its own,
as he put it.

'See that m'lad,' he said, pointing to the article in the Echo. Three years
in Borstal those lads are getting for pinchin' lifeboat rations so you'd
better liven your ideas up about who you knock round with in future,
d'yer 'ear worr I'm sayin'?'

'Yis dad,' I cried. I thought I'd heard the last about my near fatality
down the docks, but the bag had returned to haunt me. It wasn't fair, just
because I'd failed my Eleven Plus he was having a go at me and my
mam never said a word.

At one time or another during most weeks Mrs Murphy popped in to
see mam for a social visit, gabbing about the Church functions or family

problems, but the topic on this occasion was Paddy's latest escapade on the building site after he'd been sacked for drinking on the job. Spud had already told me about his dad so I drifted outside to join the lads, who were having a competition to see how long they could hang by their arms on the lamposts' cross-members without dropping off. It was the kind of game that stretched your arm muscles to the limit. Nobody got the chance of winning though, for if someone approached anywhere near the record, those watching would try to pull your trousers down, so you were left with no alternative but to let go of the bar. Spud was hopeless; he'd only hang for two seconds, whereas Tucker, who was long and skinny, and despite the fact that he was now wearing glasses, could hang all night just like a monkey.

Later that night we were larking about in the Court having a game of bum ... tit ... tit, doing no harm to anyone. All we did was sing bum ... tit ... tit ...bum ... tit ... tit, play the ukulele, touching our bums together, then chest and pretending to stretch our mickeys and twang them, that's all. Well that's all I did anyroad. Ossie couldn't have possibly stretched his, not down his short pants, they were much too tight above his knee and Spud couldn't reach his properly with his fat belly. Tucker didn't even try stretching his; he was too close to home, while Smithy, like me, also pretended to twang his mickey.

Frankie Bailey, however, slipped his out, but it was so small that we couldn't even see it, and as far as we could tell someone using a magnifying glass would have struggled. Not for old Mrs Turner though, she came outside screaming blue murder about young lads exposing themselves while their parents spent their time in pubs or in other people's houses. Within minutes the street was up in arms.

'You wicked old bitch,' Frankie Bailey's mother screeched. 'You're discreditin' young innocent boys with your big evil gob.' We stood nearby wondering whether to leg it away from the scene and leave the grown-ups to sort it out, but in the end we decided to stay and face the music.

'Shush' said Mrs Murphy cocking her ear towards the window.

'Something's goin' on outside Maggie,' she added, grabbing her coat and bowling into the Court like a tank on fire. Mam ambled behind carrying our Tommy. Mrs Smith, followed by Jock with shaving soap on his face, came to their front door. Tucker's mam, with Pixie in her arms, drew the curtains across and looked out of the window. Ossie's mam and dad had taken the baby for a walk to Marlene's house and missed all the drama. Dad and Mr Griffiths were still working, whereas Paddy was picking his winnings up from the bookie's runner in the Piggy. The rest of the neighbours who were interested in the 'shouting match' stood at open doors.

'What's goin' on ... what 'ave you been up to our Timothy?' Mrs Murphy demanded.

'Nowt mam, we were only messin' about doin' nothin' 'onest.'

'It's that vindictive old bitch over there sayin' the lads were exposin' themselves,' yelled Mrs Bailey. Jock stepped out of his doorway. 'Ye what! Dinnae make me laugh ... exposin' the'sels ... grow up woman they're only wee laddies. It's a good job yerr dinnae stay by the Dolphin bar, yir'd have something tae complain aboot then.'

Mrs Murphy's face went white with rage. 'Don't you dare suggest that my son's exposed himself,' she bawled at Mrs Turner who was now looking the other way

'Don't you know that my son's a chosen one and had the call to be a priest?' she went on. Spud turned around to us with a huge beam on his face and bowed. I began laughing until mam clipped me across my ear and told me to behave myself.

'You'll laugh the other side of your face if your dad gets wind of it,' she threatened.

Long after Mrs Turner slammed her front door conversations continued between Mrs Murphy and Mrs Bailey. 'First she 'as the cops round over her drawers gettin' nicked an' now she's on about the lads pullin' their willies out. What next?' said Frankie Bailey's mam.

'Frustration. 'Cos she's on her own.' Mrs Murphy concluded.

The incident was forgotten until next night when dad arrived from work in a right mood, demanding to know from mam 'what was going on,' and why he'd only learnt about it second-hand from Mr Griffiths as they were unloading a ship for the Blue Funnel Line.

'It's nothin' Charlie, it's not even worth talkin' about. Just an old lady with nothin' else to do but gossip an' make things up.'

'There's always two sides to a story Maggie, you know that, and there's no smoke without fire,' he carried on.

He was off again. Why couldn't he give me the benefit of the doubt like Mr Griffiths or Jock or Paddy or even Nacker's dad?

'I want a quiet word with you m'lad,' he said.

'Quiet word,' I thought. That'll be the day, the neighbours will rejoice if he resorted to those tactics.

'What's this I'm hearin' about you messin' about in the Court? What were yer up to anyway?'

'Nothin''

'What d'yer mean, nothin'? You must 'ave bin doin' somethin'.'

'We were only playin' bum ... tit ... tit, that's all.'

'Bum, tit, me bloody arse. You're eleven year old now; when are yer goin' learn to 'ave more bloody sense?' I looked at mam and put my head down. Then dad roared.

'Gerrout of my sight before I start.' I did, sharpish.

As I stood outside the kitchen window stroking Kerry, I heard dad's booming voice announcing for the umpteenth time about the wayward path I was taking.

'I've had more than enough of the other fella Maggie. He's knockin' round with the wrong crowd. Tellin' me bloody bare face-lies, then pinchin' from the docks an' saggin' school. He'll end up in bloody jail the way he's goin' on and it's up ter me to stop 'is game once and for all.' Mam didn't reply. I heard dad enter the kitchen so I moved as quick as I could into the jigger.

Final straw

It was obvious to me that something out of the ordinary was happening in our house, because every time mam and dad were talking together conversations abruptly stopped as soon as I appeared. 'Go out an' play with your mates,' they encouraged, which I found unusual to say the least. As a result of my suspicions I decided to put my earlier commando training to the test. Sneaking from the yard into the kitchen I lifted the latch without making the slightest sound; this was something I'd accomplished better than anyone. The only problem was our Kerry, she always whined whenever I came in from outside. As a precaution I thought about locking her up in the lavvie, but my heart wouldn't let me. She'd have died of fright if dad suddenly changed the time of his constitutionals. I could imagine the commotion that would cause if he walked in and found her lying on the lavvie seat.

He wouldn't have stood for that. He was dead fussy about who sat on the seat, it was something to do with the spread of germs. There was little doubt that I'd get the blame for trying to train the dog to use the lavvie instead of taking her for a walk. This was too much of a risk for me to take.

I asked our Bridie what all the secrecy was about, but she didn't know either, although in fairness to her she shared my concern that something strange was taking place.

'P'raps mam's havin' a baby,' I suggested.

'Don't be daft,' she said. She knew all about those things, I didn't, besides I wasn't interested. Mam seemed worried and upset and looked as if she'd been crying. As soon as dad nipped outside to the lavvie I approachd her.

'What's the matter mam?'

'Nothing son, it'll all come out in the wash no doubt.'

I didn't know what she meant or what would come out in the wash. I'd left nothing in my pants, my hidie-hole had been discovered; there was very little else for me to doss, all my secrets were now out. It couldn't possibly be me they were talking about, I thought. That night I heard my name mentioned again. It was me.

'I've had enough of the other fella Maggie and it's for his own good, trust me,'dad's voice boomed.

'You can't do it Charlie it's not fair on him. He'll be all on 'is own, besides think of the neighbours an' the priests, there'll be an uproar. You'll be an outcast Charlie Reilly.'

'Bugger them, d'yer think I'll lose any sleep over them? No way. I'll do what I think's right for my kids an' no-one on this earth will tell me otherwise,' he bawled.

My feet were rooted to the floor with my heart racing ten to the dozen. I was even sweating and that was with just standing still and listening. 'What's going on? Where was he sending me to?' My mind galloped on. Then mam began speaking again.

'I'll never be able to look me neighbours in the face, an' worrabout our Fanny an' Julia an' our Florrie, they'll go mad an' hit the roof.'

'Well they're goin' to have sore heads aren't they? Or else end up in the loony bin, one or the other.' He always had to have the last word. I heard mam sobbing so I coughed, opened the kitchen door and walked in.

'How long 'ave you been standin' there m'lad? I bloodywell hope you 'aven't been listenin' to me an' your mam talkin', dad growled.

'No dad I've only just come in. Our Kerry will tell yer, she always barks, yer know that.'

'Don't talk bloody soft, bark me bloody arse. This fella's goin' worse Maggie, what did I tell yer?'

'Worr 'ave a done now?' I yelled.

'Oh shurrup an' act yer age.' He picked up the Echo, rustled a few pages, folded it noisily and began reading. Mam looked at me and sighed.

'I'm goin' out,' I muttered, deliberating for a second whether to slam the door or not, but decided otherwise ... I'd only be compounding my troubles, whatever they were, I thought.

A few days later when Ossie and Spud paraded their blue blazers and caps, I realised that mam hadn't taken me for my school uniform and it was only three weeks before I started at the 'Yossers.' 'Mam when are we goin' for me new school uniform?' I asked.

'You'd better speak to your dad first James, ask 'im it's all 'is fault.' Our Bridie looked across and I detected a kind of sadness in her face as if she knew something and for a change, she wasn't gloating. 'What is it mam, go on tell me please,' I begged.

'Your dad will tell you properly when he comes in from work. All I'll say for now is that he doesn't want you to go to St Hugh's.'

'WHY!! WHAT FOR!! WHERE AM I GOIN' ?' I yelled.

Mam was crying, so was Bridie and then our Tommy started screeching because he was hungry. Our Bernadette was the only one with dry eyes.

'He's not sendin' me to an approved school is he mam?' I wailed. For the first time that day I noticed a slight twinkle in her eyes.

'Course not. D'yer think I'd let 'im do that to you, it'd be over my dead body.' She wrapped her large heavy arms round me hugging me close. A couple of large safety pins in her pinny stuck into the side of my face, but I didn't feel them, I was too upset and could hardly see with my eyes being puffed with crying.

Although the sun was shining I stayed indoors. I couldn't face my mates, not until I found out where I was being sent to. Spud called and mam said I wasn't well. She wasn't telling lies either, I wasn't well. If I had have been, I wouldn't be crying all the time. Dad had a lot to answer for when he came in from work, mam would see to that. She'd definitely have a long face on her, that's the least that she'd have. That would spoil his dinner I thought.

Dad arrived home just after half seven looking quite pleased with himself, whistling away as if he didn't have a care in the world.

'How's thing's?' He said to mam. She never answered.

'Don't tell me you've gorra kipper on yer again,' he muttered.

'An' what's the matter with you m'lad? Why aren't you playin' out with yer mates?'

'I dunno' I cried. 'Whereabouts are yer sendin' me dad ... worr 'ave I done ... what's goin' to 'appen to me?'

'CHRIST ALMIGHTY, it's a right lively 'ouse I've come 'ome to here,' he bawled, 'I've been out since seven this mornin' I could bloodywell do without this lot.' He was in a right mood, I could tell the way his face suddenly changed.

Mam slapped his dinner down so hard on the table that the gravy shot over a plate of bread and butter. He glared and she glared back. I whimpered, picking my nose for attention.

He finished his dinner, sat down, pulled his pipe out, puffed a couple of times and didn't even bother reading the Echo. After a few minutes of silence he turned to me.

'Right m'lad, I've decided to send you to Hemingford Street School instead of St Hugh's.'

I stopped crying ... I felt the colour drain from me ... I couldn't believe my ears.

'God forgive yer Charlie Reilly. You should be dam well ashamed of yourself,' mam scowled. I was still in a state of shock, I couldn't speak. I began crying again.

'Don't you start again Maggie,' dad said to mam. 'It's this fella I want ter speak to, just give me five bloody minutes okay? As I was sayin' you're goin' to Hemingford Street whether you like it or not, so you can cry till your hearts content, you're goin' an' that's it.'

'But it's a Proddy school dad, I'm a Catholic, worr am a goin' do? ' I yelled.

'Learn to stand up for yourself, that's what.'

'It's not fair Charlie Reilly an' you know it. I'm dreadin' facin' the priest, he'll go hairless, an' the Canon, he'll 'ave somethin' to say about it as well,' mam yelled. She was trying all her moves. I appreciated that. 'Maybe the Canon will change his mind,' I thought.

'The Bishop might also get involved,' she continued.

'The Pope can for all I care. He's goin', an' that's it.'

'You'll never 'ave any luck speakin' like that about the Holy Father,' mam yelled tears running down her face.

I knew then that all was lost. I went upstairs, lay on the bed and thought about stowing away to sea. Nacker would know all about it, he knew everything about ships. I slipped my jacket on and sneaked out through the back door.

'Stephen' I yelled up the lobby. Mrs Ryan popped her head round the door.

'What's come over you Jimmy Reilly, I've never known you to call him by his Christian name before.'

'I'm eleven now Mrs Ryan an' I've bin told to act me age.' She laughed.

'I'll get 'im for yer now Jimmy.' Nacker came to the door pulling his jersey over his head which was so tight that it flattened his nose like a boxer's.

'Nacker, can yer do us a favour?'

'Yeah worr is it Jim?'

'Can yer 'elp me to stowaway ter sea?'

'Bloody'ell worr 'ave you bin up to?' I told him the score. He was the first one to know and was shocked.

'You can't go ter Hemmie you're a Catholic ... you'll get murdered.'

'I know. That's why I need your help.'

He told me about a couple of lads from the North End who'd stowed away on a ship berthed in the docks. They climbed into a lifeboat and gave themselves up when they were well out at sea because their food rations ran out and they were starving, he said.

'Worr 'appened, did they end up in America?'

'No, they were only out in Liverpool Bay, the lifeboat brought them back an' they're now in Borstal.'

'So if you're goin' make sure you've got loads of grub with yer.'

'Fair enough Nacker I'll remember that,' I said.

I wondered then if I'd be better running away from home instead to London or Manchester. Maybe Mr Feeley would let me sneak on the train without a ticket. He was a practising Catholic; he'd know what I was going through.

I hadn't told Ossie or Spud yet. Mrs Murphy would take off like a bottle of pop; she was still annoyed over Sophie not being baptised in the Lauries and here's me, one of her son's best mates being forced to become a Proddy and against my will.

Paddy wouldn't like it either, he thought a lot of me I could tell; he used to spar with me in their backyard. I didn't dare mention it to dad though, just in case it made him jealous. I'll also call an' see Jock, he'd know what to do for the best, he knew loads of things and perhaps even suggest that I go to Glasgow. ' I could even learn to speak Scotch and then no one would recognise me,' I thought. And what about Tucker's dad, he was a lapsed Catholic, maybe in time I'd become one of them myself. I'd have to ask him if he'd help me.

All these things were going through my mind at once which couldn't have been good for my brain, although I knew that I'd have to put up with them for now, for I was torn between the devil and the deep blue sea.

Spud and Ossie couldn't believe my misfortune when I told them; Tucker and Smithy laughed, they thought it was dead funny.

'Fancy you becomin' one of us,' Tucker grinned 'and after givin' up all those things for Lent an' all the times you've had to go ter mass an all that,' Smithy added.

'He's still a Catholic,' replied Spud raising his voice above their laughter. Ossie didn't say much, he was a deep thinker, but after a while he came up with a solution.

'You'll 'ave to be a Proddy durin' the week Jim an' a Catholic at the weekends.'

I was more content then. 'I could live with that situation although it might cause problems on Holy Days of obligation, but I'd worry about that when the time comes,' I said.

Later that day we played cricket against a team from Patterson Street, followed by a game of 'ollies down the gutters of Vine Street. After the game ended I nipped home for a butty and found a mothers' meeting taking place in our front room. I didn't dash in straight away; I knew they were gabbing about me, so I walked in on them.

'Ah here's the poor little fella now,' Mrs Murphy gasped. Ossie's mam, Mrs McCarthy, Mrs Duffy and mam were all supping tea round the table, plotting my reprieve and dad's downfall.

'I'd get Canon Morrison to him if I were you Maggie,' Mrs Murphy suggested. Trust her to go for the big gun I thought, she doesn't believe in the small shots. Mrs Feeley favoured Father Nugent who was old and wise and down to earth.

'But he's stone deaf,' said mam. 'Charlie's bad enough with me bein' hard of hearin', he'll go doo-lally altogether if he had to bawl at him.' They rapidly adjourned the meeting when our Bridie reported seeing dad coming down the street. I thought they were wasting their time myself, for once dad made his mind up a legion of soldiers wouldn't make him change it.

Father Nugent called but dad was out. As usual mam thanked God. She was afraid of dad losing his rag and swearing. If he had have done, it would definitely put the lid on her hopes and prayers that some day he'd return to the church, although sending me to the Protestant School tested her faith and belief to the limit.

Reluctantly I traipsed along with mam to Sturlas for my uniform. Some of my mates from the Lauries were trying their new blazers on so I hid outside. When the coast was clear I slipped inside. Hemingford Street School's name had now changed to Hamilton Secondary Modern. It sounded posh to me, although I didn't feel very posh at the time. I tried a blazer on and couldn't get out of the store quick enough, even without waiting to tell mam which canister held her cheque.

Dad was in his favourite position when we arrived home, his feet spread-eagled across the fireplace though the fire wasn't lit; a pity, I wickedly thought.

'Ah you're back. Let's see what you look like in your new school uniform Jim.'

I slipped my grey pants on, they almost touched my knees, then my shirt, socks and shoes and finally my black blazer.

'Worr about your tie an' cap? ' Dad said.

'I can't wear those I'll look a sissy,' I moaned.

'Don't be so bloody stupid, put them on.' I did. 'That's better. What d'yer think Maggie? That's about the smartest he's ever looked.'

Mam nodded, she wasn't very happy at all. In Sturlas, she'd seen a couple of churchgoers from the Lauries when she collected my blazer. She was so embarrassed her face went crimson.

'I could 'ave fell through the floor when I bumped into Mrs Gary when you were trying that blazer on,' she said to me when we were leaving the shop together.

'How d'yer think I feel mam I've got ter wear it.'

'I know son. Your Grandmother would turn in her grave if she knew that you were goin' to a Protestant school.'

'Worra bout Aunt Florrie and Aunt Julia, they'll go mad as well when I tell them.'

'It's best not to tell them for now James, your dad will explode altogether if anyone else interferes.'

'Serves him right then, if I tell them.'

Secondary school

Monday morning the second of September 1949 was a day I'd have preferred forgotten. After a restless night I was woken at seven by dad and told in no uncertain manner to rise and shine and not to forget what he'd drummed into me the night before. Forget, as if I could. I lost count of the do's and don'ts during the hour-long session I was forced to endure, little wonder my head was spinning. I was relieved to go to bed out of the way even though it was still light outside.

It didn't take me long to get ready for school and by eight o'clock I was pacing up and down the backyard wondering what kind of day was ahead of me. Mam worried herself sick because I hadn't eaten my breakfast, but I couldn't face food, my stomach was turning with nerves. She knew it was serious; I'd never refused food before, not my toast anyway. After getting Bernadette ready for school mam began fussing with my hair, I hated her putting a quiff in it like a Nancy boy. I preferred it wild with my fringe flattened down over my forehead, the same as the older lads.

As usual our Bridie was dressed in her Holt Hill Convent School uniform, her blonde curly hair contrasting with the brown hat she was wearing. She kissed mam on her cheek before leaving and then glanced at me feeling sorry for myself.

'Don't let anyone pick on you and call you names Jim, stand up for yourself,' she advised.

'I will, don't you worry about it.' She meant well. She knew how I felt, even though at times we fought like cat and dog. Our Bridie was okay. I knew she was clever and in a funny way was proud that she passed the scholarship, although I'd never dream of telling her.

'It's about time you left son otherwise you're goin' to be late for school,' mam reminded me at half eight. In a tantrum I threw my cap onto the floor, pulled my socks down, put my head in my hands and yelled 'I'm not goin' ... I'm not goin' there.' Mam placed her hand on my shoulder and pulled me close.

'I know it's hard for you son, but for my sake please go.' She had tears in her eyes so how could I let her down. I picked up my cap, stuffed it in my pocket, gave her a hug, looked up and down Brookie and dashed into Charles Street before anyone had a chance to see me.

Slipping my blazer off I rolled it up and stuffed it under my arm and ran along Clevie until reaching St Werburghs parish. After passing alongside the Stork Hotel I turned into Conway Street and could see the imposing red bricked school almost in sight. I was relieved to get as far without bumping into any of my mates from the Lauries.

I looked through the railings and scanned the playground hoping to see a friendly face, but didn't recognise anyone familiar. 'If only Tucker's dad had allowed him to go to 'Hemmie' instead of Tollemach Road School I wouldn't be worried now,' I muttered. Plucking what little courage I had left in me, I eventually strolled through a small gate and fell behind a group of pupils who looked as confused as I was. We entered a large assembly hall and were immediately surrounded by a number of masters who scurried around separating new intakes from permanent ones; it was chaotic.

After a short while, a Mr Jones, form master of 1A, came over and ushered us into an empty classroom. I was in strange surrounds with new classmates, feeling extremely vulnerable and out of place.

Most of the morning I hardly opened my mouth except to answer my name and state which school I came from. When I said St Laurences everyone turned round. I looked straight ahead. I wasn't going to say anything unless they called me a 'cat lick.'

Just let them try I thought to myself. It wouldn't take me two minutes to call them 'Proddy dogs.' Nobody said a word though. I knew then that it was just curiosity. You couldn't blame them for being curious, I knew all about curiosity myself.

Whenever I was curious mam used to say 'curiosity killed the cat.' I often wondered why dad didn't practice curiosity like me, then he could have seen off the moggies who'd fouled our air-raid shelter, but I never got round to asking him.

Each class at Hamilton was divided into a four-house system, Cook, Drake, Nelson and Scott, aptly named after famous explorers. I was lucky to be placed in Drake section whose colour happened to be blue; it was a good omen for me. Blue was my favourite team's colour. I couldn't have got off to a better start.

During the afternoon the headmaster, Mr McIntosh, sent for me. I didn't know what to expect, I 'd done nothing wrong. What if there's been a mistake, I thought, and what if I shouldn't be here after all? Or maybe Canon Morrison's phoned and told him that with me being a Catholic I was supposed to go to St Hugh's where all the lads from the Lauries who'd failed the scholarship went. I was elated. I could just picture dad's face when I told him that I was going to the Yossers after all, he'd be as sick as a parrot with a hairlip.

He wouldn't be able to argue about it either, not with the Canon and Mr McIntosh on my side, they'd be far too smart for him. Then what about my uniform, I forgot about that. The shirt and trousers would be all right, but my cap, blazer and tie would have to go to Bentleys and be 'popped'. Mam would be happy, particularly during the week when she was skint.

With springs in my heels I bounded up to the headmaster's office, feeling confident that he must have realised the miscarriage of justice I had suffered and of course, the trauma that I'd been put through. He was just the person to put things right.

I couldn't help noticing how spacious his office was. Standing by the door I glanced inside not feeling in the slightest bit nervous.

He was sat at his desk, dressed in a grey striped suit and was even bigger than me sitting down. Again I wasn't bothered, for that was also in my favour - no one would dare argue the toss with him I thought.

'Come in and close the door,' Mr McIntosh commanded, his voice dead strong, not a bit like Pop Lally who stammered now and again.

'You are James Reilly, is that correct?'

'Yes Sir,' I almost shouted, sticking my chest out and standing up straight, holding my shoulders back like my dad always told me to do whenever I was slouching.

'Welcome to Hamilton Secondary Modern School.'

'Thank you Sir.'

'The reason I've sent for you Reilly is to reassure your parents that you will not be expected to attend morning assembly or take part in Religious Instruction lessons.

Your father has told me that you come from a strong Catholic background and are a regular churchgoer, am I right to assume that is correct?'

'Yes Sir.'

'All we are interested in, at this establishment, is your education. If, however, you have any problems, whether big or small, feel free to come and see me. That's all for now Reilly, return to your studies with Mr Jones.'

'Yes Sir.' I stood for a minute debating whether to tell him about my troubles, but before I had chance, he put his head down and began reading some reports on his desk. As he seemed to be busy, I decided to wait until he had a bit more time on his hands and then I'd put him in the picture about the way I'd been treated, which was real lousy, I thought.

agree with his decision. However, Aunt Florrie had an entirely different point of view and seemed quite annoyed at the way that I'd been treated. 'I'll get in touch with your Aunt Julia straight away an' we'll come down an' 'ave a word with your father,' she promised. At last I felt that something was going to be done about my plight.

A week later the delegation arrived at our house. Trust dad to be working in Bromborough. He arrived home with a right sweat on. The bus went without him at Bromborough - he was caught in a heavy downpour and soaked to the skin - and to cap it all, his dinner had burnt in the oven. With such bad luck, I knew at once my fate was sealed. They didn't stand a chance. Hemmie it was ... Hemmie was where I was staying.

Religious Philosopher

During the first few months at my new school I altered my ways and became quiet and subdued. This change in attitude allowed me to develop a routine to walk on both sides of the fence without offending either. Apart from my usual fear of bumping into my mates from the Yossers as I walked to and from school, there was also mass on Sundays to contend with. To crown it all, the priests called frequently to our house on home visits, which to my way of thinking seemed more often than before, courtesy of Mrs Murphy, I suspected.

At school I sat alone in an empty classroom during morning assembly, nevertheless I heard every word spoken, even though, subconsciously, I tried not to learn the prayers or hymns. The hymns and the music I found similar to ours and reasonably pleasant to listen to; and this fuelled my curiosity even further. Dad always accused me of being nosy, but he didn't seem to realise I was the same as everyone else, just inquisitive that's all, and as he was responsible for me being here in the first place, I could see no harm in determining the difference between Protestant and Catholic prayers and hymns.

If I was going to be half 'n half or a lapsed Catholic I wanted to know what I was letting myself into from the start; anyone in my predicament would want to. During the following weeks I watched and listened to everything uttered regarding religious subjects. After a short time I felt confident that I was in a position to make my own judgement.

The Proddy's kicked off with the Lords Prayer, the same as we did in the Lauries.

'Our Father which art in heaven ... Woah ... hold it ... we say who art in heaven, that doesn't sound right to me; still, I suppose I can live with that. I listened intently, word for word; I was just about to say Amen when to my amazement they carried on with the Lord's Prayer after it should have finished. They'd only added, 'for thine is the Kingdom, the power and the glory, for ever and ever Amen' haven't they? 'Hey that's not on,' I muttered to myself. We had the 'Our Father' first, according to the scriptures. They had no right whatsoever messing about with it like that. I also noticed that they said 'A'...men, we say Ar...men; still that's nothing worth worrying about, it's only nit-picking, but something's got to be done about the Lord's Prayer, I thought. Then again, suppose they're right and we've got it wrong? I'll have to sort that one out on my own ... in me own way,' I mumbled.

I waited for them to pray to Our Lady with the Hail Mary, but for the life of me couldn't hear it. 'That's strange,' I thought, we rattled off ten at a time, no bother at the Lauries. Maybe there's not enough time or perhaps they've said it during religious instruction lessons, which of course I didn't attend. Their hymns were better than ours though. They were in English, much easier to understand than Latin.

I then wondered if I should see the priests and explain that the Protestants were one up on us and whether it would be possible to change our hymns from Latin to English so that we could all understand what we were singing about and draw level. On second thoughts I decided to mention it to mam first, seeing she was the most religious person in our family. With me being in a position to see both sides, Father Nugent might think I was getting too big for my shoes instead of being helpful and of course, I didn't want to give him that impression, or to upset him at this stage.

On my way home from school I decided to take a peep inside St Peter's Church seeing that I was a pupil of Hemmie. It wasn't a sin. I was allowed to go in there now, but to be on the safe side I made sure that I kept my school blazer on, just in case the vicar recognised me from the Lauries. He may have remembered when we threw stones at one another and called each other names. We didn't know any different then - well I didn't myself, but now I did. If they started throwing stones there'd be nothing I could do except to stand in the middle and get pelted from both sides, for I was neither one nor the other; I was just an in-between.

I peered into the vestibule and was surprised to discover that there were no fonts with holy water, so I eased open the main doors and you could have knocked me down with a feather; the church was completely deserted. The least I'd have expected to see would be one or two old ladies praying, as you'd always find in the Lauries.

Silently I closed the door behind me and crept on my tiptoes around the back of the church, passing dark shadowed pews, which were dead creepy. On my right hand side I noticed a large baptismal font and wondered whether I'd be allowed to dip my finger and bless myself before kneeling down. I wasn't sure - you see - I didn't know the rules yet. If a baby were going to be baptised the parents wouldn't want my dirty fingers in the water, not with having liquorice on them anyway. I decided not to bother and instead walked up the aisle, knelt down and blessed myself. There were soft pads to go under your knees, not like the Lauries, which were hard and wooden, so to be honest I didn't mind kneeling on them.

I wasn't sure whether I was allowed to pray or not, for after all I only knew Catholic prayers which might get me into all sorts of trouble; it's better I say nothing, I thought, then no-one could blame me for starting a war between the two religions.

I imagined Jock walking down the aisle in the Lauries and kneeling down and praying. There'd be murder. Mrs Murphy would collapse on the spot. I could see Paddy stripped to the waist, shadow boxing outside the crypt and Spud lecturing me about the trouble I'd caused. That's without the priests and Pop Lally and the rest of the teachers getting involved. No, it's safer I see all and say nothing, I decided.

I wandered up the aisle to the altar and couldn't help noticing that there wasn't a single confessional box. I just couldn't believe my eyes. 'Wait till I tell Ossie, he'll swear I'm telling lies. He'll want to become a Proddy just like me,' I thought.

I glanced round the church, there were loads of statues of Our Lord, but not one of Our Lady. I scratched my head; I couldn't make head or tail of it. 'That's another thing I'd have to find out about,' I whispered to myself.

I was just admiring the altar when a voice roared 'GOOD AFTERNOON.' It's a good job I'd been to the lavvie otherwise I'd have been hosed out in disgrace. Shaking like a leaf, I tentatively eased my eyes around, but couldn't see a soul. Feeling goose pimples rise at the back of my neck I wondered if it was the Devil, or God, or both.

My teeth were now chattering and knees knocking. I wasn't sure whether to leg it as fast as my legs would run and then for some reason I glanced up above the doors. Two huge eyes stared down like a tawny owl. It moved, I went to open my mouth to scream. He beat me to it. It was the vicar.

'Hello young man, I have been observing you for a short while,' he said. 'Are you interested in the church?'

'Well ... er ... er ... sort of Father.' I couldn't think what to call him, I was too flustered.

'Oh I see,' he said, climbing down some secret stairs hidden away in the corner, which unusually for me, I hadn't spotted beforehand.

'So you're a new boy at Hamilton Secondary Modern School?'

'Yes Sir' I replied. I couldn't be wrong calling him Sir, could I?'

'You weren't a pupil from Cathcart Street, were you young man?'

Er ... no Sir. I went to the Lauries to be truthful Sir.'

'And you're now seeing how the other half live?' I didn't reply. I couldn't think of anything else to say. The vicar smiled. 'What's your name young man?' He asked.

'James Reilly Sir.'

'Well James, anytime you are passing St Peter's feel free to call in and say a little prayer. After all this is the house of God and everybody's welcome.'

'Thanks Sir,' I replied. 'I'll remember that.' I walked out feeling six foot tall and almost collided with a heavily built lady who was standing in the vestibule. She smiled, I smiled back. 'Hello dear,' she said to the vicar, kissing him on the side of the cheek. I couldn't believe my eyes, 'that's something I've never seen in our Church,' I thought. I was now completely mixed up and no wiser whatsoever. 'Still it's early days yet. There's plenty of time to find out and make my views known' I said to myself.

I arrived home whistling, this was the first time I'd been happy since starting at Hemmie.

'You're in a good mood James.'

'Yeah, well I'm learnin' things now mam.'

'Good, I'm pleased to hear it. You're just like me you are son, easy goin', that's what you are,' mam said, her grey blue eyes sparkling, always a sign when she was happy. Bridie glared, so I began humming another of the hymns I'd heard at school.

'He's hummin' Proddy songs again mam.'

'The more you take notice the more he'll aggravate you, ignore him.' Bridie put her head down and continued writing. I ambled alongside and nudged her arm. She screamed and hurled her homework book at me.

'Missed,' I grinned. Mam rushed towards me. I was too quick though, and fled into the street, clutching my jam butty, feeling as happy as Larry.

When mam was alone and everyone had gone to bed, I sought her advice about the problems I was encountering with determining the differences in religious beliefs; just so that I could decide for myself who was right and who was wrong.

She was unable to help me over my query about Our Lady and was at a loss to understand why Protestants didn't pray to the Holy Mother like we did, but, bearing in mind, they probably had their own prayers she said. That seemed reasonable to me. After all why shouldn't they have their own prayer book if we've got ours? I mentioned the Lord's prayer, but she couldn't see any harm at all in adding a few extra words. We'd do the same if we wanted to claim it solely for ourselves, she said, and I had to admit I fully agreed with her opinion. The tricky question however, was the fact that the vicar could get married. Mam was foxed. She couldn't for the life of her see how they could do the job properly and be married at the same time. I couldn't myself.

'Worr if it was allowed in the Catholic Church mam, an' say dad became a priest?' I asked.

'Holy Mary Mother of God,' she said, laughing and blessing herself at the same time.

'It's not impossible mam, you know worr he's like for gadgets an' ideas an' all that.'

'Don't get silly ideas into your head James, your father would be the last person on this earth who'd be a priest, believe me,' she said.

I wasn't so sure myself. If he was signing the book, you couldn't put it past him to try his hand at anything, I thought.

I lay in bed and imagined dad walking down Brookie dressed in his black suit, wearing a dog collar and the kids flying in saying 'here's Father Reilly coming,' and what about about his visits to the Murphy's and Spud's mam snivelling. Dad wouldn't have any time for that sort of nonsense; he wasn't one for snivellers. I could vividly see him telling Paddy off about his fighting.

'You're leavin' your chin wide open Paddy, keep your guard up an' throw straight lefts.'

It was great dad being a priest. I couldn't sleep properly thinking about it.

Ah! I almost forgot. What about confession? Now that would be murder for us. You could possibly be in church for weeks saying your penance. Ossie and Spud would go mad; I'd have no friends at all.

'On second thoughts I don't want you to be a priest dad,' I yelled.

'Shut up Jimmy an' go asleep, you're keepin' us awake,' our Bridie moaned.

A few weeks later Spud and I were walking with his mother down Cathcart Street, carrying her shopping bags from Rostances. As we passed alongside St Peter's Church the vicar walked out of the door and recognised me. Waving to me he shouted across the road, 'Hello James when are you calling in to see us again.'

I was as pleased as Punch, 'fancy the vicar speaking to me and he'd only seen me once,' I thought. 'I'll pop in next week vicar,' I shouted. Mrs Murphy's face paled and I honestly thought for a minute she was about to faint. Spud also looked uneasy, he didn't know what to say. Don't forget he was down on the list to become a priest himself and there was me, his mate, on friendly terms with the Proddy vicar, so in a way I could understand his shock. We arrived home in silence, not a word of thanks or even a tara - that was the least I would have expected.

I soon forgot their lack of manners when entering our backyard and smelling mam's cooking; she had spare ribs on the boil and I was starving. Two hours later Mrs Murphy, accompanied by Mrs Feeley, knocked on our door. I let them in despite having a good idea of the purpose of their visit. As I kind of expected they were reluctant to speak in front of me, so mam told me to go out and play. I couldn't disobey her in front of them even if I wanted to, but of course I knew what was coming, for after all I was eleven and a bit then.

Later that evening I strolled back home and found mam in deep conversation with dad. They immediately stopped talking.

'Sit down m'lad, I want a word with you.' The number of times he's had a word with me would fill five dictionaries, I thought.

'What's this I've been hearin' about you goin' into a Protestant Church?'

'What's wrong with it, I go to a Protestant school don't I?'

'Don't be so bloody 'ard faced. I'm askin' you a serious question,' he bawled

'I just wanted to see worr it was like for me'self that's all.'

'You're too bloody nosy for your own good. Now keep away from there, d'yer hear me?'

'Yis dad.'

'That's Mrs Murphy an' all her mates poking their noses in my business,'

I muttered to myself. 'One of these day's I'll get my own back.'

A month later I attended mass with Ossie, Spud and our mothers. We sat near the back of the church reciting the Lords Prayer. 'Amen' said the congregation. 'For thine is the Kingdom the power and the Glory,' I continued. There was a deathly silence, everyone looked round and Ossie in a fit of desperation elbowed me.

'Oh my God,' said Mrs Murphy. Mam looked ahead, all of a sudden she'd gone completely deaf. As we were leaving the church the priest called me over and had a quiet word in my ear. He knew I was acting the goat, he was smiling. At least he had a sense of humour.

After spending six months in Hemmie and without bothering anybody for their opinion I now felt in a position to draw my own conclusions about the religious divide and of course, make my mind up on which side I was going to take.

Each church was about the same size yet ours always appeared to be full. St Peter's wasn't as packed, but this was only because they had less of a congregation than the Lauries and so had fewer services. Then again we sneaked a few extra masses on the sly with our Holy Days of obligations.

We had to go to confessions … they didn't bother. That was a definite plus in their favour. And what about fasting for communion? You daren't have a crumb of bread after midnight even though you might be starving. They were two up on us already.

Then there were the hymns. Theirs were in English, ours in Latin, so it was now three nil for the Proddys. The Lords prayer came next. The Protestants added a few extra words, we were too tight, but I won't bother counting that one, because if I do we'll never catch them up. Both congregations stood outside in family groups at the end of church services, conversing with one another, except for our men who legged it to the ale houses after eleven o'clock mass to be first in for twelve o'clock opening. On reflection, I suppose the Proddys did when no one was looking.

One of the main differences between the religions was the fact that the vicar, if he wished, could marry. Now that was worth three points at least to anyone in my book and without a shadow of doubt could cause huge problems.

Imagine if your dad was a priest instead of a docker, or a boilermaker or a navvie. You'd have a dog's life. There'd be Benediction every night, confession every week, mass on Sunday, which you couldn't dodge either. Then your mates would be calling your dad Father, except your Proddy mates who'd call him Mr Reilly. Also you'd have to take his dog collars to the Chinks laundry to be starched and on top of that his suit wouldn't be allowed to be pawned, which of course would be a distinct disadvantage for mam when she was hard up during the week.

Of course there'd be no long walks on Sundays; he wouldn't have time for walks. The house would be quieter - there'd be no swearing - I don't suppose, yet I'd miss that in a way; I was used to it now, especially dad getting upset when old Mrs Connolly broke wind in her lavvie. I wonder if he'd still call her names if he were a man of the cloth? I doubt it, I thought.

The confessional problem swung it. The priests were better off staying where they were. The Catholics won that round. Summing up, there wasn't much in it. At last I could make my mind up. From now on I decided to walk in the middle of the fence. There weren't many as lucky as me, for I could join either side if I wanted to, because, without doubt, I was truly half 'n' half.

Adolescence

As time went by I had little choice but to slide into Hamilton's progressive educational programme, finding it extremely difficult at times to focus my sense of concentration, particularly in English studies which taxed my brain to the limit. Of course I had an additional advantage over my fellow pupils. During deportation periods when my class mates were having religious instructions, I was able to absorb other subjects being taught to older pupils as I sat inconspicuously at the rear of the classroom, feeling at times like a leper.

Life wasn't really tough though. It was just strange not knowing any of the lads in the beginning, but as soon I got to know my classmates they were more or less the same as my mates in the Lauries.

Mr Jones appreciated my dilemma by making me captain of Drake section and also the school junior football team, a ploy guaranteeing recognition and acceptance by the majority who played football.

Meanwhile, Ossie and Spud settled into the St Anselms College regime, although winning the scholarship also had its pitfalls. From the corner of Brookie they could be spotted a mile away wearing their light blue blazers, an advantage at times, but hazardous when the Yossers discharged their pupils simultaneously with St Anselms. On such occasions it was like the Alamo. For some unexplained reason certain pupils of the two Saints, Anselm and Hugh, appeared to have festered a deep rooted dislike for each other, frequently testing their pugilistic skills and running abilities to the extreme.

Ossie, who excelled in the latter, was often pursued by a bloodthirsty mob as far as St Anne Street, the border of our neighbourhood, but once across the boundary he stopped and shouted as loud as possible, for back up no doubt. 'Come on over here an' put your mitts up an' fight me on me own patch.' The local shopkeepers who were familiar with this spectacle, usually commented

'Here's the big ginger fella leading the field again, it must be just after half four.' Ossie was as consistent as he was predictable.

Spud, on the other hand, preferred a more peaceful approach, opting for diplomacy rather than direct confultration. This tactic wasn't always appreciated and at times he had to choose whether to defend himself or to protect his cap. His cap, the main source of the conflict, usually ended up nestling on a branch or bush hanging over the park railings. To be fair though, St Anselms wasn't the only college involved. Park High School, situated almost opposite the Yossers, took their share of combat and Birkenhead Institute pupils were vociferously taunted by other secondary schools. It appeared to be some sort of war between those who'd passed the scholarships and those who failed

Everything in our household seemed to be running normally for a change. Dad fluctuated between one shipping company and another, travelling between different docks throughout the area. He'd also sampled night shift, much to our displeasure. On those occasions it felt like we were living in a house of straw when dad was in bed. All conversations whispered, sign language practised, doors closed as if they were made of glass and even our poor little Tommy taken outside to cry. It was a wonder that Kerry's jaw wasn't clamped to prevent her yelping whenever she was hungry. At seven o'clock, after dad left for work, sighs of relief could be heard as far as the Morpeth dock.

'Jimmy ... Jimmy ... Here a minute,' Ossie yelled as we were getting dried at Livvie baths during the holidays.

'Worr is it, what's the matter?'

'Quick 'ave a look under me arm, can yer see it?' he ranted. I looked across at the unusual position of his head, as it disappeared under a thin scrawny arm, stretched above a wired section of the cubicle.

I glimpsed and couldn't see anything unusual, just a few freckles the same colour as the rest on his body, but no sign of the dreaded lurgie, or whatever it was that I was supposed to be looking for.

'Can yer see it Jim?'

'No ... worr is it?'

'A hair,' he proudly announced. I looked again, seeing it meant so much to him, before proclaiming that there was indeed a tiny sign of growth, although to be honest it took a fair degree of scanning and imagination to reach a conclusion. Still, Ossie was delighted, which was the main thing. 'Nacker's gorr em under both arms an' on his mickey,' he declared.

'Since when?' I replied. It was the first time I'd been to the baths since starting at Hemmie so I was well out of touch.

'Since he's been puttin' wagon grease on of course.'

'Wagon grease! Where'd he get that from?'

'From the railway carriages in the docks.'

'Oh' I replied. I couldn't hide my disappointment. 'Fancy me not knowing what was happening amongst my mates. That's dad's fault again for sending me to Hemmie and getting mixed up in religion an' all that. Now they've all got a start on me,' I moaned.

It was about this time I realised we were growing up. Well Nacker was anyway. Ossie had just began. Tucker hadn't any growth at all, nor had Spud, and then from out of the blue Smithy found a black curly hair under his left arm, yet strangely enough none under his right. I was still bald, but decided to scrutinise daily just in case they sprouted during the night when I was asleep and missed them. Afterwards, I became obsessed with the kitchen mirror much to dad's annoyance.

'You're goin' to break that bloody mirror the way you're goin' on m'lad,' he growled, after catching me for the umpteenth time swapping it from hand to hand.

'Don't say that Charlie, we don't want another seven years bad luck,' mam interrupted. She had a thing about mirrors. 'Your grandmother always said if you looked hard enough you'd see the Devil,' she repeatedly told me. Being of curious disposition I tried spotting him myself, but all I ever managed to see was dad's red face glaring at me from the front room. I didn't tell mam though; I knew for a fact she'd have burst out laughing and I didn't want any more trouble now that I was growing up.

At the end of my first year when school results were announced I finished sixteenth out of a possible forty and dad was pleased as Punch.

This report, to his way of thinking, represented a major improvement in my behaviour and educational progress, vindicating his decision to send me to Hemmie. Although mam was happy she still suffered bouts of uneasiness and depression whenever the priest called to enquire if I was still following my Catholic beliefs. On top of that, she was unable to report any sign of dad changing his reluctance to return to the faith and I supposed at the back of her mind she feared that one day I might follow a similar route.

As far as I was concerned I was content with my middle of the road position; not only could I walk safely through all well-known rough areas of the town, but knowing most of the hard cases from both denominations was a comforting advantage.

The second year at Hamilton was much the same as the first, except music lessons were introduced into the curriculum, a subject that tested my nervous laughter to the limit. Mr Hale, the music master, insisted that every pupil sang solo. Some lads howled like wolves, others bawled, a few sounded like girls screaming and the majority were out of tune. Unfortunately I'd inherited mam's tinny voice and couldn't even utter Do, Ray without tittering uncontrollably. Taken into account the number of adolescent voices breaking at the same time, the overall result was predictable. Of course, like the Lauries, there were dubious characters that thrived on farting or burping during live performances, making it impossible to keep a straight face. On such occasions the cane was introduced to control bad behaviour, and to improve lack of self-discipline for those who couldn't sing a note without laughing.

Spud was first of our age group to reach thirteen. He was still in short pants like the rest of us, but with being overweight his trousers were always dead tight on his heavy thighs. Spud's problem was that he just loved his grub and had difficulty evading Blackburns bakery for his daily ration of barmcakes, even though it was well off the usual route to St Anselms. With being the heaviest in the gang he often came under fire about his porky type figure, yet he remained good humoured and very rarely seemed upset by comments about his size.

'You couldn't gerra tanner up there,' Tucker joked pointing to the tightness of Spud's trousers above his knees.

'Who'd want to with his arse,' said Ossie, taking a chance that Spud didn't grip him in a headlock. Spud laughed, he frequently split his trousers and not always with over-eating.

When February arrived I became a teenager, although I didn't feel any different than before. There were no visible signs of reaching the first step on the ladder of manhood, but when Tucker found another hair under his right armpit we were dead jealous. Being teenagers we began copying the older lads by saying nudger instead of mickey, though Ossie said they called it a hampton in their school. They would, just to sound posh. In ours it was todger, yet in Smithy's it was just plain knob. Trust Birkenhead Institute to be different. Mind you, Jock always called it your wee knobby or wee friend so perhaps Smithy copied the name from his dad.

We still messed about playing football, climbing on walls and aggravating the girls who responded by chasing and wrestling us to the ground. From those encounters we progressed to innocuous games of 'catch a girl, kiss a girl,' aptly named to test even the most resilient of admirers. Spud broke his personal track record after being pursued by Irene Thomson who lived at the top end of Brookie and always had a snotty nose. We jeered at Spud as he tried hiding behind us whenever she approached and then marvelled at his seemingly improved sprinting skill. Ten minutes later he'd return breathless; Irene had gone home in tears after he refused to kiss her, so he said.

'Liar' said Ossie 'All your face is red where she's kissed yer an' there's snot on yer jacket.'

Later, Spud packed in the game altogether. We knew he was wasting his time chasing girls if he was going to be a priest, unless of course they were allowed to marry in future like the Proddies did.

Sally Dobson made a bee-line for me one night. She was the same height as I was but couldn't run as fast, so I slowed down to let her catch me. She kissed me kind of dead sloppy though, something like mam did in a way. I didn't like it very much, I preferred playing football instead. Still, with it being the dark nights we could only play dribbling under the gas light, so 'catch a girl, kiss a girl' was better than nothing I supposed.

Ossie was luckier than any of us. Mary Donovan, the best looking girl in the street fancied him, probably because of his ginger hair. Unfortunately for Mary, Ossie took the game too serious; he always did, and lost her in Price Street without giving her the chance to catch him. She had a right cob on and muttered that there was something up with him in the head, before slipping away on the quiet.

We played every night during the following weeks, hoping Mary Donovan would get fed up with Ossie's antics and chase us instead; she didn't bother though, it seemed as if we just didn't come up to scratch. One night, after relentlessly pursuing Ossie she caught him in Cottage Street. He laughed like a hyena; we heard him in Brookie, it was definitely Ossie; his voice was breaking and he was the only one out of the gang who sounded like a pig squealing when he got excited. To Mary's dismay he forgot to kiss her and at that point she gave up on him. Nevertheless, we hung round just in case she changed her mind and chased us instead, but she didn't. With having no other choice, we settled for the rest of the girls; they weren't as choosy as Mary Donovan.

I had no peace whatsoever as Sally Dobson followed me everywhere. Our Bridie called her my girl friend just to aggravate me and I hated that. Mam started skitting too, but dad didn't, he was too strict.

'Don't you be messin' round with those girls m'lad,' he informed me quite sternly

'I'm not, they're messin' round with me.'

'Well bloody chase them then. I don't want you bringin' any trouble in this house, d'yer hear?'

'Yes dad.' I couldn't understand why he bothered telling me. I was the only one who ever brought trouble into our house, which was why he always threatened me with the belt. Afterwards I heard him talking to mam about something called the 'Birds and the Bees' whatever that meant.

'It's about time I had a chat with the other fella Maggie,' he said. 'I'm worried about the way he's carryin' on lately.'

I placed my ears against the window. This method had always been an advantage to me with mam being deaf. I didn't know I was carrying on. Okay, we told dirty jokes but so did the rest of the lads, even Spud and Ossie and they went to St Anselms College.

'As long as you tell the priest when you go to confession it's alright,' Spud said.

'Worr if he doesn't gerr it,' Ossie asked.

'It can't be a good joke then can it?'

'That's fair enough,' we replied.

I haven't had a chance to have a word with the other fella yet' dad muttered to mam and as usual I happened to hear him. Next night I hung around waiting to be summoned to hear what sound advice he intended drilling into me. I was disappointed though; he never said a word even after he'd read the Echo, so I wandered outside to play, stopping by the window in case he spilled the beans in my absence.

'I thought you were goin' to 'ave a word with James, Charlie?' mam said.

I pressed my ear against the window.

'No, I've changed me mind,' he replied.

'You were all for it last night, what's happened, why 'ave you changed your tune?'

'He'll find out himself in good time.' I stood there, puzzled. What was I going to find out? Not another one of his madcap ideas, I hoped.

'So you're not goin' to tell him?' mam continued.

'No I'm not ... I had to find out about it me'self an' so can he.'

Not another word was spoken. Although I was dying to walk in and ask what I was supposed to find out for myself, I couldn't take the chance. There was no way I fancied enduring another of his lectures about being too nosy.

Chapter 5
Disaster

The second of May 1951, dad began working night shift. The first few nights after changing over from days always affected his sleeping pattern and we were blissfully aware that it was 'God help' anyone who disturbed him during the day. On Monday the 'bawlie,' yodelling under the bedroom window 'any bones to feed the rag man,' woke him at one o'clock. Although I was at school I could imagine dad's response. Tuesday's silence was shattered when the 'lecky man called just before twelve. Performing her duty which of course, she'd been thoroughly trained to do, Kerry responded by attacking him as he was about to place the meter box back in the meter cupboard. Once again dad danced down the stairs ranting and raving like a lunatic. Apart from leaving his cup of tea on the table the poor fella couldn't get out of the house quick enough, dad's erratic behaviour almost costing mam her rebate. To cap it all Kerry vanished for a few hours, but luckily she wasn't on heat. After just two days into dad's night shift mam was a nervous wreck and so were we.

Wednesday, however, was peaceful, no one called or rattled the knocker and mam, as usual, did her best to make sure that we were quiet as mice after we arrived home from school. For a change dad woke up in a good mood; it was refreshing to see him laughing and joking before he left for work. 'Good night God Bless an' don't forget to lock up properly,' he said, planting a peck on mam's cheek and ruffling our Tommy's hair before closing the front door after him. 'Goodnight and God Bless dad,' we repeated. Within minutes of dad leaving for work, the atmosphere automatically changed and 239 became the noisiest house on the block.

Of course we understood that dad needed his rest like he needed the money. The docks were still experiencing short-time working, so it was a case of taking the over-time while it was going, although it couldn't have been very pleasant working during the night, especially if like him you happened to be a light sleeper during the daytime.

Usually when dad worked night shift I slept in the same speck in the back bedroom with our Tommy and the girls shared mam's bed in the front room. I'd no sooner closed my eyes when my dreams were abruptly shattered by the noise of our door knocker being furiously rattled and as expected, Kerry brought the house down. My mind was in turmoil as I staggered out of bed, stumbled into the front room and almost collided with mam, who was making her way downstairs. After rubbing the sleep from my eyes I tentatively lifted up the bottom half of the window, stuck my head into the cold of the night and scanned the darkness to see who was rattling our door. I knew for a fact it wouldn't be dad, he never forgot his key.

From below a torch shone, the beam almost blinding me for a second. My head shot in quicker than it went out. I legged it downstairs pulling my pants up on the way, praying I'd be in time to prevent mam from opening the door, but I was too late. She was faster than I anticipated. Standing on our door step, facing her were two policemen. As quickly as I could, I crouched down and gripped Kerry round the neck to prevent her from flying to the door and attacking the policemen.

'Mrs Reilly?' they asked. Mam nodded. 'We're sorry to inform you, but we have some bad news. Your husband Charles has been involved in a serious accident and you're needed at the Borough Hospital straight away.' I stood there, my mind numb; I couldn't think what to say. Mam didn't wobble - I put my arm round her shoulder - she remained calm.

'I'll get me daughter up, she'll look after the young ones,' mam whispered. The policemen again apologised for bringing bad news and after assurance from mam that we'd be all right walking to the hospital by ourselves, they departed along the street.

Our Bridie stood at the bottom of the stairs, she'd heard everything and was crying, but I couldn't shed a tear. I was still shocked and besides I had to keep a brave face for mam's sake.

Mam gripped my arm as we stepped outside. It was a dark, drizzling, miserable morning. The gas lamp emitting a greeny flickering light was the only means of illumination in the street. We'd walked no more than a few paces when an almighty flash shattered the silence. A massive bolt of lightning struck the street lights strung between houses in readiness for the Festival of Britain celebrations. They fluttered and shook for a minute, but didn't shatter. Amazingly we hardly jumped.

'I hope that's not a bad sign James,' mam said.
She didn't utter another word as we walked up Price Street alongside the Livvie baths, before turning towards the Borough Hospital situated a couple of hundred yards away.
Dad was in casualty when we arrived. Frantic scenes greeted us as we peered into the make-shift ward, watching doctors and nurses dashing

backwards and forwards between beds that were curtained off. A matron approached mam and escorted her behind a set of mobile screens while I was ushered into a small waiting room. Alone with my thoughts I wondered what life would be like without dad. It was something I couldn't bear to imagine. An hour later mam appeared, her face the colour of chalk. I put my arms round her and she hugged me tight.

'Is he dead mam?'

'No son, but not far off it,' she whispered.

'The priest is comin' to give your dad the last rites.'

'Does he know about it?' I asked. She looked me straight in the eye 'Of course he doesn't, you should know your father by now son.'

'Is it Father Nugent who's coming mam?'

'No, it's a young priest from Our Lady's.'

'That's okay then, he wont mind him, will he?'

Through deserted streets we made our way home; it was five in the morning. Mam linked my arm, she wasn't much bigger than me; I was four foot nine; she was four eleven.

'You'll 'ave to be my little man now son,' she said and I almost cried, but I didn't.

'Course I will mam, you know I will.'

Aunt Fan opened the door; she was with our Bridie. The fire was lit and the teapot placed on the table. Bernadette and Tommy were still asleep. Mam hugged Aunt Fan and Bridie. I watched the three of them hug each other with tears dripping down their faces.

Kerry looked at me as if she knew about dad, so I ruffled her head and decided to take her for a walk. Six o'clock chimed and lights began appearing in upstairs windows as householders began rising for the beginning of another day, but all I could think about was dad fighting for his life and bleeding to death. Shuddering at the thought, I tried switching my mind off, thinking instead about football and school and everything else, yet my thoughts kept returning to dad.

Frustrated, I booted a tin can - it rattled down the street - a dog barked. Kerry immediately responded, a door hurriedly opened and quickly closed. A black and white mongrel came haring towards us so I grabbed Kerry, picked her up and waited for the dog to attack. It growled, then thought better; I was in no mood to be kind. It cocked its leg up and peed on Mrs Donovan's front step right over the empty milk bottles then shot away down the street.

After walking as far as the park entrance, I made my way home to find Tucker's dad talking to mam in the front room. Like dad, he too was working night shift, but unloading a different ship. He'd heard about the accident and was devastated. He told us that dad had been crushed against the side of a bogie by numerous fifteen hundred weight bundles of pig iron, swung from a crane; the news was all over the docks.

A continual stream of neighbours called over the next couple of hours including Mrs Murphy. She was sorry to hear about dad yet delighted that he'd received the last rites.

'Most people don't get a second chance in this life Maggie,' she said. 'Charlie's fortunate you know,' she added. 'Fortunate,' I thought. I couldn't believe my ears. I knew someone who definitely wouldn't agree with her and he was lying in the Borough Hospital right now. Of course I didn't say anything, it wouldn't have done me much good anyway, I'd have only been accused of being cheeky.

'Think positive wee man, yir faither's as hard as steel,' Jock Smith told me after calling to offer his sympathy to mam. Paddy and Ossie's dad uttered similar sentiments.

At eight o'clock mam again returned to the hospital, this time with Aunt Fan. I tagged along and parked on a bench across the road by the Bowling Green waiting for them to re-emerge.

'Your dad's still with us thank God,' mam said, when she eventually appeared.

'He's still unconscious an' critical though,' she added.

By dinner hour we'd had more visitors than I could remember in ten years. Mam's sisters and her brothers, Uncle Bob and Uncle Frank (both bosses on the docks) called to see us, offering mam all kinds of advice. Bridie and I sat there listening and no one objected; we were both surprised. We were forever being told that children should be seen and not heard, a saying often quoted by dad even when we were teenagers. It now looked as if times were about to change.   •

Over the following weeks, mam lived through a nightmare. She was constantly called to the hospital at all hours of the day and night. Dad was slipping away, recovering, slipping away again and even the priests were backwards and forwards like yo- yo's. The last rites were given as often as absolutions were dished out after Saturday morning confessional stints. Although dad remained unconscious, I vowed to tell him how many last rites he'd received, assuming he recovered. I knew for a fact he wouldn't believe me, yet still I continued counting them anyway.

As days turned into weeks dad had numerous operations. His pelvis, legs, kidneys and ribs had been extensively crushed and there was little doubt that more than his fighting spirit and fitness would be needed if he were to survive.

Eventually both Bridie and I returned to school leaving mam to struggle on. There was very little we could do to help by staying at home anyway. Dad had no savings and with five mouths to feed it was little wonder that mam didn't know if she was coming or going. After the accident I walked along with her to the Clearing House in Corporation Road to collect dad's last wage, it was an experience difficult to forget. Cardboard collection boxes had been placed in the centre of the floor with the names of dockers killed or badly maimed scribbled on the sides. I was shocked at the vast number of casualties. This made me realise that the docks wasn't a safe haven to play or sag school after all, but an extremely hazardous place to work.

I watched dockers open their pay packets and drop coins into various boxes, while mam was escorted to the front of the queue. Both Bridie and I were given similar treatment weeks later when collecting dad's sick pay benefit from the union office in Berner Street. It was a known fact that dockers paid respect to women and children and always made exceptions on such occasions.

As time went by I was lucky enough to get a paper round for Connolly's newsagents and with help from a few mates obtained a weekend job on a milk round. Although rising early curbed my leisure time, eleven bob a week boosted the family budget and meant a difference between having a couple of meals on the table or doing without. We were by no means poor; in fact we were well off compared to many large families who struggled with meagre wages and poverty that existed at the time. However, it was normal for lads to have spare time jobs such as milk and paper rounds, or helping out at the butchers, or even loading and unloading goods at the market, always acknowledged as one of the best places to find work on Saturdays; so I was no different than anyone else.

In line with other hospitals, children below a certain age were not allowed to visit adults, so I set about making enquiries to see if there was any possibility of me breaching that particular rule in the hope of seeing dad who'd been in the Borough Hospital for five months. After discussing the situation with Nacker, he came up with a solution. He said that he'd get in touch with Tommy Collins, a mate of his, who had a paper round that included the Borough Hospital. He then suggested that I would be willing to give Tommy a helping hand with his early morning paper round which included the hospital, for nothing. Tommy, naturally agreed. Nacker never changed, he was always on hand to help any of us ever we were in a fix.

Nervously I entered dad's ward, humping a large green canvas bag slung across my shoulder, and gradually made my way from bed to bed. Upon reaching the bottom of the ward, I thought I'd got my bearings wrong until I spotted a bed, hidden behind a curtained section in the left-hand corner of the room. Peeping behind the partition I found dad. He was lying with his his head propped on starch white pillows. I had to look twice - I didn't recognise him - he was so thin and yellow, even as yellow as Mr Chung from the Chinese Cafe. His hair had receded further - his eyes were closed - I stood motionless for a minute, frozen to the spot and then somehow, plucked up courage, leaned across and gripped his hand.

'Dad ... dad,' I whispered 'it's me Jimmy.' His eyes flickered for a second.

I looked into his dilated pupils at the colour of his eyes, which were as yellow as his skin. He gripped my hand, squeezed it and closed his eyes again. I had a lump the size of a golf ball in my throat. Before leaving I glanced across at dad once more, put my head down and quickly slipped out of the ward; pleased I'd seen him, but shocked at his condition.

That evening I told mam of my visit to the hospital.

'I thought it wouldn't be long before you found your way into there James,' she said.

'Your granny always said, where there's a will, there's a way.'

'Or a relative,' I answered. She laughed. It was great to see her laugh. She hadn't had much to laugh at for months.

It was somewhere near this time that Spud dropped into longies. He'd expanded so fast the shops didn't sell short pants to fit him anymore. At least he suited the conversion, Ossie didn't. No sooner had Mrs Feeley bought him a pair of greys than he was showing off, parading round the street as if he owned it, but the pants were so baggy everyone said he resembled a red headed Charlie Chaplin. He didn't mind taking the flack though; he'd changed for the better since he'd won the scholarship to St Anselms College. A year earlier and he'd have sulked and gone home whinging.

Before the start of my third year, with dad still in hospital and funds desperately low, mam constantly worried over not being able to afford new clothes for the girls. Bridie needed a school uniform and shoes and Bernadette a new dress. I wasn't bothered about my blazer being tight; the buttons were of little consequence to me anyway, and besides, they were never fastened. All I needed though was new pants. Mam managed to get the girls' clothes on the tick and somehow found a few bob to buy me a pair of black 'longies' from Rostances as they were cheaper than greys and saved her a few bob for something more vital.

Christmas arrived and passed uneventfully. The house just wasn't the same without dad. Father Nugent paid mam an unexpected visit during the festive season, still optimistic that dad would return to the faith after his close encounter with death. I wasn't convinced though; dad wasn't out of the woods yet; how he'd react when he came home was anyone's guess.

Young men from the Saint Vincent de Paul Society began visiting us and bringing secondhand clothes, their sincerity and generousity was always appreciated by mam. Whether dad would have felt the same was hard to predict. He wasn't one for accepting charity, but beggars couldn't be choosers and everything given was given with a good heart.

By the time Easter arrived one of dad's kidneys had been removed. The operation was another blow to his progress, setting his recovery back even further. Poor mam, desperate for some kind of a job suffered bouts of depression, but her hands were tied with Tommy being so young. Although Bridie and I had long ceased arguing all we could do was to offer mam moral support; there was little else we could do anyway to ease the situation.

Our clothes were washed and dried overnight to remove the shabbiness brought on by wear and tear and whenever a major repair was needed mam, who had never been very good with a needle, did her best to overcome her handicap. On one such occasion I split my pants delivering milk to one of the top flats in Hamilton Square so mam clamped the rip with a few well-spaced dog stitches in white cotton; it was fortunate we had black shoe polish at the time.

At the beginning of the following week Father Nugent arrived at our house with Mrs Murphy. I opened the door and couldn't help noticing a sort of triumphant look on Mrs Murphy's face that made me suspicious about the reason for their visit. However, as soon as they began talking about Novena's, Benediction and the forthcoming trip to Lourdes, I quickly pushed my suspicions to the back of my mind. While mam made a pot of tea for the visitors, I popped round the corner to see Ossie.

Although he was busy doing his homework, he seemed glad of the opportunity to have a break. The house was dead quiet since Marlene had left. She'd taken baby Sophie to stay at her mother's in Brassey Street because of the constant bickering between her and Mrs Feeley. Ossie wasn't bothered now that the novelty of having a baby in close ·proximity had worn off. He was learning Latin and French at school and found it difficult to focus on his studies when the house was full, blaming the noisy distractions for his lack of concentration. He had also sampled the slipper for falling asleep during lectures. This was an experience I had encountered on a number of occasions from the P.E teacher for not showing enough interest in gymnastics. The slipper or the pain didn't bother me, my main worry always concerned my trousers and if they'd stand up to the pressure whenever I had to bend over to be whacked.

At nine o'clock I returned home to be greeted by our Bridie's war cry.

'Here's our Jimmy now mam.'

'What's up mam, what's the matter?' I asked, as she came from the kitchen carrying a pot of tea.

'I won't beat about the bush, James,' she said. 'I'll come straight to the point. I've been speakin' to Father Nugent about transferrin' you to St Hugh's.'

'ST HUGH'S! What for mam, I'm happy where I am at Hemmie,' I yelled.

'Well son I thought it would be nice for you to finish your education in a Catholic School - that's all - what do you think?' I couldn't think - I couldn't believe my ears.

All the hassle I'd endured, the detours, hiding from my mates, sitting with older lads during R.I. lessons and morning assembly; I'd conquered the lot over a period of time and now mam, having succumbed to pressure from Mrs Murphy and Father Nugent, was contemplating casting me back in the opposite direction.

'Why can't they leave well alone instead of sticking their big noses into my business,' I muttered to myself. 'Worr about dad, he'll go mad, you know what he's like mam,' I protested.

'He won't get to know. Besides we've had no dammed luck in this house since he put you in the Protestant school in the first place. Your poor grandmother would turn in her grave if she knew what's been happening in this house,' she lamented.

'If she keeps on turnin' she'll soon be out,' I replied. I know it was lousy thing to say, but I couldn't help it. I was in a fearful mood.

'Don't be so damned cheeky, that's another thing I've noticed about you lately m'lad.'

Mam looked depressed at my attitude. She wasn't normally as snappy. I could read her thoughts and knew that as far as she was concerned transferring me to St Hugh's was in my best interest. I looked at the sadness in her face and thought of the way she'd fought tooth and nail with dad to stop me going to Hemmie in the first place and I felt really sorry for her.

'Okay mam if it makes you happy I'll go,' I said, 'but don't forget I've only got me Hemmie blazer an' I'll get murdered if I turn up wearing that at the Yossers.'

Two weeks to the day I made my way along Park Road South and reported to Mr Lafferty, the headmaster of St Hugh's. Due to circumstances I had little choice but to go without a blazer and wear an over-sized jersey given by the S.V.P., which fortunately covered the pockets of my dependable black pants. Somehow or other mam managed to achieve a crease down both legs without scorching them, no mean feat considering the old flat iron was heated by the gas flame on the stove. She'd also obliterated the ever-present creases around the crotch without damaging the dog-stitches, another accomplishment worthy of note.

'This is the new boy, James Reilly,'Mr Lafferty announced to my form master Mr MacPherson, after escorting me to the classroom. I couldn't help noticing the looks of astonishment on the faces of the lads who knew me from the Lauries. No wonder they were surprised, I thought. Anyone would be surprised seeing someone appear for school three years later than he should have done. At break time I spotted Cleary, fortunately he wasn't in my class but in a lower grade. He glared at me just the same and called me a dirty stinking Proddy dog. I laughed in his face; I wasn't scared of him anymore. He was just a bully, and besides the Yossers had a no-fighting policy in or outside school, a comforting barrier when accosted by the likes of Cleary.

Whenever indifferences occurred arguments were settled by having what was known as 'grudge fights'. These bouts took place after school finished on Fridays and pennies collected from spectators were donated to help the poor kids living overseas.

Cleary didn't offer me out, but knowing him like I did he was liable to sneak up behind me when I was walking home down Park Road East and punch me in the ribs.

Similar to Hamilton, St Hugh's practised a strict no-nonsense approach towards unruly pupils. I was surprised and deterred at the ferocity certain teachers adopted to keep their charges in check. Mr Grant, a very tall teacher with doleful thyroid type eyes, meted out punishment at the slightest interruption to his lesson. Big Frankie Thompson caught his attention, he didn't like Frankie, I don't think he liked anyone.

'Out ... yes you Thompson, out' he bawled.

'Who me, worr 'ave a done Sir?' Frankie replied.

'Out' he said removing a long thin cane from a cupboard in the corner of the room.

'Watch this Jimmy,' Tony Byrne whispered.

'Byrne and the new boy, step out here,' Mr Grant roared. We trudged out.

Frankie held his hand up; he was almost as tall as Mr Grant. He whacked him six times on one hand, Frankie never flinched.

'The other one now,' he ordered. Frankie raised his right hand.

'Nicotine ... have you been smoking Thompson?'

'It looks like Sir,' he replied.

Granties face twisted in anger. He dished out six, followed by a further six on his left hand. Frankie scornfully looked at him and said 'Is that the best you can do?'

I'd never seen a teacher lose his rag completely. He began whacking Thomo across his buttocks with all his might and everyone cheered. Meanwhile Tony pushed me into a corner out of the way. Fortunately for all concerned, the melee attracted the attention of Mr O'Neil, who was teaching a geography lesson to first year old pupils in the next classroom. Within minutes he had everything under control. After restoring order he took Mr Grant to one side and escorted him to the staff room to calm down. Tony and I were hoping in a way he wouldn't return and that we'd get away with our misdemeanour. This wasn't to be our lucky day, for shortly afterwards Mr Grant appeared with his memory still intact and accordingly we each received four of the best, the minimum punishment dished out.

The following Saturday morning Spud asked me if I'd help him to carry his mother's shopping from the Maypole and I was more than willing to oblige. Mrs Murphy often bought a few extra groceries for mam, despite at times being short of money herself. After loading the bags at the Maypole we trundled down Exmouth Street and turned into Conway Street. Outside Liversedge's fishing tackle shop we stopped for a minute to allow Mrs Murphy the chance to have a breather before proceeding into the top end of Cathcart Street. No sooner had we turned the corner than we bumped into vicar Bates and his wife.

'Hello young man,' he shouted. 'Is this your mother and brother?'

'Indeed we're not,' Mrs Murphy replied quite sharpish.

'Go on James, why don't you tell the vicar about your new school,' she added, walking on ahead.

'I'm back on the other side now Vicar,' I yelled. 'Me dad's in hospital after nearly gettin' killed on the docks, so me mam's put me into the Yossers.'

'Oh, I am sorry to hear about your father,' he replied, coming across the road to where I was standing. 'How distressing for you to be taken out of Hamilton Secondary School you poor dear. You must be traumatised with all the changes,' his wife interrupted.

I didn't know about being traumatised. I felt as if I'd been transferred from Everton to Liverpool and then given a free transfer back again without even kicking a ball.

At this particular time I couldn't really convey my feelings properly so I smiled and nodded in reply to her concern.

'We'll pray for your father and all of your family, James,' the vicar called as I made my way in pursuit of Mrs Murphy.

'Thanks vicar,' I replied.

Mrs Murphy's pace was slow and ponderous so I easily caught up with her.

'Did you tell him that you're back where you belong now James?' she asked.

'Indeed I did Mrs Murphy and he's offered to pray for us,' I mischievously added.

'My God,' she said. 'The cheek of it. You should 'ave told him you don't need anymore prayers, you've got all your own parish prayin' without them lot getting' involved.'

'Yeah I know, but there's still only one God up there accordin' to me dad, so I don't suppose it matters who prays for him,' I replied.

A month later Spud left St Anselms and joined the priesthood to finish his education. Mrs Murphy was ecstatic. We were surprised and didn't think for a moment that he'd answer 'the call.' We were all wrong.

'Fancy us 'aving a priest as a best mate' said Ossie.

'Father Spud doesn't sound right does it Jim?'

'No, it 'ill have to be Father Timothy Murphy from Brookie' I replied.

1953

For almost two years dad had spent the best part of his time in hospital. After the pain and suffering since his accident he was finally coming home for good. Watching him walking down Brookie carrying a small canvas case, I couldn't believe my eyes; he'd lost so much weight that his brown suit seemed as if it was three times too big for him. As soon as he entered the front room mam threw her arms around him and was immediately followed by both girls who hugged and kissed him. He then bent down and tried lifting young Tommy but found him too heavy so he ruffled his hair instead. He then turned to me and hugged me before shaking my hand.

After enjoying a cup of tea and easing himself into his chair it was noticable the amount of space either side of him. Kerry glanced across and for a minute I thought she was about to commit suicide by crawling next to him. She'd developed a habit of making herself comfortable in dad's chair over the past twelve months and I, more than anyone else, was fully aware through personal experiences of course that in many cases old habits died hard. I had little doubt her demise would be rapid if she didn't watch herself.

The neighbours said how well dad looked, but to me and my mates he didn't. Mind you, unlike adults we told the truth. Mrs Murphy, fishing for compliments, said it was the parish prayers that had saved him. Dad pretended not to hear. Despite receiving numerous last rite sacraments he wasn't one for broadcasting his beliefs or disbeliefs. Continuing her devout Catholic crusade Mrs Murphy gave mam a bottle of holy water from Lourdes. 'Slip that in Charlie's tea Maggie an' let me know how he goes on,' she whispered.

Mam did, on the sly, of course. Dad got the runs and blamed the bread from the Co-op. That was all he'd eaten all day. I knew about the holy water after hearing Mrs Murphy talking to mam. For a change I was rumbled for 'ear-wigging' and warned by mam not to open my big mouth in front of dad. I was more than happy to oblige. The last thing I wanted was for him to have a relapse.

Having joined 'The penny in the pound fund,' when the docks were booming dad now qualified to benefit from the scheme. Within weeks of returning home he was given the opportunity to recuperate in the Lake District, followed by two more pleasant weeks of spring sunshine and rest at nearby Arrowe Park Convalescent home. The month away worked wonders for him; upon his return he looked fitter and healthier than ever.

On the following Friday, Father Nugent paid us a visit and dad made no attempt to perform his usual dash to the lavvie. Instead he stayed in his chair by the fire. Mind you his legs were playing him up at the time.

'Nice to see you out and about Charles,' the priest said, shaking hands 'and how are you feeling?'

'Not bad, considerin' father. Could be better I suppose, but there's far worse cases out there than me, so I'm not complainin'.'

Mam fussed about making a pot of tea. 'Nip across the street an' ask Mrs Barton if she can lend me a cup of sugar 'til tomorrow James,' she asked. 'Tell her I've got Father Nugent here,' she yelled as I left.

'What difference would that make to Mrs Barton,' I thought. She was a Protestant. It looked as if mam was cracking up already.

Father Nugent sipped his tea, without biscuits. Mam hadn't bought any since dad's accident. Just as he was about to leave she looked behind Our Lady's statue as if expecting some sort of a miracle to happen and a two bob bit to suddenly appear, despite telling us often enough that miracles rarely happened wherever money was concerned.

Mam continued fussing about around the dresser and even I knew that she was grasping at straws. The last time I'd seen a couple of two bob pieces behind Our Lady's statue, both were used in the meters when the gas and the 'lecky ran out at the same time. As a last resort she fumbled in her purse, knowing quite well it contained only coppers, so in desperation she turned to dad.

'Have you got any change on yer for the priest Charlie?' she asked.

'Don't talk bloody daft woman where d'yer think I've got change from?' he replied. Father Nugent stood by the door ready to leave. Mam searched her old handbag. She looked flustered. Then dad took over.

'You can't give what you 'avent got Maggie,' he said raising his voice.

'Yes Maggie, Charlie's right,' said Father Nugent, aware of the annoyance in dad's tone.

'Perhaps next time round your fortunes will be better, that's if God spares you,' the priest added.

'I hope he does,' dad quickly replied. 'I wouldn't like to go to me grave owin' a few bob to the parish collection. The devil would 'ave a field day,' he added.

'Goodnight an' God Bless,' Father Nugent said closing the door firmly behind him. Dad smiled, shaking his head from side to side. There was little doubt in any of our minds that he was back on the road again.

'I don't think it's funny Charlie it's downright embarrassin' not 'avin' a penny to your name an' not even 'avin' two bob to give to the church,' mam muttered.

'Don't make me laugh woman, me leg an' me kidney's are playin' me up,' he replied.

Nacker, who was first to leave school out of our gang, achieved his ambition by joining the New Zealand Shipping Line with a position as a galley boy. On the day of his maiden voyage we walked along Clevie with him to Woodside Ferry before crossing the river to the Pier Head. Just like his dad he was full of confidence. He even walked the same way, rolling his shoulders in rhythm with each step.

A few weeks after dad returned from convalescence I left school, but continued working on the milk as a full time employee. Dad never mentioned my school progress or lack of it and naturally mam didn't broach the subject either. Whether he'd have been aware at the time of my transfer to St Hugh's was debatable. Still, deep down I suspected that he would have eventually discovered the deception. Nothing in the past had escaped his detection and I for one wouldn't gamble that the accident had dented his astuteness.

Ossie remained at St Anselms College, unsure whether to carry on and further his education or to follow his dad onto the railways, not as a manual worker but an office wallah. Tucker, as expected, left school at Easter, joining Gordon Allisons as an apprentice fitter. Smithy was hesitant about leaving school, he just couldn't make his mind up whether to stay on at Birkenhead Institute or move to his grandmother's house in Glasgow.

After the ups and downs of the two previous years the wind seemed to change direction for our family with dad returning to the docks. At first he found the work tiring, so to compromise his weakness he began a course of training in the backyard with the help of his dependable chest expanders and arm springs. Meanwhile the union's legal department began gathering momentum in his fight for compensation, a claim that had been ongoing since his accident.

One day a letter arrived regarding the outcome of dad's case and as a result, he was summoned for an appointment with his solicitors in Liverpool. A couple of hours later he returned home looking totally dejected.

'Go out with your mates while me an' yer mam discuss something important son,' he said to me. Our Bridie was allowed to remain, only because she was studying French at the time. Later that evening when we were alone she whispered that dad had lost his case.

From what she gathered dad shouldn't have been in the vicinity of the accident, but working with his own gang further down the quay. However, what was regarded as customary for dockers to work the 'welt', dad, following tradition, acted as a stand in for the bogie driver. This common practice allowed his colleague the opportunity of slipping away for a quick cup of tea, content that his job was covered during his absence. Seizing upon this unofficial practice, the firm was adamant that there wouldn't have been an accident if dad had remained on his own job. The cause of the mishap wasn't even mentioned. Bad lighting conditions and the unfortunate crane driver's involvement were accepted as part of the course at the time.

The solicitor appealed against the judgement and within a matter of weeks dad received notification to appear again. As a compromise the firm put forward a settlement for loss of earnings, an offer his solicitor, in conjunction with the union officials advised him to accept.

Nine hundred pounds to any working man was a fortune and dad received it in cash. He didn't have a bank account, very few working class people did, so using what he considered as a safe alternative, he hid it under the floorboards in our bedroom.

Of course I wasn't supposed to know about his little secret, but very little escaped my swivelling eyes and as soon as the coast was clear I prised up the floorboards to enjoy counting the enormous fortune; I felt like a millionaire with all that dosh running through my hands. I knew I was dicing with death and if caught by dad he would have skinned me alive, but I was always inclined to live dangerously; it seemed as if taking risks and liberties ran through my blood.

The time dad chose to go on a spree was like three Christmas's rolled into one. After giving mam a bundle of notes to kit us out with new clothes, he set off for Grange Road to buy items of bedroom furniture from Brown Brothers & Taylors. It felt kind of strange trying on pants, jerseys, new shoes and mam paying cash. As soon as we arrived home our secondhand clothes were discarded and bagged. Little Tommy gave them to the 'bawlie' and was delighted to receive two small goldfish and a balloon, a bargain in anyone's book I thought. Dad also made a donation to the S.V.P. in appreciation of their assistance during our 'run of bad luck' as he put it. He had a lot of time for the Saint Vincent de

Paul's Society. They didn't discriminate between different denominations. If you were poor and down and out they did all in their power to help, these were solid principles that appealed to his way of thinking.

Despite gentle hints from various quarters of how grateful he should be to God for his recovery dad still refused to attend mass. Mam said he'd go in his own time. I wasn't as optimistic myself. I just couldn't imagine dad walking down the aisle alongside Paddy Murphy, then kneeling down and praying, it wouldn't be like him. If he ever did I knew for a fact that I wouldn't be able to keep a straight face, so in a purely selfish way I was happy with his present position. Saving my own skin always ranked high on my list of priorities.

The Emerald Isle

I found it hard to believe my ears when mam told us we were going to Ireland for our holidays. Rising from poverty to riches within a matter of months was unbelievable.

Now hearing the news that dad had already booked us on the overnight ferry from Liverpool to Dublin was the icing on the cake. Without telling anyone he'd replied to an advert in the Catholic Universe for us to stay at a guesthouse in Bray, a small seaside resort on the outskirts of Dublin. All he was waiting for was confirmation regarding the accommodation.

With increasing excitement the family looked forward to our first holiday together. It was bound to be controversial; dad's unpredictability would guarantee that. Our date of departure was the twenty fourth of June. The night before, we had two new suitcases packed tightly with everything in sight squeezed into them. Kerry was staying at home guarding the house, from what no one could ascertain. Then I thought on. 'Worra bout dad's money?'

Seeing that I wasn't supposed to know about the cash I had to pretend not to notice dad making extra journeys upstairs. On the sly though, I watched him like a hawk and took more than a healthy interest in his activities by counting the number of times he carried his metal box down with him. Although I was tempted to suggest a new place to doss his cash, I was in a funny predicament. There was no way I would dare to mention about the money; he'd have gone mad altogether if he knew I'd discovered his secret hoard, so I racked my brains and tried forecasting whereabouts he'd stash it. His choice of hideout, however, even surprised me.

I just couldn't believe my eyes after I caught him shovelling the coal in the air raid shelter. What a place to hide all that money I felt like saying. 'A couple of moggies would be handy now to stink the place out,' I said under my breath, but since Kerry's arrival they'd steered clear of the backyard and the air raid shelter.

On the day of our departure we walked round to Clevie carrying the cases between us and boarded the number ten bus to Woodside. It seemed strange that we, the Reilly's, were leaving the house together dressed up like ten bob notes. A number of neighbours stood on their steps wishing us luck and telling us to enjoy ourselves. Mrs Feeley and Mrs Murphy hugged mam and Paddy gave dad the address of his brother who lived in the centre of Dublin.

No sooner had we arrived at the Prince's dock and boarded the vessel than dad began issuing orders. 'Grab that speck over there son, don't budge and stay were you are 'til I sort yer mam and the kids out with a berth.' I sat in between two fella's drinking bottles of Guinness and although it wasn't much of a speck the lavvies were handy so I didn't have to worry about sorting out my bearings. Dad appeared after ten minutes full of beans and bursting with enthusiasm. 'D'yer mind squeezin' over an' lettin' a little fella in, lads?' he asked the two drinkers. 'Not at all, not at all,' they replied.

The crossing was dead stormy and as I sort of expected, dad was up and down all night, walking back an' forth stretching his legs. He paid no attention to the freezing wind, or to the fact that I was wearing summer clothes and couldn't stop myself from shivering like a jelly. I also felt seasick and here we were only going to Ireland. 'I'd have been no good if I 'd stowed away to sea,' I muttered to myself, thinking about Nacker and his dad sailing the ocean waves and more than likely sleeping below deck in a nice warm cabin; not like us getting our heads blown off.

'Get that fresh air down yer son,' dad insisted. Fresh air, it was so fresh it would have lifted me off my feet if I'd been daft enough to follow his meandering along the main deck. The majority of the passengers sitting in our location found the sanctuary of the bar a more comfortable alternative, including the two fella's drinking Guinness. They moved indoors when the ship suddenly tilted and sent sprays of Guinness splattering on the bulkhead above us. Naturally they cursed. Dad grinned; he was made up with the extra room. I wasn't, they kept the wind off me. At half six dad called out to me for the umpteenth time that morning.

'Jimmy come over here, you can see the coastline now.' Still feeling as sick as a dog I wasn't particularly interested about the coastline, but I knew that if I didn't show an effort he'd bawl until I did. With legs like jelly I staggered over the slippery wooden deck as the ship rolled like a pig's bladder caught in the Mersey current. White sprays rose above the bow showering down our side of the vessel, the starboard side, according to dad's nautical lecture narrated before we set sail.

Dad was standing alone leaning over the side, his face bright red. What little hair he had was vertical with his collar and he was also grinning like a Cheshire cat. I wondered how on earth his teeth managed to stay in place and what would happen if they blew out and landed in the bar or the saloon. He wouldn't be so cheerful then, I thought, and neither would anyone else sitting there.

The coastline was grey and murky, not very impressive to the naked eye at that hour of the morning, and personally, I couldn't see what all the fuss was about. A few more curious, sleepy-eyed passengers emerged, probably woken by dads enthusiastic yells. 'Maybe they thought he'd seen a whale' I mutterted to myself.

Despite dad's exciteable oration when describing the geographical landmarks on the horizon, they didn't stay out long. They had more sense than we did.

We disembarked at half seven. Mam, Bridie, Bernadette and Tommy seemed quite refreshed unlike me, I felt like a wet rag doll; dad didn't look any different, he never did.

'How far's Bray dad?' I asked, when observing the distance to the end of the huge shed that lay in front of us.

'Wait here' he said, 'while I go and scan the coast' Within minutes he returned, 'Right come on, this way.' he urged.

A taxi stood waiting. This was the first time any of us had been in one; dad was really putting on the style, mam couldn't believe her eyes. We travelled through Dublin like royalty. The similarities to Liverpool were noticeable. There were large buildings, pubs on every corner, busy streets, and the grey mist rising from the Liffey reminded us of a bleak day on the Mersey in March. Eventually we joined the coast road taking us above Dun Laoghaire, then into Blackrock, finally arriving in Bray just in time for breakfast.

The Commemara Guest House, a large three-storey terraced house with a small garden in the front, held a prominent position near the seaside and Mr and Mrs Lynch were the proprietors. Mrs Lynch opened the door for us. She had a kind face with smiling eyes, similar to mam's, and her hair was tied up in a bun. 'Welcome to Bray and to The Connemara Guest House,' she said shaking hands with mam and dad. We trundled in behind, I was lugging a suitcase almost as big as I was.

'Berty,' she called 'Come an' meet Mr and Mrs Reilly and their family.'

The hall door opened and a huge pot-bellied man appeared wearing the biggest pair of brown corduroys I'd ever seen in my life. He held a garden rake in one hand and a small sack of spuds in the other. Dad looked like a midget beside him and I felt like a midget's midget. Mr Lynch carried the cases upstairs without any effort, while his wife fussed around in the kitchen.

'Breakfast is ready.' Mrs Lynch called to us as we sat like lead soldiers in the front parlour. I'd never seen the likes of the breakfast before. There was bacon, egg, sausage, fried bread, beans and loads of toast, besides cereal. 'Dont be makin' a pig of yourself,' dad warned, before I started eating. I didn't, he did though. He didn't leave a bean but I left a couple on purpose. This was to stop him complaining when I attacked the toast.

Amazingly we had our own bedroom; it was the first time we hadn't slept top and bottom in our lives. I was in the back room with Tommy, the girls were next door and mam and dad had the best room. It was dead posh with walnut wardrobes, real class, just like the ones we'd seen at the flicks.

From the bedroom window my keen eyes observed an orchard in the back garden with apples as red as our back kitchen door. Without a second thought I changed as quickly as possible, determined to be the first of our family to explore this wonderful vision.

Before going downstairs, however, dad issued his customary do's an' don't instructions, commands that became a highlight of the holiday.

'Don't you dare touch those apples, m'lad,' he warned.

I wandered outside and enjoyed the luxury of being able to sit in the shade of an apple tree without panicking about getting caught or chased. It was an experience I found most satisfying.

The apples were dead rosy and to be honest, for the devilment, I was tempted to touch one just to feel if they were any different than ours back home, but instinctively I thought twice; the curtain in mam's room moved slightly, I was being watched.

I sat there in my own world, day-dreaming of the apple orchards that we'd raided during our expeditions from town when we were young. I then imagined that I was eight again and pictured how I'd react to being cast into a heaven like this, surrounded by masses of apples and pears. Out of curiosity, I wondered how often apples dropped off the trees without anyone touching them and if I'd still be quick enough to catch any before they hit the grass.

'You can take an apple if you like,' a deep Irish voice echoed. Startled, I turned round to find Mr Lynch standing on the far side of the garden leaning against a small shed. I didn't hear him approach. I thanked him for his offer and told him my name was Jimmy, just in case he needed an extra hand in the garden or should he want me to help myself again to an apple, then he'd know what to call me.

I chose a large red juicy apple and strolled inside the house rubbing it on my new jersey. Dad's eyes almost popped out of his head when I approached him.

'Worr 'ave I bloodywell told yer,' he growled. He couldn't shout too loudly, he wouldn't have wanted to create a bad impression. This was something I intended to exploit while inside the house. Outdoors, well, that would be a different proposition altogether.

We were up bright and early for our first day out in Dublin. Before leaving 'The Connemara' Mr Lynch provided dad with a list of timetables for trains and buses. It was Monday morning and we, the Reilly's, were about to descend on 'Molly Malone's territory, the first of many excursions around the ancient city.

When disembarking in Grafton Street we were mesmerised at the sheer volume of busy traffic engulfing the city. Meanwhile Dad held the street map like a proper tourist; there was no denying that he definitely looked the part. Besides wearing a sports jacket and greys he also sported a brown trilby with a fancy band, it was without doubt the smartest we'd ever seen him dressed. I felt the proper thing to do, was to compliment him on his appearance.

'Dad looks like James Cagney,' I said.

'Don't be so bloody funny, you,' he growled.

'I'm not dad, you look the ringer of him, doesn't he Bride?'

'Yeah, Jim's right, you do look like him with that trilby on dad.'

'Well then,' he answered tilting his trilby to one side and appearing to swagger slightly. He loved the gangster pictures and so his reply was predictable. 'I suppose I do in a way.' Mam smiled. She was dying to laugh and so were we, but it was more than we dared, he'd have made a holy show of us.

If we thought the walks around Birkenhead, Liverpool and Merseyside were bad enough they were nothing compared with Dublin. Dad clung to the street map like a bible, pursuing every landmark of note, including monuments of numerous patriots that he'd read about in the library and unfortunately for us were scattered all over the city.

We traipsed up and down O'Connell Street, over the Liffy to St Stephens Green, back as far as the Abbey Theatre, on to St Patrick's Cathedral, mam was worn out. Dad gave running commentaries about Charles Parnell, Daniel O'Connell, the Post Office siege, the North South divide, the 1916 uprising and all Irish politics rolled into one, it was worse than being at school.

'Right Charlie, we've had more than enough for today,' mam finally declared, resting her feet at a small café that we'd managed to find while dad was plotting further incursions into the dock area of the city. Glancing through the window I was fascinated by the number of priests riding bikes; I'd never seen as many in my life. Cyclists covered both sides of the road, driving towards each other through spaces barely wide enough for a bike to go through. 'D'yer think Spud will end up coming over here an' learn to become a proper priest, dad?' I asked.

'I doubt it, I think it's his mother pushin' him too much me'self,' he replied.

'But he got 'the call' dad.'

'What bloody call? Worra yer talkin' about anyway, talk bloody sense.' I thought I was, but obviously I wasn't.

'Anyway, I couldn't see him riding a bike if he does come over here,' I continued.

'He wouldn't be carryin' all that fat if he were my lad. Paddy's got him soft; he'll bloody regret it one of these days though. You can't beat walkin' for exercise, that's what I say.' Mam glanced across so I rapidly dropped the subject when she winked at me on the sly.

Dad picked up the menu and ordered a plate of fish, chips and peas for each of us, with a few slices of bread and Irish butter. By this time, with all the walking and fresh air down our lungs we were starving. No sooner had the waitress placed the food on the table than our plates were cleared without leaving a scrap. After finishing his meal dad slipped across the road for a newspaper, he liked keeping in touch with the latest gossip whichever side of the sea it happened to be. Meanwhile mam called the waiter over after a colourful poster caught her eye. 'You've never lived till you've sampled a Sweet Aften', it said. This seemed to appeal to her taste buds. 'Can we 'ave five Sweet Aftens please?' she asked.

'Five, are you sure, madam?' the waiter replied, scratching his head and looking bemused. Mam counted her fingers without including dad in her calculations.

'Yes five please.' Then dad appeared.

The waiter came across carrying a tray with five ciggies on a serviette. 'Here you are missus, Five Sweet Aftens,' he said and placed them on the table. Mam looked bewildered. Dad glared at me. 'Who are they for?' he growled.

'Not me,' I swiftly replied.

'There's been a mistake Charlie. The kids are still hungry so I asked for five Sweet Aftens an' the waiter probably hasn't understood me,' she said.

'Bloody 'ell, no wonder he hasn't. I can't turn me back for five minutes. Sweet Aftens are ciggies, woman,' he muttered. The waiter smiled.

'Five puddin's please mate,' dad asked, looking round to see if anyone else besides us had heard the conversation. No one seemed bothered, so he casually opened the paper, lit up and puffed away on his pipe.

Everyday during the week we visited most tourist attractions, including a peaceful day at Phoenix Park. The break allowed mam to relax for the first time on our holiday. If the food hadn't been so good she'd have lost at least a stone.

'Can we go to County Cork an' kiss the blarney stone, dad?' I pleaded, seeing he was in a good mood.

'No we 'avent got time, besides you're likely to swallow it.' He laughed, he thought it was funny. I didn't and pulled a face. 'Come on, can't yer take a joke son?' he said. I sulked; I always did when he caught me out. Dad couldn't take a joke himself so how did he expect me to.

On Thursday a group of Americans booked in the 'The Connemara.' Since the day of our arrival we'd been warned to be on our best behaviour, but to be on the safe side dad issued another caution just in case our memories had been impaired with pounding the beat around Dublin.

In Mrs Lynch's parlour, taking pride of place was a huge piano. Dad immediately forbade us to venture anywhere near it. For some reason he seemed paranoid about this particular piece of furniture. 'Worra 'ave told yer. Gerra away from there,' he grimaced even if we touched the lid. Out of devilment I lifted it on purpose just to see his face. 'Put it bloody down,' he snarled almost spitting venom through his false teeth.

On Friday night we wandered back to the guesthouse after strolling along the promenade. As we were about to remove our coats, music from the piano and voices singing from the parlour reached our ears. The Americans, it seemed, were really enjoying themselves, so out of curiosity we stood by the door listening to their version of 'Danny Boy.' Although we didn't really know them properly they were friendly folk and we were invited to join them.

As dad made himself comfortable between Bridie and Bernadette on the couch, I managed to squeeze into a tiny space alongside the cat on the easy chair, while mam took our Tommy to bed. There were four people in the group, three men and one lady. They weren't very old, perhaps in their middle to late twenties. After applauding their performance, Mr Lynch introduced them to us. We shook hands; they were the first Americans I'd ever spoken to properly. The only other time I'd seen Americans apart from on the flicks were servicemen who congregated outside Hamilton Square Station. This was after the war had finished when we cadged chewing gum from them. I smiled to myself thinking what would happen if I said 'any gum chum.' Dad would never get over it.

They asked if any of us could sing, we shook our heads.

'None of them take after their father,' dad interrupted. We looked at the door - it was closed. 'Come on Bud, join in and entertain us,' the tallest Yank said.

'Charlie Reilly's the name lad, not Bud.' We giggled - he glared - we put our heads down.

'Sorry Charlie, no offence meant.'

'None taken lad.' We nudged each other; dad was in that kind of a mood.

'Would you care for a glass of Bourbon Sir?' the lady asked dad.

'I very rarely touch the stuff love, but to be sociable an' seein' we're all enjoyin' ourselves in ol' Ireland, I'll join yer and drink to all yer health, so I will.'

We nudged each other again. I stood up, Bridie followed, gripping Bernadette's hand. 'We'll just take our Bernie upstairs dad.' He nodded - we slipped quietly out.

An hour and a half later we returned with mam. Dad was hogging the middle of the floor, his face redder than Paddy Murphy's on a Saturday night.

'Plato, my friends was Socrates' favourite pupil,' he rambled. The Americans looked bored. Mr Lynch, with a huge grin on his face held a massive tumbler full to the brim with Potheen and Mrs Lynch, sitting alongside him was nursing a glass of wine. Another middle-age couple waltzed around the floor, serenading each other singing 'If you ever go across the sea to Ireland.'

'What's your occupation Charlie?' one of the Americans asked.

'I'm a dock.er,' dad slurred.

'Gee you're norra brain surgeon are you Charlie?'

'Don't be bloody funny lad, course I'm not.'

'So you're just an ordinary M.D Charlie?'

'Not ordinary lad, I'm a Birken'ead docker an' proud of it.'

'Well it's an honour to have a professional person in our company Sir,' the lady said, topping dad's glass up with a drop more Bourbon.

Mam moved over and eased dad into an easy chair. His eyes were half closed, we laughed. I whispered to Bridie,'fancy dad bein' called Bud and then taken for a doctor all in the same night.' She giggled uncontrollably. Someone put a record on; it was John McCormack, dad's favourite singer. He came to life.

'I'll take you home again Kathleen,' his throaty voice crackled.

Bridie blushed, I burst out laughing and mam told me to be quiet for my own sake. I took her advice. They all clapped, dad was off again.

'It's a long way to Tipperary,' he crooned.

Mr Lynch snored loudly and Mrs Lynch nudged him in the ribs. He stood up, staggered a few paces and fell over the cat. Two of the Americans attempted to pick him up while dad carried on singing with his eyes closed. There was little doubt he was savouring every second of his moment of fame.

Bridie cringed again, I put my fingers in my ears and mam just smiled, she'd heard him before. Dad bowed, straightened up, staggered backwards and sat down flattening a large aspidistra plant that was placed between the dresser and the door.

'Christ Almighty, what's that,' he spluttered. Mam was up like a flash.

'Come on Charlie time for bed, you've had enough for now.'

Mrs Lynch looked distressed. The Yanks were laughing. They began singing the 'Stars and Stripes.' Dad joined in, Mr Lynch followed and Mrs Lynch had a face on her like thunder. So did mam. We were lapping it up.

With help from our American friends dad was half carried, half dragged upstairs and plonked on the bed, still singing his head off. We remained downstairs watching a combined Irish, American operation, trying to lift Mister Lynch from the floor onto the couch. There was no way he could be taken upstairs; he was much too heavy. As a last resort they rolled him across the room and hauled him under the window cill, his place of rest for the night.

It was hilarious; he kept snoring his head off and shouting in his sleep. Mrs Lynch belted him a couple of times, on the sly of course when she thought no one was looking, yet I spotted her all right. She had the cheek to smile; then again she didn't know that Mister Lynch and me were best of friends. Unknown to her he allowed me to help myself to the apples from the orchard and now and again gave me a swift drag on his pipe in the shed where he dossed his Potheen. Although I fancied tasting the Potheen he never offered. I did, however, keep nix while he had a decent guzzle and from that moment on I was in his good books. I was that kind of a lad ... I got on well with everyone.

Next morning, dad, full of remorse, profusely apologised to Mrs Lynch for the damage caused to her aspidistra plant and as a gesture of goodwill offered to buy her a new one. I was made up with the whole situation, especially as dad couldn't face his bacon and egg, so as a favour I helped him out with his breakfast. The Americans didn't appear for breakfast and to crown it all poor Mr Lynch was banished from the house. Unfortunately, he'd spewed and peed himself at the same time, stinking the parlour out, and what's more the cat had vanished so he couldn't blame her like any normal fella would have done. We couldn't help hearing a holy commotion going on as he was being evicted and I, more than anyone else, felt really sorry watching Mrs Lynch hosing him down with freezing water.

After breakfast I popped down to the shed and found him consoling himself with a little help from the Potheen. He was dressed in an old pair of overalls and wellies, his normal clothes lying in a heap. Considering his early morning shower he didn't look too bad. I had a feeling he'd been down that road before.

We had a smashing time next day with dad having a thick head. 'It's a pity he doesn't hit the bottle more often' I said to mam. She agreed, even though he was nowty all day. By the time Saturday arrived he was in one

of his pious moods, enquiring to mam, in front of Mrs Lynch, about us going to confession in preparation for Holy Communion next day.
'The family that prays together, stays together,' said Mrs Lynch.
'Aye tis' true' said dad. I glanced over at mam, her eyes were smiling.
'I always find it gratifying to see families going to mass together,' Mrs Lynch continued.
'True,' said dad. I spluttered out loud.
'Worr a you laughin' at m'lad?'
'Nothin'.'
'You get locked up for laughin' at nothin' over here.'
'Tis true,' said Mrs Lynch. It was contagious; dad had an ally already. Next morning we were up bright and early dressed in our best clothes ready for eight o'clock mass. Mrs Lynch was preparing breakfast for our return and the smell of the bacon had me wishing I was a Proddy, but it was only wishful thinking, I was back amongst the home side again. Watching mam link dad's arm, we found it amazing ... He was going to mass ... we couldn't believe it. He'll probably wait outside I thought, but against all odds he entered the church.

I stood next to our Bridie in church as far away from dad as possible. I knew for a fact I'd burst out laughing if I heard him praying. I just couldn't look at him. I said a few silent prayers to Our Lady that the congregation wouldn't sing any hymns. If they did it would be curtains for me altogether. I had visions of getting excommunicated from the church for disrupting the service, so I bit the side of my cheek for practice, just in case the organist drummed up a hymn and dad joined in. Luck was with me however, for it turned out to be a normal mass in Ireland, much the same as back home in the Lauries.

Mam led the way to communion, dad didn't bother; half a miracle had already been achieved with him going to mass in the first place. It would have been totally unreasonable to expect a full miracle to occur after so many years had passed since he's seen the inside of a church.

We arrived back just before nine, the Americans were having their breakfast.
'Mornin' doc,' they said.
'Mornin' guys,' dad replied. I tried my best to contain my sniggers.
'Stop your bloody titterin' for Christ sake,' he roared.
'CHARLIE! Stop swearin' you've just been to mass,' mam remonstrated.
'That bloody fella would make anyone swear, even if you didn't want to,' he replied.
I looked down at the floor then over my shoulder and through the

window, watching Mr Lynch raking his vegetable patch. He was content with his lot, despite his disposition. I wouldn't mind his kind of life, I thought.

Mrs Lynch brought our breakfast to us on a large tray. Dad, however, was still in a bad mood and kept glaring at me. To avoid his dirty looks, I gazed at the ceiling watching two fly's dive bombing from the chandelier. I glanced at dad's bald head in the mirror and wished they were pigeons who'd just been fed. Then I realised that I'd just been to church and swiftly said a good act of contrition in case I choked on my bacon and egg for having evil thoughts about him.

With sadness we left Ireland on Tuesday night. It had been an unforgettable experience. We were the luckiest family in town; there weren't many that could afford the luxury of a holiday together. Despite dad's funny ways, it was all down to his thoughtfulness that we were able to sample life on the other side of the fence.

I liked the food and having our own room with a big double bed with just our Tommy to share - and what about the bathroom and inside lavvie - that was really living it up.

Then there was Mr Lynch; he was great as well. But Brookie was okay; we were used to life in the town.

Before leaving Dublin mam spent a few hours choosing holy pictures and statues while dad stocked up with pipe tobacco. We were content to buy sweets, different types rarely seen at home.

During our holiday Bridie suggested we track down Blessed Matt Talbot's house in Dublin to see if we could obtain a picture of him. This was to be a surprise for mam. She was delighted and added it to her collection of saints in her prayer book. We were disappointed for not finding time to trace Spud's relatives, but Dublin was full of Murphy's so it was a tall order finding their particular clan in the first place.

'They'll understand' said dad. Unlike Birkenhead, Dublin was a big place.

Mr and Mrs Lynch told dad to keep in touch and looked forward to seeing us again. As a surprise Mr Lynch gave me a bag of prize apples and pears for my journey and although I had every intention of taking them home as souvenirs my eyes were bigger than my belly and I scoffed them on the overnight trip.

Dad's day of reckoning

Everywhere seemed dull and miserable when we eventually arrived in our street. It was early morning and the town hadn't properly woken up, although we were wide awake, dad made sure of that. He'd given everyone an early morning call before we entered Liverpool Bay whether they wanted it or not. I suppose this was just enthusiasm on his part, although you'd have thought we'd been to America instead of Ireland the way he carried on.

As soon as dad put the key in the door Kerry nearly brought the house down. She was made up to see us judging by her welcome. As expected Aunt Fan had spoilt her while we were away, but from now on, her holiday and ours were over, it was back to reality.

After dinner dad went for a walk. No sooner had he turned the corner into Cathcart Street than Mrs Murphy emerged, followed by Ossie's mam. They headed straight for our front door. I ambled into the back kitchen as mam sorted out small souvenirs, medals, holy pictures and miniature bottles of water from Knock. Dad, as usual, was on the agenda after mam mentioned the miracle of him going to mass.

'Isn't it wonderful Charlie going to mass without any pressure at all,' she said.

'It's been a long time but thank God half me prayers have been answered,' she continued.

'Only half' said Mrs Murphy. 'Didn't he receive the Holy Sacraments, Maggie?'

'Of course not. We almost collapsed with shock when he went to mass in the first place, didn't we James?' she called to me.

'We did, an' you'll wait a long time for the other half of your miracle, unless we move to Dublin mam,' I answered. Mrs Murphy didn't appear to appreciate my reply or pessimism.

'The kids these days 'ave too much to say, don't they Rene?' she remarked to Mrs Feeley.

'We'd 'ave been swiped across our faces just for openin' our mouths in front of our elders,' she continued.

Mam ignored her. Mrs Murphy seemed to have forgotten that I was now working and growing up. Before our holidays I'd even used my dad's razor to remove a bit of bum fluff from above my top lip, without him knowing of course, so as far as I was concerned I was entitled to my opinion, vex or please.

The holiday had worked wonders for dad, he looked healthier and fitter than he had for ages and strangely his temperament seemed calmer. Father Nugent called to our house full of the joys of spring and for the second time on record dad didn't dash out to the lavvie. He stood his ground and mam was delighted. You could tell by her face that she had every confidence that he'd soon be going to mass at the Lauries with Paddy Murphy.

'How did you enjoy Ireland, Charles?' Father Nugent enquired.

'Not bad father, it was a nice change and thank God we could afford it.'

With dad thanking God, Father Nugent unwisely assumed he was in the presence of a fully-fledged convert and jumped in feet first.

'So can we look forward to seeing you at mass on Sunday, Charles?'

'No, father, I don't make promises I can't keep.'

Mam looked uncomfortable as she poured the tea out. It was noticeable that a plate of biscuits, having been placed on the table in anticipation of a celebration, remained untouched.

'Oh!' Said Father Nugent. 'I respect your point of view Charles, but when you do decide don't forget that the Lord in his infinite mercy welcomes all sinners back with open arms.'

I quickly moved into the back kitchen. You could never tell how dad was likely to react; he was touchy at times. His reply, however, left me in no doubt whatsoever that he'd definitely mellowed.

'Okay Father, I get the gist, let's leave it at that eh?'

Mam escorted Father Nugent to the door, slipping him two half crown pieces on the quiet, a donation which seemed to please him. After thanking her once again he made his way in the direction of the Murphy's. Meanwhile dad sat in his chair, chuckling away.

'Nice try, eh Maggie, you've got ter hand it to him for perseverance.'

Dad's next battle was with the housing department. During the following months he began a relentless barrage on Mr Benny, the Council chief, to have us re-housed. Now that Bridie was sixteen and a half and I'd turned fifteen, it was apparent we were growing up with little privacy. As a result the couch became my bed and I couldn't have been happier. Apart from having the fire to myself, no one objected even when our Kerry crawled on the bottom of the couch to keep my feet warm, while at the same time deterring any cockroaches or stray mice from approaching our speck.

Now that I was earning a living, although it was only on the milk round, I began frequenting Livvie Baths with dad on Saturday mornings, enjoying the luxury of a nice hot soak in a real bath. Ireland had certainly spoilt us; we were after the good things in life now.

A few weeks later I came flying in with great news. I'd been promised a job as a galley boy with Elders and Fife on the skin boats to West Africa. Dad, however, didn't share my enthusiasm and nearly hit the roof.

'Over my dead body are yer goin' to sea at fifteen,' he bawled.

'Worr am I gonna do? I can't stay on the milk all me life' I yelled.

'Use your loaf lad, an' gerra trade otherwise you'll end up like me on the docks' he advised.

Apprenticeship

Three weeks after my ambition to go to sea had been shattered I met up with Chunkie and Scullo, two mates from Hemmie. They were serving their time for a small contractor in Liverpool as apprentice electricians.

'Why not try our firm Jim,' they said. 'They're still lookin' for lads yer know.'

'Me! I'm dead scared of electricity. I wouldn't 'ave a clue how to go about it.' I answered.

'There's nowt to it, you'll be all right with us, it's dead easy 'onest,' they reassured.

With words of encouragement ringing in my ears I decided to chance my luck.

On the following Friday after donning my best shirt and polishing my shoes, back and front, I set off over the water on the ferry for my one and only interview since leaving school at Easter. The office, a mid-Victorian terraced house situated between Slater Street and Hanover Street was easy to find, for prominently displayed in bold letters on the right of the pillar by the front door was a sign. 'The Pitts Electrical Company Ltd.'

Confidently I ambled through the large open front door and entered a musty lobby. Being inquisitive I glanced into a room on my right which looked to me like a converted workshop, but there was no sign of life.

'Is there anyone at home,'.I yelled, as I normally would on Friday's milk round, while waiting to get paid. There was no reply so I trudged up a row of dark stairs adorned with a single shade-less light bulb hanging perilously from a stranded maroon cord. Daylight appeared from under a door at the top and so I knocked. Amazingly the door seemed to open on its own, and facing me, behind a huge desk, sat a grey haired old fella.

'So you're Jimmy Reilly an' you want to be a spark eh?' I nodded. I couldn't speak for a minute, I didn't know what to say, this was a different world to me.

'You're not very big are yer lad?' He continued, scrutinising me from head to toe as if deliberating whether I'd stay a midget all my life. After several humm's he eventually spoke.

'I suppose you'll come in handy for crawlin' under floorboards lad.'

'I don't mind doin' anythin' Sir,' I stuttered.

'For starters son, don't call me Sir, it's Mac to you an' everyone else round here,' he added. I couldn't help noticing a smile on his face.

'You know some of the lads workin' here I believe?'

'Yeah they're me mates from school.'

'Okay young Reilly you can start on Monday on eight pence an hour, 'ow does that sound?'

'Great,' I gasped. I couldn't conceal my excitement, me an apprentice, wait till I get home an' tell me mam an' dad' that was my first thought. We didn't get the indentures that the lads in the shipyards received, but who cared? Not me. I was dead chuffed with myself as I legged it from Woodside without stopping.

'Mam ... mam, guess what ... go on guess ... go on,' I pleaded.

'You've got the job James.'

'How did you know?' I replied.

'I said a little prayer to St Anthony, that's how I know. Now come here an' give me a big hug,' she said wrapping her arms round me. I didn't pull away, I was made up. I'd never been as happy in my life.

At first dad didn't believe me, he thought I was romancing until Chunkie called to see how I went on at the interview; it was only then that he believed me.

'Make sure you look after it m'lad. You've been given an opportunity to better yourself so don't start messin' about, d'yer 'ear what I'm sayin'?'

'Yes dad.'

I met Chunkie, Scullo and Phil outside Hamilton Square Station at half seven on Monday morning. Mam wrapped my butties in greaseproof paper from the cornflake packet instead of the Sunday newspaper, I was honoured. The train was chock-a- block with a crush of pin stripes and thick khaki overcoats, the moth balls mingling with odours of paint, grease and flatulence, pongs the turned-up noses of the bowler hat brigade attributed to the winter worn faces of the flat caps.

Arriving at the office we fell in line with a crowd of young lads milling around the workshop, while the tradesmen, outnumbered at least six to one, stood in a group smoking near the doorway. The electricians were in all shapes and sizes and judging by the expressions on their faces they had difficult days ahead. On reflection, it couldn't have been very inspiring for them, trying to teach us raw recruits the rudiments of the game.

After gulping a swift cup of tea each spark climbed the stairs to receive his daily-allocated job from Mac before returning to the workshop and commandeering a lad to retrieve his toolbox and materials before setting off for the day.

I watched intensely as the older lads positioned themselves near tradesmen they preferred working with and wondered which spark I would be assisting on my first day. An old fella looking a picture of laughs appeared on the scene, moaning and groaning about drawing the short straw. I glanced in his direction and had a sinking feeling I could be his companion for the day.

'He's only sending me to the stinkin' tannery again,' he muttered. Upon hearing the word 'tannery' the lads moved as if they'd been attacked by a swarm of bees. Obviously, I was unaware that they'd all assisted Ted Snypy at one time or another on some of these rather unpleasant jobs, while he supervised and moaned as they struggled doing the bulk of the work.

'Which of youse lads is free to 'elp me today?' he asked. There was no response. Then his heavily bagged eyes seemed to glance in my direction, but to my delight he didn't appear to be impressed with what he saw.

'The new kid, Christ he doesn't look as if he could burst a wet Echo,' he moaned. After a few minutes of silence he bawled. 'Right short arse, come with me.' I wasn't too sure whether he was speaking to me or not, so all I said was 'which one of us do yer mean like?'

'Oh we've got a comedian on our books 'ave we,' he growled. 'You're no relation to Arthur Askey by any chance are yer?'

I felt my face going as red as a beetroot, but how was I to know that he was looking at me in the first place? As I'd never heard of Arthur Askey I tried my best to retrieve the situation. 'I don't know but I'll ask me mam if he's a relative on her side of the family when I gerr 'ome tonight,' is all I said.

'Come 'ere yer cheeky little buggar an' pick that toolbox up an' a couple of coils of cable while you're at it,' he scowled. 'I'll straighten you out me'lad if it's the last thing I do.'

I struggled down the steps; my arms pulled almost out of their sockets while Snypy strode out in front with bib and brace ovies tucked under his arm.

'Best of luck Jimmy,' Chunkie yelled. Judging by Snypy's long face I needed it.

I arrived home worn out. Dad was off work. All he was interested in was how I'd fared and what I'd learnt. I told him I was being exploited and he didn't appear to be happy with my attitude.

'Exploited! Exploited ... you don't know the bloody meaning of the word. You're on the bottom of the pile now lad, just do as you're bloody told an' don't answer your elders back' he bawled. It was all right for him; he had no idea what it was like to crawl through stinking voids doing all the work and constantly being warned about not going fast enough. Mam was more sympathetic. 'If you don't like it son pack it in' she said. Dad almost fell off his perch. I left them arguing and walked round the corner to Ossie's for a bit of peace.

Farewell to Brookie

I was getting on for seventeen when dad's perseverance with the housing department finally paid off. He had continually badgered them over a period of fifteen months so it was more than likely to get him off their backs that we were eventually promised a transfer. Tucker's family had already departed to the north end of the town. Their new house located in the vicinity of the Nanny Goat mountains was an area Mr Griffiths seemed quite happy to move to.

Ossie left school at sixteen to begin working for an insurance company in Liverpool. Keeping in line with the Feeley's tradition he loved smart clothes and not to be outdone by anyone else he went to the office dressed to kill. Nobody could deny he looked the part. Of course we never told him. He was bad enough as it was with showing off, but then again he'd always been a show-off.

Spud, on the other hand, rarely came home. He did, however, write frequently, corresponding on a regular basis with Ossie who was an acknowledged letter writer. Smithy, who seemed to have more ambition than the lot of us, frequently visited Glasgow to stay with his grandmother. It was only a matter of time, he said, before he'd make this a permanent move. We rarely set eyes on Nacker; he tended to sign on for long voyages.

Our Bridie was at teaching college and missed all the drama. The last time I'd seen dad as excited was after he'd heard she'd passed the scholarship. No sooner had I lifted the latch to the entry door than he came tearing into the yard, holding a brown envelope, waving it like a flag. At first I thought he'd come up on the football pools.

'We've gorra a new house,' he raved, 'with a bathroom an' a garden an' all that.'

Mam just smiled.

'Whereabouts dad?' I tentatively asked, hoping it wasn't stuck out in the wilds where new developments had began springing up.

'The Woodchurch Estate,' he beamed.

'What! The Ponderosa' ...Bloody'ell that's out in the sticks.'

'Hey cut that bloody language out in front of your mother an' show some respect m'lad.'

I didn't reply ... I just laughed; he'd quietened down considerably since I'd begun serving my time; in fact we hardly had a cross word. As long as I responded to his early morning alarm call for work and paid mam for my keep he was happy.

At first I had mixed feelings about the move. Living in town had its advantages, such as getting to and from work and being in close proximity with my mates.

My doubts, however, began diminishing when thoughts of having hot water in the taps, an inside lavvie and a bathroom entered my head. I still aired my views about the distance from town though, but dad, as usual, had the last word.

'There's plenty of buses an' don't forget there's always shank's pony,' he jovially insisted. Five or six miles were nothing to him; he'd practised all his life. We could either like it or lump it, we had little choice.

When the removal van stopped outside our door I felt more a feeling of sadness than jubilation; leaving town for the last time felt kind of strange.

It was late Saturday morning, a time of day usually quiet, but on this occasion a surprising number of neighbours congregated in small groups. It seemed as though they sensed the inevitable was happening and Brookie would soon be deserted, with communities lost forever.

Besides Tucker's family, the Bailey's and M'cCarthy's had moved on. An exodus on a grand scale had begun.

We didn't have much furniture ourselves, although it was still necessary to hire a van, a far distant cry to the time that we left Queensbury Street and dad pushed our possessions on a handcart. I must admit I felt downhearted when our front door was closed for the last time, but as dad said, it was high time we moved on and for once I didn't contradict him.

By one o'clock we arrived in our new house. By seven, I was back down town at Ossie's. By ten we were well away, talking rubbish. We'd only been drinking a short time. The smell of the barmaid's apron was enough to see us off. Due to my inebriated state I missed the last bus and slept at Smithy's on the couch. Next morning I trooped home and heard dad bawling even before I reached our house.

'Just wait 'til the other fella gets in ... Just wait ... This is a respectable house so he'd better liven his ideas up or he'll be lookin' for new digs.' For an excuse I told him I'd got lost. He eventually calmed down: he was still on a high with the novelty of having a bathroom and inside lavvie and two gardens, one in the front and one in the back.

Over the following months I found it difficult to adjust and couldn't keep away from town. Every weekend I called at Ossie's or Smithy's and often stayed the night. Soon afterwards Jock finished up at Lairds after deciding to move back to Glasgow. He'd secured a job at John Brown's shipyard in Clydebank, despite Lairds having plenty of work on at the time, but as he said, it was time he returned to his native city to be close to his mother who was feeling the strains of old age.

Sadly our gang appeared to be falling apart. During a drinking session in the Observatory Pub in Oxton Road, we made a pact and arranged to meet in five years time. For some unknown reason we decided to make it on the twentieth of June 1961 at the Stork Hotel in Price Street.

'We'll be dead old by then,' said Ossie, after writing all the details down in his works diary. 'Yeah we'll all be in our twenties,' Tucker added.

A lot of water passed down the Mersey during those five years. Mrs Murphy moved to Claughton, but remained in the Lauries parish. Spud was still at Ushaw, County Durham, continuing his vocational training, while Paddy toiled on the building sites, spending most of his money and time on drinking sessions.

The Feeley's moved to Woodland Road, a slightly more up-market terraced house than Brookie, and Ossie failed his medical for the army. I was the first to know, he couldn't tell me quick enough. He was always a jammy bugger. We were green with envy and then to cap it all Tucker was called up by the Cheshire Regiment with the possibility of losing his trade. This naturally was a bitter blow for him.

Nacker remained at sea to avoid National Service, even though he'd married a girl from Lower Tranmere and was just nineteen at the time

Smithy joined the police force in Glasgow, his choice of profession causing quite a reaction from the lads. I wasn't surprised, I knew all about his ambition for years.

Dad became a part-time gardener, in a fashion, and also a television addict.

Unsurprisingly, as time passed by he went deaf. Accordingly the tele was always switched on full blast. Just like his younger days he was still addicted to western and gangster films. Like father, like son, is a phrase often quoted and for both of us old habits died hard. He tended to leave the front door open as he did down town. Occasionally I walked in unannounced. Dad was so wrapped up with gangsters and molls killing one another that he didn't notice me. I could never resist the temptation … I switched the main power supply off.

'MAGGIE … MAGGIE … the two bob's gone in the meter,' he bawled almost jumping out of his chair and frightening the life out of poor old Kerry, who at that time was on her last legs.

I switched it back on again … just as he turned round.

'Stop your bloody messin' about m'lad or I'll bloodywell shift yer,' he hollered.

Mam laughed, it tickled her, she still had her sense of humour.

Our new parish, St Michael and All Angels had recently been constructed and mam became a regular parishioner. The priest often popped in to see dad, but like his fellow clergy from the Lauries, he couldn't persuade him to go to church. I knew dad almost as much as mam did, he was just stubborn. It was a game to him. He again took ill and was taken to hospital where he received the last rites, as he had on countless occasions. When he came out of hospital the priest brought communion to the house. Out of respect dad didn't refuse. Mam was elated and phoned Mrs Murphy straight away.

She always had a soft spot for dad and prayed for him every night, so she told mam. Dad didn't know of course, he didn't like being in debt with anyone. 'Thank God Maggie, at last me prayers have been answered,' she exclaimed placing the phone down. Her faith in prayers trebled instantly with one short phone call.

When dad recovered he resumed his usual routine, fully aware that the mountain had come to Mohammed. It made no difference to him or to his point of view.

'You don't have to go to church to lead a decent and respectable life,' he often proclaimed. He'd never change, it wasn't in his make up; dad was a one off.

Epilogue

20th June 1961

Ossie was propping the bar up with Nacker next to him when we entered the Stork Hotel. Both wore flashy short sleeve shirts and were supping Guinness.

'Two pints of best bitter Oz,' I yelled, watching him observe our approach through the mirror above the till. Tucker grinned as we slapped each other on the backs and shook hands.

Smithy pulled out at the last minute; he had a court case to attend. We knew about Spud, there was no way he could have made the reunion, not with being on retreat in a remote abbey somewhere out in the bush. Naturally they were as disappointed as much as we were. We'd waited a long time for our get-together and had so much to talk about.

Elvis Presley's 'Wooden Heart' broke our conversation. We joined in the singing, with everyone in the bar. It was before the rock and roll explosion. After the music finally ended, we chatted about old times and eventually ended up getting plastered. The steamrollers hadn't moved in then.

They did later, flattening Brookie, but not our memories.